Lisa Gardner is the *New York Times* bestselling author of fourteen novels. Her FBI Profiler novels include *Say Goodbye*, *Gone* and *The Killing Hour*. Her Detective D.D. Warren series includes *Live to Tell*, *Alone*, *Love You More*, *Catch Me* and *The Neighbour*, which won the International Thriller Writers' Award in 2010. She lives with her family in New England.

Praise for *The Killing Hour*:

'With tight plotting, an ear for forensic detail and a dash of romance, this is a truly satisfying sizzler in the tradition of Tess Gerritsen and Tami Hoag' *Publishers Weekly*

'Gardner keeps us guessing . . . She also keeps us on edge' *LA Times*

Praise for *Catch Me*:

'Well-wrought suspense . . . Gardner skillfully tacks back and forth . . . Fans should enjoy the numerous cameos by characters from other Gardner novels' *Publishers Weekly*

'Gardner brings the ingredients to a rolling boil . . . Irresistible high-wire melodrama' *Kirkus Reviews*

Praise for *Love You More*:

'Lisa Gardner's books come with a built-in set of hands. They reach up out of the pages, grab you by the lapels, and hold you until you've read to the final, suspense-filled sentence. And *Love You More* is no exception' Linwood Barclay

'Lisa Gardner is an amazing writer. Her characters are multi-dimensional and believable, and they tell the kinds of stories that grip you right from the first page' Karin Slaughter

Praise for *Live to Tell*:

'Gardner has another hit on her hands' *Kirkus Reviews*

'An utterly gripping if profoundly ~~...~~ ~~...~~ould cause sleepless nights' *Irish Ind~~...~~*

By Lisa Gardner

The Perfect Husband
The Other Daughter
The Third Victim
The Next Accident
The Survivors Club
The Killing Hour
Alone
Gone
Hide
Say Goodbye
The Neighbour
Live to Tell
Love You More
Catch Me

LISA GARDNER

the Killing Hour

headline

First published in Great Britain in 2003 by Orion Publishing Group

This paperback edition first published in 2012 by
HEADLINE PUBLISHING GROUP

4

Cataloguing in Publication Data is available from the British Library

ISBN 978 0 7553 9645 0

Typeset in Sabon by Avon DataSet Ltd,
Bidford-on-Avon, Warwickshire

Printed and bound in Great Britain by Clays Ltd, St Ives plc

Headline's policy is to use papers that are natural, renewable and
recyclable products and made from wood grown in sustainable forests.
The logging and manufacturing processes are expected to conform to
the environmental regulations of the country of origin.

HEADLINE PUBLISHING GROUP
An Hachette UK Company
338 Euston Road
London NW1 3BH

www.headline.co.uk
www.hachette.co.uk

the Killing Hour

Acknowledgments

A little bit of research went into the making of this novel. In the absolutely, highly recommended, great-way-to-spend-a-weekend department, I was privileged to once again visit the FBI Academy and learn more about life amid an active Marine base. I have done my best to recreate the facilities and culture of the Academy. In regard to some of the anecdotes and traditions, however, buyer beware. The Academy is a living, breathing institution, undergoing constant change depending on the year, the class, and Bureau needs. As fast as one agent told me a story of a hallowed tradition during his Academy days, another agent would confess he'd never heard of such a thing. Being a crafty writer, I sifted through the various anecdotes, selected the ones I liked best and delivered them here as the gospel truth. That's my story and I'm sticking to it.

As much as I enjoy interviewing FBI agents, I confess I was totally blown away by the nice men and women I met via the US Geological Survey team of Richmond, Virginia. I needed some experts on the great outdoors and boy, did I hit the mother lode. Not only were the team members very patient when explaining to me the intricacies of properly analyzing water samples, but they came up with a dynamite list of cool places to kill people. They also gave my husband and me a personal tour of their recommended crime scenes, which had us on good behavior for weeks.

Following is the rather extensive list of nice folks who took time away from their very busy lives just to answer my phone calls. These people gave me correct information with the best of intentions. What happened to it after that is entirely my fault.

FIRST, THE EARTH EXPERTS:

Jim Campbell, Subdistrict Chief, US Geological Survey
David Nelms, Hydrologist, US Geological Survey
George E. Harlow, Jr, P.G., Hydrologist, US Geological Survey
Randall C. Orndorff, Geologist, US Geological Survey
William C. Burton, Geologist, US Geological Survey
Wil Orndorff, Karst Protection Coordinator, Virginia Department of Conservation and Recreation
Wendy Cass, Park Botanist, Shenandoah National Park
Ron Litwin, Palynologist, US Geological Survey

SECOND, THE DRUG EXPERTS:

Margaret Charpentier
Celia MacDonnell

THIRD, THE PROCEDURE EXPERTS:

Special Agent Nidia Gamba, FBI, New York
Dr Gregory K. Moffatt, PhD, Professor of Psychology, Atlanta Christian College
Jimmy Davis, Chief of Police, Snellville Police Department, GA

FOURTH, THE SUPPORTING CAST:

Melinda Carr, Diana Chadwick, Barbara Ruddy, and Kathleen Walsh for their invaluable proofreading assistance
My husband, Anthony, who didn't have to make any chocolate this time, but was required to unpack an entire house while I tended to deadline. Love, let's never move again.

Also, my deepest thanks to Kathy Sampson, who generously bought her daughter, Alissa Sampson, a 'cameo' appearance in this novel as part of a charity auction. I'm never sure if it's a good thing to be a character in one of my novels, but I appreciate Kathy's donation and hope Alissa enjoys the book.

And finally, in loving memory of my grandmother, Harriette Baumgartner, who supplied me with my favorite paperbacks, baked the best chocolate chip cookies in the world, and taught us all a dozen different ways to play solitaire. Here's to you, Grandma.

Happy reading,
Lisa Gardner

Prologue

The man first started noticing it in 1998. Two girls went out to a bar, never came home again. Deanna Wilson and Marlene Mason were the first set. Roommates at Georgia State U, nice girls by all accounts, their disappearance didn't even make the front pages of the *Atlanta Journal-Constitution*. People disappear. Especially in a big city.

Then, of course, the police found Marlene Mason's body along Interstate 75. That got things going a bit. The fine folks of Atlanta didn't like one of their daughters being found sprawled along an interstate. Especially a white girl from a good family. Things like that shouldn't happen around here.

Besides, the Mason case was a head-scratcher. The girl was found fully clothed and with her purse intact. No sign of sexual assault, no sign of robbery. In fact, her corpse looked so damn peaceful, the passing motorist who found her thought she was sleeping. But Mason was DOA. Drug overdose, ruled the ME (though Mason's parents vehemently denied their daughter would do such a thing). Now where was her roommate?

That was an ugly week in Atlanta. Everyone looking for a missing college coed while the mercury climbed to nearly a hundred degrees. Efforts started strong, then petered out. People got hot, got tired, got busy with other things. Besides, half the state figured Wilson had done it – offed her roommate in some dispute, probably over a boy, and that was that. People watched *Law & Order*. They knew these things.

A couple of hikers found Wilson's body in the fall. It was all the way up in the Tallulah Gorge, nearly a hundred miles away. The body was still clad in Wilson's party clothes, right down to her three-inch heels. Not so peaceful in death this time, however. For one thing, the scavengers had gotten to her first. For another, her skull was shattered into little bits. Probably from taking a header down one of the granite cliffs. Let's just say Mother Nature had no respect for Manolo Blahnik stilettos.

Another head-scratcher. When had Wilson died? Where had she been between that time and first vanishing from a downtown Atlanta bar? And had she offed her roommate first? Wilson's purse was recovered from the gorge. No sign of any drugs. But strangely enough, neither was there any sign of her vehicle or her car keys.

The Rabun County Sheriff's Office inherited that corpse, and the case once again faded from the news.

The man clipped a few articles. He didn't really know why. He just did.

In 1999, it happened again. Heat wave hit, temperatures – and tempers – went soaring, and two young girls went out to a bar one night and never made it back. Kasey Cooper and Josie Anders from Macon, Georgia. Maybe not such nice girls this time. Both were underage and never should've been drinking except that Anders's boyfriend was a bouncer at the bar. He claimed they weren't 'hardly tipsy at all' when he last saw them climbing into Cooper's white Honda Civic. Their distraught families claimed that both girls were track-and-field stars and wouldn't have gone anywhere without a fight.

People got a little more nervous this time. Wondered what was going on. Two days later, they didn't have to wonder anymore. Josie Anders's body was found along US 441 – ten miles from the Tallulah Gorge.

The Rabun County Sheriff's Office went into hyperdrive. Rescue teams were organized, search dogs hired, the National Guard called in. The *Atlanta Journal-Constitution* gave it front-page coverage. The strange double-disappearance so like the one the summer before. And exactly what happened when a person went missing in this kind of heat?

The man noticed something he'd missed before. It was small, really. A minor little note under Letters to the Editor. It read: 'Clock ticking ... planet dying ... animals weeping ... rivers screaming. Can't you hear it? Heat kills . . .'

And then the man knew why he'd started the scrapbook.

They never did find Kasey Cooper in the gorge. Her body didn't turn up until the November cotton harvest in Burke County. Then, three men operating a cotton picker got the surprise of their lives – a dead girl right smack in the middle of thousands of acres of cotton fields, still wearing a little black dress.

No broken bones this time. No shattered limbs. The ME ruled that nineteen-year-old Kasey Cooper died from multiple organ failure, most likely brought on by severe heat stroke. In other words, when she'd been abandoned out in the middle of that field, she'd still been alive.

An empty gallon jug of water was discovered three miles from her mummified corpse. Her purse was another five miles away. Interestingly enough, they never did find her vehicle or her car keys.

People grew more nervous now. Particularly when someone in the ME's office let it leak that Josie Anders also died from a drug overdose – a fatal injection of the prescription drug Ativan. Seemed sinister somehow. Two sets of girls in two different years. Each, last seen in a bar. In both cases the first girl was found dead along a major road. And in both cases, the second girl seemed to suffer a fate that was far, far worse ...

Lisa Gardner

The Rabun County Sheriff's Office called in the Georgia Bureau of Investigation. The press got excited again. More banner headlines in the front pages of the *Atlanta Journal-Constitution*. GBI SEEKS POSSIBLE SERIAL KILLER. Rumors flew, articles multiplied and the man clipped each one diligently.

He had a cold feeling growing in his chest now. And he started to tremble each time the phone rang.

The GBI, however, were not nearly so sensational about the case. Investigation ongoing, a spokesperson for the state police declared. And that's all the GBI would say. Until the summer of 2000 and the very first heat wave.

It started in May. Two pretty, young Augusta State University students headed to Savannah one weekend and never returned home. Last known sighting – a bar. Vehicle – MIA.

This time, the national media descended. Frightened voters hit the streets. The man pawed furiously through stacks of newspapers while the GBI issued meaningless statements such as 'We have no reason to suspect a connection at this time'.

The man knew better. People knew better. And so did the letters to the editor. He found it Tuesday, May 30. Exact same words as before. 'Clock ticking ... planet dying ... animals weeping ... rivers screaming. Can't you hear it? Heat kills ...'

Celia Smithers's body was found along US 25 in Waynesboro, just fifteen miles from the cotton-field crime scene where Kasey Cooper had been found six months before. Smithers was fully clothed and clutching her purse. No sign of trauma, no sign of sexual assault. Just one dark bruise on her left thigh, and a smaller, red injection site on her upper left arm. Cause of death – an overdose of the prescription tranquilizer, Ativan.

The public went nuts; the police immediately went into high gear. Still missing, Smithers's best friend, Tamara McDaniels. The police, however, didn't search the Burke County cotton fields. Instead, they sent volunteers straight to the muddy banks of the Savannah River. Finally, the man thought, they were starting to understand the game.

He should've picked up the phone then. Dialed the hastily established hotline. He could've been an anonymous tipster. Or maybe the crazy whacko that thinks he knows everything.

He didn't though. He just didn't know what to say.

'We have reason to believe Ms. McDaniels is still alive,' reported GBI Special Agent Michael 'Mac' McCormack on the evening news. 'We believe our suspect kidnaps the women in pairs, killing the first woman immediately, but abandoning the second in a remote location. In this case, we have reason to believe he has selected a portion of the Savannah River. We are now assembling over five hundred volunteers to search the river. It is our goal to bring Tamara home safe.'

And then Special Agent McCormack made a startling revelation. He had also been reading the letters to the editor. He now made an appeal to speak to the author of the notes. The police were eager to listen. The police were eager to help.

By the eleven o'clock news, search-and-rescue teams had descended upon the Savannah River and the suspect finally had a name. The Eco-Killer, Fox News dubbed him. A crazed lunatic who no doubt thought that killing women really would save the planet. Jack the Ripper, he ain't.

The man wanted to yell at them. He wanted to scream that they knew nothing. But of course, what could he say? He watched the news. He obsessively clipped articles. He attended a candlelight vigil organized by the frantic parents of poor Tamara McDaniels – last seen in a tight black skirt and platform heels.

No body this time; the Savannah River rarely gives up what she has taken.

But 2000 hadn't ended yet.

July. Temperatures soared above one hundred degrees in

the shade. And two sisters, Mary Lynn and Nora Ray Watts, met up with friends at T.G.I. Friday's for late-night sundaes to beat the heat. The two girls disappeared somewhere along the dark, windy road leading home.

Mary Lynn was found two days later alongside US 301 near the Savannah River. The temperature that day was 103 degrees. Heat index was 118. Her body contained a faintly striped brown shell crammed down her throat. Bits of grass and mud were streaked across her legs.

The police tried to bury these details, as they'd buried so many others. Once again, an ME's office insider ratted them out.

And for the first time the public learned what the police had known – what the man had suspected – for the past twelve months. Why the first girl was always left, easy-to-discover, next to a major road. Why her death came so quickly. Why the man needed two girls at all. Because the first girl was merely a prop, a disposable tool necessary for the game. She was the map. Interpret the clues correctly, and maybe you could find the second girl still alive. If you moved quickly enough. *If* you beat the heat.

The task force descended, the press corp descended, and Special Agent McCormack went on the news to announce that given the presence of sea salt, cord grass, and the marsh peri-winkle snail found on Mary Lynn's body, he was authorizing an all-out search of Georgia's 378,000 acres of salt marshes.

But which part, you idiots? the man scribbled in his scrapbook. *You should know him better than that by now. Clock is* TICKING!

'We have reason to believe that Nora Ray is still alive,' Special Agent McCormack announced, as he had announced once before. 'And we're going to bring her home to her family.'

Don't make promises you can't keep, the man wrote. But

finally, he was wrong.

The last article in an overstuffed scrapbook: July 27, 2000. Nora Ray Watts is pulled half-naked from the sucking depths of a Georgia salt marsh. The Eco-Killer's eighth victim, she'd survived fifty-six hours in hundred-degree heat, burning sun, and parching salt, by chewing cord grass and coating herself in protective mud. Now, a newspaper photo shows her exuberantly, vibrantly, triumphantly alive as the Coast Guard chopper lifts her up into the blue, blue sky.

The police have finally learned the game. They have finally won.

Last page of the scrapbook now. No news articles, no photos, no evening news transcripts. In the last page of the scrapbook, the man wrote only four neatly printed words: *What if I'm wrong?*

Then, he underlined them.

The year 2000 finally ended. Nora Ray Watts lived. And the Eco-Killer never struck again. Summers came, summers went. Heat waves rolled through Georgia and lambasted the good residents with spiking temperatures and prickling fear. And nothing happened.

Three years later, the *Atlanta Journal-Constitution* ran a retrospective. They interviewed Special Agent McCormack about the seven unsolved homicides, the three summers of crippling fear. He simply said, 'Our investigation is ongoing.'

The man didn't save that article. Instead, he crumpled it up and threw it into the trash. Then he drank long and heavily deep into the night.

It's over, he thought. It's over, I'm safe, and it's as simple as that.

But he already knew in his heart that he was wrong. For some things, it's never a matter of if, but only a matter of when . . .

1

'God it's hot. Cacti couldn't take this kind of heat. Desert rock couldn't take this kind of heat. I'm telling you, this is what happened right before dinosaurs disappeared from the Earth.'

No response.

'You really think orange is my color?' the driver tried again.

'Really is a strong word.'

'Well, not everyone can make a statement in purple plaid.'

'True.'

'Man-oh-man is this heat killing me!' The driver, New Agent Alissa Sampson, had had enough. She tugged futilely on her 1970's polyester suit, smacked the steering wheel with the palm of her hand, then blew out an exasperated breath. It was ninety-five outside, probably one hundred and ten inside the Bucar. Not great weather for polyester suits. For that matter, it didn't work wonders for bulletproof vests. Alissa's suit bled bright orange stains under her arms. New Agent Kimberly Quincy's own mothball-scented pink-and-purple plaid suit didn't look much better.

Outside the car, the street was quiet. Nothing happening at

Billiards; nothing happening at City Pawn; nothing happening at the Pastime Bar-Deli. Minute ticked into minute. Seconds came and went, as slowly as the bead of sweat trickling down Kimberly's cheek. Above her head, still fastened to the roof but ready to go at any minute, was her M-16.

'Here's something they never tell you about the disco-age,' Alissa muttered beside her. 'Polyester doesn't breathe. God, is this thing going to happen or *what?*'

Alissa was definitely nervous. A forensic accountant before joining the Bureau, she was highly valued for her deep-seated love of all things spreadsheet. Give Alissa a computer and she was in hog heaven. This, however, wasn't a back-room gig. This was front-line duty.

In theory, at any time now, a black vehicle bearing a two-hundred-and-ten-pound heavily armed suspected arms dealer was going to appear. He might or might not be alone in the car. Kimberly, Alissa, and three other agents had orders to halt the vehicle and arrest everyone in sight.

Phil Lehane, a former New York cop with the most street experience, was leading the operation. Tom Squire and Peter Vince were in the first of the backup vehicles. Alissa and Kimberly were in the second backup. Kimberly and Tom, being above-average marksmen, had cover duty with the rifles. Alissa and Peter were in charge of tactical driving, plus, had handguns for cover.

In consummate FBI style, they not only planned and dressed for this arrest, but they had practiced it in advance. During the initial run-through, however, Alissa had tripped when getting out of the car and had landed on her face. Her upper lip was still swollen and there were flecks of blood on the right-hand corner of her mouth.

Her wounds were superficial. Her anxiety, however, now went bone deep.

'This is taking too long,' she was muttering now. 'I thought he was supposed to appear at the bank at four. It's four-ten. I don't think he's coming.'

'People run late.'

'They do this just to mess with our minds. Aren't you boiling?'

Kimberly finally looked at her partner. When Alissa was nervous, she babbled. When Kimberly was nervous, she grew clipped and curt. These days, she was clipped and curt most of the time. 'The guy will show up, when the guy shows up. Now chill out!'

Alissa thinned her lips. For a second, something flared in her bright blue eyes. Anger. Hurt. Embarrassment. It was hard to be sure. Kimberly was another woman in the male-run world of the Bureau, so criticism coming from her was akin to blasphemy. They were supposed to stick together. Girl power, the Ya Ya Sisterhood, and all that crap.

Kimberly went back to gazing at the street. Now she was angry, too. Damn. Double-damn. Shit.

The radio on the dash suddenly crackled to life. Alissa swooped up the receiver without bothering to hide her relief.

Phil Lehane's voice was hushed but steady: 'This is Vehicle A. Target now in sight, climbing into his vehicle. Ready, Vehicle B?'

'Ready.'

'Ready, Vehicle C?'

Alissa clicked the receiver. 'Ready, willing, and able.'

'We go on three. One, two, THREE.'

The first siren exploded across the hot, sweltering street, and even though Kimberly had been expecting the noise, she still flinched in her seat.

'Easy,' Alissa said dryly, then fired the Bucar to life. A blast of hot air promptly burst from the vents into their faces, but now both were too grim to notice. Kimberly reached for her rifle. Alissa's foot hovered above the gas.

The sirens screamed closer. Not yet, not yet . . .

'FBI, stop your vehicle!' Lehane's voice blared over a bullhorn two blocks away as he drove the suspect closer to their side street. Their target had a penchant for armor-plated Mercedes and grenade launchers. In theory, they were going to arrest him while he was out running errands, hopefully catching him off guard and relatively unarmed. In theory.

'Stop your vehicle!' Lehane commanded again. Apparently, however, the target didn't feel like playing nice today. Far from hearing the screech of brakes, Alissa and Kimberly caught the sound of a gunning engine. Alissa's foot lowered farther toward the gas.

'Passing the movie theater,' New Agent Lehane barked over the radio. 'Suspect heading toward the pharmacy. Ready . . . Go.'

Alissa slammed the gas and their dark blue Bucar shot forward into the empty street. A sleek black blur appeared immediately to their left. Alissa hit the brakes, swinging the back end of their car around until they were pointed down the street at a forty-five degree angle. Simultaneously, another Bucar appeared on their right, blocking that lane.

Kimberly now had a full view of a beautiful silver grill gunning down on them with a proud Mercedes logo. She popped open the passenger's door while simultaneously releasing her seat belt, then hefted her rifle to her shoulder and aimed for the front tire.

Her finger tightened on the trigger.

The suspect finally hit his brakes. A short screech. The smell of burning rubber. Then the car stopped just fifteen feet away.

'FBI, hands on your head! HANDS ON YOUR HEAD!'

Lehane pulled in behind the Mercedes, shouting into the bullhorn with commanding fury. He kicked open his door, fit his handgun between the opening made between the window frame and the door and drew a bead on the stopped car. No hands left for the bullhorn now. He let his voice do the work for him.

'Driver, hands on your head! Driver, reach over with your left hand and lower your windows!'

The black sedan didn't move. No doors opening, no black tinted windows rolling down. Not a good sign. Kimberly adjusted her left hand on the stock of the rifle and shrugged off the rest of her seat belt. She kept her feet in the car, as feet could become targets. She kept her head and shoulders inside the vehicle too. On a good day, all you wanted the felon to see was the long black barrel of your gun. She didn't know if this was a good day yet.

A fresh drop of sweat teared up on Kimberly's brow and made a slow, wet path down the plane of her cheek.

'Driver, put your hands up,' Lehane ordered again. 'Driver, using your left hand, lower all four windows.'

The driver's side window finally glided down. From this angle, Kimberly could just make out the silhouette of the driver's head as fresh daylight surrounded him in a halo. It appeared that his hands were held in the air as ordered. She eased her grip slightly on her rifle.

'Driver, using your left hand, remove the key from the ignition.'

Lehane was making the guy use his left hand, simply to work the law of averages. Most people were right-handed, so they wanted to keep that arm in sight at all times. Next, the driver would be instructed to drop the car key out the open window, then open the car door, all with his left hand. Then he would be ordered to step slowly out of the car, keeping both hands up at all times. He would slowly pivot 360 degrees so they could visually inspect his form for weapons. If he were wearing a jacket, he would be asked to hold it open so they could see beneath his coat. Finally, he would be ordered to walk toward them with his hands on his head, turn, drop to his knees, cross his ankles and sit back on his heels. Then they would finally move forward and take their felony suspect into custody.

Unfortunately, the driver didn't seem to know the theories behind a proper felony vehicle stop. He still didn't lower his hands, but neither did he reach for the key in the ignition.

'Quincy?' Lehane's voice crackled over the radio.

'I can see the driver,' Kimberly reported back, gazing through the rifle sight. 'I can't make out the passenger side, however. Tinted windshield's too dark.'

'Squire?'

Tom Squire had cover duty from Vehicle B, parked twenty feet to the right of Kimberly. 'I think . . . I think there might be someone in the back. Again, hard to tell with the windows.'

'Driver, using your left hand, remove the key from the ignition.' Lehane repeated his command, his voice louder now, but still controlled. The goal was to remain patient. Make the driver come to you, do not relinquish control.

Was it Kimberly's imagination, or was the vehicle now slowly rocking up and down? Someone was moving around . . .

'Driver, this is the FBI! Remove the key from the ignition!'

'Shit, shit, shit,' Alissa murmured beside Kimberly. She was sweating hard, streams of moisture pouring down her face. Leaning half out of the car, she had her Glock .40 aimed between the crack between the roof of their vehicle and the open door. Her right arm was visibly shaking, however. For the first time, Kimberly noticed that Alissa hadn't fully removed her seat belt. Half of it was still tangled around her left arm.

'Driver—'

The driver's left hand finally moved. Alissa exhaled forcefully. And in the next instant, everything went to shit.

Kimberly saw it first. 'Gun! Backseat, driver side—'

Pop, pop, pop! Red mushroomed across their front windshield. Kimberly ducked and dove out of the vehicle for the shelter of her car door. She came up fast and spread cover fire above the top of her window. More *pop, pop, pop.*

'Reloading rifle,' she yelled into the radio.

'Vince reloading handgun.'

'Taking heavy fire from the right, backseat passenger window!'

'Alissa!' Kimberly called out. 'Cover us!'

Kimberly turned toward her partner, frantically cramming fresh rounds into the magazine, then realized for the first time that Alissa was no longer to be seen.

'Alissa?'

She stretched across the front seats. New Agent Alissa Sampson was now on the asphalt, a dark red stain spreading across her cheap orange suit.

'Agent down, agent down,' Kimberly cried. Another pop, and the asphalt exploded two inches from Alissa's leg.

'Damn,' Alissa moaned. 'Oh damn that *hurts!*'

'Where are those rifles?' Lehane yelled.

Kimberly shot back up, saw the doors of the Mercedes were now swung open for cover and bright vivid colors were literally exploding in all directions. Oh, things had definitely gone FUBAR now.

'Rifles!' Lehane yelled again.

Kimberly hastily scrambled back to her side, and got her rifle between the crack of the car door. She was frantically trying to recall protocol. Apprehension was still the goal. But they were under heavy fire, possible loss of agent life. Fuck it. She started firing at anything that moved near the Mercedes.

Another *pop*, her car door exploded purple and she reflexively yelped and ducked. Another *pop* and the pavement mushroomed yellow one inch from her exposed feet. Shit!

Kimberly darted up, opened fire, then dropped back behind the door.

'Quincy, rifle reloading,' she yelled into the radio, her hands shaking so badly now with adrenaline that she fumbled the release and had to do it twice. Come on, Kimberly. Breathe!

They needed to regain control of the situation. She couldn't get the damn rounds into the magazine. Breathe, breathe, breathe. Hold it together. A movement caught the corner of her eye. The car. The black sedan, doors still open, was now rolling forward.

She grabbed her radio, dropped it, grabbed it again, and yelled 'Get the wheels, get the wheels.'

Squire and Lehane either heard her or got it on their own because the next round of gunfire splattered the pavement and the sedan came to an awkward halt just one foot from Kimberly's car. She looked up. Caught the startled gaze of the man in the driver's seat. He bolted from the vehicle. She leapt out from behind her car door after him.

And a moment later, pain, brilliant and hot pink, exploded across her lower spine.

New Agent Kimberly Quincy went down. She did not get up again.

'Well, that was an exercise in stupidity,' FBI supervisor Mark Watson exclaimed fifteen minutes later. The vehicle-stop drill was over. The five new agents had returned, paint-splattered, overheated, and technically half-dead to the gathering site on Hogan's Alley. They now had the honor of being thoroughly dressed down in front of their thirty-eight fellow classmates. 'First mistake, anyone?'

'Alissa didn't get her seat belt off.'

'Yeah. She unfastened the clasp, but didn't pull it back. Then when it came time for action . . .'

Alissa hung her head. 'I got a little tangled, went to undo it—'

'Popped up and got shot in the shoulder. That's why we practice. Problem number two?'

'Kimberly didn't back up her partner.'

Watson's eyes lit up. A former Denver cop before joining the Bureau ten years ago, this was one of his favorite topics. 'Yes, Kimberly and her partner. Let's discuss that. Kimberly, why didn't *you* notice that Alissa hadn't undone her seat belt?'

'I did!' Kimberly protested. 'But then the car, and the guns . . . It all happened so fast.'

'Yes, it all happened so fast. Epitaph of the dead and untrained. Look – being aware of the suspect is good. Being conscious of your role is good. But you also have to be aware of what's right beside you. Your partner overlooked something. That's her mistake. But you didn't catch it for her, and that was your mistake. Then she got hit, now you're down a man, and that mistake is getting bigger all the time. Plus, what were you doing just leaving her there on the pavement?'

'Lehane was yelling for rifle support—'

'You left a fellow agent exposed! If she wasn't already dead, she certainly was after that! You couldn't drag her back into the car?'

Kimberly opened her mouth. Shut her mouth. Wished bitterly, selfishly, that Alissa could've taken care of herself for a change, then gave up the argument once and for all.

'Third mistake,' Watson demanded crisply.

'They never controlled the car,' another classmate offered up.

'Exactly. You stopped the suspect's car, but never controlled it.' His gaze went to Lehane. 'When things first went wrong, what should you have done?'

Lehane visibly squirmed. He fingered the collar of his brown leisure suit, cut two sizes too big and now bearing hot pink and mustard yellow paint on the left shoulder. The paint guns used by the actors in the drills – aka the bad guys – stained everything in sight, hence their Salvation Army wardrobe. The exploding shells also hurt like the dickens, which was why

Lehane was holding his left arm protectively against his ribs. For the record, the FBI Academy trainees weren't allowed paint guns but used their real weapons loaded with blanks. The official explanation was that their instructors wanted the trainees to get a feel for their firearms. Likewise, they all wore vests to get used to the weight of body armor. That all sounded well and good, but why not have the actors shoot blanks as well?

The students had their theories. The brightly exploding paint shells made getting hit all the more embarrassing. And the pain wasn't something you forgot about anytime soon. As Steven, the class psychologist, dryly pointed out, the Hogan Alley live-action drills were basically classic shock therapy on a whole new scale.

'Shot out the tires,' Lehane said now.

'Yes, at least Kimberly eventually thought of that. Which brings us to, the Deadly Deed of the Day.'

Watson's gaze swung to Kimberly. She met his look, knew what it meant, and stuck her chin up.

'She abandoned the cover of her vehicle,' the first person said.

'Put down her weapon.'

'Went after one suspect before she finished securing the scene.'

'Stopped providing cover fire—'

'Got killed—'

'Maybe she missed her partner.'

Laughter. Kimberly shot the commentator a thanks-for-nothing glare. Whistler, a big burly former Marine – who sounded like he was whistling every time he breathed – smiled back. He'd won Deadly Deed of the Day yesterday when, during a bank robbery of the Bank of Hogan, he went to shoot a robber and hit the teller instead.

'I got a little lost in the moment,' Kimberly said curtly.

'You got killed,' Watson corrected flatly.

'Merely paralyzed!'

That earned her another droll look. 'Secure the vehicle first. Control the situation. Then give pursuit.'

'He'd be gone—'

'But you would have the car, which is evidence, you'd have his cohorts to flip on him, and best of all, you'd still be alive. A bird in the hand, Kimberly. A bird in the hand.' Watson gave her one last stern look, then opened up his lecture to the rest of the class. 'Remember, people, in the heat of the moment, you have to stay in control. That means falling back on your training and the endless drills we're making you do here. Hogan's Alley is about learning good judgment. Taking the high-risk shot in the middle of a bank holdup is not good judgment.' Whistler got a look. 'And leaving the cover of your vehicle, and your fellow agents, to pursue one suspect on foot, is not good judgment.' A fresh glance at Kimberly. Like she needed it.

'Remember your training. Be smart. Stay controlled. That will keep you alive.' He glanced at his watch and clapped his hands. 'All right, people, five o'clock, that's a wrap. For God's sake, go wash all that paint off. And remember, folks – as long as it remains this hot, drink plenty of water.'

2

Twenty minutes later, Kimberly stood blessedly alone in her small Washington Hall dorm room. Given this afternoon's debacle, she'd thought she'd have a good cry. She now discovered that as of week nine of the Academy's sixteen-week program, she was officially too tired for tears.

Instead, she stood naked in the middle of the tiny dorm room. She was staring at her reflection in a full-length mirror, not quite believing what she saw.

The sound of running water came from her right; her roommate, Lucy, fresh off the PT course, was showering in the bathroom they shared with two other classmates. Behind her, came the sounds of gunfire and the occasional exploding artillery. The FBI Academy and National Academy classes were done for the day, but Quantico remained a busy place. The Marines conducted basic training just down the road. The DEA ran various exercises. At any given time, on the sprawling 385-acre grounds, someone was probably shooting something.

When Kimberly had first arrived here back in May, first

stepped off the Dafre shuttle bus, she'd inhaled the scent of cordite mixed with fresh-cut lawn and thought she'd never smelled anything quite so nice. The Academy seemed beautiful to her. And surprisingly inconspicuous. The sprawling collection of thirteen oversized beige brick buildings looked like any kind of 1970s institution. A community college maybe. Or government offices. The buildings were ordinary.

Inside wasn't much different. A serviceable, blue-gray carpet ran as far as the eye could see. Walls were painted bone-white. Furniture was sparse and functional – low-slung orange chairs, short, easily assembled oak tables and desks. The Academy had officially opened its doors in 1972, and the joke was the decorating hadn't changed much since.

The complex, however, was surprisingly inviting. The Jefferson Dormitory, where visitors checked in, boasted beautiful wood trim as well as a glass-enclosed atrium, perfect for indoor barbecues. Over a dozen long, smoked-glass corridors connected each building and made it seem as if you were walking through the lush, green grounds, instead of remaining indoors. Courtyards popped up everywhere, complete with flowering trees, wrought-iron benches, and flagstone patios. On sunny days, trainees could race woodchucks, rabbits, and squirrels to class as the animals bounded across the rolling lawns. At dusk, the glowing amber eyes of deer, foxes, and raccoons appeared in the fringes of the forest, peering at the buildings with the same intensity the students used to stare back. One day, around week three, as Kimberly was strolling down a glass-enclosed corridor, she turned her head to admire a white flowering dogwood, and a thick black snake suddenly appeared among the branches and dropped to the patio below.

In the good news department, she hadn't screamed. One of her classmates, a former Navy man, however, had. Just startled, he told them all sheepishly. Honestly, just startled.

Of course, they had all screamed a time or two since. The instructors would've been disappointed otherwise.

Kimberly returned her attention to the full-length mirror, and the mess that was her body now reflected there. Her right shoulder was dark purple. Her left thigh yellow and green. Her rib cage was bruised, both her shins were black and blue, and the right side of her face – from yesterday's shotgun training – looked like someone had gone after her with a meat mallet. She turned around and gazed at the fresh bruise already forming on her lower back. It would go nicely with the giant red mat burn running up the back of her right thigh.

Nine weeks ago, her five-six frame had been one hundred and fifteen pounds of muscle and sinew. As a life-long workout junkie, she'd been fit, trim, and ready to breeze through physical training. Armed with a master's degree in criminology, shooting since she was twelve, and hanging out with FBI agents – basically her father – all of her life, she'd strode through the Academy's broad glass doors like she owned the joint. Kimberly Quincy has arrived and she's still pissed off about September 11. So all you bad people out there, drop your weapons and cower.

That had been nine weeks ago. Now, on the other hand . . .

She'd definitely lost badly needed weight. Her eyes held dark shadows, her cheeks were hollowed out, her limbs looked too thin to bear her own weight. Her shoulders were slightly hunched, the posture of a woman who's been beat one too many times. And her fingernails were torn and ragged where she'd started biting them.

She looked like a washed-out version of her former self. Bruises on the outside to match the bruises on the inside.

She couldn't stand the sight of her own body. She couldn't seem to look away.

Inside the bathroom, the water shut off with a rusty clank. Lucy would be out soon.

Kimberly raised her hand to the mirror. She traced the line of her bruised shoulder, the glass cool and hard against her fingertips.

And, unbidden, she remembered something she hadn't thought of for six years now. Her mother, Elizabeth Quincy. Dark, softly curling brown hair, fine patrician features, her favorite ivory silk blouse. Her mother was smiling at her, looking troubled, looking sad, looking torn.

'I just want you to be happy, Kimberly. Oh God, if only you weren't so much like your father . . .'

Kimberly's fingers remained on the mirrored glass. She closed her eyes, however, for there were some things that even after all these years she still could not take.

Another sound from the bathroom; Lucy raking shut the curtain. Kimberly opened her eyes. She moved hastily to the bed and grabbed her clothes. Her hands were trembling. Her shoulder ached.

She pulled on dark blue running shorts and a light blue FBI T-shirt.

Six o'clock. Her classmates would be going to dinner. Kimberly went to train.

Kimberly had arrived at the FBI Academy in Quantico, Virginia, the third week of May as part of NAC 03-05 – meaning her class was the fifth new agent class to start in the year 2003.

Like most of her classmates, Kimberly had dreamt about becoming an FBI agent for most of her life. To say she was excited to be accepted would be a little bit of an understatement. The Academy accepted only six percent of applicants – a lower acceptance rate than even Harvard's – so Kimberly had been more like giddy, awestruck, thrilled, flabbergasted, nervous, fearful, and amazed all in various turns. For twenty-four hours, she'd kept the news to herself. Her own special secret, her own special day. After all the years of educating and training and trying and wanting . . .

She'd taken her acceptance letter, gone to Central Park, and just sat there, watching a parade of New Yorkers walk by while wearing a silly grin on her face.

Day two, she'd called her father. He'd said, 'That's wonderful, Kimberly,' in that quiet, controlled voice of his and she'd babbled, for no good reason, 'I don't need anything. I'm all set to go. Really, I'm fine.'

He'd invited her to dinner with him and his partner, Rainie Conner. Kimberly had declined. Instead, she'd sheared off her long, dirty blond hair and clipped down her fingernails. Then she'd driven two hours to the Arlington National Cemetery, where she sat in silence amid the sea of white crosses.

Arlington always smelled like a fresh mowed lawn. Green, sunny and bright. Not many people knew that, but Kimberly did.

Arriving at the Academy three weeks later was a lot like arriving at summer camp. All new agents were bundled into the Jefferson Dormitory where supervisors rattled off names and crossed off lists, while the new trainees clutched their travel bags and pretended to be much cooler and calmer than they really felt.

Kimberly was summarily handed a bundle of thin white linens and an orange coverlet to serve as her bedding. She also received one threadbare white towel and one equally threadbare washcloth. New agent trainees made their own beds, she was informed, and when she wanted fresh sheets, she was to pack up the old bunch and go to linen exchange. She was then handed a student handbook detailing all the various rules governing life at the Academy. The handbook was twenty-four pages long.

Next stop the PX, where, for the bargain-basement price of $325, Kimberly purchased her new agent uniform – tan cargo pants, tan belt, and a navy blue polo shirt bearing the FBI Academy logo on the left breast. Like the rest of her classmates, Kimberly purchased an official FBI Academy lanyard, from which she hung her ID badge.

ID badges were important at the Academy, she learned. For one thing, wearing ID at all times kept students from being summarily arrested by Security and thrown out. For another thing, it entitled her to free food in the cafeteria.

New agents must be in uniform Monday through Friday from eight A.M. to four-thirty P.M., they learned. After four-thirty, however, everyone magically returned to being mere mortals and thus could wear street clothes – excluding sandals, shorts, halters, tube tops or tank tops. This was afterall, the Academy.

Handguns were not permitted on Academy grounds. Instead, Kimberly checked her Glock .40 into the Weapons Management Facility vault. In return, she received what the new agents fondly referred to as a 'Crayola Gun' or 'Red Handle' – a red plastic gun of approximately the same weight and size as a Glock. New agents were required to wear the Crayolas at all times, along with fake handcuffs. In theory, this helped them grow accustomed to the weight and feel of wearing a handgun.

Kimberly despised her Red Handle. It seemed childish and silly to her. She wanted her Glock back. On the other hand, the various accountants, lawyers, and psychologists in her class, who had zero firearms experience, loved the things. They could knock them off their belts, drop them in the halls, and sit on them without shooting themselves or anyone else in the ass. One day, Gene Yvves had been gesturing so wildly, he whacked his Crayola halfway across the room, where it hit another new agent on the head. Definitely, the first few weeks, it had been a good idea that not everyone in the class was armed.

Kimberly still wanted her Glock back.

Once piled high with linens, uniforms, and toy handguns, the new agent trainees returned to the dorms to meet their roommates. Everyone started out in the Madison and Washington dormitories, two people to a room and two rooms sharing a bath. The rooms were small but functional – two single beds, two small oak desks, one big bookshelf. Each bathroom, painted vivid blue for reasons known only to the janitor, had a small sink and a shower. No tub. By week four, when everyone's bruised and battered bodies were desperate for a long, hot soak, several agents rented hotel rooms in neighboring Stafford purely for the bathtubs. Seriously.

Kimberly's roommate, Lucy Dawbers, was a thirty-six-year-old former trial lawyer who'd had her own two-thousand-dollar-a-month Boston brownstone. She'd taken one look at their spartan quarters that first day and groaned, 'Oh my God, what have I done?'

Kimberly had the distinct impression that Lucy would kill for a nice glass of Chardonnay at the end of the day. She also missed her five-year-old son horribly.

In the good news department – especially for new agents who didn't share particularly well, say perhaps, Kimberly – somewhere around week twelve, new agents became eligible for private rooms in 'The Hilton' – the Jefferson Dormitory. These rooms not only were slightly bigger, but entitled you to your very own bathroom. Pure heaven.

Assuming you survived until week twelve.

Three of Kimberly's classmates already hadn't.

In theory, the FBI Academy had abandoned its earlier, boot camp ways for a kindler, gentler program. Recognizing how expensive it was to recruit good agents, the Bureau now treated the FBI Academy as the final training stage for selected agents, rather than as a last opportunity to winnow out the weak.

That was in theory. In reality, testing started week one. Can you run two miles in less than sixteen minutes? Can you do fifty pushups in one minute? Can you do sixty sit-ups? The shuttle run must be completed in twenty-four seconds, the fifty-foot rope must be climbed in forty-five seconds.

The new agent trainees ran, they trained, they suffered through body fat testing and they prayed to fix their individual weaknesses – whether that was the shuttle run or the rope climb or the fifty pushups, in order to pass the three cycles of fitness tests.

Then came the academics program – classes in white-collar crime, profiling, civil rights, foreign counterintelligence, organized crime and drug cases; lessons in interrogation, arrest tactics, driving maneuvers, undercover work, and computers; lecture series on criminology, legal rights, forensic science, ethics, and FBI history. Some of it was interesting, some of it was excruciating, and all of it was tested three times over the course of the sixteen weeks. And no mundane high-school scale here – it took a score of 85 percent or higher to pass. Anything less, you failed. Fail once, you had an opportunity for a make-up test. Fail twice, you were 'recycled' – dropped back to the next class.

Recycled. It sounded so innocuous. Like some PC sports program – there are no winners or losers here, you're just recycled.

Recycling mattered. New agents feared it, dreaded it, had nightmares about it. It was the ominous word whispered in the halls. It was the secret terror that kept them going up over the towering Marine training wall, even now that it was week nine and everyone was sleeping less and less while being pushed more and more and the drills were harder and the expectations higher and each day, every day, someone was going to get awarded the Deadly Deed of the Day . . .

Besides the physical training and academics, new agents worked on firearms. Kimberly had thought she'd have the advantage there. She'd been taking lessons with a Glock .40

for the past ten years. She was comfortable with guns and a damn good shot.

Except firearms training didn't involve just standing and firing at a paper target. They also practiced firing from the sitting position – as if surprised at a desk. Then there were running drills, belly crawling drills, night firing drills, and elaborate rituals where they started out on their bellies, then got up and ran, then dropped down, then ran more, then stood and fired. You fired right-handed. You fired left-handed. You reloaded and reloaded and reloaded.

And you didn't just use a handgun.

Kimberly got her first experience with an M-16 rifle. Then she fired over a thousand rounds from a Remington Model 870 shotgun with a recoil that nearly crushed her right cheek and shattered her shoulder. Then she expelled over a hundred rounds from a Heckler & Koch MP5/10 submachine gun, though that at least had been kind of fun.

Now they had Hogan's Alley, where they practiced elaborate scenarios and only the actors actually knew what was going to happen next. Kimberly's traditional anxiety dreams – leaving the house naked, suddenly being in a classroom taking a pop quiz – had once been in black and white. Since Hogan's Alley, they had taken on vivid, violent color. Hot pink classrooms, mustard yellow streets. Pop quizzes splashed with purple and green paint. Herself, running, running, running down long endless tunnels of exploding orange, pink, purple, blue, yellow, black, and green.

She awoke some nights biting back weary screams. Other nights, she simply lay there and felt her right shoulder throb. Sometimes, she could tell that Lucy was awake, too. They didn't talk those nights. They just lay in the dark, and gave each other the space to hurt.

Then at six A.M. they both got up and went through it all over again.

Nine weeks down, seven to go. Show no weakness. Give no quarter. Endure.

Kimberly wanted so desperately to make it. She was strong Kimberly, with cool blue eyes just like her father's. She was smart Kimberly with her B.A. in psychology at twenty-one and her master's in criminology at twenty-two. She was driven Kimberly, determined to get on with her life even after what happened to her mother and sister.

She was infamous Kimberly, the youngest member of her class and the one everyone whispered about in the halls. *You know who her father is, don't you? What a shame about her family. I heard the killer nearly got her, too. She gunned him down in cold blood . . .*

Kimberly's classmates took lots of notes in their eagerly awaited profiling class. Kimberly took none at all.

She arrived downstairs. Up ahead in the hall, she could see a cluster of green shirts chatting and laughing – National Academy students, done for the day and no doubt heading to the Boardroom for cold beer. Then came the cluster of blue shirts, talking up a storm. Fellow new agent trainees, also done for the day, and now off to grab a quick bite in the cafeteria before hitting the books, or the PT course, or the gym. Maybe they were mentoring each other, swapping a former lawyer's legal expertise for a former Marine's firearms training. New agents were always willing to help one another. If you let them.

Kimberly pushed her way through the outside doors. The heat slammed into her like a blow. She made a beeline for the relative shade of the Academy's wooded PT course and started running.

Pain, Agony, Hurt, the signs read on the trees next to the path. Suck it in. Love it!

'I do, I do,' Kimberly gasped.

Her aching body protested. Her chest tightened with pain. She kept on running. When all else failed, keep moving. One foot in front of another. New pain layering on top of the old.

Kimberly knew this lesson well. She had learned it six years ago, when her sister was dead, her mother was murdered and she stood in a Portland, Oregon, hotel room with the barrel of a gun pressed against her forehead like a lover's kiss.

3

Twenty-year-old Tina Krahn had just stepped out the front door of her stifling hot apartment when the phone rang. Tina sighed, doubled back into the kitchen and answered with an impatient hello while using her other hand to wipe the sweat from the back of her neck. God, this heat was unbearable. The humidity level had picked up on Sunday, and hadn't done a thing to improve since. Now, fresh out of the shower, Tina's thin green sundress was already plastered to her body, while she could feel fresh dewdrops of moisture trickle stickily down between her breasts.

She and her roommate Betsy had agreed half an hour ago to go anyplace but here. Betsy had made it to the car. Tina had made it to the door, and now this.

Her mother was on the other end of the line. Tina promptly winced.

'Hey, Ma,' she tried with forced enthusiasm. 'How are you?' Her gaze went to the front door. She willed Betsy to reappear so she could signal she needed a minute longer. No such luck. Tina tapped her foot anxiously and was happy her mother was a thousand miles away in Minnesota, and couldn't see her guilty expression.

'Well, actually I'm running out the door. Yeah, it's Tuesday. Just the time zones are different, Ma, not the days.' That earned her a sharp rebuke. She grabbed a napkin from the kitchen table, swiped it across her forehead, then shook her head when it immediately became soaking wet. She patted her upper lip.

'Of course I have class tomorrow. We weren't planning on drinking ourselves silly, Ma.' In fact, Tina rarely drank anything stronger than ice tea. Not that her mom believed her. Tina had gone away to college – egads! – which Tina's mother seemed to equate with choosing a life of sin. There was alcohol on college campuses, you know. And fornication.

'I don't know where we're going, Ma. Just . . . out. It's like . . . a gazillion degrees this week. We gotta find someplace with air-conditioning before we spontaneously combust.' Lord, did they.

Her mother was instantly concerned. Tina held up a hand, trying to cut off the tirade before it got started.

'No, I didn't mean that literally. No, really, Ma, I'm all right. It's just hot. I can handle some heat. But summer school is going great. Work is fine—'

Her mother's voice grew sharper.

'I only work twenty hours a week. Of course, I'm focusing on my studies. Really, honestly, everything's fine. I swear it.' The last three words came out a smidgeon too high. Tina winced again. What was it with mothers and their internal radars? Tina should've quit while she was ahead. She grabbed another napkin and blotted her whole face. Now she was no longer sure if the moisture was solely from the heat, or from nerves.

'No, I'm not seeing anyone.' That much was true.

'We broke up, Ma. Last month. I told you about it.' Kind of.

'No, I'm not pining away. I'm young, I'll survive.' At least that's what Betsy, Vivienne, and Karen told her.

'Ma—' She couldn't get in a word.

'Ma—' Her mother was still going strong. Men are evil. Tina was too young to date. Now was the time to focus on school. And her family, of course. You must never forget your roots.

'Ma—' Her mother was reaching her crescendo. Why don't you just come home? You don't come home enough. What are you, ashamed of me? There's nothing wrong with being a secretary you know. Not all young ladies get the wonderful opportunity to go off to college . . .

'*Ma!* Listen, I gotta run.'

Silence. Now she was in trouble. Worse than her mother's lectures was her mother's silence.

'Betsy's out in the car,' Tina tried. 'But I love you, Ma. I'll call you tomorrow night. I promise.'

She wouldn't. They both knew it.

'Well, if anything, I'll call you by the weekend.' That was more like it. On the other end of the phone, her mother sighed. Maybe she was mollified. Maybe she was still hurt. With her, it was always hard to know. Tina's father had walked out when she was three. Her mother had been going at it alone ever since. And yeah she was bossy and anxious and downright dictatorial on occasion, but she also worked ferociously to get her only daughter into college.

She tried hard, worked hard, loved hard. And Tina knew that more than anything in the world, her mother worried that it still wouldn't be enough.

Tina cradled the phone closer to her damp ear. For a moment, in the silence, she was tempted. But then her mother sighed again, and the moment passed.

'Love you,' Tina said, her voice softer than she intended. 'Gotta run. Talk to you soon. Bye.'

Tina dropped the phone back on the receiver before she changed her mind, grabbed her oversized canvas bag and headed out the door. Outside, Betsy sat in her cute little Saab convertible, her face also shiny with sweat and gazing at her questioningly.

'Ma,' Tina explained and plunked her bag in the backseat.

'Oh. You didn't . . .'

'Not yet.'

'Coward.'

'Totally.' Tina didn't bother opening the passenger side door. Instead she perched her rump up on the edge of the car, then slid down into the deep, beige leather seat. Her long legs stuck up in the air. Ridiculously high brown cork sandals. Hot pink toenails. A small red ladybug tattoo her mother didn't know about yet.

'Help me, I'm melting!' Tina told her friend in a dramatic voice as she threw the back of her hand against her forehead. Betsy finally smiled and put the car into gear.

'Tomorrow it's supposed to be even hotter. By Friday, we'll probably break one hundred.'

'God, just kill me now.' She straightened up, self-consciously checked the knot holding her heavy blond hair, and then fastened her seat belt. Ready for action. In spite of her lighthearted tone, however, her expression was too somber, the light gone out of her blue eyes and replaced now by four weeks of worry.

'Hey, Tina,' Betsy said after a moment. 'It's going to be all right.'

Tina forced herself to turn around. She picked up Betsy's hand. 'Buddy system?' she asked softly.

Betsy smiled at her. 'Always.'

The sun setting was one of the most beautiful sights in the world to him. The sky glowed amber, rose, and peach, firing the horizon with dying embers of sunlight. Color washed across the clouds like strokes of an artist's brush, feathering white cumulus billows with iridescent hues from gold to purple to finally – inevitably – black.

He had always liked sunsets. He remembered his mother bringing him and his brother out to the front porch of the rickety shack every evening after dinner. They would lean against the railing and watch the sun sink behind the distant rim of mountains. No words were spoken. They learned the reverent hush at an early age.

This was his mother's moment, a form of religion for her. She would stand alone, in the western corner of the porch, watching the sun descend, and for a brief moment, the lines would soften in her face. Her lips would curve into a slight smile. Her shoulders would relax. The sun would slip beneath the horizon and his mother would sigh long and deep.

Then the moment would end. His mother's shoulders would return to bunched-up tension, the worry lines adding ten years to her face. She would usher them back into the house and return to her chores. He and his brother would do their best to help her, all of them careful not to make too much noise.

It wasn't until he was much older, nearly an adult, that the man wondered about these moments with his mom. What did it say about her life that she relaxed only when the sun eased down and signaled the end of the day? What did it mean that the only time she seemed happy was when daylight drew its last gasping breath?

His mother died before he could ask her these questions. Some things, he supposed, were for the best.

The man walked back into his hotel room. Though he'd paid for the night, he planned on leaving in the next half hour. He wouldn't miss this place. He didn't like structures built out of cement, or mass-produced rooms with only one window. These were dead places, the modern-day version of tombs, and the fact that Americans were willing to pay good money to sleep in these cheaply constructed coffins defied his imagination.

He worried sometimes that the very fakeness of a room like this, with its garish comforter, particle-board furniture, and carpet made with petroleum-based fibers would penetrate his skin, get into his bloodstream and he'd wake up one morning craving a Big Mac.

The thought frightened him; he had to take a moment to draw deep breaths. Not a good idea. The air was foul, rank with fiberglass insulation and plastic ficus trees. He rubbed his temples furiously, and knew he needed to leave more quickly.

His clothes were packed in his duffel bag. He had just one thing left to check.

He wrapped his hand in one of the bathroom towels, reached with his covered hand beneath the bed, and slowly pulled out the brown attaché case. It looked like any other business briefcase. Maybe full of spreadsheets and pocket calculators and personal electronic devices. His, however, wasn't.

His carried a dart gun, currently broken down, but easy to reassemble in the field. He checked the inside pocket of the attaché case, pulled out the metal box, and counted the darts inside. One dozen hits, preloaded with five hundred and fifty milligrams of Ketamine. He had prepared each dart just this morning.

He returned the metal box and pulled out two rolls of duct tape, heavy duty, followed by a plain brown paper bag filled with nails. Beside the duct tape and nails, he kept a small glass bottle of chloral hydrate. A backup drug, which thankfully he'd never had to use. Next to the chloral hydrate, he had a special insulated water bottle he'd been keeping in the minibar freezer until just fifteen minutes ago. The outside of the container froze, helping keep the inside contents cool. That was important. Ativan crystalized if not kept refrigerated.

He felt the bottle again. It was ice cold. Good. This was his first time using this system and he felt a little nervous. The plastic drinking bottle seemed to do the trick, though. The things you could buy for $4.99 from Wal-Mart.

The man took a deep breath. He was trying to remember if he needed anything else. It had been a while. Truth be told, he was nervous. Lately, he'd been struggling a bit with dates. Things that happened a long time ago, seemed bright as day, whereas yesterday's events took on a hazy, dreamlike quality.

Yesterday, when he had arrived here, three years ago blazed in his mind with vivid, Technicolor detail. This morning, however, things already started to fade and curl at the edges. He was worried that if he waited much longer, he'd lose the memories altogether. They'd disappear into the black void with his other thoughts, his nonflaming thoughts, and he'd be left sitting at the edges again, waiting helplessly for something, anything, to float to the top.

Crackers. Saltines. And water. Gallon jugs. Several of them.

That's right, he had these things in the van. He'd gotten them yesterday, also from Wal-Mart, or maybe it had been K mart – now see, that detail had disappeared, slipped into the pit, what was he supposed to do? Yesterday. He'd bought things. Supplies. At a very big store. Well, what could the name matter anyway? He'd paid cash, right? And burned the receipt?

Of course, he had. Even if his memory played tricks on him, it was no excuse for stupidity. His father had always been adamant on that point. The world was run by dumb fuck idiots who couldn't find their own assholes with a flashlight and two hands. His sons, on the other hand, must be better than that. Be strong. Stand tall. Take your punishment like a man.

The man finished looking around. He was thinking of fire again, the heat of flames, but it was too soon so he let that thought go, willed it into the void, though he knew it would never stay. He had his travel bag; he had his attaché case. Other supplies in the van. Room already wiped down with ammonia and water. Leave no trace of prints.

All right.

Just one last item to grab. In the corner of the room, sitting on the horrible, fake carpet. A small rectangular aquarium covered in his own yellow faded sheet.

The man slipped the strap of his duffel bag over his shoulder, followed by the strap for his attaché case. Then he used both arms to heft up the heavy glass aquarium. The sheet started to slip. From inside the yellow depths came an ominous rattle.

'Shhhh,' he murmured. 'Not yet, my love, not yet.'

The man strode into the blood-red dusk, into the stifling, heavy heat. His brain fired to life. More pictures came to his mind. Black skirts, high heels, blond hair, blue eyes, red blouse, bound hands, dark hair, brown eyes, long legs, scratching nails, flashing white teeth.

The man loaded up his van, got behind the wheel. At the last minute, his errant memory sparked and he patted his breast pocket. Yes, he had the ID badge as well. He pulled it out and inspected it one final time. The front of the plastic rectangle was simple enough. In white letters against the blue backdrop, the badge read Visitor.

He flipped the ID over. The back of the security card was definitely much more interesting. It read: Property of the FBI.

The man clipped the ID badge to his collar. The sun sank, the sky turned from red to purple to black.

'Clock ticking,' the man murmured. He started to drive.

4

'What's up, sugar? You seem restless tonight.'

'Can't stand the heat.'

'That's a strange comment coming from a man who lives in Hotlanta.'

'I keep meaning to move.'

Genny, a tight-bodied redhead with a well-weathered face but genuinely kind eyes, gazed at him speculatively through the blue haze of the smoky bar.

'How long have you lived in Georgia, Mac?' she asked over the din.

'Since I was a gleam in my daddy's eye.'

She smiled, shook her head and stubbed out her cigarette in the glass ashtray. 'Then you won't ever move, sugar. Take it from me. You're a Georgian. Stick a fork in you, you're done.'

'You just say that because you're a Texan.'

'Since I was a gleam in my great-great-great-grandpappy's eyes. Yanks move around, honey. We Southerners take root.'

GBI Special Agent Mac McCormack acknowledged the point with a smile. His gaze was on the front door of the crowded bar again. He was watching the people walk in, unconsciously seeking out young girls traveling in pairs. He should know better. On days like this, when the temperature topped ninety, he didn't.

'Sugar?' Genny said again.

He caught himself, turned back to her, and managed a rueful grin. 'Sorry. I swear to you my mother raised me better than this.'

'Then we'll never let her know. Your meeting didn't go well today, did it?'

'How did you—'

'I'm a police officer, too, Mac. Don't dismiss me just because I'm pretty and got a great set of boobs.'

He opened his mouth to protest, but she cut him off with a wave of her hand, then dug around in her purse until she found a fresh cigarette. He held up a light and she smiled her gratitude, though the lines were a bit tighter around her eyes. For a minute, neither one of them said a word.

The bar was hopping tonight, flesh pressed against flesh, with more people still pouring through the doors. Half of them, of course, were their fellow National Academy classmates – detectives, sheriffs, and even some military police enrolled in Quantico's eleven-week course. Still, Mac wouldn't have expected the bar to be this busy on a Tuesday night. People were fleeing their homes, probably trying to escape the heat.

He and Genny had arrived three hours ago, early enough to stake out hard-to-find seats. Generally the National Academy students didn't leave Quantico much. People hung out in the Boardroom after hours, drinking beer, swapping war stories, and by one or two in the morning, praying that their livers wouldn't fail them now. The big joke was that the program had to end week eleven, because no one's kidneys could survive week twelve.

People were restless tonight, though. The unbearable heat and humidity had started moving in on Sunday, and reportedly were working their way to a Friday crescendo. Walking outside was like slogging through a pile of wet towels. In five minutes your T-shirt was plastered to your torso. In ten minutes, your shorts were glued to your thighs. Inside seemed little better, with the Academy's archaic air-conditioning system groaning mightily just to cool things to eighty-five.

People started bailing from Quantico shortly after six, desperate for any sort of distraction. Genny and Mac had followed shortly thereafter.

They'd met the first week of training, eight weeks ago. Southerners had to stick together, Genny had teased him, especially in a class overrun with fast-talking Yanks. Her gaze, however, had been on his broad chest when she'd said this. Mac had merely grinned.

At the age of thirty-six, he'd figured out by now that he was a good-looking guy – six two, black hair, blue eyes, and deeply tanned skin from a lifetime spent running, cycling, fishing, hunting, hiking, canoeing, etc. You name it, he did it and he had a younger sister and nine cousins who accompanied him all the way. You could get into a lot of trouble in a state as diverse as Georgia, and the McCormacks prided themselves on learning each lesson the hard way.

The end result was a leanly muscled physique that seemed to appeal to women of all ages. Mac did his best to bear this hardship stoically. It helped a great deal that he was fond of women. Really, truly fond. A little *too* fond, according to his exasperated mother, who was dead-set on gaining a daughter-in-law and oodles of grandkids. Maybe someday, he supposed. At the moment, however, Mac was completely wed to his job, and days like this, boy didn't he know it.

His gaze returned to the doorway. Two young girls walked in, followed by another two. All were chatting happily. He wondered if they would leave that way. Together, alone, with newly met lovers, without. Which way would be safer? Man, he hated nights like this.

'You gotta let it go,' Genny said.

'Let what go?'

'Whatever's putting lines on that handsome face.'

Mac tore his gaze away from the door for the second time. He regarded Genny wryly, then picked up his beer and spun it between his fingers. 'You ever have one of those cases?'

'The kind that gets beneath your skin, soaks into your blood, jumps into your brain and haunts your dreams, until five, six, ten, twenty years later you still sometimes wake up screaming? No sugar, I wouldn't know a thing about that.' She stubbed out her cigarette, then reached in her purse for another.

'Sugar,' Mac mocked gently, 'you're lying through your teeth.' He held up a lighter again and watched how her blue eyes appraised him even as she leaned toward his hands and accepted the flame.

She sat back. She inhaled. She exhaled. She said abruptly, 'All right, pretty boy. There's no dealing with you tonight, so you might as well tell me about your meeting.'

'It never happened,' he said readily.

'Blew you off?'

'For bigger fish. According to Dr Ennunzio, it's now all terrorism all the time.'

'Versus your three-year-old case,' she filled in for him.

He grinned crookedly, leaned back, and spread out his darkly bronzed hands. 'I have seven dead girls, Genny. Seven little girls who never made it home to their families. It's not their fault they were murdered by a plain-vanilla serial killer and not some imported terrorist threat.'

'Battle of the budgets.'

'Absolutely. The Behavioral Science Unit has only one forensic linguist – Dr Ennunzio – but the nation has thousands of whackos writing threats. Apparently, letters to the editor are low on the list of priorities. Of course, in my world, these letters are about the only damn lead we have left. National Academy prestige aside, my department didn't send me here for continued education. I'm supposed to meet this man. Get his expert input on the only decent lead we have left. I go back to my department without so much as saying boo to the fine doctor, and I can kiss my ass good-bye.'

'You don't care about your ass.'

'It would be easier if I did,' Mac said, with his first trace of seriousness all night.

'You ask anyone else in Behavioral Science for help?'

'I've asked anyone who'll give me the time of day in the hall for help. Hell, Genny, I'm not proud. I just *want* this guy.'

'You could go independent.'

'Been there, done that. Got us nowhere.'

Genny considered this while taking another drag from her cigarette. Despite what she might think, Mac hadn't let the great set of boobs fool him. Genny was a sheriff. Ran her own twelve-man office. In Texas, where girls were still encouraged to become cheerleaders or better yet, Miss America. In other words, Genny was tough. And smart. And experienced. She probably had *many* of those cases that got under an investigator's skin. And given how hot it had become outside, how hot it would be by the end of the week, Mac would appreciate any insight she could give him.

'It's been three years,' she said at last. 'That's a long time for a serial predator. Maybe your guy wound up in jail on some other charge. It's been known to happen.'

'Could be,' Mac acknowledged, though his tone said he wasn't convinced.

She accepted that with a nod. 'Well how about this, big boy? Maybe he's dead.'

'Hallelujah and praise the Lord,' Mac agreed. His voice still lacked conviction. Six months ago he'd been working on buying into that theory. Hell, he'd been looking forward to embracing that theory. Violent felons often led violent lives and came to violent ends. All the better for the taxpayers, as far as Mac was concerned.

But then, six months ago, one single letter in the mail . . .

Funny the things that could rock your world. Funny the things that could take a three-year-old frustrated task force and launch it from low-burn, cooling their heels to high-octane, move, now, now, now in twenty-four hours or less. But he couldn't mention these things to Genny. These were details told only on a need-to-know basis.

Like why he really wanted to talk to Dr Ennunzio. Or why he was really even in the great state of Virginia.

Almost on cue, he felt the vibration at his waist. He looked down at his beeper, the sense of foreboding already gathering low in his belly. Ten numbers stared back up at him. Atlanta area code. And the other numbers . . .

Damn!

'I gotta go,' he said, bolting to his feet.

'She that good looking?' Genny drawled.

'Honey, I'm not that lucky tonight.'

He threw thirty bucks on the table, enough to cover his drinks and hers. 'You got a ride?' His voice was curt, the question unconsciously rude, and they both knew it.

'No man's that hard to replace.'

'You cut me deep, Genny.'

She smiled, her gaze lingering on his tall athletic build, her eyes sadder than she intended. 'Sugar, I don't cut you at all.'

Mac, however, was already striding out the door.

Outside, the heat smacked the grin off of Mac's face. Merry blue eyes immediately turned dark, his expression went from teasing to grim. It had been four weeks since he'd last received a call. He'd been beginning to wonder if that was it.

GBI Special Agent Mac McCormack flipped open his cell phone and furiously started dialing.

The person picked up after the first ring. 'You are not even trying,' an eerily distorted voice echoed in his ears. Male, female – hell, it could've been Mickey Mouse.

'I'm here, aren't I?' Mac replied tightly. He stopped in the Virginia parking lot, looking around the dark, empty space. The phone number always read Atlanta, but lately Mac had begun wondering about that. All a person had to do was use a cell phone with a Georgia number, then he could call from anywhere with the same effect.

'He's closer than you think.'

'Then maybe you should stop speaking in riddles and tell me the truth.' Mac turned right, then left. Nothing.

'I mailed you the truth,' the disembodied voice intoned.

'You sent me a riddle. I deal in information, buddy, not childish games.'

'You deal in death.'

'You're not doing much better. Come on. It's been six months. Let's end this dance and get down to some business. You must want something. I know I want something. What do you say?'

The voice fell silent for a moment. Mac wondered if he'd finally shamed the caller, then in the next instant he worried that he'd pissed off the man/woman/mouse, His grip tightened on his phone, pressing it against the curve of his ear. He couldn't afford to lose this call. Damn he hated this.

Six months ago, Mac had received the first 'letter' in the mail. It was a newspaper clipping really, of a letter to the editor of the *Virginian-Pilot*. And the one short paragraph was horribly, hauntingly similar to other editorial notes, now three years past: planet dying . . . animals weeping . . . rivers screaming . . . can't you hear it? heat kills . . .

Three years later, the beast was stirring again. Mac didn't know what had happened in between, but he and his task force were very, truly frightened about what might happen next.

'It's getting hot,' the voice singsonged now.

Mac looked around the darkness frantically. No one. Nothing. Dammit! 'Who are you?' he tried. 'Come on, buddy, speak to me.'

'He's closer than you think.'

'Then give me a name. I'll go get him and no one will be hurt.' He changed tack. 'Are you scared? Are you frightened of him, because trust me, we can protect you.'

'He doesn't want to hurt them. I don't think he can help himself.'

'If he's someone you care about, if you're worried for his safety, don't be. We have procedures for this kind of arrest, we'll take appropriate measures. Come on, this guy has killed seven girls. Give me his name. Let me solve this problem for you. You're doing the right thing.'

'I don't have all the answers,' the voice said, and for a moment, it sounded so plaintive, Mac nearly believed him. And then, 'You should've caught him three years ago, Special Agent. Why oh why didn't you guys catch him?'

'Work with us and we'll get him now.'

'Too late,' the caller said. 'He never could stand the heat.'

The connection broke. Mac was left in the middle of the parking lot, gripping his impossibly tiny phone and cursing a blue streak. He punched send again. The number rang and rang and rang, but the person didn't pick up and wouldn't until Mac was paged again.

'Damn,' Mac said again. Then, 'Damn, damn, damn.'

He found his rental car. Inside it was approximately two hundred degrees. He slid into the seat, leaned his forehead against the steering wheel, then banged his head against the hard plastic three times. Six phone calls now and he was no closer to knowing a single goddamn thing. And time was running out. Mac had known it, had been feeling it, since the mercury had started rising on Sunday.

Tomorrow Mac would check in with his Atlanta office, report the latest call. The task force could review, rework, reanalyze . . . And wait. After all this time, that's about all they had left – the wait.

Mac pressed his forehead against the steering wheel. Exhaled deeply. He was thinking of Nora Ray Watts again. The way her face had lit up like the sun when she had stepped from the rescue chopper and spotted her parents standing just outside of the rotor wash. The way her expression had faltered, then collapsed thirty seconds later after she'd excitedly, innocently asked, 'Where is Mary Lynn?'

And then her voice with that impossible reedy wail, over and over again. 'No, no, no. Oh god, please *no*.'

Her father had tried to prop her up. Nora Ray sank down on the tarmac, curling up beneath her army blanket as if that could protect her from the truth. Her parents finally collapsed with her, a huddle of green grief that would never know an end.

They won that day. They lost that day.

And now?

It was hot, it was late. And a man was writing letters to the editor once again.

Go home, little girls. Lock the doors. Turn out the lights. Don't end up like Nora Ray Watts who ran out with her younger sister for a little ice cream one night and ended up abandoned in a desolate part of the coast, frantically burying herself deeper into the muck, while the fiddler crabs nibbled on her toes, the razor clams slashed open her palms, and the scavengers began to circle overhead.

5

Fredericksburg, Virginia
10:34 P.M.
Temperature: 89 degrees

'I'm ready,' Tina said two inches from Betsy's ear. In the pounding noise of the jam-packed bar, her roommate didn't seem to hear her. They were outside Fredericksburg, at a little hole-in-the-wall joint favored by college students, biker gangs, and really loud Western bands. Even on a Tuesday night, the place was jamming, the people so thick and the base so loud Tina didn't know how the roof stayed on over their heads.

'I'm ready,' Tina tried again, shouting louder. This time, Betsy at least turned toward her.

'What?' Betsy yelled.

'Time ... to ... go ... *home*,' Tina hollered back.

'Bathroom?'

'HOME!'

'Oooooh.' Her roommate finally got it. She looked at Tina more closely and her brown eyes instantly softened with concern. 'You okay?'

'Hot!'

'No kidding.'

'Not feeling . . . so well.' Actually, she was feeling horrible. Her long blond hair had come untangled from its knot and was plastered against her neck. Sweat trickled down the small of her back, over her butt, and all the way down her legs. The air was too heavy. She kept trying to draw deep, gulping breaths, but she still wasn't getting enough oxygen. She thought . . . She thought she might be sick.

'Let me tell the others,' Betsy said immediately, and headed out to the jostling dance floor where Viv and Karen were lost amid the sea of people.

Tina closed her eyes and promised herself she would not projectile vomit in the middle of a crowded bar.

Fifteen minutes later, they had pushed their way outside and were walking toward Betsy's Saab, Viv and Karen bringing up the rear. Tina put her hand against her face. Her forehead felt feverish to her.

'Are you going to make it?' Betsy asked her. After screaming to be heard in the bar, her voice cracked three decibels too loud in the parking lot's total silence. They all winced.

'I don't know.'

'Girl, you had better tell me if you're going to be sick,' Betsy warned seriously. 'I'll hold your head over the toilet, but I draw the line at puking in my car.'

Tina smiled weakly. 'Thanks.'

'I could go get you some club soda,' Karen offered from behind her.

'Maybe we should just wait a minute,' Viv said. She, Karen, and Betsy all drew up short.

Tina, however, had already climbed into Betsy's Saab. 'I just want to go home,' she murmured quietly. 'Please, let's go home.'

She closed her eyes as her head fell back against the seat. With her eyes closed, her head felt better. Her hands settled upon her stomach. The music faded away. Tina let herself drift off to desperately needed sleep.

It seemed to her that they had no sooner left the parking lot, than she was awakened by a savage jerk.

'What the—' Her head popped up. The car lurched again and she grabbed the dash.

'Back tire,' Betsy said in disgust. 'I think I got a flat.'

The car lurched right and that was enough for Tina. 'Betsy,' she said tightly. 'Pull over. *Now!*'

'Got it!' Betsy jerked the car onto the right-hand shoulder of the road. Tina fumbled with the clasp of her seat belt, then fumbled with the door. She got out of the car and sprinted down the embankment into the nearby woods. She got her head down just in time.

Oh, this was not fun. Not fun at all. She heaved up two cranberry and tonics, then the pasta she'd had for dinner, then anything else she'd ever eaten for the last twenty years. She simply stood there, hands braced upon her thighs as she dry-heaved.

I'm going to die, she thought. I was bad and now I'm being punished and my mom was right all along. There is no way in the world I'm going to be able to take this. Oh God, I want to go home.

Maybe she cried. Maybe she was just sweating harder. With her head between her knees, it was hard to be sure.

But slowly her stomach relented. The cramping eased, the worst of the nausea seemed to pass. She staggered upright, put her face up to the sky, and thought she'd kill for an ice cold shower right about now. No such luck. They were in the middle of nowhere outside of Fredericksburg. She'd just have to wait.

She sighed. And then for the first time, she heard the noise. A non-Betsy noise. A non-girls-out-on-the-town noise. It sounded high, short, metallic. Like the slide of a rifle, ratcheting back.

Tina slowly turned toward the road. In the hot humid dark, she was no longer alone.

Kimberly never even heard a noise. She was an FBI trainee, for God's sake. A woman experienced with crime and paranoid to boot. She still never heard a thing.

She stood alone at the Academy's outdoor firing range, surrounded by 385 acres of darkness with only a small Mag flashlight. In her hands, she held an empty shotgun.

It was late. The new agents, the Marines, hell even the National Academy 'students' had long since gone to bed. The stadium lights were extinguished. The distant bank of towering trees formed an ominous barrier between her and civilization. Then there were the giant steel sidewalls, designed to segregate the various firing ranges while stopping high-velocity bullets.

No lights. No sounds. Just the unnatural hush of a night so hot and humid not even the squirrels stirred from their trees.

She was tired. That was her best excuse. She'd run, she'd pumped iron, she'd walked, she'd studied, then she'd downed three gallons of water and two PowerBars and headed out here. Her legs were shaky. Her arm muscles trembled with fatigue.

She hefted the empty shotgun to her shoulder, and went through the rhythms of firing over and over again.

Place butt firmly against right shoulder to absorb the recoil. Plant feet hip-width apart, loose in the knees. Lean slightly forward into the shot. At the last minute, as your right finger squeezes the trigger, pull forward with your left hand as if the gun were a broom handle you were trying to tear in half. Hope against hope, you don't fall once more on your butt. Or smash your shoulder. Or shatter your cheek.

Live ammunition was limited to supervised drills, so Kimberly had no real way of knowing how she was doing.

Still, lots of the new agents came out after hours to go through the motions. The more times you handled a weapon, the more comfortable it felt in your hands.

If you did it enough times, maybe it would become instinctive. And if it became instinctive, maybe you'd survive the next firearms test.

She leaned into her next practice 'shot'. Went a little too far, and her rubbery legs wobbled dangerously. She reached out a hand, had just caught herself, and then, in the pitch darkness beside her, she heard a man say, 'You shouldn't be out here alone.'

Kimberly acted on instinct. She whirled, spotted the hulking, threatening form, and whipped the empty shotgun at the man's face. Then, she ran.

A grunt. Surprise. Pain. She didn't wait to find out. The hour was late, the surroundings remote, and she knew too well that some predators preferred it if you screamed.

Footsteps. Hard and fast behind her. In her initial panic, Kimberly had sprinted toward the trees. Bad idea. Trees were dark, sheltered, and far away from help. She needed to cut back toward the Academy buildings, back toward lights, population, and the FBI police. The man was already gaining on her.

Kimberly took a deep breath. Her heart was pounding, her lungs screaming. Her body was too abused for this kind of business. Good news, adrenaline was a powerful drug.

She focused on the footsteps behind her, trying to separate their staccato beat from her heart's frantic hammering. He was gaining. Fast. Of course. He was bigger and stronger than her. At the end of the day, the men always were.

Fuck him.

She homed in on his rhythm, timed it with her own. One, two, three—

The man's hand snaked out for her left wrist. Kimberly

suddenly planted her feet, pirouetted right. He overshot her completely. And she took off at warp nine for the lights.

'Jesus!' she heard the man swear.

It made her smile. Grim and fierce. Then the footsteps were behind her again.

Is this how her mother had felt? She had fought bitterly in the end. Her father had tried to protect Kimberly from the details, but a year later, on her own, Kimberly had looked up all the articles in the *Philadelphia Inquirer*. High Society House of Horrors, the first banner headline had declared. Then it had gone on to describe the trail of blood that ran from room to room.

Had her mother known then that the man had already killed Mandy? Had she guessed that he would come after Kimberly next? Or had she simply realized, in those last desperate minutes, that beneath the silk and pearls she was an animal, too? And all animals, even the lowest field mice, fight to live in the end.

The footsteps had closed in on her again. The lights were too far away. She wasn't going to make it. It amazed her how coolly she accepted this fact.

Time's up, Kimberly. No actors, here. No paint guns, no bulletproof vests. She had one last ploy.

She counted his footsteps. Timed his approach. And then, in the next heartbeat as he was upon her, his giant form swooping down on her own, she dropped to the ground and curled her arms protectively over her head.

She saw the man's face, faintly caught by the distant lights. His eyes went wide. He tried to draw up short, his arms flailing wildly. He made one last desperate move, careening left to spin around her.

Kimberly adroitly stuck out her leg. And he went flat on his face on the ground.

Ten seconds later, she flipped him over on his back, dropped down on his chest and placed the silver blade of her serrated hunting knife against his dark throat.

'Who the fuck are you?' she asked.

The man started to laugh.

'Betsy?' Tina called nervously. No answer. 'Bets?'

Still nothing. And then it hit Tina the second thing that was wrong. There were no other sounds. Shouldn't she be hearing car doors opening or closing? Or even Betsy heaving as she dragged the spare to the ground? Surely there should be some noise. Other cars. Crickets. The wind in the trees.

But there was nothing. Absolutely nothing. The night had gone completely, deathly still.

'This isn't funny anymore,' Tina said weakly.

Then she heard a twig snap. And then she saw his face.

Pale, somber, maybe even gentle above the black collar of his turtleneck. How in the world could someone wear a turtleneck in this heat, Tina thought.

Then, he hefted up the rifle and leveled it against his shoulder.

Tina stopped thinking. She bolted for the trees.

'Stop laughing. Why are you laughing? Hey, stop!'

The man laughed harder, a steady ripple of spasms moving down his large frame and tossing her from side to side as easily as if she were a small boat caught in a rough wake. 'Toppled by a woman,' he gasped with an unmistakable southern accent. 'Oh, please, honey . . . don't tell my sister.'

His sister? What the hell?

'All right. That's it. Move one more muscle and I will slit your throat.' Kimberly must've sounded more impressive this time. The man finally stopped laughing. That was better. 'Name?' she asked crisply.

'Special Agent Michael McCormack.'

Kimberly's eyes widened. She had a sudden bad feeling. 'FBI?' she whispered. Oh no, she'd taken out a fellow agent. Probably her future boss. She wondered who would make the call to her father. '*You know, Quincy old fellow, you were a star among stars here at the Bureau; but I'm afraid your daughter is just too, er,* freaky *for us.*'

'Georgia Bureau of Investigation,' the man drawled. 'State police. We've always had a soft spot for the Bureau, though, so we stole your titles.'

'You little—' She was so angry she couldn't think of a word. She whacked his shoulder with her left hand, then remembered, oh yeah, she had a knife. 'You're with the National Academy,' she accused him, in the same tone of voice others used for addressing vermin.

'And you're a new agent . . . obviously.'

'Hey, I still have a knife at your throat, mister!'

'I know.' He frowned at her, his easy tone throwing her for another loop. Was it her imagination, or had he just shifted to get more comfortable beneath her? 'Why are you carrying a knife?'

'They took away my Glock,' she said without thinking.

'Of course.' He nodded as if she were very wise, instead of a highly paranoid aspiring federal agent. 'If I might ask a personal question, ma'am. Umm, where do you hide the blade?'

'I beg your pardon!' She could definitely feel his gaze on her body now, and she immediately blushed. It was hot. She'd been working out . . . So the nylon shorts and thin blue T-shirt didn't cover much. She was training after hours, for God's sake, not preparing for an interview. Besides, it was amazing the things you could strap to the inside of your thigh.

'Why did you chase me?' she demanded, pressing the tip of her knife deeper against his throat.

'Why did you run?'

She scowled, pursed her lips, then tried another tack. 'What are you doing out here?'

'Saw the light. Thought I'd better investigate.'

'Ah ha! So I'm not the only one who's paranoid.'

'That's true, ma'am. It would appear that we're both equally paranoid. I can't stand the heat. What's your story?'

'I don't have a story!'

'Fair enough. You're the one with the knife after all.'

He fell silent and seemed to be waiting for her to do something. Which was an interesting point. What was she going to do now? New Agent Kimberly Quincy has just made her first apprehension. Unfortunately, he was a fellow law enforcement officer whose title was already bigger than hers.

Damn. Double damn. God she was tired.

All at once, the last of the adrenaline left her, and her body, pushed too hard too fast, simply collapsed. She slid off the man's chest and let her aching limbs sprawl in the relative comfort of the thick green grass.

'Long day?' Southern boy asked, making no effort to get up.

'Long life,' Kimberly replied flatly, then promptly wished she hadn't.

Super cop didn't say anything more, though. He tucked his hands beneath his head and appeared to be studying the sky. Kimberly followed his gaze and for the first time noticed the clear night sky, the sea of tiny, crystal stars. It was a beautiful night, really. Other girls her age probably went for walks during nights like this. Held hands with their boyfriends. Giggled when the guy tried to steal a kiss.

Kimberly couldn't even imagine that sort of life. All she'd ever wanted was this.

She turned her head toward her companion, who seemed content with the silence. Upon closer inspection, he was a big guy. Not as big as some of the ex-Marines in her class, but he was over six feet tall and obviously very active. Dark hair, bronzed skin, very fit. She'd done good to take him out. She was proud of herself.

'You scared the shit out of me,' she said at last.

'That was uncalled for,' he agreed.

'You shouldn't skulk around at night.'

'Damn straight.'

'How long have you been in the program?'

'Arrived in June. You?'

'Week nine. Seven to go.'

'You'll do fine,' he said.

'How do you know?'

'You outran me, didn't you? And trust me, honey, most of the beautiful women I've chased haven't gotten away.'

'You are so full of shit!' she told him crossly.

He just laughed again. The sound was deep and rumbly, like a jungle cat's purr. She decided she didn't like Special Agent Michael McCormack very much. She should move, get away from him. Her body hurt too much. She went back to gazing at the stars.

'It's hot out,' she said.

'Yes ma'am.'

'You said you didn't like the heat.'

'Yes ma'am.' He waited a heartbeat, then turned his head. 'Heat kills,' he said, and it took her another moment to realize that he was finally serious.

Tree branches scratched at her face. Shrubs grabbed her ankles, while the tall grass tangled around her sandals and tried to pull her down. Tina pressed forward, panting hard, heart in her throat, as she careened from tree to tree and tried frantically to get one foot in front of the other.

He wasn't running behind her. She heard no stampede of

footsteps or angry commands to halt. He was quieter than that. Stealthier. And that frightened her far more.

Where was she going? She didn't know. Why was he after her? She was too afraid to find out. What had happened to Betsy? The thought filled her with pain.

And the air was hot, searing her throat. And the air was wet, burning her lungs. And it was late, and she'd run away from the road, instinctively heading downhill, and now she realized her mistake. There would be no savior for her down in these deep dark shadows. There would be no safety.

Maybe if she could get far enough ahead. She was fit, active, agile. She could find a tree, climb high above his head. She could find a ravine, duck low and curl up so small and tight he'd never see her. She could find a vine, and soar away like Tarzan in the animated Disney movie. She would like to be in a movie now. She would like to be anywhere but here.

The log came out of nowhere. A dead tree probably felled by lightning decades ago. She connected first with her shin, couldn't bite back her sharp scream of pain, and went toppling down the other side. Her palms scraped savagely across a thorny shrub. Then her shoulder hit the rock-hard ground and her breath was knocked from her body.

The faint crackle of twigs behind her. Calm. Controlled. Contained.

Is this how death comes? Slowly walking through the woods?

Tina's shin throbbed. Her lungs refused to inhale. She staggered to her feet anyway and tried one more step.

A faint whistle through the dark. A short stabbing pain. She looked down and spotted the feathery dart now protruding from her left thigh. What the . . .

She tried to take a step. Her mind commanded her body, screamed with primal urgency: *Run, run, run!* Her legs buckled. She went down in the knee-high grass as a strange, fluid warmth filled her veins and her muscles simply surrendered.

The panic was receding from her consciousness. Her heart slowed. Her lungs finally unlocked, giving easily into that next soft breath. Her body started to float, the woods spinning away.

Drugs, she thought. Doomed. And then even that thought wafted out of her reach.

Footsteps, coming closer. Her last image, his face, gazing down at her patiently.

'Please,' Tina murmured thickly, her hands curling instinctively around her belly. 'Please . . . Don't hurt me . . . I'm pregnant.'

The man simply hefted her unconscious form over his shoulder and carried her away.

Nora Ray Watts had a dream. In her dream it was blue and pink and purple. In her dream the air felt like velvet and she could spin around and around and still see the bright pinpricks of stars. In her dream, she was laughing and her dog Mumphry danced around her feet and even her worn-out parents finally wore a smile.

The only thing missing, of course, was her sister.

Then a door opened. Yawned black and gaping. It beckoned her toward it, drew her in. Nora Ray walked toward it, unafraid. She had taken this door before. Sometimes she fell asleep these days, just so she could find it again.

Nora Ray stepped inside in the shadowy depths—

And in the next instant, she was jerked awake. Her mother stood over her in the darkened room, her hand on her shoulder.

'You were dreaming,' her mother said.

'I saw Mary Lynn,' Nora Ray countered sleepily. 'I think she has a friend.'

'Shhh,' her mother told her. 'Let her go, baby. It's only the heat.'

6

'Get out of bed.'
  'No.'
  'Get out of bed!'
  'No.'
  'Kimberly, it's seven o'clock. Get up!'
  'Can't make me.'
  The voice finally disappeared. Thank God. Kimberly sank blissfully back down into the desperately needed blackness. Then . . . a bolt of ice-cold water slapped across her face. Kimberly jerked upright in the bed, gasping for breath as she frantically wiped the deluge from her eyes.
  Lucy stood beside her, holding an empty water pitcher, and looking unrepentant. 'I have a five-year-old son,' she said. 'Don't mess with me.'
  Kimberly's gaze had just fallen on the bedside clock. Seven-ten A.M.
  'Aaaagh!' she yelped. She jumped out of bed and looked wildly around the room. She was supposed to be . . . supposed to do . . . Okay, get dressed. She bolted for the closet.

'Late night?' Lucy asked with a raised brow as she trailed behind Kimberly. 'Let me guess. Physical training or firearms training or both?'

'Both.' Kimberly found her khaki pants, tore them on, then remembered she was supposed to report to the PT course first thing this morning, and ripped back off her khakis in favor of a fresh pair of blue nylon shorts.

'Nice bruises,' Lucy commented. 'Want to see the one on my ass? Seriously, I look like a side of beef. I used to be a trial lawyer, you know. I swear I once drove something called a Mercedes.'

'I thought that's what drug dealers had.' Kimberly found her T-shirt, yanked it on while walking into the bathroom, then made the mistake of looking in the mirror. Oh God. Her eyes looked like they'd collapsed into sunken pits.

'I spoke to my son last night,' Lucy was saying behind her. 'Kid's telling everyone I'm learning to shoot people – but only the bad ones.'

'That's sweet.'

'You think?'

'Absolutely.' Kimberly found the toothpaste, brushed furiously, spit, rinsed, then made the mistake of looking in the mirror a second time, and fled the bathroom.

'You look like hell,' Lucy said cheerfully. 'Is that your strategy? You're going to scare the bad guys into surrendering with your looks?'

'Remember which one of us is better with a gun,' Kimberly muttered.

'Yeah, and remember which one of us is better with a pitcher of water!' Lucy brandished her weapon triumphantly, then, with a final glance at the clock, replaced the pitcher on top of her desk and headed for the door. Then she paused. 'Seriously, Kimberly, maybe you should curtail the midnight sessions for a bit. You have to be conscious to graduate.'

'Have fun shooting,' Kimberly called after her exiting roommate while frantically lacing her sneakers. Lucy was gone. And in another second, Kimberly was also out the door.

Kimberly was a lucky girl after all. She could pinpoint the exact moment when her whole career fell apart. It happened at eight twenty-three A.M. That morning. At the FBI Academy. With only seven weeks to go.

She was tired, disoriented from too little sleep and a strange midnight chase with a Georgia special agent. She'd been pushing herself too hard. Maybe she should've listened to Lucy after all.

She thought about it a lot. Later, of course. After they'd taken away the body.

Things started out fine enough. PT training wasn't so hard. Eight A.M., they did some pushups, then some sit-ups. Then the good old jumping jacks everyone learns in grade school. They looked like a sea of blue-clad kids. All obediently standing in line. All obediently going through the motions.

Then they were sent out to run three miles, using the same course Kimberly had jogged just last night.

The PT course started in the woods. Not a difficult path. Hell, it was paved. That would be one hint of where to go. The signs were another hint. Run! Suck it in! Love it! *Endure.*

They started as a herd, then gradually thinned out as people found their individual paces. Kimberly had never been the fastest in her class. She generally wasn't the slowest either.

Except this morning. This morning she almost immediately fell behind.

Vaguely, she was aware of her classmates pulling ahead. Vaguely she was aware of her own labored breathing as she struggled to keep up. Her left side ached. Her feet were sluggish. She stared down at the blacktop, willing one foot to land in front of the other.

She didn't feel well. The world tilted dangerously, and she thought for a moment that she was honestly going to faint. She just made it off the path and grabbed a tree for support.

God, her side hurt, the muscle stitched so tight it felt as if it had a vice-grip on her lungs. And the damn air was so hot already, filled with so much humidity that no matter how many times she inhaled, she couldn't get enough oxygen. She was drowning. She was an FBI new agent, a woman who'd been running all of her life, and now she was going to drown standing in the early morning sun.

She headed deeper into the woods, desperately seeking shade. Green trees whirled sickeningly, while goose bumps suddenly burst out across her arms. She started shivering uncontrollably.

Dehydration or heat sickness, she thought idly. Is that good enough for you yet, Kimberly, or would you like to take this self-destructive streak a step further?

The woods spun faster. A faint roaring filled her ears while black dots spotted in front of her eyes. Breathe, Kimberly. Come on, honey, breathe.

She couldn't do it. Her side wouldn't unlock. She couldn't draw a breath. She was going to pass out in the woods. She was going to collapse onto this hard, leaf-strewn ground and all she wanted was for the dirt to feel cool against her face.

And then the thoughts rushed her all at once.

Last night, and the genuine terror that had seized her by the throat when she'd seen a strange man standing beside her. She had thought . . . What? That it was her turn? That death had come for every other woman in her family? That she'd barely escaped six years ago, but that didn't mean death was done with her yet?

She thought that she spent too much time with crime scene photos, and though she would never tell anyone, sometimes she saw the pictures move. Her own face appeared on those lifeless bodies. Her own head topped shattered torsos and bloodied limbs.

And sometimes she had nightmares where she saw her own death, except she never woke up the moment before dying, the way sane people did. No, she dreamt it all the way through, feeling her body plummet over the cliff and smash into the rocks below. Feeling her head slam through the windshield of the shattered car.

And never once in her dreams did she scream. No, she only thought, *finally*.

She couldn't breathe. More black dots danced in front of her vision. She grabbed another tree limb, and hung on tight. How had the air gotten this hot? What had happened to all the oxygen?

And then, in the last sane corner of her mind, it came to her. She was having an anxiety attack. Her body had officially bottomed out, and now she was having an anxiety attack, her first in six years.

She staggered deeper into the woods. She needed to cool down. She needed to draw a breath. She had suffered this kind of episode before. She could survive it again.

She careened through the underbrush, unmindful of the small twigs scratching her cheeks or the tree limbs snatching at her hair. She searched desperately for cooler shade.

Breathe deep, count to ten. Focus on your hands, and making them steady. You're tough. You're strong. You're well trained.

Breathe, Kimberly. Come on honey, just breathe.

She staggered into a clearing, stuck her head between her knees and worked on sucking air until with a final, heaving gasp, her lungs opened up and the air whooshed gratefully into her chest. Inhale. Exhale. That's it, breathe . . .

Kimberly looked down at her hands. They were quieter now, pressed against the hollow plane of her stomach. She forced them away from her body, and inspected her splayed fingers for signs of trembling.

Better. Soon she would be cool again. Then she would resume jogging. And then, because she was very good at this by now, no one would ever know a thing.

Kimberly straightened up. She took one last deep breath, then turned back in the direction of the PT course ... and realized for the first time that she was not alone.

Five feet in front of her was a well-worn dirt path. Wide and very smooth, probably used by the Marines for their training. And right smack in the middle of that path, sprawled the body of a young girl in civilian clothes. Blond hair, black sandals, and splayed tanned limbs. She wore a simple white cotton shirt and a very short, blue-flowered skirt.

Kimberly took one step forward. Then she saw the girl's face, and then she knew.

The goose bumps rippled down her arms again. A shiver snaked up her spine. And in the middle of the hot, still woods, Kimberly began to frantically look around, even as her hand flew to the inside of her leg and found her knife.

First rule of procedure, always secure the crime scene.

Second rule of procedure, call for backup.

Third rule of procedure, try hard not to think of what it means, when young blond women aren't even safe at the Academy. For this girl was quite dead, and by all appearances, it had happened recently.

7

'One more time, Kimberly. How did you end up off the PT course?'

'I got a stitch in my side, I went to the side of the course. I was trying to walk it out, and . . . I don't think I realized how far I had wandered.'

'And you saw the body?'

'I saw something up ahead,' Kimberly said without blinking. 'I headed toward it, and then . . . Well, you know the rest.'

Her class supervisor, Mark Watson, scowled at her, but finally leaned back. She was sitting across from him in his bright, expansive office. Mid-morning sun poured through the bank of windows. An orange monarch butterfly fluttered just outside the glass. It was such a beautiful day to be talking about death.

At Kimberly's cry, two of her classmates had come running. She'd leaned forward and taken the girl's pulse by then. Nothing, of course, but then Kimberly hadn't expected any signs of life. And it wasn't just the girl's wide, sightless brown eyes that spoke of death. It was her violently stitched up mouth, some kind of thick black thread sealing her waxy lips in macabre imitation of Raggedy Ann. Whoever had done this had made damn well sure the girl had never screamed.

The second classmate promptly threw up. But not Kimberly.

Someone had fetched Watson. Upon seeing her grisly find, he had immediately contacted the FBI police as well as the Naval Criminal Investigative Service. Apparently, a death on the Academy's front door did not belong to the FBI, but rather to NCIS. It was their job to protect and serve the Marines.

Kimberly and her classmates had been hastily led away, while young Marines in dark green camouflage and more sophisticated special agents in white dress shirts descended upon the scene. Now, somewhere in the deep woods, real work was being done – death investigators photographing, sketching, and analyzing; an ME examining a young girl's body for last desperate clues; other officers bagging and tagging evidence.

While Kimberly sat here. In an office. As far away from the discovery as a well-meaning FBI supervisor could bring her. One of her knees jogged nervously. She finally crossed her ankles beneath the chair.

'What will happen next?' she asked quietly.

'I don't know.' Her supervisor paused. 'I'll be honest, Kimberly, we've never had this kind of situation before.'

'Well, that's a good thing,' she murmured.

Watson smiled, but it was thin. 'We had a tragedy a few years ago. A National Academy student dropped dead on the firearms course. He was relatively young, which led to speculation. The ME determined, however, that he had died of a sudden massive coronary. Still tragic, but not so shocking given the sheer quantity of people who pass through these grounds in any given year. This situation, on the other hand . . . A facility of this kind relies heavily on good relations with the neighboring communities. When word gets out that a local girl has been found dead . . .'

Lisa Gardner

'How do you know she's local?'

'Playing the law of averages. She appears too young to be an employee, and if she were either FBI or Marine, someone at the scene would've recognized her. Ergo, she's an outsider.'

'She could be someone's sweetheart,' Kimberly ventured. 'The mouth . . . Maybe she talked back one too many times.'

'It's possible.' Watson was eyeing her speculatively, so Kimberly pressed ahead.

'But you don't think so,' she said.

'Why don't I think so?'

'No violence. If it were a domestic situation, a crime of passion, she would show signs of battery. Bruises, cuts, abrasion. Instead . . . I saw her arms and legs. There was hardly a scratch on her. Except for the mouth, of course.'

'Maybe he only hit her where no one would see.'

'Maybe,' her tone was doubtful. 'It still doesn't explain why he would dump the body on a secured Marine base.'

'Why do you think the body was dumped?' Watson asked with a frown.

'Lack of disturbance at the scene,' Kimberly answered immediately. 'Ground wasn't even stirred up until I crashed in.' Her brow furrowed; she looked at him quizzically. 'Do you think she was alive when he brought her onto the grounds? It's not that easy to access the base. Last I saw, the Marines were operating at condition Bravo, meaning all entrances are guarded and all visitors must have proper ID. Dead or alive, not just anyone can access Academy grounds.'

'I don't think we should—'

'That doesn't make sense, either, though,' Kimberly persisted, her frown deepening. 'If the girl's alive, then she would have to have clearance, too, and two security passes are harder to find than one. So maybe she was dead. In the trunk of the car. I've never seen the guards search a vehicle, so she wouldn't be too hard to sneak in that way. Of course, that

68

theory implies that the man knowingly dumped a body *on* Quantico grounds.' She shook her head abruptly. 'That doesn't make sense. If you lived here and you killed someone, even accidentally, you wouldn't take the remains into the woods. You'd hightail it off the base, and get the evidence as far away from here as possible. Leaving the body here is just plain stupid.'

'I don't think we should make any assumptions at this time,' Watson said quietly.

'Do you think he's trying to make a personal statement against the Academy?' Kimberly asked. 'Or against the Marines?'

At that comment, Watson's brows fired to life. Kimberly had definitely crossed some unspoken line, and his expression firmly indicated that their conversation was now over. He sat forward and said, 'Listen, the NCIS will be handling the investigation from here on out. Do you know anything about the Naval Criminal Investigative Service?'

'No—'

'Well you should. The NCIS has over eight hundred special agents, ready to be deployed anywhere around the globe at a moment's notice. They've seen murder, rape, domestic abuse, fraud, drugs, racketeering, terrorism, you name it. They have their own cold case squad, they have their own forensics experts, they even have their own crime labs. For heaven's sake, these are the agents who were called upon to investigate the bombing of the USS *Cole*. They can certainly handle one body found in the woods at a Marine base. Is that understood?'

'I didn't mean to imply—'

'You're a rookie, Kimberly. Not a special agent, but a new agent. Don't forget that difference.'

'Yes sir,' she said stiffly, chin up, eyes blazing at the unexpected reprimand.

Her supervisor's voice finally softened. 'Of course, NCIS

will have some questions for you,' he allowed. 'Of course you will answer to the best of your ability. Cooperation with fellow law enforcement agencies is very important. But then you're done, Kimberly. Out of the picture. Back to class. And – this should go without saying – as quiet as a church mouse.'

'Don't ask, don't tell?' she asked dryly.

Watson didn't crack a smile. 'There are many times in an FBI agent's career when she must be the soul of discretion. Agents who can't be prudent don't belong on the job.'

Kimberly's expression finally faltered. She stared down at the carpet. Watson's tone was so stern, it seemed to border almost on threatening. She had found the body accidentally. And yet . . . He was treating her almost as if she were a troublemaker. As if she'd personally brought this upon the Academy. The safe course would be to do exactly as he said. To get up, seal her lips, and walk away.

She'd never been good at playing it safe.

She lifted her gaze and looked her supervisor in the eye. 'Sir, I'd like to approach NCIS about assisting with the investigation.'

'Did you just hear anything I said?'

'I have some experience in these matters—'

'You know *nothing* about these matters! Don't confuse personal with professional—'

'Why not? Violent death is violent death. I helped my father after my mother's body was found. I'm now seven weeks from becoming a full-fledged FBI agent. What would it hurt to jump the gun a little? After all, I found her.' Her tone was possessive. She hadn't meant to sound that way, realized it was a misstep, but it was too late to call it back now.

Watson's face had darkened dangerously. If she thought he'd appeared stern before, he was downright intimidating now. 'Kimberly . . . Let's be frank. How do you think you're doing as a new agent?'

'Hanging in there.'

'Do you think that's the best goal for a new agent?'

'Some days.'

He smiled grimly, then steepled his hands in front of his chin. 'Some of your instructors are worried about you, Kimberly. You have an impeccable resume, of course. You consistently score ninety percent or higher on your exams. You seem to have some skills with firearms.'

'But?' she gritted out.

'But you also have an attitude. Nine weeks here, Kimberly, and by all accounts you have no close friends, allies, or associates. You offer nothing to your classmates. You take nothing from them. You're an island. Law enforcement is ultimately a human system. With no connections, no friends, no support, how far do you think you're going to get? How effective do you think you can be?'

'I'll work on that,' she said. Her heart was beating hard.

'Kimberly,' he said, gently now, and she winced further. Anger could be deflected. Gentleness was to be feared. 'You know, you're very young.'

'Growing up all the time,' she babbled.

'Maybe now is not the right time for you to join the Bureau—'

'No time like the present.'

'I think if you gave yourself a few more years, more space between now and what happened to your family . . .'

'You mean forget about my mother and sister?'

'I'm not saying that.'

'Pretend I'm just another accountant, looking for a little more excitement in my life?'

'Kimberly—'

'I found a corpse! Is that what this is about? I found a blight on the Academy's front porch and now you're kicking me out!'

'*Stop it!*' His tone was stern. It finally shocked Kimberly into silence and in the next instant she realized everything she had just said. Her cheeks flamed red. She quickly looked away.

'I would like to go back to class now,' Kimberly murmured. 'I promise not to say anything. I appreciate the task NCIS has before it, and I wouldn't want to do anything to compromise an ongoing investigation.'

'Kimberly . . .' Her supervisor's tone was still frustrated. It appeared he might say something more, then he just shook his head. 'You look like hell. You obviously haven't slept in weeks, you've lost weight. Why don't you go to your room and get some rest? Take this opportunity to recuperate. There's no shame in slowing down a little, you know. You're already one of the youngest applicants we've had. What you don't accomplish now, you can always accomplish later.'

Kimberly didn't reply. She was too busy biting back a bitter smile. She had heard those words before. Also from an older man, a mentor, someone she had considered a friend. Two days later, he'd put a gun to her head.

Please don't let her tear up now. She would not cry.

'We'll talk again in a few days,' Watson said in the ensuing silence. 'Dismissed.'

Kimberly headed out of his office. She walked down the hall, passing three groups of blue-clad students and already hearing the whispers beginning again. Were they talking about her mother and sister? Were they talking about her legendary father? Or maybe they were talking about today, and the new body she of all people had managed to find?

Her eyes stung more fiercely. She pressed the heels of her hands against her temples. She would not give in to pity now.

Kimberly marched to the front doors. She burst back into the blistering hot sun. Sweat immediately beaded across her brow. She could feel her T-shirt glue itself stickily to her skin.

But she did not return to her room. NCIS would want to talk to her. First, however, they would want to finish up at the scene. That gave her a solid hour before anyone would come looking for her.

An hour was enough.

Kimberly made a beeline for the woods.

8

Quantico, Virginia
11:33 A.M.
Temperature: 89 degrees

'Time of death?'

'Hard to tell. Body temperature reads nearly ninety-five, but the current outside temp of eight-nine would impede cooling. Rigor mortis appears to be just starting in face and neck.' The white-clad ME paused, rolled the body slightly to the left and pressed a gloved finger against the red-splotched skin, which blanched at his touch. 'Lividity's not yet fixed.' He straightened back up, thought of something else, and checked the woman's eyes and ears. 'No blowfly larvae yet, which would happen fast in this heat. Of course, the flies prefer to start in the mouth or an open wound, so they had less opportunity here . . .' He seemed to consider the various factors one last time, then delivered his verdict. 'I'm going to say four to six hours.'

The other man, probably an NCIS special agent, looked up from his notes in surprise. 'That fresh?'

'That's my best guess. Hard to know more until we cut her open.'

'Which will be?'

'Tomorrow morning.'

74

The special agent stared at the ME.

'Six A.M.?' the ME tried again.

The special agent stared harder.

'This afternoon,' the ME amended.

The special agent finally cracked a smile. The ME sighed heavily. It was going to be one of *those* cases.

The investigating officer returned to his notes. 'Probable COD?'

'That's a little trickier. No obvious knife or gunshot wounds. No petechial hemorrhages, which rules out strangulation. No bleeding in the ears, which eliminates some brain traumas. We do have a large bruise just beginning to form on the left hip. Probably occurred shortly before death.' The coroner lifted up the girl's blue-flowered skirt, eyed the contusion again, then shook his head. 'I'm going to have to do some blood work. We'll know more then.'

The investigating officer nodded. A second man, also clad in khakis and a white dress shirt, moved in to snap more shots with a digital camera, while several grim-faced Marines stood guard along the yellow-ribbon-draped scene. Even in the deep shade of the woods, the heat and humidity were impossible to escape. Both NCIS special agents had sweated through their long-sleeve shirts, while the young sentries stood with moisture rolling down their chiseled faces.

Now the second special agent, a younger man with the requisite buzz-cut hair and squared-off jaw, looked down the heavily wooded path. 'I don't see drag marks,' he commented.

The ME nodded and moved to the victim's black sandals. He picked up her foot and studied the heel of her shoe. 'No dirt or debris here. She must've been carried in.'

'Strong man,' the photographer said.

The first special agent gave them both a look. 'We are on a Marine base cooccupied by FBI trainees; they're all strong men.' He nodded back toward the victim. 'What's with the mouth?'

The ME put his hand on her cheeks, turned her head side to side. Then suddenly, he flinched and snatched his hand away.

'What?' the older agent asked.

'I don't . . . Nothing.'

'Nothing? What kind of nothing?'

'Trick of the light,' the ME muttered, but he didn't put his hand back on the girl's face. 'Looks like sewing thread,' he said curtly. 'Thick, maybe like what's used for upholstery. It's certainly not medical. The stitching is too rudimentary to be a professional's. Just small flecks of blood, so the mutilation probably occurred postmortem.'

There was a green leaf caught in the girl's tangled blond hair. The ME distractedly pulled it free and let it flutter away. He moved on to her hands, flung above her head. One was curled closed. Gently, he unrolled her fingers. Inside her grip, nestled against her palm, was a jagged green-gray rock.

'Hey,' he called to the younger special agent. 'Want to get a picture of this?'

The kid obediently came over and snapped away. 'What is it?'

'I don't know. A rock of some kind. Going to bag and tag?'

'Right.' The kid fetched an evidence container. He dropped the rock in and dutifully filled out the top form.

'No obvious defensive wounds. Oh, here we go.' The ME's gloved thumb moved up her left arm to a red, swollen patch high on her shoulder. 'Injection mark. Just the faintest bruising, so it probably occurred right before death.'

'Overdose?' the older agent asked with a frown.

'Of some kind. An intramuscular injection isn't very common for drugs; they're generally administered intravenously.' The ME lifted the girl's skirt again. He inspected the inside of her thighs, then moved down to between her toes. Finally, he inspected the webbing between her index finger and thumb. 'No track marks. Whatever happened, she's not a habitual user.'

'Wrong place at the wrong time?'

'Possibly.'

Older Special Agent sighed. 'We're going to need an ID right away. Can you print her here?'

'I'd prefer to wait until the morgue, when we can test her hands for blood and skin samples. If you're in a real hurry, though, you can always check her purse.'

'What?'

The ME smiled broadly, then took pity on the Naval cop. 'Over there, on the rock *outside* the crime scene tape. The black leather backpack thingy. My daughter has one just like it. It's very hip.'

'Of all the stupid, miserable, incompetent . . .' Older Special Agent wasn't very happy. He got the kid to photograph the purse, then had two sentries expand the crime scene perimeter to *include* the leather bag. Finally, with gloved hands, he retrieved the item. 'Note that we need to take full inventory,' he instructed his assistant. 'For now, however, we'll detail the wallet.'

The kid set down the camera and immediately took up the paper and pencil.

'Okay, here we go. Wallet, also black leather . . . Let's see, it contains, a grocery store card, a Petco card, a Blockbuster card, another grocery store card, and . . . no driver's license. There's thirty-three dollars in here, but no driver's license, no credit cards, and for that matter, no kind of any card bearing a person's name. What does that tell us?'

'He doesn't want us to know her ID,' the kid said eagerly.

'Yeah.' Older Special Agent was frowning. 'How about that? You know what? We're missing something else. Keys.' He shook the bag, but there was no telltale jingle. 'What kind of person doesn't have keys?'

'Maybe he's a thief? He's got her address from the license, plus the house keys . . . It's not like she's going to come home anytime soon.'

'Possibly.' But the Naval officer was looking at the stitched-up mouth and frowning. From her vantage point behind a tree, Kimberly could read his thought: What kind of thief stitched up a woman's mouth? For that matter, what kind of thief dumped a body in the middle of a Marine base?

'I need to fetch paper bags for the hands,' the ME reported. 'They're back in my van.'

'We'll walk with you. I want to review a few more things.' The older Naval officer jerked his head toward his counterpart, and the younger man immediately fell into step. They headed off down the dirt path, leaving the sprawling corpse alone with the four sentries.

Kimberly was just considering how to make a stealthy exit herself, when a strong hand snapped around her wrist. In the next instant, a second hand smothered her mouth. She didn't bother with screaming; she bit him instead.

'Damn,' a deep voice rumbled in her ear. 'Do you ever talk first and shoot later? I keep running into you, I'm not gonna have any hide left.'

Kimberly recognized the voice. She relaxed against his large body, but grudgingly. In return, he removed both hands.

'What are you doing here?' she whispered, casting a furtive glance at the crime scene attendants. She turned to face Special Agent Mac McCormack and he frowned.

'What happened to you?' He held up a silencing hand. 'Wait, I don't want to see the other guy.'

Kimberly touched her face. For the first time she felt the zigzag welts creasing her nose and cheeks with flecks of dried blood. Her scramble through the woods had taken its toll after all. No wonder her supervisor had tried to send her to her room.

'What are you doing here?' she asked again, voice low.

'Heard a rumor. Decided to follow it up.' His gaze briefly skimmed down her body. 'I heard a young new agent made the find. I take it you had the honors? Little ways off the PT course, don't you think?'

Kimberly simply glared at him. He shrugged and returned both of their attentions to the crime scene.

'I want that leaf,' his voice rumbled in her ear. 'You see the one the ME pulled out of the victim's hair—'

'Not proper protocol.'

'You tell him, honey. I want that leaf. And as long as you're here, you might as well help me get it.'

She jerked away from him. 'I will not—'

'Just distract the sentries. Strike up a conversation, bat those baby blues and in sixty seconds, I'll be in and out.'

Kimberly frowned at him. 'You distract the guards, I'll grab the leaf,' she said.

He looked at her as if she were slightly slow. 'Honey,' he drawled. 'You're a *girl*.'

'So I can't grab a leaf?' Her voice rose unconsciously.

He covered her mouth with his palm again. 'No, but you surely have a bit more natural *appeal* to young men than I do.' He glanced down the wooded path at the direction the ME and two Naval investigators had gone. 'Come on, sugar. We don't have the rest of our lives.'

He's an idiot, she thought. Sexist, too. But she nodded anyway. The ME had been grossly negligent to pull the leaf out of the girl's hair, and it would be best if someone retrieved it.

Mac motioned to the left pair of guards and how he wanted her to draw them to the front. Then he'd go in from the back.

Thirty seconds later, taking a deep breath, Kimberly made a big production of walking from the woods right onto the dirt path. She made a sharp left and walked straight up to the pair of sentries.

'I just need to see the body for a moment,' she said breezily.

'This area is restricted, ma'am.' The first sentry spoke in clipped tones, his gaze fixed somewhere past her left ear.

'Oh, I'm sure it is.' Kimberly waved her hand negligently and stepped forward.

The young sentry made a discreet move left and without seeming to exert any real effort, blocked her path.

'Excuse me,' Kimberly said firmly. 'But I don't think you understand. I have clearance. I'm part of the case. For heaven's sake, I was the first officer at the scene.'

The Marine frowned at her, unimpressed. The other pair of Marines had moved closer, obviously prepared to offer backup. Kimberly flashed them a sickeningly sweet smile. And watched as Special Agent McCormack eased into the clearing behind them.

'Ma'am, I must ask you to depart,' the first sentry said.

'Where's the crime scene log?' Kimberly asked. 'Just get the log and I'll show you where I'm signed in.'

For the first time, the Marine hesitated. Kimberly's instincts had been right. These guys were just foot soldiers. They knew nothing about investigative procedure, or law enforcement jurisdiction.

'Seriously,' she pressed, taking another step closer and getting everyone antsy now. 'I'm New Agent Kimberly Quincy. At approximately oh-eight twenty-two hundred I found the victim and secured the scene for NCIS. Of course I want to follow up with this case.'

Mac was halfway to the body now, moving with surprising stealth for a big guy.

'Ma'am, this area belongs to the Marines. It is restricted to the Marines. Unless you are accompanied by the appropriate officer, you may not enter this area.'

'Who's the appropriate officer?'

'Ma'am—'

'Sir, I found that girl this morning. While I appreciate that you're doing your job, I'm not leaving a poor, young girl like that to a bunch of camo-clad men. She needs one of her own around. Simple as that.'

The Marine glared at her. She'd definitely crossed some line in his mind over to wacky. He sighed and seemed to be struggling to find his patience.

Mac was now at the area where they had both seen the leaf flutter to the ground. He was on his hands and knees, moving carefully. For the first time, Kimberly realized their problem. There were many dried up leaves on the ground. Red, yellow, brown. What color had been in the girl's hair? Oh God, she already didn't remember.

The backup sentries had edged closer. They had their hands on the stocks of their rifles. Kimberly brought up her chin and dared them to shoot her.

'You need to leave,' the first sentry repeated.

'No.'

'Ma'am, you depart on your own or we will forcefully assist you.'

Mac had a leaf now. He held it up, seemed to be frowning at it. Was he also wondering what color it should be? Could he remember?

'Lay a hand on me and I will sue you for sexual harassment.'

The Marine blinked. Kimberly blinked, too. Really, as threats went, that was a pretty good one. Even Mac had turned toward her and appeared sincerely impressed. The leaf in his hand was green. All at once, she relaxed. That made sense. The leaves already at the scene were old, from last fall. A green leaf, on the other hand, had probably been brought in with the body. He had done it. *They* had done it.

The backup sentries were now right behind the first pair. All four sets of male gazes stared at her.

'You need to leave,' the first Marine said again, but he no longer sounded as forceful.

'I'm just trying to do right by her,' Kimberly said quietly.

That seemed to disarm him further. His stare broke. He glanced down at the dirt path. And Kimberly found herself still talking.

'I had a sister, you see. Not that much older than this girl here. One night, a guy got her drunk, tampered with her seat belt, and drove her straight into a telephone pole. Then he ran away, leaving her there all alone, her skull crushed against the windshield. She didn't die right away, though. She lived for a while. I've always wondered . . . Did she feel the blood trickling down her face? Did she know how alone she was? The medics would never tell me, but I wonder if she cried, if she understood what was happening to her. That's gotta be the worst thing in the world. To know that you're dying, and nobody is coming to save you. Of course, you don't have to worry about such things. You're a Marine. Someone will always come for you. We can't say the same, however, for the women of the world. I sure couldn't say the same for my sister.'

Now all the Marines were looking down. That was okay. Kimberly's voice had gotten huskier than she intended. She was afraid of the expression that must be on her face.

'You're right,' she said abruptly. 'I should go. I'll come back later, when an investigating officer is here.'

'That would be best, ma'am,' the Marine said. He still would not look her in the eye.

'Thank you for your help.' She hesitated, then just couldn't help herself. 'Please take care of her for me.'

Then Kimberly turned quickly, and before she did anything even more stupid, disappeared back down the path.

Two minutes later, she felt Mac's hand upon her arm. She took one look at his somber expression and knew he'd heard everything.

'Did you get the leaf?' she asked.

'Yes, ma'am.'

'Now would you like to tell me why you're really here?'

And Mac said, 'Because all these years later, I've been waiting for him.'

9

Quantico, Virginia
12:33 P.M.
Temperature: 95 degrees

'It started in nineteen-ninety-eight. June fourth. Two college roommates went out to a tavern in Atlanta and never came home. Three days later, the first girl's body was found near Interstate seventy-five just south of the city. Four months later, the second girl's remains were found a hundred miles away in Tallulah Gorge State Park. Both girls were found fully clothed and with their purses; no signs of robbery or sexual assault.'

Kimberly frowned. 'That's different.'

Mac nodded at her. They were in a corner of the Crossroads Lounge, huddled over a small table, heads together and voices low. 'Next year, nineteen-nine-nine. First heat wave of the year doesn't hit until July. Two high school girls in Macon, Georgia, sneak into a local bar on July tenth. Never seen alive again. First girl's body is found four days later, this time next to US four forty-one, which happens to be near the Tallulah Gorge State Park. Second girl is found . . .'

'Inside the gorge?' Kimberly tried gamely.

'Nope. Burke County cotton field. One hundred and fifty

miles away from the gorge. It's the gorge that we searched, however, so nobody discovered her body until the cotton harvest in November.'

'Wait a minute.' Kimberly held up a hand. 'It takes all the way until November to find a girl's body in a field?'

'You've never been to Burke County. We're talking eight hundred square miles of cotton. The kind of place where you can drive all day without ever hitting a paved road. There ain't *nothing* out in Burke County.'

'Except a dead body.' Kimberly leaned forward intently. 'Both girls fully clothed again? No sign of sexual assault?'

'The best we can tell,' Mac said. 'It's difficult with the second girl of each pair, given the condition of their bodies. But for the most part, yes, all four girls are found wearing their party clothes and looking relatively . . . peaceful.'

'Cause of death?'

'It varies. For the girls left next to roadways, an overdose of benzodiazepine, the prescription drug Ativan. He injects the lethal dose into their left shoulders.'

'And the second girls?'

'We don't know. It looks like a fall may have been what killed Deanna Wilson. For Kasey Cooper, exposure, maybe, or dehydration.'

'They were abandoned alive?'

'It's a theory.'

She wasn't sure she liked how he said that. 'You said you found their purses. What about ID?'

Mac's turn to frown. He was obviously thinking of the girl they'd found that day, and the lack of ID in her wallet. 'They did have their driver's licenses,' he admitted. 'IDing the bodies was never an issue. No keys, though. For that matter, no cars. We've never recovered a single vehicle.'

'Really?' Kimberly's scowl deepened. She was fascinated in spite of herself. 'Okay, continue.'

'Two thousand,' Mac said crisply, then promptly rolled his eyes. 'Bad year, two thousand. Brutally hot summer, no rain. May twenty-ninth we're already in the mid-nineties. Two students from Augusta State University head to Savannah for a girls' weekend. They never come home. Tuesday morning, a motorist finds the first girl's body next to US twenty-five in Waynesboro. Can you guess where Waynesboro is?'

Kimberly thought about it a minute. 'The cotton field place. Burke County?'

He smiled, a flash of white against his dark skin. 'You catch on quick. That's one of the rules of the game, you see: the first body of the new pair is always left near the second girl of the last pair. Maybe he likes the continuity, or maybe he's giving us a fighting chance at finding the second body in case we missed it the previous year.' He paused for a second and eyed her appraisingly. 'So for this new pair, where's the second girl?'

'Not in Burke County?'

'You're cheatin'.'

'Well, he hasn't repeated an area. So you can assume not the gorge and not a cotton field. Process of elimination.'

'Georgia has nearly sixty thousand square miles of mountains, forests, coastline, swamplands, peach orchards, tobacco fields, and cities. You're gonna need to eliminate more than that.'

Kimberly acknowledged the point with a slight shrug. Unconsciously she worried her lower lip. 'Well, you said it was a game. Does he leave you clues?'

His answering smile was dazzling. 'Yes, ma'am. Second rule of the game – for it to be competitive, you gotta leave clues. Let's go back to the very first girl, found outside of Atlanta. Girl's laid out next to a major interstate, remember? We have no signs of violence, no sexual assault, so that means no blood, no semen, none of the normal trace evidence you might expect to collect in a homicide case. But here's something interesting. The body's clean. Very clean. Almost as if someone has washed the victim's legs, arms, and shoes. We not only lack hair and fiber, we can't even find traces of spilled beer on her shoes or a stray peanut in her hair. It's like the girl's been . . . sanitized.'

'All of her?' Kimberly asked sharply. 'Then you can no longer be sure of lack of sexual assault.'

Mac shook his head. 'Not all of her. Just the parts . . . exposed. Hair, face, limbs. My best guess? He wipes them down with a sponge. It's like . . . he's wiping a slate clean. And then he starts his work.'

'Oh my God,' Kimberly breathed. She was no longer sure she wanted to know what had happened next.

'They're a map,' Mac said quietly. 'That's why the first girl exists. That's why she's left next to a major road and easily found. Maybe why she gets a quick and relatively painless death. Because she doesn't matter to him. She's just a tool, a guide to where the real game is being played out.'

Kimberly was leaning forward again. Her heart had started pounding, neurons firing to life in her brain. She could feel where this was headed now. Almost see the dark, twisted road open up before her. 'What are the clues?'

'From the first girl, we found a feather in her hair, a crushed flower beneath her body, traces of rock on her shoe, and a business card in her purse. The crime lab followed protocol and took samples of everything. And then . . . nothin'.'

'Nothing?'

'Nothin'. You ever been to a real crime lab, Kimberly? And by that, I don't mean the FBI lab. The Feds have money, no doubt about it. I mean what the rest of us working stiffs get to use.'

Kimberly shook her head.

'We have equipment. Lots of equipment. But unless it's

fingerprints or DNA – God's honest truth – it's as worthless as an unmatched sock. We don't have databases. So sure, we collect soil samples, but it's not like we can scan them into some giant computer and have a matching location magically blip across the screen the way they do in some of those crime shows. Frankly, we operate on tight budgets and tight budgets mean forensics is mostly reactionary. You take samples and someday, if you have a suspect, then you have a reference sample to work with. You take your dirt from the crime scene and hope it matches dirt from the bad guy's yard. That's as good as it gets.

'In other words, we collected the rock sample, the feather, the flower and we knew they were worthless to us. So we sent them out to real experts who might be able to make something of them. And then we waited nine months.'

Kimberly closed her eyes. 'Oh no,' she said.

'Nobody knew,' he said quietly. 'You have to understand, nobody ever expected the likes of this man.'

'He abandoned the second girl in the gorge, didn't he?'

'With a gallon jug of water. Wearing high heels. In nearly a hundred degree heat.'

'But if you had interpreted the clues in time . . .'

'You mean, if we'd identified the white flower as persistent trillium, a rare herb found growing only in a five-point-three square mile area in all of Georgia – an area inside the Tallulah Gorge? Or if we'd realized the feather belonged to the peregrine falcon, which also makes its home in the gorge? Or if we'd understood that the granite in the rocks found ground into her shoes matched samples taken from the cliffs, or that the business card found in her purse belonged to a customer service representative from Georgia Power, the company that just so happens to own and manage the gorge? Sure, if we'd known that stuff, then maybe we could've found her. But most of those reports didn't come in for months, and poor

Deanna Wilson was dead and buried by then.'

Kimberly hung her head. She was thinking of a poor young girl lost alone and bewildered in the middle of a hostile forest. Trying to hike her way out over uneven terrain in party heels and a little black dress. The burning, scorching heat. She wondered if the girl had drunk the water quickly, convinced someone would find her soon. Or if she had rationed it from the start, already fearing the worst.

'And the second pair of girls?' she asked quietly.

Mac shrugged. His eyes were dark and somber. He was trying to appear nonchalant, the callused professional, but it wasn't quite working. 'We still didn't know any better. The minute the first body appeared outside of the gorge, that's the connection everyone made. We have someone who kidnaps girls and likes to hide 'em in the gorge. Given the extreme heat, the Rabun County Sheriff's Office did the logical thing and threw all resources at searching the state park. It took another week to realize she wasn't there, and even then, it was hard to be sure.'

'What were the clues?'

'Josie Anders had white lint on her red top, dried mud on her shoes, four kernels in her purse, and a phone number scribbled on a cocktail napkin wadded up in her front pocket.'

'The lint and kernels have something to do with cotton?' Kimberly guessed.

'Upon further examination, the lint proved to be linters, made from raw cottonseed. The kernels were cotton kernels. The mud turned out to be high in organic matter. And the phone number belonged to Lyle Burke, a sixty-five-year-old retired electrician, living in Savannah, who'd never heard of the two girls, let alone Roxie's bar, which was where they were last seen alive.'

'Burke County,' Kimberly said.

Mac nodded. 'Cotton's not a fair clue in a state like Georgia.

There's only ninety-seven counties that grow the stuff. But by throwing in the phone number . . . I think in his own way, the man considered it sporting. Now we had only eight hundred square miles to search. If we'd been paying attention—' His voice broke off harshly. He turned away from her for a minute, his hand knotting and unknotting in a restless, frustrated motion.

'When did you start putting it together?' Kimberly asked.

'Two months after Kasey Cooper was found in the cotton field. The last of the evidence reports came in, and we made the connections after the fact. Gee, we've had two girls disappear in pairs. In both instances, one girl is found right away, next to a major road. And in both instances, the second girl isn't found for a long time, and when she is found, it's in a remote and dangerous area. The first girls, however, have evidence that ties them to the second location. Gee, maybe if we figure out those clues sooner, we can find the second girl in time. Good golly, Miss Molly, that might make some sense.' Mac blew out a breath of air. He sounded disgusted, but then he shrugged philosophically and got on with it.

'We assembled a task force. Not that the public knew. We worked behind the scenes at that point, identifying some of the best experts on Georgia – biologists, botanists, geologists, entomologists, etc., and getting them thinking about this guy and where he might strike next. The goal was to be proactive. Failing that, at least we'd already have the experts in place to give us real-time answers should the man strike again.'

'What happened?' Kimberly asked.

'The year two thousand,' he said bluntly. 'The year we'd thought we'd gotten smart. Instead, everything went to hell in a hand basket. Two more kidnappings, three girls dead.' Mac glanced at his watch. He shook away the rest of what he was going to say, and startled them both by taking her hand instead. 'But that was then. This is now. If this is the Eco-Killer, Kimberly, we don't have much time. The clock is ticking. Now here is what I need you to do next.'

10

Special Agent Mac McCormack was going to get her kicked out of the FBI Academy. Kimberly thought about it dispassionately as she drove through Quantico's winding roads on her way to the main highway. She'd showered after talking to Mac. She'd changed into the appropriate uniform of khaki cargo pants and a navy blue FBI Academy shirt. Then she'd tucked her good ol' Crayola gun into a holster on the waistband of her pants and attached handcuffs to her belt. As long as she was going to trade in on the cachet of being a new agent, she might as well look the part.

She could've told Mac no. She thought about that, too, as she drove. She didn't really know the man. Good looks and compelling blue eyes aside, he had no claim on her. She wasn't even sure she believed his story yet. Oh sure, this Eco-Killer guy had probably ravaged the state of Georgia. But that was three years ago. In a state hundreds of miles away. Why would some Georgian nut suddenly turn up in Virginia? Better yet, why would a Georgian nut leave a dead body on the FBI's doorstep?

It didn't make sense to her. Mac saw what he needed to see. He wasn't the first cop to be obsessed by a case and he wouldn't be the last.

None of which explained why Kimberly had just blown off her afternoon classes, a violation that could get her written up. Or why she was now driving to a county ME's office, after her supervisor had explicitly told her to stay away from the case. That little act of insubordination could get her kicked out.

And yet from the minute Mac had made his request, she'd agreed. She wanted to speak to the ME. She wanted to con her way into an autopsy of a poor young girl she'd never met.

She wanted . . . She wanted to know what happened. She wanted to know the girl's name and the dreams she'd once had. She wanted to know if she'd suffered, or if it'd been quick. She wanted to know what mistakes the unidentified subject might have made, so she could use those mistakes to track him down and find justice for a young girl who deserved better than to be abandoned like garbage in the woods.

In short, Kimberly was projecting. As a former psych student, she recognized the signs. As a young woman who'd lost her sister and mother to violent deaths, she couldn't stop if she tried.

She had found the victim. She'd stood alone with her in the dark shadows of the woods. She couldn't walk away from her now if she tried.

Kimberly followed the address she'd received from the Marine base. She'd asked about the NCIS investigator while there, only to discover he'd already left to observe the victim's autopsy at the morgue.

In the good news department, Special Agent Kaplan's presence at the autopsy gave Kimberly a better excuse for insinuating herself into the procedure. She'd just come to talk to him, but hey, as long as she was there . . .

In the bad news department, an experienced special agent

was probably going to be a bit savvier about a new agent trying to horn in on his investigation than an overworked ME.

That's why Mac had volunteered her for this mission after all. No one was going to let another cop into the case. A mere student, on the other hand . . . Play to your weaknesses, he'd advised her. No one ever suspects the small, bewildered rookie.

Kimberly parked her car outside the nondescript five-story building. She took a deep breath. She wondered if her father had ever felt this nervous before a case. Then again, had he ever gone off the beaten path? Risked everything to learn the truth for yet another dead girl in a world of so many murdered blondes?

Her cool remote father. She couldn't picture it. Somehow that bolstered her spirits. She squared her shoulders and got on with it.

Inside the odor hit her at once. Too antiseptic, too sterile. The smell of a place that definitely had things to hide. She went to the glass-enclosed receptionist area, made her request, and was grateful when the woman buzzed her straight through.

Kimberly followed a long corridor with stark walls and linoleum floors all the way to the back. Here and there metal gurneys were shoved up against bone-colored walls. Steel gray doors led off other places, security boxes demanding access codes she didn't have. The air was colder in here. Her footsteps rang out with a startling echo, while the fluorescent lights buzzed overhead.

Her hands were trembling at her side. She could feel the first trickle of sweat slide stickily down her back. Being inside this cool place should've been a welcome relief from the stifling outdoor heat. It wasn't.

At the end of the hallway, she pushed through a wooden door into a new lobby area. This is where the ME's offices were housed. She pressed a buzzer, and wasn't horribly surprised when a door cracked open, and Special Agent Kaplan poked out his head.

'You lookin' for the ME? He's busy.'

'Actually, I'm looking for you.'

Special Agent Kaplan straightened in the doorway. This close Kimberly could see the faint sheen of silver mixed into his dark, buzz-cut hair. He had a weathered face, stern eyes, and thin lips that reserved judgment before smiling. Not a cruel man, but a hard one. He was the guy after all, who kept all of the Navy plus the Marines in line.

Oh, this was not going to be easy.

'New Agent Kimberly Quincy,' Kimberly said, and stuck out her hand.

He accepted the handshake. His grip was firm, his expression wary. 'You had quite a ride.'

'I understand you have questions for me. Given my schedule, I thought it might be easier if I found you. At the Marine base, they said you were here. So I decided to make the drive.'

'Your supervisor know you left the Academy?'

'I didn't mention it to him directly. When I spoke with him this morning, however, he underscored the importance of cooperating fully with NCIS's investigation. Naturally I assured him I would do whatever I could to help.'

'Uh huh,' Kaplan said. And that was it. He stood, he stared, and he let the silence drag on and on and on. If this man had kids, they *never* snuck out at night.

Kimberly's fingers desperately wanted to fidget. She stuck them into her pockets and wished once more she were carrying her Glock. It was tough to project confidence when you were armed with a red-painted toy.

'I understand you visited my crime scene,' Kaplan said abruptly.

'I stopped by.'

'Gave the boys quite a scare.'

'With all due respect, sir, your boys scare easily.'

Kaplan's lips finally cracked into a ghostly semblance of a smile. 'I told them the same,' he said, and for a moment they were coconspirators. Then the moment passed. 'Why are you crowding my case, New Agent Quincy? Hasn't your father taught you better than that?'

Kimberly's shoulders immediately went rigid. She caught the motion, then forced herself to remain loose and breathe easy. 'I didn't apply to the Academy because my interests ran to sewing.'

'So this is an academic study to you?'

'No.'

That made him frown. Good, keep him guessing. 'I'll ask one more time: why are you here, New Agent Quincy?'

'Because I found her, sir.'

'Because you found her?'

'Yes, sir. And what I start, I like to finish. My father taught me that.'

'It's not your case to finish.'

'No sir. It's your case to finish. Absolutely. I'm just a student. But I'm hoping you'll be kind enough to let me watch.'

'Kind? No one calls me kind.'

'Letting a green rookie watch an autopsy and puke her guts out won't change your image, sir.'

Now he did smile. It changed the contours of his whole face, made him handsome, even approachable. The human in him came out, and Kimberly thought she had hope yet.

'You ever see an autopsy, New Agent Quincy?'

'No sir.'

'It's not the blood that will get you. It's the smell. Or maybe the whine of the buzz saw when it hits the skull. Think you're up to it?'

'I'm pretty sure I'll be sick, sir.'

'Then by all means, come on back. The things I gotta do to

96

educate the Feebies,' Kaplan muttered. He shook his head. Then he opened the door and let her into the cold, sterile room.

Tina was going to be sick. She was trying desperately to control the reflex. Her stomach was clenching, her throat tightening. Bile surged upward. Bitterly, harshly, she forced it back down.

Her mouth was duct-taped shut. If she started vomiting now, she was terrified she'd drown.

She curled up tighter in a ball. That seemed to alleviate some of the cramping in her lower abdomen. Maybe it bought her another few minutes. And then? She didn't know anymore.

She lived in a black tomb of darkness. She saw nothing. She heard very little. Her hands were behind her back, but at least not taped too tight. Her ankles seemed bound as well. If she wiggled her feet, she could get the tape to make a squishy sound, and earn herself some extra room.

The tape didn't really matter, though. She'd figured that out hours before. The real prison wasn't the duct tape around her limbs. It was the locked plastic container that held her body. It was too dark to be sure, but given the approximate size, the metal gate in the front, and the holes that marked the top – where she could press her cheek – she had a feeling that she'd been thrown into a very large animal carrier. Honest to goodness. She was trapped in a dog crate.

She'd cried a bit in the beginning. Then she'd gotten so angry she'd thrashed against the plastic, hurtling herself at the metal door. All she had to show for that tantrum was a bruised shoulder and banged up knees.

She'd slept after that. Too exhausted by fear and pain to know what to do next. When she'd woken up, the duct tape had been removed from her mouth and a gallon jug of water was in the crate with her, along with an energy bar. She'd been tempted to refuse the offering out of spite – she was no trained monkey! But then she'd thought of her unborn baby, and she'd consumed the water greedily while eating the protein bar.

She thought the water might have been drugged, though. Because no sooner had she drank it, than she fell deeply asleep. When she woke up again, the tape was back over her mouth, and the wrapper from the energy bar had been taken away.

She'd wanted to cry again. Drugs couldn't be good. Not for her. And not for her unborn child.

Funny, four weeks ago, she hadn't even been sure she wanted a baby. But then Betsy had brought home the Mayo Clinic book on child development and together they'd looked at all the pictures. Tina knew now that, at six weeks past conception, her baby was already half an inch long. It had a big head with eyes but no eyelids and it had little arms and little legs with paddle-like hands and feet. In another week, her baby would double to being one-inch long and the hands and feet would develop tiny webbed fingers and teensy little toes until her baby looked like the world's cutest lima bean.

In other words, her baby was already a baby. A tiny, precious something Tina couldn't wait to hold one day in her arms. And Tina had better enjoy that moment because her mother would be killing her shortly thereafter.

Her mom. Oh God, even the thought of her mother made her want to weep. If anything happened to Tina . . . Life was too unfair sometimes, to a grown woman who had worked so hard in the hope that her daughter would have a better life.

Tina had to be more alert. She had to pay more attention. She wasn't going to just disappear like this, dammit. She refused to be a stupid statistic. She strained her ears again. Struggled for some hint of what might be going on.

Tina was pretty sure she was in a vehicle. She could feel movement, but it confused her that she couldn't see. Maybe the crate was in the back of a covered pickup bed, or a blacked-out van. She didn't think it was night, though without being able to glance at her watch she had no idea how much time had passed. She'd slept for a long while, she thought. The drugs, then the fear, having taken their toll.

She felt isolated. The pitch black was too sterile, devoid of even the soft whisper of someone else's breath, let alone whimpers of fear. Whatever else was back here, she was pretty sure she was the only living thing. Maybe that was a good thing. Maybe she was the only person he'd kidnapped then. He'd taken just her.

But somehow, she doubted that and it made her want to weep.

She didn't know why he was doing this. Was he a pervert, who kidnapped college girls to take them to his sick hideaway where he would do unspeakable things? She was still fully clothed, however. Down to her three-inch sandals. He'd also left her her purse. She didn't think a pervert would do such a thing.

Maybe he was a slave trader. She'd heard stories. A white girl could fetch a lot of money overseas. Maybe she'd end up in a harem, or working in some sleazy bar in Bangkok. Well, wouldn't they be in for a big surprise when their pretty young thing suddenly grew big and fat. That would teach them to snatch first and talk later.

Her child born into slavery, prostitution, porn . . .

The bile rose up in her throat again. She grimly fought it back.

I can't be sick, she tried telling her tummy. You have to give me a break. We're in this together. I'll figure out a way to get out of the crate. You have to hold down all food and water. We don't have much to work with here, you know. We have to make these calories count.

Which was very important actually, because as perverse as it sounded, the less Tina had to eat, the worse her nausea became. Basically, food made her sick and lack of food made her sicker.

Belatedly, Tina was aware that the motion was decelerating. She strained her ears and detected the slight squeak of brakes. The vehicle had stopped.

Immediately her body tensed. Her hands fumbled behind her. They found her black shoulder bag, gripping it tight like a weapon. Not that it would do her any good with her hands bound behind her back. But she had to do something. Anything was better than simply waiting for what would happen next . . .

A door suddenly rolled back. Bright sunlight penetrated the vehicle, making her blink owlishly, and in the next instant, she was aware of an intense wall of heat. Oh God, it was boiling outside. She shrunk back, but couldn't avoid the scorching air.

A man stood in the open doorway. His features were a black shroud haloed by the sunlight behind him. His arm came up and a cellophane package fell between the plastic bars. Then another and another.

'Do you have water?' he asked.

She tried to speak, then remembered the tape over her mouth. She did have water, but she wanted more, so she shook her head.

'You should ration your supplies more carefully,' the man scolded.

She wanted to spit at him. She shrugged instead.

'I'll give you another jug. But that's it. Understood?'

What did he mean by that's it? That's it before he set her free? Or that's it before he raped her, killed her, or sold her to a bunch of sick twisted men?

Her stomach was roiling again. She closed her eyes to savagely fight it back.

Next thing she felt was a prick on the arm. A damn needle. The drugs, oh no . . .

Her muscles melted as if trained. She slumped against the side of the dog crate, the world already fading away. The kennel door opened. A jug of water materialized in her crate.

A hand casually ripped the tape from her mouth. Her lips stung. Blood trickled from the corner of her mouth.

'Eat, drink,' the man said quietly. 'By nightfall, you're going to need your strength.'

The kennel door snapped shut. The van door rolled closed. No more sunlight. No more heat.

Tina slid down to the floor of the dog crate. Her legs came up. Her body curled up protectively around her belly. Then the drugs won this battle and swept her far away.

11

They hadn't gotten very far with the postmortem. Kimberly wasn't surprised. Most autopsies were scheduled for days after the recovery of the body, not hours. Either things were slow at the moment, or an NCIS investigation carried some hefty weight.

Special Agent Kaplan introduced her to the medical examiner, Dr Corben, and then to his assistant, Gina Nitsche.

'Your first post?' Nitsche asked, wheeling in the body with quick efficiency.

Kimberly nodded.

'If you're gonna puke, don't ask, just leave,' Nitsche said cheerfully. 'I got enough to clean up after this.' She continued talking briskly, while unzipping the body bag and folding back the plastic. 'I'm called a diener. Technically speaking, Dr Corben is the prosector. He'll handle all the protocol and I'll do what I'm told. Usual procedure is that the body arrives a day or two earlier and is logged in, in a separate area. We inventory clothes and possessions, take the weight, give the body an official tag with an ID number. Given time constraints, however,' Nitsche shot Kaplan a look, 'this time we're doing it all as we go. Oh, and while I'm thinking about it, there's a box of gloves on the side table. The cupboard has extra caps and gowns. Help yourself.'

Kimberly glanced toward the cupboard uncertainly, and Nitsche, as if she were reading her mind, added, 'You know, 'cause sometimes they splatter.'

Kimberly went to the cupboard and found herself a cap to cover her short feathery hair and a gown to cover her clothes. She noticed that Special Agent Kaplan followed her over and also snagged a set of protective gear. He'd brought his own pair of gloves. She borrowed her pair from the ME's supply.

Nitsche had finished unwrapping the body now. First she'd pulled back the external layer of heavy-duty plastic. Next, she'd unfolded a plain white sheet. Finally, she unpeeled the internal layer of plastic, much like a dry cleaning bag, which was what came into contact with the corpse's skin. Nitsche folded each layer down around the base of the gurney. Then she methodically inventoried the dead girl's clothing and jewelry, while Dr Corben prepped the autopsy table.

'I inventoried her purse before coming in,' Nitsche said conversationally. 'Poor thing had brochures from a travel agency for Hawaii. I've always wanted to go to Hawaii. Do you think she was going with a boyfriend? Because if she was going with a boyfriend, well then he's available again, and God knows I need someone to take me away from here. All right. We're ready.'

She wheeled the gurney over to the cutting table. She and Dr Corben had obviously done this many times before. He moved to the head. She moved to the feet. On the count of three, they slid the now naked corpse from the gurney onto the metal slab. Then Nitsche wheeled the gurney away.

'Testing, testing,' Dr Corben said into his recording equipment. Satisfied that it was working, he got down to business.

First, the ME catalogued the victim's naked body. He described her sex, age, height, weight, and hair and eye color. He commented that she appeared in good health (other than the fact that she was dead? Kimberly thought), then noted that she had good teeth (things they never tell you during a dental exam – someday some ME will *know* if you've *really* flossed). He also listed the presence of a tattoo, shape of a rose, approximately one-inch in size, on the deceased's upper left breast.

Victim and deceased. Dr Corben used those words a lot. Kimberly began to think this was the heart of her problem. She never thought in terms of victim or deceased. Instead, she thought in terms such as young, pretty, blond, girl. If she was supposed to be a dispassionate, world-weary death investigator, she hadn't achieved it yet.

Dr Corben had moved on to perceived injuries. He described the large bruise on the girl's – the victim's – upper left hip, his gloved hand poking and prodding at the waxy skin. 'Victim has presence of large ecchymosis, approximately four inches in diameter, on the upper left thigh. Center area is red and swollen, approximately one and a half inches around puncture site. It's an abnormal amount of bruising for an intramuscular injection. Perhaps the result of inexperience or a large bore needle.'

Special Agent Kaplan frowned at that and made a gesture with his hand. Dr Corben snapped off the minirecorder in his hand. 'What do you mean a large bore needle?' Kaplan asked.

'Different needle gauges have different thicknesses. For example, in the medical community, when we give injections we use an eighteen-gauge needle which slides very easily into a vein. Administered correctly, it can be done with relatively little bruising. Now this injection site has a great deal of bruising. And not just of the muscle area. This center spot where it's red and swollen – that's where the needle punctured the skin. The size of the aggravation leads me to believe that either it was a needle wielded with a fair amount of force, really, truly stabbed into the thigh, or it was an abnormally large needle.'

Kaplan narrowed his eyes, considering the possibilities. 'Why would someone use a bigger needle?'

'Different sized needles are used for a variety of different procedures.' Dr Corben's brow furrowed. 'Sometimes to inject large amounts of a substance at a faster rate, you need a larger-bore needle. Or when mixing substances, you would use a larger needle. Now here's something interesting. The second injection site, the arm. Note the relatively small amount of aggravation we see here. Just the slightest swollen spot. That's more like what we would typically see – consistent with a standard eighteen-gauge needle. Granted, the limited amount of bruising is also due to the fact she died shortly thereafter. But either way, this injection is clearly more skillfully done. Either it's two different needles, or it's two very different . . . approaches toward intramuscular injections.'

'So first she's injected in the hip,' Kaplan mused slowly. 'Forcefully and/or with a very large needle. Then, later, she's injected in the arm. But more controlled, more carefully. How much time occurred between the two?'

Dr Corben frowned. He resumed studying the first bruise with his fingers. 'Given the large size, it had time to develop. But notice the coloring is all purple and dark blues? None of the green and yellow tinges that happen later. I'd say twelve to twenty-four hours between the hip puncture and the injection into the arm.'

'Ambush,' Kimberly murmured.

Special Agent Kaplan turned on her. He had the hard stare again. 'Come again?'

'Ambush.' She forced herself to speak up louder. 'The first bruise . . . If it could be caused by more force, then maybe it's from an ambush. How he gains initial control. Later, when she's already subdued, he can take more time for the final injection.'

She was thinking of what Mac had said about the Georgia murders. How the girls found first always had bruises on their hips, plus a fatal injection mark on their upper left arms. She'd never heard of such an MO before. What were the odds that two different killers were using it in two different states?

Dr Corben had the recorder back on. He rolled the body onto its back, noted the absence of bruises and contusions, then finished his initial exam by narrating the condition of the mouth. Nitsche handed him some kind of standardized form, and he quickly and efficiently sketched each one of the external injuries he'd noted in the protocol.

They moved onto her hands. They had been bagged at the scene. Now Nitsche pulled off the paper bags and both prosector and diener leaned close. Dr Corben scraped beneath each nail. Nitsche collected the samples. Next Dr Corben swathed around each nail bed with a Q-tip, testing for traces of blood. He looked up at Kaplan and shook his head. 'No signs of defensive wounds,' he reported. 'No skin, no blood.'

Kaplan sighed and resumed leaning against the wall. 'Not my lucky day,' he murmured.

As the victim's hands had now been examined for evidence, Nitsche brought over an inkpad for fingerprinting. The body, however, had achieved full rigor since being found and the stiff fingers refused to cooperate.

Dr Corben moved up to assist her. He worked the first joint of the girl's index finger until with a faint popping sound, the rigor broke. Nitsche started inking, and Dr Corben methodically worked his way through both hands, each popping sound echoing faintly in the cold tile room and bringing up bile in the back of Kimberly's throat.

I will not be sick, she promised herself. And then – Oh God, this is only the external exam.

Fingerprinting done, Dr Corben moved down the body to between the girl's – the deceased's – legs. While the condition of her clothing had been inconsistent with rape, he still had to examine the body itself.

'No bruising of the inner thighs, no lacerations of the labia majora or labia minora,' Dr Corben reported. He combed the pubic hair and Nitsche collected the loose strands in another bag. Then he picked up three swabs.

Now Kimberly had to look away. The young girl was dead. Far beyond insults or injury. But Kimberly couldn't watch. Her fingers were knotted, her breathing shallow. She was once more aware of the strong smell of the room, and the feel of sweat on her back. She noticed out of the corner of her eye that Kaplan was now intently studying the floor.

'From the external exam,' Dr Corben concluded shortly, 'there is no evidence of sexual assault. Now then, let's get her cleaned up.'

Kimberly's eyes flew open. Nitsche had just moved into position and she and Dr Corben were now hosing down the body. Kimberly's bewilderment must have shown on her face, because Dr Corben spoke up above the spray of water: 'After concluding the external exam, we wash the body before making the first incision. You don't want factors from the outside – dirt, fiber, debris – contaminating the internal organs and confusing your findings. The outside had its stories to tell. Now, it's the inside's turn.'

Dr Corben matter-of-factly turned off the hose, passed out plastic goggles, and picked up a scalpel.

Kimberly went green. She was trying hard. She had seen crime scene photos, dammit. She wasn't a novice to violent death.

But she felt herself sway on her feet anyway. She told herself to hold it together, but then she looked at the young girl's face, and that did it completely.

'Oh my God,' she gasped, 'what is in her mouth?'

It was there, unmistakable now, the shadow of the thing Dr Corben had sensed earlier. First the girl's left cheek bulged, pale and waxy. Then with dazzling speed, her right cheek went, until it looked like she was puffing up her mouth while staring at them with her dead brown eyes.

Kaplan was fumbling with his holster. Kimberly was fumbling, too. He brought out a gun. She brought out a red plastic toy. Shit, damn. She dropped down to her ankle, without ever taking her gaze off the girl's face.

'Stand back,' Kaplan said.

Dr Corben and his attendant needed no urging. Nitsche's gaze was wide and fascinated. Dr Corben had that pale tight look from earlier in the day. 'It could be gasses from decomp,' he tried vainly. 'She was out in intense heat.'

'The body just achieved full rigor. It's not that far along,' Kaplan muttered tightly.

The cheeks bulged again. Moved from side to side.

'I think . . .' Kimberly's voice came out too faintly. She licked her lips, tried again. 'I think there's something in there. In her mouth. That's why he stitched it shut.'

'Holy shit!' Nitsche said with awe.

'Mother of God,' Kaplan said with more levity.

Kimberly stared at Dr Corben. His right hand was shaking badly. She was pretty sure nothing like this had ever happened in one of his postmortems before. The look on his face said he'd retire before letting it happen again. 'Sir,' she said as calmly as she could, 'you have the scalpel. You need . . . You need to cut the stitching.'

'I will not!'

'Whatever's in there has gotta come out. It's better on our terms than its.'

Kaplan was nodding slowly. 'She has a point. We need to do the autopsy. So whatever's there, needs to go.'

Dr Corben looked at them both wildly. He definitely was thinking of an argument. He definitely wanted to argue. But then his scientific mind seemed to reassert itself. He glanced at the body again, watched the horrible distortion of its face, and slowly, very slowly, nodded.

'Eye gear on,' he said at last. 'Masks, gloves. Whatever it is, I want us to be prepared.' And then, almost as an afterthought. 'Gina, stand next to the special agent.'

Nitsche moved hastily behind Kaplan's large build. Kimberly straightened up and worked on her own composure. Knees slightly bent, legs ready to move. She put on her goggles, her Crayola long since discarded on the floor, and her favorite hunting knife now in her hand.

Dr Corben moved gingerly. He got just close enough to be able to touch the girl's stitched-up mouth with his scalpel, without his body being in the line of fire for Kaplan's gun.

'On the count of three,' Dr Corben said tightly. 'One. Two. Three.'

The scalpel went slash, slash. Dr Corben fell back from the body, his feet already scrambling. And a dark, mottled shape exploded from its unwanted prison and hurtled halfway across the tiled floor.

One moment Kimberly was alone in her corner of the room. The next, she saw the unmistakable, brown-splotched shape of a coiled rattler. The viper reared up with an ominous hiss.

Kaplan's Glock exploded in the tiny room, and Kimberly hurled her knife.

12

Mac was standing outside a classroom, asking Genny if she happened to know of a good botanist in the state of Virginia, when the blurred form of a blue-clad figure came roaring down the hall. The next instant, he felt a sharp pain in his left shoulder, just had time to look up in surprise, and promptly got whacked again by his favorite new agent.

'You did not say anything about snakes!' Kimberly Quincy swung a solid right; he barely dodged left. 'You did *not* say *anything* about leaving live *vipers* in their *mouths*!' She followed with a jab to the ribs; he fell back three steps. For a tiny thing, she really could hit.

'You lying, manipulating, cold-hearted bastard!' She took a good wind-up and he came to his senses just in time to block the blow, twist her arm behind her back, and turn her into the solid restraint of his body. She, of course, tried to flip him over her back.

'Sugar,' he murmured in her ear. 'I appreciate your enthusiasm, but maybe you'd like to wait 'til we're alone.'

He felt the outrage scream through her stiffened frame, but

then his words must've penetrated. She seemed to become aware of their surroundings. For example, as students generally didn't assault other students in the halls of the Academy, she now had everyone's full attention. Genny's gaze was most amused. She had it locked on Mac's face with blatantly unconcealed interest.

'Just practicing a little drill,' Mac drawled out loud. 'You know, always happy to help out a new agent.' He gingerly released Kimberly's arm. She didn't hit him, or stomp on his foot, so he figured he was making some progress. 'Now then, darlin', why don't we go outside where we can discuss other ways for ambushing a possible suspect?'

He hightailed it for the double doors. After another awkward moment, Kimberly scrambled after him. She managed to make it all the way around the corner of the building, to a somewhat isolated flagstone patio before she went after him again.

'Why didn't you warn me about the stitched-up mouth!' she yelled.

He threw up his hands in surrender. 'Warn you about what? I still don't know what you're talking about!'

'He left a rattlesnake in her mouth. A real live rattler!'

'Well that'll put hair on your chest. Did you hit the rattler as hard as you hit me?'

'I threw a knife at it!'

'Of course.'

She scowled. 'But I missed. Special Agent Kaplan shot it with his gun.'

Ah, no wonder she was pissed. Her big moment, and she missed throwing a knife at a striking viper. The girl did have her standards.

'I want my Glock!' she was still raging.

'I know, honey, I know.' His arms had come down. He was thinking hard. 'A live snake,' he said at last. 'I didn't see that coming. Once he left an alligator's egg down a girl's throat. And for the last one, Mary Lynn, he used a snail. But I never . . . A live rattler. Damn, give a guy three years and he goes and gets mean.'

And that frightened him. God, that frightened him all the way down to his big Southern bones.

Kimberly didn't seem to have heard him. Her hands were rubbing her arms compulsively, as if she were trying to ward off a chill in hundred-degree heat. She was also holding herself carefully, her shoulders hunched, her spine too stiff, a woman made out of glass and trying not to shatter.

Shock, he realized. Quantico's newest badass had been given quite a scare, and her system still hadn't recovered. He belatedly pulled out one of the wrought iron chairs and gestured to the seat. 'Come on. Sit. Take a minute. Autopsy's over, honey. Nothin' can happen to you here.'

'Tell that to the dead girl,' Kimberly said roughly, but she accepted the chair and, for a moment, they both simply sat in silence.

Kimberly didn't know it yet, but Mac had been doing his own investigative work that afternoon. For starters, he'd inquired all about her. And boy, it had been quite an education. In the good news department, his current partner-in-solving-crime came with a genuine law enforcement pedigree. Her father had reputedly been a brilliant profiler in his day. Handled a lot of cases, put away a lot of very bad guys.

Rumor had it that his daughter had inherited his brains and aptitude for anticipating the criminal mind.

Bad news, however – the daughter was also regarded as a little bit of a head case. Didn't like authority figures. Didn't like her fellow classmates. Didn't seem to actually like much of anyone, which may explain why every time Mac ran into her, she was trying to kill him.

Of course, then there was what had happened to her family.

Losing most of your relatives to a homicidal maniac was bound to make an impression on you. Perhaps Mac should just be grateful she hadn't actually inflicted bodily harm on him yet.

Mac stole another glance beneath the cover of his eyelids. Kimberly's gaze was off in the distance, her eyes unfocused, her shoulders slumped. She appeared profoundly exhausted, haggard beyond measure with deep shadows bruising her eyes and a patchwork of red scratches still welting her skin.

The girl definitely wasn't sleeping at night. And that was before she'd met him.

'Was it an overdose?' he asked at last.

She seemed to rouse herself from her daze. 'I don't know the results of the tox screen. But she was hit first – and forcefully – by something in the upper left thigh. Later, probably after twelve to twenty-four hours had passed, she received the fatal injection in her upper left arm.'

'Intramuscular injections?' Mac asked.

'Yes.'

'All her clothes were intact? Her purse? No sexual assault?'

'Yes on all accounts.'

'What about defensive wounds? Blood, skin, anything?'

'Nothing.'

'Shit,' Mac said heavily.

She nodded.

'They have an ID?'

'Not yet. They took her prints. They'll need time to run them through the system.'

'We need to know who she is,' Mac murmured. 'We'll need a list of her friends and family, who she was out with last night. Where they went, what was the make and model of their car . . . Jesus.' He ran a hand through his hair, his mind beginning to race. 'It's already been at least twelve hours . . . Jesus. Who's in charge of the case?'

'Special Agent Kaplan.'

'I'd better go talk to him.'

'Good luck,' Kimberly snorted.

'He let you watch the autopsy.'

'Only because I promised to throw up.'

'Did you?'

'I was thinking about it,' she admitted. 'But the rattler put a damper on things. Then Kaplan exploded its head, and then we all had to debate how carefully to clean up snake guts, as you could consider them evidence.'

'You had quite a first autopsy,' Mac said seriously.

'Yeah,' she sighed. She seemed rather surprised by the notion herself. 'I think other ones will be easier after this.'

'I think they will be.'

They both lapsed back into silence, Kimberly probably thinking of the snake she still wished she'd killed; Mac contemplating past cases that were at least three years old and now once more loomed larger than life.

The heat settled in on them, rolling in like a heavy blanket and pressing them deep into their chairs while their clothing glued to their skin. Mac used to not mind heat like this. It was perfect for sitting outdoors, next to his parents' pool. Put on a little Alan Jackson, drink a lot of homemade lemonade. And later, when dusk fell, watch the fireflies flicker and dart amid the purple-tinged air.

He didn't think of idyllic summer days anymore. Summer had become the enemy, when heat waves would roll in, and girls would no longer be safe, even when traveling in pairs.

He needed to call Atlanta. He needed to figure out how to best approach this Special Agent Kaplan. And then they were going to need resources. ASAP. The best experts they could find. A botanist, biologist, a forensic geologist, an entomologist, and God knows what other kind of ologists. Was there an expert on snakes? They should find someone who knew everything about rattlers and what it signified when one burst out of a dead girl's mouth.

Then there was the rock, of course, which Mac hadn't even gotten to see. And the leaf they'd recovered this morning, but he'd had no luck at all tracing it. And that's just the clues/evidence he knew off the top of his head.

He needed the body, that was the deal. The clothes would be good to study as well. And her purse, her hair, her sandals. This guy liked to leave clues in the damnedest places, and it sounded like he was refining his technique all of the time. A live rattlesnake crammed into a body . . .

Shit. Just plain . . . shit.

Nearby doors opened. Mac heard footsteps approach, then a shadow fell across their patio. A man stood in front of them. Mac didn't recognize him, but he could tell from the look on Kimberly's face that she did.

'Kimberly,' the man said quietly.

'Dad,' she said with equal reserve.

Mac's eyebrows had just disappeared beneath his hairline, when the man, older, trim, and very impressive looking in a deep gray suit, turned toward him.

'And you must be Special Agent McCormack. Pierce Quincy. Pleased to meet you.'

Mac accepted the man's handshake. And then he knew. A funny grin came across his face. The bottom dropped out of his stomach, and he heard a faint ringing in his ears. He had been so concerned that the NCIS had done nothing in the past eight hours. But, apparently, they had done something after all.

Pierce Quincy shouldn't know his name. Former FBI agent Pierce Quincy should have no reason to know anyone at the National Academy. Unless he had been explicitly told to look for Mac. And that could only mean . . .

'If you two would follow me, we need to have a meeting,' Quincy was saying in that carefully modulated voice.

'You shouldn't be here,' Kimberly said tightly.

'I was invited.'

'I didn't call you!'

'I would never presume that you did.'

'Dammit, did they tell you about the body?'

'Kimberly—'

'I am doing just fine!'

'Kim—'

'I don't need help, especially from you!'

'K—'

'Turn around. Go home! If you love me at all, please for God's sake just go away.'

'I can't.'

'Why not!'

Pierce Quincy sighed heavily. He didn't say anything right away. He simply reached out a hand and touched his daughter's battered face. She flinched. And his arm instantly dropped back to his side, as if burned.

'We need to have a meeting,' Quincy said again, turning toward the front of the building. 'If you'll please just follow me.'

Mac finally rose. Kimberly much more grudgingly shoved back her chair. They both fell in step behind her father, Mac's arm settling lightly around her waist.

'I think we're in trouble,' Mac murmured in Kimberly's ear.

And she said bitterly, 'You have no idea.'

13

Quincy led them to an office in the main administrative wing. The sign on the door read Supervisor Mark Watson. Inside, the man in question was leaning against the edge of his desk, facing two guests. The first person, Mac recognized as being the NCIS officer from the crime scene. The second person was actually a very attractive woman. Late thirties, Mac would guess. Gorgeous, long chestnut hair. A face that was startlingly angular, more arresting than classically beautiful. Definitely not FBI. For one thing, she already looked annoyed as hell with Watson.

'Kimberly!' the woman said. She stood the moment Kimberly walked in the room, and gave the girl a quick hug.

'Rainie,' Kimberly acknowledged. She offered the woman a faint smile, but immediately appeared wary again as Watson pushed away from his desk. It was clearly the supervisor's show. He was now holding up his hands and awaiting everyone's attention.

He started with the introductions: Rainie turned out to be Lorraine Conner, Quincy's partner in Quincy & Conner

Investigations out of New York; the NCIS officer was Special Agent Thomas Kaplan from General Crimes out of Norfolk.

Quincy & Conner Investigations, Watson announced, had been retained by NCIS to assist with the case. Given the location of the body on Marine grounds and near FBI facilities, the powers-that-be had determined the presence of independent consultants would be in everyone's best interest. Translation: Everyone was keenly aware of what it would mean if the bad guy turned out to be one of their guys and it looked like they'd tried to cover it up. Score one for the politicians.

Mac settled in next to the door, which had now been closed for privacy. He noted that Kaplan stood next to Watson, while Quincy had taken the seat next to Rainie Conner. Kimberly, on the other hand, had put as much distance between herself and her father as possible. She stood in the far corner of the room, arms crossed in front of her chest, and chin up for a fight.

So everyone had their alliances. Or lack thereof. Now they could get down to business.

Mark Watson addressed his opening comments to Kimberly. 'I understand you saw Special Agent Kaplan earlier today, New Agent Quincy.'

'Yes, sir.'

'I thought we had reached an understanding this morning. This is NCIS's case. You are not to go near it.'

'As part of my pledge to cooperate with NCIS,' Kimberly replied evenly, 'I found the officer in charge in order to volunteer my statement. At the time, interestingly enough, he was about to observe the autopsy of the body. I asked if I could join him. He graciously let me in.' Kimberly smiled stiffly. 'Thank you, Special Agent Kaplan.'

Watson turned to Kaplan, who shrugged big Marine shoulders. 'She told me her name. She asked permission. What the hell, I let her join us.'

'I never lied,' Kimberly spoke up promptly. 'And I never misrepresented my interests.' She scowled. 'I did, however, miss the snake. For that I apologize.'

'I see,' Watson said. 'And earlier in the day, when you directly violated my orders and attempted to revisit the crime scene, were you also thinking of the urgency of NCIS's investigation?'

'I was looking for Special Agent Kaplan—'

'Don't play me for dumb.'

'I was curious,' Kimberly immediately amended. 'It didn't matter. The Marines obediently chased me away.'

'I see. And what about *after* you harassed the Marines in the woods, New Agent Quincy? What about the *hour* you then spent talking to Special Agent McCormack, after you were explicitly told *not* to discuss your find with anyone in the Academy? How would you care to explain that?'

Kimberly stiffened. Her gaze flickered to Mac, uncertain now, while he swallowed back a fresh curse. Of course: their meeting in the Crossroads Lounge. In full view of everyone. Stupid, stupid, stupid.

This time, Watson didn't wait for Kimberly to reply. He was on a roll – or maybe he was aware of just how tense Quincy had grown in the seat opposite him.

'Imagine my surprise,' Watson continued, 'when I discovered that far from returning to her room as requested, my student first wandered into the woods, and then was seen in animated discussion with a National Academy student who just happens to have once worked a case bearing a startling resemblance to the homicide discovered this morning. Were you sharing information with Special Agent McCormack, Kimberly?'

'Actually, I was getting information from him.'

'Really. I find that extremely interesting. Particularly since ten minutes ago, he became Special Agent Kaplan's primary suspect.'

Lisa Gardner

'Oh for heaven's sake,' Mac burst out. 'I'm doing my best to help with a case that is only the beginning of one long, hot nightmare. Do you have any idea what you've waded into the middle of—'

'Where were you last night?' Special Agent Kaplan interrupted curtly.

'I started the night at Carlos Kelly's in Stafford. Then I returned to Quantico, where I ran into New Agent Quincy on the firing ranges. It doesn't matter—'

Kaplan's gaze had swung to Kimberly. 'What time did you see him on the ranges?'

'Around eleven. I didn't look at my watch—'

'Did you see him go back to the dorms?'

'No.'

'Where was he headed?'

'I don't know. I was heading back to the dorms. I didn't pay attention to him!'

'So in other words,' Kaplan homed in on Mac, 'no one knows where you were after eleven-thirty last night.'

'Don't you think it's an awfully big coincidence,' Watson spoke up, 'that we should just happen to get a homicide that bears so many resemblances to one of your past cases, *while* you're staying here at the Academy?'

'It's not coincidence,' Mac said. 'It was planned.'

'*What?*' Watson finally drew up short. He shot a glance at Kaplan, who appeared equally perplexed. Apparently, they'd both been big fans of the Georgia-cop-as-a-killer theory. Why not? Get a dead body at eight A.M., wrap up the case before six P.M. It made for good headlines. Assholes.

'Perhaps,' Quincy interjected quietly, 'you should let the man speak. Of course,' he added dryly, 'that's only the advice of the independent consultant.'

'Yes,' Rainie seconded beside him. 'Let him speak. This is finally getting to be good.'

'Thank you,' Mac said stiffly. He shot Quincy and Rainie a grateful look, while carefully avoiding Kimberly's gaze. How must she feel right about now? Hurt, confused, betrayed? He had honestly meant none of those things, and yet there was nothing he could do about that now.

'You can verify everything I'm about to say with my supervisor, Special Agent in Charge Lee Grogen from the Atlanta office. Yes, starting in ninety-eight, we had a string of murders similar to the one you discovered today. After the third incident, we formed a multi-jurisdictional task force in charge of the investigation. Unfortunately, seven murders later, the man we were seeking, the so-called Eco-Killer, simply vanished. No new crimes, nothing. The task force started out with over a thousand leads. Three years later, our work is down to a trickle. Until six months ago. When things went hot again.

'We got a letter in the mail. It contained a newspaper clipping of a letter to the editor similar to the ones our guy used to send the *Atlanta Journal-Constitution*. Except this letter wasn't sent to a Georgia paper. It was sent to the *Virginian-Pilot*. And then I started getting phone calls—'

'You,' Quincy interrupted. 'Or the task force?'

'Me. On my cell phone. Hell if I know why, but lucky me has received six calls now. The caller's voice is always distorted by some kind of electronic device and he/she/it always has the same message – the Eco-Killer is getting agitated again. He's going to strike. Except this time, he's picked Virginia as his favorite playground.'

'So your department sent you here,' Watson spoke up. 'Why? To be a watchdog? To magically prevent another crime? You didn't even make anyone aware of your concerns.'

Mac started getting angry again. 'For the record, I told everybody who would listen about my goddamn concerns. But let's face it, around here, cold cases are a dime a dozen;

everybody comes bearing that one investigation that's still keeping them up at night. Best I could do was get a preliminary meeting with a forensic linguist in the BSU – Dr Ennunzio – and show him the letters to the editor. What he thinks, however, I don't know 'cause he's been dodging my calls ever since. And now here we are. I got a good lead a bad way, and you're barking up the wrong tree, you paranoid piece of shit.'

'Well that summarizes things nicely,' Rainie said.

Watson's face had developed a red mottled look above his regulation red tie. Mac just kept staring him in the eye. He was angrier than he should be, making enemies when he needed allies. He didn't care. Another girl was dead, and Mac was tired of standing in an office, discussing a case these guys would never understand in time to make a difference.

'I still see no compelling evidence between this body and what happened in Georgia,' Kaplan spoke up finally. 'Did the caller tell you this so-called Eco-Killer was going to strike this week?'

'Not specifically.'

'Did he tell you it would be at the FBI Academy?'

'Can't say that he did.'

'Did he give you a reason why this killer has done nothing for three years?'

'Nope.'

'Or why he would move from Georgia to Virginia?'

'Nope.'

'In other words, the caller has told you nothing at all.'

'You got me, sir. That is the major weakness of our investigation. Five years later, we still know nothin', and today hasn't changed a thing. So maybe we can wrap this up now, so I can get back out there and you know, do something.'

The former Marine ignored him, turning his attention to the rest of the suits instead. 'So what we're really left with is a letter to the editor written six months before the body was found today. It's too far-fetched,' he said flatly. 'Some Georgian serial killer, who does nothing in three years, suddenly delivers a body to Quantico grounds, while only notifying a National Academy student. It doesn't make any sense.'

'Should he have called you instead?' Rainie asked. Her voice held just the barest hint of sarcasm and Mac liked her immensely for it.

'That's not what I'm saying—'

'Or maybe he should've explained himself better in one of his notes?'

'Now that's not a half-bad thought! If this guy is leaving notes, where's the one for this body? Seems to me he likes to take credit for his crimes. So where's the ownership?'

'It's been three years,' Rainie said. 'Maybe he's had a change of heart.'

'Listen,' Mac interjected tightly. He could feel the urgency growing in his voice. Vainly, he tried to swallow it down. But he just didn't have time for this. They didn't understand; without the proper paperwork and memos they never would understand. And maybe that's what the Eco-Killer grasped better than any of them suspected. No bureaucracy moved fast, particularly one involved in law enforcement. No, law enforcement agencies moved painfully slow, dotting i's, crossing t's, and covering asses along the way. While a lone girl was dropped off in some surreal wilderness terrain, clutching her gallon of water, wearing her party clothes, and probably wondering what was gonna get her next.

'There's more than a damn letter. The Eco-Killer has rules, Rules of the Game, we call them, and we're seeing plenty of them in this murder. At least enough to convince me.' Mac ticked off his first finger, 'One, he only strikes when it's a heat wave.'

'It's July, we have plenty of heat waves,' Watson objected up.

Lisa Gardner

Mac ignored the FBI agent. 'Two, the first girl is always found with clothing and purse intact. No sign of robbery, no sign of sexual assault. Body has one bruise in the thigh or buttocks, but cause of death is an overdose of the tranquilizer Ativan, injected into the upper left arm.'

Watson skewered Kimberly with a look. 'Well, you really didn't spare him any of the details, did you?'

'I went and looked for myself!' Mac spoke up sharply. 'Dammit, I've been waiting for this moment for three long years. Of course I paid a visit to your crime scene. New agents aren't the only people who can go skulking around in the woods—'

'You had no right—'

'I had every right! I know this man. I have studied him for five goddamn years. And I'm telling you, we don't have time for this kind of bullshit. Don't you get it yet? This girl isn't the only victim. Rule number three: he always kidnaps in pairs, because the first girl is just a map. She's a tool to help you find where the real game is going down.'

'What do you mean where the real game is going down?' Rainie asked.

'I mean there's another girl out there, right now. She was traveling with this girl, maybe her sister or roommate or best friend. But she was with the first victim when they were both ambushed, and now she's been taken somewhere. He picked out the place ahead of time. It's somewhere geographically unique, but also very, very treacherous. In our state he chose a granite gorge, a vast farming county, then the banks of the Savannah River, and finally marshlands around the coast. He likes places exposed, with natural predators such as rattlesnakes and bears and bobcats. He likes places isolated, so even if the girls roam for days they still won't run into anyone who can offer them help. He likes places that are environmentally important, but no one thinks about them anymore.

124

'Then he turns these girls loose, drugged, dazed, and confused, and waits to see what will happen next. In this kind of heat, some of them probably don't make it more than hours. But some of them – the smart ones, the tough ones – they might make it days. Maybe even a week. Long, tortured days, without food, without water, waiting for someone to come and save them.'

Rainie was looking at him in rapt fascination. 'How many times did he do this before?'

'Four. Eight girls kidnapped. Seven dead.'

'So you got one back alive.'

'Nora Ray Watts. The last girl. We found her in time.'

'How?' Quincy spoke up.

Mac took a deep breath. His muscles were bunching again. He grimly fought his impatience down. 'The man leaves clues on the first body. Evidence, that if you interpret correctly, will narrow down the location of the second girl.'

'What kind of clues?'

'Flora and fauna, soil, sediment, rocks, insects, snails, hell whatever he can dream up. We didn't understand the significance in the beginning. We bagged and tagged according to SOP, merrily trotted evidence off to the labs, and found only dead bodies after that. But hey, even we can be taught. By the fourth pair of kidnappings, we had a team of experienced specialists in place. Botanists, biologists, forensic geologists, you name it. Nora Ray had been traveling with her sister. Mary Lynn's body was found with substance on her shirt, samples of vegetation on her shoes and a foreign object down her throat.'

'Down her throat?' Kaplan spoke up sharply. Mac nodded his head. For the first time, the NCIS agent seemed to have gained real interest.

'The sediment on her shirt proved to be salt. The vegetation on her shoes was identified as *Spartina alterniflora*. Cord grass.

And the biologist identified the foreign object as a marsh periwinkle shell. All three elements were consistent with what you would find in a salt marsh. We focused the search and rescue teams on the coast, and fifty-six hours later, a Coast Guard chopper spotted Nora Ray, frantically waving her bright red shirt.'

'She couldn't help you identify the killer?' Rainie asked.

Mac shook his head. 'Her last memory is of her tire going flat. The next she knew, she woke up ravenously thirsty in the middle of a damn marsh.'

'Was she drugged?' Watson this time.

'Bruise still fading on her left thigh.'

'He ambushes them?'

'Our best guess – he scopes out bars. He looks for what he wants – young girls, no specific coloring required, traveling in pairs. I think he follows them to their car. While they get in, he drops a tack or two behind their back tire. Then he simply has to follow. Sooner or later the tire goes flat, he pulls over as if offering to help, and boom, he has them.'

'Sneaks up on them with a needle?' Watson asked skeptically.

'No. He nails them with a dart gun. Like the kind a big game hunter might use.'

In the quiet room, came the unmistakable sound of sharply indrawn breaths. Mac regarded them all stonily. 'You think we haven't done our homework? For five years, we've been hunting this man. I can tell you his profile. I can tell you how he hunts his victims. I can tell you he doesn't always get his way – after the fact, we learned about two different pairs of girls who got flat tires and had a man pull over behind them. They refused to roll down their windows, however, and they got to live another day.

'I can tell you that Mary Lynn, whose body we found the earliest, tested positive for a second drug – ketamine, which is used by vets and animal control officers for its quickly subduing effect. I can tell you ketamine is a controlled substance, but also readily available on the streets as kids use it in rave parties, calling it Kit Kat or Special K. I can tell you Ativan is also controlled, and also used by vets. But pursuing all vets got us nowhere. As did investigating members of various hunting groups, the Appalachian Mountain Club, or the Audubon Society.

'I can tell you the man is growing angrier. He went from striking once a year, which takes a tremendous amount of control in a serial killer, to striking twice in twelve weeks. And I can tell you the man's game only gets tougher. The first time, if we'd been paying attention, one of the clues was a rare herb found only in a five-mile radius in all of Georgia. Identify that herb, and we would've gotten the girl for sure. The last time, for Nora Ray Watts, the clues only led us to salt marshes. There are nearly four hundred thousand acres of salt marshes in Georgia. Quite frankly, Nora Ray was the proverbial needle in a haystack.'

'And yet you found her,' Kimberly said.

'She kept herself alive,' Mac replied tightly.

Quincy, however, was regarding him intently. 'Four hundred thousand square miles is not a feasible search area. A chopper could not pick out a lone girl when covering that kind of terrain. You knew something else.'

'I had a theory,' Mac said grudgingly. 'Call it geographic profiling.'

'The victims were related somehow? Had areas of geography in common?'

'No. The bodies did. When you put them on the map and identified the direction in which they were facing—'

'He used them as compasses,' Quincy breathed.

'Maps,' Mac said quietly. 'The guy sees the first girls as nothing but maps. So why not line up Mary Lynn's body to point to her sister? She's just a tool after all. Anything for the sake of his game.'

'Jesus,' Rainie murmured. And all around the room, they were silent.

After a moment, Kaplan cleared his throat. 'The victim this morning, she wasn't aligned in any particular manner. In fact, her arms and legs were spread in four different directions.'

'I know.'

'It's another inconsistency.'

'I know.'

'She did have a rock in her hand, though,' Kaplan was saying, his eyes appraising Mac's. 'And a snake in her mouth. Can't say I've seen much of that.'

'She also had a leaf in her hair,' Mac said. 'The ME pulled it out at the scene. I retrieved it later. I'll fetch it when we're done.'

'You've destroyed chain of custody,' Watson spoke up immediately.

'So paddle my behind. You want the leaf or not?'

'It just doesn't make sense,' Kaplan was saying, still looking troubled. 'On the one hand, the snake. Seems to indicate something off the business-as-usual map. On the other hand, all you really have in common is a letter to the editor written six months ago. Otherwise . . . It's been three years between bodies and this is the wrong state for your man. Could be related. Or your caller could just be some asshole jerking your chain, and this body a matter of chance. You got an equal shot of going either way.'

Around the room, others slowly started to nod. Kaplan, Quincy, Rainie. Only Kimberly remained apart. Mac was proud of her for that.

'I have a theory,' he said abruptly. They looked at him, and he took that as an invitation.

'When this man started in ninety-eight, the first clues were obvious and easy. He ramped up pressure from there. Clues which were more difficult to find. Conditions which were harsher for the victims. A rapid escalation in time. He anticipated our own learning curve and to keep his game competitive, he remained one step ahead.

'Until the year two thousand. When we finally, seven bodies later, got it right. We saved the girl. And he quit. Because we'd finally won the game.'

Mac looked at Quincy. 'Serial killers don't quit,' the profiler said obediently.

'Yeah, but they don't always know that, do they?'

Quincy nodded thoughtfully. 'Sometimes they try. Bundy broke out of jail twice and both times he swore he'd stop attacking women. He'd quit, live a quiet life and get away scott free. Except he couldn't. He underestimated the physiological and emotional need he had to kill. In fact, the more he tried not to kill, the worse the compulsion became. Until he attacked five girls in a single night.'

'I think this guy tried to stop,' Mac said, watching as Rainie and Kaplan closed their eyes. 'Except the compulsion, like you said, just grew and grew and grew. Until he had to start again . . .

'It's not the old game,' Mac told them grimly. 'We won the old game. So now it's a new game. One where the victim's limbs will no longer serve as compass points. One where the map contains a live, lethal rattlesnake. And one where the body is left outside the FBI Academy because what point is there to inventing a game if you can't get the best to come out to play?

'In the year two thousand, this man killed three girls in twelve weeks. If this is the same man, if this is a new game, then whatever he's doing now, I promise you, it's going to be much, much worse. So sorry if I offend you ladies and gentlemen, but I can't just stand around talking about this anymore. You don't get to talk this case. You don't get to write up detective activity reports or create timelines of events. From the second that first body is found, the clock starts ticking. Now, if you want to have any chance at finding the second victim alive, then believe you me, get off your butts and get to work. 'Cause there's another girl out there, and I just hope to hell it's not already too late.'

14

He was getting tired now. He'd been awake for close to forty-eight hours, and driving for a solid sixteen. The sun, bright and strong for most of the day, had helped keep him going. Daylight, however, was at long last beginning to fade. Behind him, the horizon was streaked with the vivid pinks and bright oranges of a dying sun. Ahead of him, in the thick wilderness into which he drove, the sun had already lost the war.

Darkness crowded under the thick canopy of trees. Shadows grew and lengthened, forming deep wells of black that swallowed up the world beyond sixty feet. Trees took on twisted, unnatural shapes, with leaves few and far between. Now, the landscape was interrupted only by doublewide trailers that squatted in the middle of fields, surrounded by the shells of burnt out cars, and old electrical appliances.

The man didn't have to worry about anyone noticing his approach.

Kids didn't play in these lawns. People didn't sit out on these front porches. Here and there he saw lone bloodhounds, scrawny dogs with drooping faces and jutting hipbones, sitting dispirited on broken-down steps. Otherwise, only the steady line of road-killed possums marked his way.

Life still existed around here. Not everyone could afford to move. And some people simply got used to the smell that constantly permeated the air. A cross between rotten eggs and burning garbage. A heavy, acrid smell that made old folks gag while bringing tears to the eyes of strangers. A smell that made even the locals wonder if the high rate of cancer among their neighbors was really so random after all.

This place was still Virginia. But technically, most of the state would like to forget this place ever existed. Virginia was supposed to be beautiful, famous for its green mountain ranges and wonderful sandy beaches. Virginia is for lovers, the tourism board liked to declare. It wasn't supposed to look like this.

The man took the right-hand fork in the road, leaving pavement behind and traveling on dirt. The van jostled and bounced noisily, the steering wheel jerking beneath his hands. He held it without much visible effort, though his muscles were tired and he still had several more rigorous hours to go. He would have some coffee after this. Take a minute to stretch out his arms and legs. Then there would be more work to do.

Life was about effort. Take your punishment like a man.

The thick canopy of trees gave way. His van suddenly burst into a clearing, where the dusky sky grew brighter and illuminated a scene straight out of a nightmare.

Yawning piles of sawdust stretched all the way up to the sky, still steaming from the compressed heat trapped in the middle and covered with a white film some people thought was dust, but was really a thin coating of fungus. To his left, ramshackle sheds with busted-out windows and teetering walls vainly attempted to shelter long conveyors lined with rusted belts and ending with giant saw blades. The teeth on the multiple blades appeared black in the fading light. Smeared with blood? Oil? It was anyone's guess.

This place had finally been closed down a few years ago. Too late. Tucked away in this backwoods shithole, the mill had already spent twenty years polluting streams, killing off surface vegetation, and doing far greater damage beneath the earth.

He'd seen the mill in action when he was younger. Watched workers attack tree trunks with gas-powered chain saws. No one wore protective eye gear. Few bothered with hats. Men strode around in loose flannel shirts, the excess material just waiting to get caught beneath the right hungry blade.

Coffee cups were tossed straight to the ground. Crumpled up Coke cans formed an expanse of mini landmines. Old saw blades were yanked off the equipment and carelessly tossed aside. Walk around unaware and scratch up your pant leg. Walk around too unaware, and lose a limb.

That's the kind of place this was. And the mountains of sawdust had yet to spontaneously combust. Once that happened, there would be no hope for anything around here. Or anyone.

The stupid fucks. They destroyed the land, then called it quits, and had the gall to think that made things right.

The man got out of his van, reenergized by his outrage, and the bugs instantly swarmed his face. Mosquitoes, yellow flies, tiny gnats. They came en masse, attracted by the smell of fresh blood and salty sweat. The man waved his hand around his head, but knew it was useless. Dusk was the hour for mosquitoes. And also for the brown bats, which were already swooping overhead and preparing to feast.

In the back of the van, the girl didn't stir. He'd administered 3.5 mg of Ativan four hours ago. She should be out for another two hours, if not four. That was important for the journey ahead.

First, he took care of himself. He donned a pair of thick blue coveralls. The material was a synthetic, thin but rubbery to the touch. As a general rule, he avoided unnatural fibers, but it was unavoidable here. The latest water test he'd done had revealed a pH-level of 2.5; in other words, this water was so acidic, it would literally eat away cotton and peel away skin. Synthetic suit, it was.

Over his coveralls, the man donned a thick pair of canvas boots, then a thick pair of gloves. Around his waist went his care pack – extra water, saltine crackers, waterproof matches, a Swiss army knife, a handheld LED light, a compass, one extra loop of nylon rope, and two extra clamps.

Next, moving quickly, he turned his attention to the girl. This one was a brunette, not that it really mattered to him. She wore some kind of skimpy, yellow-flowered dress that did little to cover her long, tanned limbs. She looked like a runner, or a natural athlete. Maybe that would help her in the days to come. Maybe it wouldn't.

He gritted his teeth, bent down, and hefted her unconscious form up over his shoulder. His arms screamed while his back groaned. She was not a heavy girl, but he was not a big man, and his body was already fatigued by forty-eight hours of intensive effort. Then he was standing, and the worst of the strain was over.

She got a suit of her own. For the entry. He dressed her the same way one might attend a doll. Flopping each limb into place. Tucking feet and hands where appropriate. Snapping the suit up tight.

Then he strapped her to the body board. At the last minute, he remembered her purse and the jug of water. Then he remembered her face, how close it would be to the acidic sludge, and pulled the hood as tightly as he could over her face.

He stood and the world went black.

What? Where? He needed to . . . He must . . .

He was standing in an old sawmill. He had a girl with him. He was outside his van.

The world spun again, black void threatening as he wobbled a little on his feet and clutched frantically at his temples. What? Where? He needed to . . . He must . . .

He was standing in an old sawmill. That's right. He had a girl with him . . . He rubbed his temples harder, trying to hold it together through a fresh burst of pain. Concentrate, man, focus. He was outside his van; he was wearing blue coveralls. He had his survival pack. The body board was already loaded with water; the girl was strapped on board. Everything was all set.

Except that confused him even more. Why couldn't he remember getting it all set? What had happened?

The black holes, he realized faintly. They came more and more frequently these days. The future and the past, both slipping through his fingers with frightening speed. He was an educated man. Someone who prided himself on intelligence, strength, and control. But he, too, was part of nature's web. And nothing lived forever. Everything of beauty died.

Lately, he'd been dreaming so often of the flames.

The man reached down, he attached his line to the body board, swung the rope over his shoulder and started to pull.

Seventeen minutes later, he had arrived at the opening of a small hole in the ground. Not many people would notice it, just another sinkhole in a state whose limestone foundation was more hole-riddled than Swiss cheese. This opening was special, though. The man had known it since his youth, and understood even back then its full potential.

First he had to fasten his rope around the thick trunk of a nearby tree, forming a rough belay. He stationed his feet for balance, then used the rope to carefully lower the body board down through the hole deep into the bowels of the earth. Ten minutes later, he heard the small splash of the board landing. He tied off one end of the rope around the tree, and rappelled down the other, also disappearing into the foul-smelling earth.

He landed standing upright in knee-deep water. Fading light forty feet above. Endless darkness all around.

Most people never looked past the sawmill above. They didn't understand that in Virginia, there was often a whole other ecosystem far below.

He turned on his headlight, identified the cavern's narrow passageway to his right, and got on his hands and knees to crawl. The girl floated after him, the board's rope tied once more to the belt at his waist.

Within minutes the passageway shrunk. He extended his narrow frame, body flattening carefully into the oily stream of rancid water. He was protected in synthetic shrinkwrap; he still swore he could feel the water lapping away at his skin, sluicing off his cells, eroding him down to his very bones. Soon the water would get into his brain, and then he would have no hope left. Ashes to ashes. Dust to dust.

The smells were richer now. The stifling decay of layers and layers of bat guano, now melted into an oozing morass that squished around his hands and knees. The sharp, pungent odor of sewage and waste. The deeper, more menacing smell of death.

He moved slowly, feeling his way even with the light. Bats startled easily and you didn't need a panicked, rabid creature flying at your face. Ditto the raccoons, though he'd be surprised if any of them could survive this passageway anymore. Most of what had once lived here had probably died years ago.

Now there was just this rancid water, corroding away the last of the limestone walls and spreading its slow, insidious death.

The body board bobbed along behind him, bumping him from time to time in the rear. And then, just when the ceiling was shrinking dangerously low, forcing his face closer and closer to that putrid water, the tunnel ended. The room opened up, and he and the girl spilled out into a vast, expansive cavern.

The man shot immediately to his feet, embarrassed by his own need to stand, but doing it nonetheless. He compulsively took giant gulps of air, his sudden need for oxygen outweighing his apprehension of the smell. He needed to feel his chest expand and contract. He needed to flex his fingers and toes. He looked down, and was genuinely surprised by how badly his hands were shaking.

He should be stronger than this. He should be tougher. Forty-eight hours without sleep, even he was starting to go.

He wasted another thirty seconds regaining his composure, then belatedly went to work on the rope at his waist. He was here, the worst of it was over, and he was aware once again of just how fast the clock was ticking.

He fetched the girl from the mini-stretcher. He laid her out on a ledge away from the dark running stream, and quickly stripped the coveralls from her body. Purse went beside her. Bottle of water as well.

Forty feet above, an eight-inch diameter pipe formed a makeshift skylight in the ceiling. When daylight came, she would be greeted by a narrow shaft of light. He thought that gave her a sporting chance.

He retied the board to his waist, and ready now for his exit, gave the brunette one last glance.

She was propped up near a small pool of water. This water wasn't polluted like the stream. Not yet. It was replenished from the rain and put up a better fight.

This water rippled and surged with the promise of life. Things moved beneath the pitch-black surface. Things that lived and breathed and fought. Things that bit. Some things that slithered. And many things that wouldn't care for intruders in their home.

The girl was moaning again.

The man bent over. 'Shhhh,' he whispered in her ear. 'You don't want to wake up just yet.'

The water surged again. The man turned his back on the girl and left.

15

'She doesn't look very good,' Rainie said.

'I know.'

'What the hell happened to her eye? It looks like she's gone ten rounds with Tyson.'

'Shotgun training would be my guess.'

'She's definitely lost weight.'

'It's not supposed to be easy.'

'But you're worried about her. Come on, Quince. Give up the ghost. You'd like to go punch Watson's lights out. Pretty please. I'll hold him down for you.'

Quincy sighed. He finally put down the case file he was reading – the homicide notes from the Georgia case years ago. These were just summary documents, of course. The original detective reports, evidence sheets, and activity logs probably took up enough boxes to fill a small family room. They both hated working off case summary reports – almost by definition, the documents were filled with erroneous assumptions and conclusions. Here, however, they had to make do.

The page Quincy currently had open was labeled 'Profile: Atlanta Case #832.' Rainie's hands itched reflexively. GBI's profile of the Eco-Killer, no doubt. She'd like to read that report herself, particularly after listening to that Georgian cop's take on things. But Quincy had grabbed the file first. He'd probably read it long into the night, pinching the bridge of his nose in that gesture which meant he was thinking too hard and giving himself a headache.

'If I say anything, she'll just get angry,' he said now.

'That's because she's your daughter.'

'Exactly. And my daughter hates for me to be involved in her life. My daughter believes pigs will fly before she'll accept help from me.'

Rainie frowned at him. She was sitting Indian-style in the middle of the orange-covered bed. This was only her fourth time at Quantico and the place never failed to intimidate the crap out of her. The grounds practically screamed reputable-law-enforcement-agents-only. Even though she and Quincy had been together for six years, they were still given separate rooms – they were unmarried, you know, and the Academy did have its sense of propriety.

Rainie knew the way the world worked. She would never have been allowed through those hallowed gates if she hadn't had Quincy to vouch for her. Not way back when, and not now. Thus, she could understand some of Kimberly's issues, having taken the long route to elite law enforcement herself.

'I don't think she's going to make it,' Rainie said flatly. 'She looks too haggard around the eyes. Like a dog that's been beat too many times.'

'The training pushes you. It's meant to test your level of endurance.'

'Oh bullshit! You think Kimberly lacks endurance? My God, she held up even after a madman killed Bethie. She remained functional and alert when that same madman came after her. I was with her, remember. Kimberly has plenty of endurance. She doesn't need a bunch of numbnuts in suits to prove otherwise.'

'I don't think Watson would care to be labeled a numb-nut.'

'Oh, now you're just pissing me off.'

'Apparently.' Quincy threw up his hands. He'd discarded his suit jacket after their meeting with Watson and Kaplan. Sequestered in his room, he'd even gone so far as to roll up the cuffs of his white dress shirt and loosen his tie. He still looked like an FBI agent, and Rainie had the overwhelming compulsion to fight with him, if only to mess him up a little. 'What do you want me to do?' he asked.

'Stop being an agent.'

'I am not an agent!'

'Oh for the love of God. There is no agent more agent than you. I swear you have pin-striped ties encrypted into your DNA. When you die, the coffin is going to read Property of the FBI.'

'Did you just think that up off the top of your head?'

'Yep, I'm on a roll. No changing the subject. Kimberly's in trouble. You've seen her, and you've seen how Watson is treating her. It's only a matter of time before things come to a head.'

'Rainie . . . Not that you're going to want to hear this, but Watson is an experienced Academy supervisor. Maybe he has a point.'

'What? Are you fucking mad?'

Quincy sighed deeply. 'She disobeyed orders,' he said, in his infuriating calm, rational sort of way. 'Even if she had good reasons, she still disobeyed orders. Kimberly is a new agent. This is the life she chose, and the whole beginning of her career is going to be defined by doing what she's told. If she can't do that, maybe the FBI isn't the right organization for her.'

'She found a body. When you were training here, how many bodies did you find? Uh huh. That's what I thought. She has the right to be a little rattled.'

'Rainie, look at these crime scene photos. You tell me. Who does this girl look like?'

Rainie grudgingly turned her gaze to the photos, currently spread out on the foot of the bed. 'Mandy,' she said without hesitation.

Quincy nodded somberly. 'Of course she looks like Mandy. It's the first thing I noticed and the first thing you noticed. Yet Kimberly hasn't mentioned anything about it.'

'If she so much as whispers that the victim reminds her of her dead sister, they'll cart her out of here in a straightjacket for sure.'

'And yet the victim must remind her of her sister. Isn't that the whole point?'

Rainie scowled. He was leading her down some psycho-babble trail. She could nearly feel the trap closing in. 'You're working the case,' she countered.

'I've worked over three hundred homicides. I've had a bit more time to develop objectivity about these things.'

'But you saw the resemblance.'

'I did.'

'Does it bother you, Quincy?'

'What? That a victim should look so much like Mandy, or that Mandy is still gone, and I never did a damn thing to help her?' His question was harsh. Rainie took that as an invitation to slide off the bed. He stiffened when she first touched his shoulders. She expected that. After all these years, they each still had their barriers and self-defenses. It didn't used to bother her so much. But lately it had been making her sad.

'You hurt for her,' she whispered.

'For Kimberly? Of course I do. She's picked a hard path. It's just sometimes . . .' He blew out a breath.

'Go on.'

'Kimberly wants to be tough. She wants to be strong. I understand that. After everything that happened to her, a desire for some level of invincibility is natural. And yet . . . Does shooting a gun make you omnipotent, Rainie? Does pushing yourself to run six miles every day mean you'll never be a victim? Does engaging in every kind of physical combat imaginable mean you'll never lose?' He didn't wait for her answer; none was necessary. 'Kimberly seems to honestly believe that if she can become an FBI agent, no one will ever hurt her again. Oh God, Rainie, it is so damn hard to watch your child repeat your own mistake.'

Rainie slid her arms around his shoulder. She leaned her head against Quincy's chest. Then, because there were no words to comfort him, no way of denying the truth of what he said, she went to the one topic that was always safe. Work. Dead bodies. A good, intriguing homicide case.

'Do you think the Georgian hunk is right?' she asked.

'The Georgian hunk?'

'I'm only thinking of Kimberly. I'm very altruistic that way. So, you grabbed the case file first. What do you think of his allegation that the Georgian Eco-Killer is now hunting Virginian prey?'

'I don't know yet,' Quincy said reluctantly. His hand came up and rested on the back of her neck. After another moment, he stroked her hair. She closed her eyes, and thought for a moment that things might be all right.

'The Eco-Killer is an interesting case, remarkable almost more for what the investigators don't know about the killer, than for what they do. For example, seven homicides later, the investigators have recovered no murder weapon, identified no primary murder scene, and not recovered a single bit of trace evidence such as hair, fiber, blood, or semen. In fact, the killer seems to have spent only the barest amount of time with each of the victims, limiting the opportunity for evidence transfer. He simply strikes, kills and runs.'

'An efficiency freak.'

Quincy merely shrugged. 'Most killers are driven by blood lust. They don't just want to kill, they want to savor their victim's pain and suffering. In contrast, this is the coldest string of murders I've ever seen. The UNSUB has little apparent interest in violence and yet, he is extraordinarily deadly.'

'He's into gamesmanship,' Rainie said, thinking about the unidentified subject. 'For him the sport isn't the kill, but setting up the bodies, and establishing his riddles. Then he writes his notes, ensuring he'll receive credit for his crime.'

'He writes the notes,' Quincy agreed. 'Giving his game an environmental slant. Now do we believe this man really cares about the environment, or is this yet another aspect of this game? I don't know enough yet, but I'm fairly certain that even the notes are just another type of prop. The man is setting a stage. He is like the great Oz, hiding behind a curtain and pulling all the strings. But to what end? What does he really want – and what does he really get – out of doing all this? I don't have that answer yet.'

'So what are the similarities between the Georgia case and this one?' Rainie prodded.

'Cause of death,' Quincy said promptly. 'There aren't too many serial predators who kill using prescription tranquilizers. At least not male killers.'

'Women love poison,' Rainie said knowingly.

'Exactly. Your dear friend Watson, however, also raised some good points. First, the Georgian Eco-Killer always dumped the first victim near a major road, where his 'map' per se, could be easily found. Following that pattern, the victim could still be left on the Marine base, but should be near such roads as MCB-4 or MCB-3. A dirt jogging path isn't quite the same. Second, the stitched-up mouth bothers me. It shows an increased need for violence, post-mortem mutilation of the victim, let alone the very obvious symbol of the victim keeping her mouth shut.'

'Or the killer is engaging in a more dangerous game, as Special Agent McCormack theorizes.'

'True. The new location, however, bothers me as well. I've only just glanced at the Georgia profile, but one of the main assumptions is that the man is local. His knowledge of certain areas is too intimate to be an outsider. In fact, the very nature of his game is that of someone who lives in and loves his surroundings. That's not the kind of person who simply shifts to a whole new state.'

'Maybe he felt the police were getting too close.'

'It's possible. For his game to work in Virginia, however, he'd have to do his homework.'

'What about the phone calls?' Rainie switched gears. 'It seems more than coincidental that McCormack should start getting anonymous tips that the Eco-Killer would strike in Virginia right before the discovery of a new body. Seems to me, the caller might know something.'

'The anonymous tips are what make it interesting,' Quincy agreed. He sighed again, then rubbed his temple. 'Seems at the end of the day, we have six reasons why the cases shouldn't be related, and half a dozen reasons why they should. Now we need a tiebreaker.' He looked at her. 'You know what? We need to know the victim's ID. Right now, we have one body, which may or may not bear resemblance to another case. If, however, we had concrete evidence that *two girls* had been kidnapped . . .'

'Then it would definitely point to the Eco-Killer,' Rainie filled in.

'Then I would definitely pay more attention to the Georgia case.'

'Has Kaplan checked missing person reports?'

'He has someone going through old files. No new cases, however, have opened up in the last twenty-four hours. At least not for a young woman.'

'How sad,' Rainie murmured. 'To be kidnapped and murdered, and have no one even realize that you're gone yet.'

'Most colleges are on break,' Quincy said with a shrug. 'If our victim is a student, the lack of a regular schedule might make it take longer for anyone to notice that she's disappeared.'

'Maybe that's why there's no ID,' Rainie said after a moment. 'If we don't know who she is, we can't know for sure that she – or a companion – is missing. The Eco-Killer has bought himself some time.'

Quincy eyed her speculatively. 'But doesn't that work both ways?'

'He either is the Eco-Killer and doesn't want us to know it yet,' she said slowly.

'Or someone has done their homework,' Quincy concluded quietly. 'Someone has committed murder, and now is seeking to cover his tracks by sending us off on a wild goose chase.'

There had been a time, back in Rainie's small-town deputy days, when she would've dismissed such a theory as too wild and outlandish. But that was before the shooting that had permanently scarred her community. That was before six years ago, when she'd helped Quincy protect what was left of his family from a savage madman. She knew well by now, better than most, that many predators weren't just into the kill – they also honestly enjoyed the thrill of the hunt and the challenge of a well-played game.

'Where do you want to start?' she asked.

'We start where we always start. Close to home. Right here.' His arms finally went around her waist. He drew her up against his chest. 'Come on, Rainie,' he murmured in her ear. 'Tell me the truth. Haven't you always wanted to tear apart the FBI Academy?'

'You have no idea.'

And then, a moment later: 'I'm trying,' he whispered.

'I know,' she said, and closed her eyes against the fresh sting of tears.

16

Kimberly sat alone in her dorm room. Lucy had returned briefly, dumping one pile of books on the cluttered desk, before scooping up the next.

'Wow, you look worse than you did this morning,' she said by way of greeting.

'Been working on it all day,' Kimberly assured her.

'Finding a corpse must be hard on a girl.'

'So you heard.'

'Everyone's heard, my dear. It's the hottest topic around. This your first corpse?'

'You mean other than my mother and sister?'

Lucy stilled in front of the desk. The silence grew long. 'Well, I'm off to study group,' she said finally. She turned, her expression gentle. 'Want to come along, Kimberly? You know we don't mind.'

'No,' Kimberly said flatly.

And then Lucy was gone.

She should sleep. Supervisor Watson was right. Her nerves were frayed, the adrenaline rush gone and leaving her feeling

148

heavy and empty all at once. She wanted to tip over on the narrow bed. Slip into the blessed numbness of sleep.

She'd dream about Mandy. She'd dream about her mother. She wasn't sure which dream would hurt her worse.

She could find her father over at the Jefferson Dormitory. He would talk to her, he always did. But she knew already the look she'd see on his face. Slightly distracted, slightly puzzled. A man who had just started a terribly important assignment, and even as he listened to his daughter lament, the other half of his brain would be reshuffling crime scene photos, murder books, investigator logs. Her father loved her. But she and Mandy had come to understand early on that he mostly belonged to the dead.

She couldn't stand the empty room. She couldn't stand the sound of footsteps in the hall. People meeting friends, sharing laughs, swapping stories, having a good time. Only Kimberly sat alone, the island she'd worked so hard to become.

She left the room, too. She took her knife and disappeared down the hall.

Outside it was hot. The dark, oppressive heat greeted her like a wall. Ten p.m. and still this unbearably sticky out. Tomorrow would be punishing for sure.

She slogged forward, feeling blotches of dark gray sweat bloom across the front of her T-shirt, while more moisture began trailing down the small of her back. Her breath came out in shallow pants, her lungs laboring to find oxygen in air that was 90 percent water.

She could still hear fading laughter. She turned away from it and headed toward the welcoming dark of the firing ranges. No one came out here this time of night. Well, almost no one.

The thought came only briefly, and then she knew just how much trouble she was in.

'Been waitin' for you,' Special Agent Mac McCormack drawled softly, pushing away from the entrance to the ranges.

'You shouldn't have.'

'I don't like to disappoint a pretty girl.'

'Did you bring a shotgun? Well then, too bad.'

He merely grinned at her, his teeth a flash of white in the dark. 'I thought you'd spend more time with your father.'

'Can't. He's working the case and I'm not allowed.'

'Being family doesn't entitle you to some perks?'

'You mean like a sneak peek of homicide photos? I think not. My father is a professional. He takes his job seriously.'

'Now how many years of therapy has it taken you to say that in such a calm, clear voice?'

'More than most suspect,' she admitted grudgingly.

'Come on, sugar. Let's take a seat.' He headed out into the green field of the range without looking back. It amazed her how easy it was to follow him.

The grass was nice. Soft beneath her battered body. Cool against her bare, sweat-slicked legs. She lay back, with her knees pointed at the sky and her short, serrated hunting knife snug against the inside of her left leg. Mac lay down beside her. Close. His shoulder brushing hers. She found his proximity faintly shocking, but she didn't move away.

He'd showered since their meeting with Kaplan and Watson. He smelled like soap and some kind of spicy men's aftershave. She imagined that his hair was probably still damp. For that matter, his cheeks had appeared freshly shaven when he'd walked through the glow cast by the streetlight. Had he cleaned up for her? Would it matter if he did?

She liked the smell of his soap, she decided, and left it at that.

'Stars are out,' he said conversationally.

'They do that at night.'

'You noticed? Here I thought you driven new agent types were too busy for those kinds of things.'

'In personal combat training, we get to spend a lot of time on our backs. It helps.'

He reached over and brushed her cheek. The contact was so unexpected, she flinched.

'A blade of grass,' he said calmly. 'Stuck to your cheek. Don't worry, honey. I'm not gonna attack you. I know you're armed.'

'And if I wasn't?'

'Why then I'd roll you right here and now, of course. Being a testosterone-bound male who's prone to that kind of violent, brutish behavior.'

'I don't mean it that way.'

'You don't like touching much, do you? I mean, biting, flipping and beating the bejesus out of me aside.'

'I'm not ... used to it. My family was never very demonstrative.'

He seemed to consider that. 'If you don't mind me saying, your father seems wound a bit tight.'

'My father is wound way tight. And my mother came from an upper-class family. As you can imagine, holidays were a gay, frolicking time in our home. You wouldn't believe the boisterous outbreaks.'

'My family's loud,' he volunteered casually. 'Not big, but definitely demonstrative. My father still grabs my mother around the waist and tries to lure her into dark corners. As an adult, I appreciate their relationship. As a kid ... Hell, we were scared to death not to announce ourselves before walking down a darkened hall.'

Kimberly smiled faintly. 'You got an education?'

'Heavens yes. It's sweet though, I suppose. My father's a civil engineer who designs roads for the state. My mother teaches high school English. Who would've thought they'd be so happy?'

'Siblings?'

'One sister. Younger, of course. I terrorized her for most of our childhood. On the other hand, every time I fell asleep in the family room, she put makeup on my face and took pictures. So I guess it evens itself out. Plus, I'm the only man you'll ever meet who understands just how hard it is to remove waterproof mascara. And I guess I'll never run for political office. The photos alone would ruin me.'

'What does she do now?'

'Marybeth's a kindergarten teacher, so in other words, she's tougher than most cops. Has gotta be to keep all those little critters in line. Maybe when they fall asleep, she puts makeup on their faces, too. I'm too scared to ask.'

'So you're the only police officer in your family.'

'I have a cuz who's a fireman. That's pretty close.'

She smiled again. 'They sound like fun.'

'They are,' he agreed, and she heard the genuine affection in his voice. 'I mean, they could still use some good training and all. But as families go, they're keepers. Do you miss your mother and sister?' he asked abruptly.

'Yes.'

'Should I shut up?'

'Would you obey me if I said yes?'

'No. I suppose I need some training, too. Besides, the stars are out. You should always talk when you're lying beneath the stars.'

'I hadn't heard that before,' Kimberly said, but she turned her face up toward the night sky, feeling the hot air against her face, and it did make it easier. 'My family wasn't happy. Not in the typical way. But we tried. I give us credit for that. We wanted to be happy, so we tried. I guess you could say we were earnest.'

'Your parents divorced?'

'Eventually. When we were teens. But the problems were way before that. The usual cop stuff. My father had a demanding job, worked long hours. And my mom...She'd been raised expecting something different. She would've done well with a banker, I think. Or even a doctor, the hours would've been just as bad, but at least her husband would've held a title with a certain level of decorum. My father, on the other hand, was an FBI profiler. He dealt in death, violent death, extreme violent death each and every day. I don't think she ever got used to that. I don't think she ever stopped finding it distasteful.'

'It's a good job,' Mac said quietly.

She turned toward him, finding herself surprisingly serious. 'I think so. I was always proud of him. Even when he had to leave in the middle of birthday parties or missed them altogether. His job sounded so larger-than-life to me. Like something a superhero would do. People got hurt. And my father went to save the day. I missed him, I'm sure I had tantrums, but mostly I remember feeling proud. My daddy was cool. For my sister, however, it was another story.'

'Older or younger?'

'Mandy was older. She was also . . . different. High strung. Sensitive. A little wild. I think my first memory of her is her being yelled at for breaking something. She struggled with our parents. I mean, really, truly struggled. They were so by-the-book and she was so color-outside-the-lines. And life was harder for her in other ways. She took things to heart too much. One harsh word and she was wounded for days. One wrong look and she'd be devastated. She had nightmares, was prone to crying jags and had genuine fits. My father's job terrified her. My parents' divorce shattered her. And adulthood didn't get much easier.'

'She sounds intense.'

'She was.' For a moment, Kimberly was silent. 'You know what gets to me, though? You know what's truly ironic?'

'What?'

'She needed us. She was exactly the kind of person that my father and I have sworn our lives to protect. She wasn't tough.

She made bad choices. She drank too much, she dated the wrong men, she believed anyone's pack of lies. God, she desperately needed someone to save her from herself. And we didn't do it. I spent so much of my childhood resenting her. Crying, complaining Mandy who was always upset about something. Now, I just wonder why we didn't take better care of her. She was in our own family. How could we fail her so completely?'

Mac didn't say anything. He touched her cheek again. Gently. With his thumb. She felt the slow rasp of his work-roughened skin all the way down to her jaw line. It made her shiver. Then it made her want to close her eyes, and arch her neck like a cat.

'Another blade of grass?' she whispered.

'No,' he said softly.

She turned toward him then, knowing her eyes said too much, knowing she needed more armor, but helpless to find it now.

'They don't believe you,' she said softly.

'I know.' His fingers traced along her jaw, lingered at the curve of her ear.

'My father's good. Very good. But like all investigators, he's meticulous. He's going to start at the very beginning and have to work his way toward your conclusion. Maybe on another case it wouldn't matter. But if you're right, and there's another girl already out there . . .'

'Clock's ticking,' Mac murmured. The rough pads of his fingers returned along her jaw, then feathered down her neck. She could feel her chest rising and falling faster. As if she were running once more through the woods. Was she running toward something this time, or was she still running away?

'You're very relaxed about all this,' she said brusquely.

'The case? Not really.' His fingers stopped moving. They rested at the base of her neck, his fingers bracing her collarbone and her skittering pulse. He was gazing at her with an intense look. A man about to kiss a woman? A cop obsessed with a difficult case? She was no good at this sort of thing. The Quincy women had a long history of being unlucky at love. In fact, the last man her mother and Mandy thought they had loved had killed them both. That was female intuition for you.

She wished suddenly that she didn't think of her family so much. She wished suddenly that she really were an island, that she could be born again without any attachments, without any past. What would her life have become if her family hadn't been murdered? Who would've Kimberly Quincy been then?

Kinder, softer, gentler? The kind of woman capable of kissing a handsome man under the stars? Maybe a woman actually capable of falling in love?

She turned her head away. Pulled her body away from his touch. It didn't matter anymore. She suddenly hurt too much to look him in the eye.

'You're going to work this, aren't you?' she asked, giving him her back.

'I did a little reading on Virginia this afternoon,' he said conversationally, as if she hadn't just jerked away. 'Did you know this state has over forty thousand square acres of beaches, mountains, rivers, lakes, bays, swamps, reservoirs, and caverns? We're talking several major mountain ranges offering over a thousand miles of hiking trails. Two million acres of public land. Then we have the Chesapeake Bay, which is the largest coastal estuary in the United States. Plus, four thousand caverns and several reservoirs that have been formed by flooding complete towns. You want rare and ecologically sensitive? Virginia has rare and ecologically sensitive. You want dangerous? Virginia has dangerous. In short, Virginia is perfect for Eco-Killer, and hell yes, I'm definitely gonna pursue a few things.'

'You don't have jurisdiction.'

'All's fair in love and war. I called my supervisor. We both believe this is the first solid lead we've had in months. If I take off from the National Academy to do a little sidebar exploration, he's not gonna cry any rivers. Besides, your father and NCIS are moving too slow. By the time they realize what we already know, the second girl will be long dead. I don't want that, Kimberly. After all these years, I'm tired of being too late.'

'What will you do?'

'First thing tomorrow morning, I'm meeting with a botanist from the US Geological Survey team. Then I'll take it from there.'

'Why are you meeting a botanist? You don't have the leaf anymore.'

'I don't have the original,' he said quietly. 'But I might have scanned a copy.'

She turned sharply. 'You copied evidence.'

'Yep.'

'What else?'

'Gonna run to Daddy?'

'You know me better than that!'

'I'm trying to.'

'You really are obsessed with this, you know. You could be wrong. This case could have no bearing on the Eco-Killer or those girls in Georgia. You missed your man the first time. Now you see what you want to see.'

'It's possible.' He shrugged. 'Does it matter? A girl is dead. A man did it. Whether he's my guy or someone else's guy, finding the son of a bitch will make the world a better place. Frankly, that's good enough for me.'

Kimberly scowled. It was hard to argue with that kind of logic. She said abruptly, 'I want to go with you.'

'Watson will have your hide.' Mac sat up, brushing the grass from his hands and already shaking his head. 'He'll kick you out so far so fast it'll be days before you feel the bruise on your butt.'

'I can take personal leave. I'll talk to one of the counselors. Plead emotional distress from finding a dead body.'

'Ah honey, you tell them you got emotional distress from finding a corpse, and they'll kick you out for sure. This is the FBI Academy. You can't handle a corpse, you're in the wrong line of work.'

'It's not his call. The counselor says yes, I get to go, simple as that.'

'And once he learns what you're really doing?'

'I'm on leave. What I do in my personal time is my business. Watson has no authority over me.'

'You haven't been in the FBI very long, have you, Kimberly?' Mac asked dryly.

Kimberly's chin came up. She understood his point. She agreed with his point, which was why her heart was pounding so hard in her chest. Pursuing this case would earn her her first political enemy. Let alone a less-than-stellar start to her career. She'd waited twenty-six years to become an FBI agent. Funny, how easy it seemed to throw it all away now.

'Kimberly,' Mac said abruptly as if reading her thoughts, 'you know that this won't bring your mother or sister back, don't you? That no matter how many murderers you hunt down, none of it changes the fact that your family is still dead, and you still didn't save them in time?'

'I've been to their graves, Mac. I know how dead they are.'

'And you're just a rookie,' he continued relentlessly. 'You know nothing about this guy, you're not even fully trained. Your efforts probably won't make one iota of difference. Think about that before you throw away your career.'

'I want to go.'

'Why?'

She finally smiled at him, though she knew the look must

appear strained on her face. There was the million-dollar question. And honestly, there were so many answers she could give. That Watson had been right this morning, and nine weeks later she had no friendships or allegiances among her own classmates. In fact the closest she'd come to feeling any loyalty was for a dead body she'd found in the woods.

Or that she did feel survivor's guilt, and she was tired of holidays spent in fields of white crosses. Or that she had a morbid need to chase after death, having once felt its fingers brush across the nape of her neck. Or that she was her father's daughter after all. No good with the living, desperately attached to the dead, particularly when the body bore such a startling resemblance to Mandy.

So many possible answers. She surprised herself then, by going with the one that was closest to the truth. 'Because I want to.'

Mac stared at her a heartbeat longer, then suddenly, finally, nodded in the dark. 'All right. Six a.m. Meet me in the front of Jefferson. Bring hiking gear.'

'And Kimberly,' he added, as they both rose and dusted off the grass. 'Don't forget your Glock.'

17

Nora Ray's mother was still watching TV. She slumped on their old brown sofa, wearing the same faded pink bathrobe she'd worn for the past three years. Her short dark hair stood up around her face, gray showing at the roots, where it would remain until Nora Ray's grandmother visited again and forcefully took her daughter in hand. Otherwise, Abigail Watts rarely moved from the sofa. She sat perfectly hunched, mouth slightly agape, eyes fixed straight ahead. Some people turned to booze, Nora Ray thought. Her mother had Nick@Nite.

Nora Ray still remembered the days when her mother had been beautiful. Abigail had risen at six every morning, fixing her hair in hot rollers and doing her makeup while her hair set. By the time Nora Ray and Mary Lynn made it downstairs for breakfast, their mother would be bustling around the kitchen in a nice floral dress, pouring coffee for their father, setting out cereal for them, and prattling away cheerfully until seven-oh-five on the dot, at which point she would grab her purse and head to work. She had been a secretary at a law firm back then. Not great money, but she'd enjoyed the job and the two partners who ran the place. Plus, it gave her an aura of prestige in the tiny blue-collar neighborhood where they lived. Working at a law firm . . . Now that was respectable work.

Nora Ray's mother hadn't been to the office now in years. Nora Ray didn't even know if she'd ever officially quit. More like she'd walked out one day after getting a call from the police, and she'd never been back since.

The lawyers had been nice about it. They'd volunteered their services for a trial that never happened in a case where the perpetrator was never caught. They kept Abigail on the payroll for a while. Then they put her on a leave of absence. And now? Nora Ray couldn't believe her mom still had a job after three years. No one was that nice. No one's life stayed frozen for that long a period of time.

Except, of course, for Nora Ray's family. They lived in a time warp. Mary Lynn's room, painted sunshine yellow and lined with blue ribbons and horse trophies, remained exactly the same day after day. The last pair of dirty jeans she'd tossed in the corner were still waiting for an eighteen-year-old girl to come home and throw them in the wash. Her hairbrush, filled with long strands of brunette hair, sat on top of her dresser. A tube of pink lip gloss was half-opened next to the brush. Ditto the tube of mascara.

And still taped to the mirror above the dresser was the letter from Albany State University. *We are proud to inform you that Mary Lynn Watts has been formally accepted into the freshman class of 2000 . . .*

Mary Lynn had wanted to study veterinary sciences. Someday she could work full-time saving the horses she loved so much. Nora Ray was going to become a lawyer. Then they would buy farms side-by-side in the country where they could ride horses together every morning, before reporting to their high-paying and no doubt highly rewarding jobs. That's what they had talked about that summer. Giggled about, really.

Especially that last night, when it had been so friggin' hot, they had decided to head out for ice cream.

In the beginning, right after Nora Ray came home and Mary Lynn didn't, things had been different. People stopped by, for one thing. The women brought casseroles and cookies and pies. The men showed up with lawnmowers and hammers, wordlessly attending to small details around the house. Their little home had hummed with activity, everyone trying to be solicitous, everyone wanting to make sure that Nora Ray and her family were all right.

Her mother had still showered and put on clothes in those days. Bereft of a daughter, she at least clung to the skeletal fabric of everyday life. She got up, put her hair in rollers, and started the pot of coffee.

Her father had been the worst back then. Roaming from room to room while constantly flexing his big, work-calloused hands, a dazed look in his eyes. He was the man who was supposed to be able to fix anything. He'd built their deck one summer. He did odd jobs around the neighborhood to help pay for Mary Lynn's horse camp. He painted their house like clockwork every three years and kept it the neatest one on the block.

Big Joe could do anything. Everyone said that. Until that day in July.

Eventually people stopped coming by so much. Food no longer magically appeared in the kitchen. Their lawn was no longer mowed every Sunday. Nora Ray's mom stopped getting dressed. And her father returned to his job at Home Depot, coming home every night to join her mother on the couch, where they would sit like zombies in front of a score of mindless comedies, the TV spraying their faces with brightly colored images deep into the night.

While weeds took over their lawn. And their front porch sagged with neglect. And Nora Ray learned how to cook her mother's casseroles while her own dreams of law school drifted further and further away.

People in the neighborhood whispered about them now. *That sad family in the sad little house on the corner. Did you hear what happened to their daughter? Well, let me tell you . . .*

Sometimes Nora Ray thought she should walk around with a scarlet letter attached to her clothes, like the woman in that book she'd read her senior year of high school. Yes, we're the family that lost a daughter. Yes, we're the ones who actually fell victim to violent crime. Yes, it could happen to you, too, so you're right, you should turn away when we walk too close and whisper behind our backs. Maybe murder is contagious, you know. It's found our house. Soon, it'll find yours.

She never said these things out loud, however. She couldn't. She was the last functioning member of her family. She had to hold it together. She had to pretend that one daughter could be enough.

Her mother's head was starting to bob now, in that way it did right before sleep. Her father had already called it a night. He had work in the morning and that made him somewhat more normal, in this strange little pattern they called their lives.

Abigail finally succumbed. Her head fell back. Her shoulders sank into the deep comfort of their overstuffed sofa, bought during happier times and meant for happier days.

And Nora Ray finally stepped into the room. She didn't turn off the TV. She knew better by now; the sudden absence of TV voices awakened her mother faster than any shrieking alarm. Instead, she merely took the remote from the pocket of her mother's faded bathrobe and slowly turned down the volume.

Her mother started to snore. Soft little wheezes of a woman who hadn't moved in months, yet remained exhausted beyond her years.

Nora Ray clenched her hands by her side. She wanted to stroke her mother's face. She wanted to tell her everything would be all right. She wanted to plead for her real mother to come back to her because sometimes she didn't want to be the strong one. Sometimes, she wanted to be the one who curled up and cried.

She set the remote on the coffee table. Then she tiptoed back to her room, where the air conditioning was permanently cranked to a frosty fifty-eight and a full pitcher of water sat by her bed at all times.

Nora Ray buried herself under the thick comfort of her bedcovers, but she still didn't fall immediately asleep.

She was thinking of Mary Lynn again. She was thinking of their last night, driving back from T.G.I. Friday's, and Mary Lynn chatting away merrily in the driver's seat.

'Uh oh,' her sister was saying. 'I think we just got a flat. Oh wait. Good news. Some guy's pulled in behind us. Isn't that neat, Nora Ray? The world is just filled with good people.'

The man was tired. Very, very tired. Shortly after two A.M. he completed his last chore and wearily called it a night. He returned the van to where it belonged, and though his muscles truly ached now, he took the time to wash the vehicle, inside and out, by the comforting glow of lantern light. He even crawled under the van and hosed down the undercarriage. Dirt could tell stories. Didn't he know.

Next he pulled out the dog carrier. He sponged it down with ammonia, the sharp, pungent scent stinging his senses back into hyper alertness, while also destroying any evidence of fingerprints.

Finally, he took inventory. He should wash down the aquarium, too, though what could it prove? That he once had a pet snake? No crime in that. Still, you didn't want to leave things to chance.

You didn't want to be one of those dumb fucks his father talked about, who couldn't find their assholes with a flashlight and their own two hands.

The world was spinning. He felt the gathering storm clouds in the back of his brain. When he got tired, the spells grew worse. The black holes grew to tremendous size, swallowing not just hours and minutes, but sometimes consuming entire days. He couldn't afford that now. He had to be sharp. He had to be alert.

He thought of his mother again and the sad look she wore every time she watched the sun die in the sky. Did she know the planet was dying? Did she understand even back then that anything that was beautiful could not belong long on this earth?

Or was she simply afraid to go back inside, where his father would be waiting with his quick temper and hamlike fists?

The man did not like these thoughts. He didn't want to play this game anymore. He jerked the aquarium from the inside of the van. He dumped its grass and twig matting into the woods. Then he dumped in half of a bottle of ammonia and went to work with his bare hands. He could feel the harsh chemical burn his skin.

Later the runoff from this little exercise would seep into a stream, and kill off algae, bacteria, and cute little fishes. Because he was no better, you know. No matter what he did, he was still a man who drove a car and bought a refrigerator and probably once kissed a girl who used a can of aerosol spray on her hair. Because that's what men did. Men killed. Men destroyed. Men beat their wives, abused their kids, and took a planet and warped it into their own twisted image.

His eyes were running now. Snot poured from his nose and his chest heaved until his breath came out in savage gasps. The harsh scent of ammonia, he thought. But he knew better. He was once again thinking of his mother's pale, lonely face.

He and his brother should have gone back inside with her. They could've walked through the door first, judged the mood, and if it came to it, taken their punishment like M-E-N. They didn't though. Their father came home, and they ran away into the woods, where they lived like gods on pokeweed salad, wild raspberries, and tender fiddleheads.

They turned to the land for shelter, and tried not to think about what was happening back in one tiny cabin in the woods. At least that's what they'd done when they could.

The man turned off the hose. The van was washed, the aquarium cleansed, the whole project sanitized within an inch of its life. Forty-eight hours later, it was over.

He was tired again. Bone-deep weary in a way that people who had never killed could never appreciate. But it was over. Now, at long last, he was done.

He took his kill kit away with him. Later, he tucked it beneath his mattress before finally crawling into bed.

His head touched the pillow. He thought of what he had just done. High heels, blond hair, blue eyes, green dress, bound hands, dark hair, brown eyes, long legs, scratching nails, flashing white teeth.

The man closed his eyes. He slept the best he had in years.

18

Quincy jerked awake to the sound of the phone ringing. Instinct bred of so many other calls in the middle of so many other nights led him to reach automatically toward the nightstand. Then the ringing penetrated a second time, shrill and insistent, and he remembered that he was at the FBI Academy, staying in a dorm room, where the lone phone sat on the desk halfway across the room.

He moved quiet and quick, but it was no longer necessary. Even as he cut off the third ring, Rainie was sitting up sleepily in the bed. Her long chestnut hair was tousled around her pale face, drawing attention to the striking angles of her cheeks and the long, bare column of her neck. God she was lovely first thing in the morning. For that matter, she was lovely at the end of a long day. All these years later, day in, day out, she never failed to take his breath away.

He looked at her, and then, as happened too often these days, he felt a sharp pain in his chest. He turned away, cradling the phone between his shoulder and his ear.

'Pierce Quincy.'

And then a moment later. 'Are you sure? That's not what I meant – Kimberly . . . Well, if that's what you want to do. Kimberly . . .' Big sigh again. The beginning of a headache already building in his temples. 'You're a grown adult, Kimberly. I respect that.'

It didn't do him any good. His last surviving daughter had ended yesterday angry with him and had apparently started today even madder. She slammed down the phone. He returned his own receiver much more gently, trying not to notice how his hands shook. He had been trying to mend the bridge with his mercurial daughter for six years now. He hadn't made much progress yet.

In the beginning, Quincy had thought Kimberly simply needed time. After the intense episode of what happened to their family, of course she harbored a great deal of rage. He had been an FBI agent, a trained professional, and still he'd done nothing to save Bethie and Amanda. If Kimberly hated him, he couldn't blame her. For a long time, he had hated himself, too.

Now, however, as year advanced into year, and the raw ache of loss and failure began to subside, he wondered if it wasn't something more insidious than that. He and his daughter had gone through a harrowing experience. They had joined forces to outwit a psychopath as he'd hunted them down one by one. That kind of experience changed people. Changed relationships.

And it built associations. Perhaps Kimberly simply couldn't view him as a father anymore. A parent should be a safe harbor, a source of shelter amid turbulent times. Quincy was none of those things in his daughter's eyes. In fact, his presence was probably a constant reminder that violence often struck close to home. That real monsters didn't live under the bed. They could be very attractive, fully functioning members of society, and once they targeted you, not even a smart, strong, professionally trained father could make any difference.

It still amazed Quincy how easy it was to fail the ones you loved.

'Was that Kimberly?' Rainie asked from behind him. 'What did she want?'

'She's leaving the Academy this morning. She talked one of the counselors into giving her a leave of absence for emotional distress.'

'Kimberly?' Rainie's voice was incredulous. 'Kimberly who would walk barefoot through fire before asking for a pair of shoes, let alone a fire extinguisher? No way.'

Quincy merely waited. It didn't take long. Rainie had always been exceptionally bright. She got it in the next instant.

'She's going to work the case!' she exclaimed suddenly. In contrast to his reaction, however, she threw back her head and laughed. 'Well what do you know. I told you the Georgian was a hunk!'

'If Supervisor Watson finds out,' Quincy said seriously, 'her career will be over.'

'If Watson finds out, he'll simply be mad he didn't get to save the second girl first.' Rainie bounded out of bed. 'Well, what do you want to do?'

'Work,' Quincy said flatly. 'I want the ID on the victim.'

'Yes, sir!'

'And maybe,' he mused carefully, 'it wouldn't hurt to pay a visit to the forensic linguist, Dr Ennunzio.'

Rainie regarded him in surprise. 'Why Pierce Quincy, are you beginning to believe in the Eco-Killer?'

'I don't know. But I definitely think that my daughter is much too involved. So let's work, Rainie. And let's work fast.'

Kimberly and Mac drove toward Richmond mostly in silence. She learned that his taste in radio stations ran toward country music. In turn, she taught him that she didn't function well without a morning cup of coffee.

They had taken his car; the rented Toyota Camry was nicer than her ancient Mazda. Mac had thrown a backpack filled with supplies into the trunk. Kimberly had added hiking boots and a duffel bag filled with her sparse collection of clothes.

She'd retrieved her gun first thing this morning, turning in the plastic Crayola along with her handcuffs. She signed a few forms, relinquished her ID, and that was that. She was officially on leave from the FBI Academy. For the first time since she was about nine years old, she was not actively aspiring to be a federal agent.

She should feel anxious, guilt-stricken, and horrified, she thought. So many years of her life she was suddenly throwing away on a whim. As if she ever did anything on a whim. As if her life had ever held a hint of the whimsical.

And yet, she didn't feel horrible. No shortness of breath that would indicate an oncoming anxiety attack. No bunched muscles or pounding headache. In all honesty, she actually felt the lightest she had in weeks. Maybe, beneath her sleep-deprived haze, she was even a little giddy.

What that meant, she didn't want to know.

They made good time getting to Richmond. Mac handed her a printed-out e-mail, and she navigated to the offices of the US Geological Survey team, which were located in an office park north of the city. First glance wasn't what Kimberly had expected. The office park, for one thing, was plunked down in the middle of suburban sprawl. They passed a community college, a housing development, and a local school. There were lovely sidewalks shaded by graceful trees, wide expanses of deep green yards, and brightly flowering pink and white crepe myrtle trees.

The USGS office building, too, was different than what she had pictured. One story of brick and glass. Newer. Lots of windows. Nicely landscaped with more crepe myrtle trees and God knows what kind of bushes. Definitely a far cry from the usual government décor of monochromatic malaise.

So a nice building in a nice place. Kimberly wondered if Mac knew that the FBI Richmond field office was literally right down the street.

She and Mac got out of the car, pushed their way through the heavy glass door and were immediately greeted by the waiting receptionist.

'Ray Lee Chee,' Mac said. The receptionist smiled at them brightly, then led the way.

'He's a botanist?' Kimberly asked as she followed Mac down the wide, sunny hall.

'Geographer, actually.'

'What's a geographer?'

'I think he works on maps.'

'You're bringing our leaf to a mapmaker?'

'Genny knows him. He went to school with her brother or something like that. Apparently he has a background in botany and he said he could help.' Mac shrugged. 'I have no jurisdiction; it's not like I can order up any expert I want in the state.'

The receptionist had arrived at an interior office. She gestured to the partially opened door, then turned back down the hall, leaving Kimberly alone with Mac, already wondering if this wasn't some kind of fool's errand.

'Mr Chee?' Mac asked, poking his head through the doorway. A short, well-built Asian man promptly fired back his desk chair and popped up to greet them.

'Oh God, don't call me that. Ray, by all means, or I'll keep looking around for my father.'

Ray pumped Mac's hand vigorously, then greeted Kimberly with the same enthusiasm. The geographer was younger than Kimberly would've thought, and definitely not a dried-out academic. He sported khaki shorts and a short-sleeved shirt made out of one of those micro-fibers favored by hikers for wicking the sweat from their bodies.

Now, he gestured them into his paper-jammed office, then bounced back into his chair with about four times the necessary energy. His biceps bulged even when sitting and his hands were moving a mile a minute around his desk, looking for God knows what.

'So Genny said you needed my help,' Ray stated brightly.

'We're trying to identify a leaf. I understand you have some experience in that sort of thing.'

'Spent my undergrad days studying botany,' Ray said, 'before I moved into geography. For that matter, I also studied zoology and for a brief stint in time, auto mechanics. Seemed kind of funky at the time. On the other hand, when our truck gets stuck out in the field, everyone's happy to have me along.' He turned toward Kimberly. 'Do you talk?'

'Not before coffee.'

'You need some java? I brewed the world's strongest batch in the kitchenette just half an hour ago. Stuff will knock the ZZZs right out of you, while putting some hair on your chest.' He held up both of his hands, which were trembling with caffeine jitters. 'Want some?'

'Mmmm, I think I'll wait.'

'Well, suit yourself, but after the first sixteen ounces or so, I'm telling you it's not so bad.' His dark gaze rebounded to Mac. 'So where's the leaf?'

'Well, actually, we brought you a picture.' Mac dug into his folder and pulled out the piece of paper.

'That's all you got? A *picture*?'

'It's a scanned image. Actual size. Front and back.' Ray kept staring at him and finally Mac shrugged ruefully. 'Sorry, man. It's all we got.'

'A real leaf would be better, you know. I mean, *much* better. What's this for again?'

'It's a piece of evidence in a case.'

'Like from a crime scene?' Ray's face brightened. 'If I ID

this, can it be used to catch the bad guy or locate a corpse? Like they do on *CSI*?'

'Absolutely,' Mac assured him.

'Groovy.' Ray accepted the paper with more enthusiasm. 'A picture is definitely tougher, but I like a challenge. Let's see what you got.'

He took out a magnifying glass and studied the image for a second. 'Well, let's start with the basics. It's an angiosperm – to you, a broadleaf tree. Given the oval shape with pointed tip and coarse-tooth margins, it's most likely from the *Betula* family – some kind of birch.' He looked up. 'Where did you find this again?'

'I'm afraid I can't comment further on that subject.'

Ray resumed staring at the picture. He frowned. 'This is really all you've got? No bark, no flowers, no twig?'

'That's it.'

'Well, then you also like a challenge.' Ray's desk chair shot back. He jerked to a stop in front of the bookshelf across the way and rapidly skimmed titles. His fingers settled on a big volume labeled *Gray's Manual of Botany*. 'In the good news, bad news department, birch is one of the larger tree families with a number of species commonly found here in Virginia. If you're into history, the old Appalachian mountaineers used to make birch beer from the sap of black birch trees, which tastes a bit like wintergreen. They came close to harvesting all of the black birches in the mountains to make the stuff, then synthetic wintergreen oil was developed, and the mountaineers moved on to making moonshine. All's well that ends well, you know.'

He shot back to his desk, propelling his chair as easily as a small automobile, while his fingers rapidly flipped through the thick index guide. Peering over his shoulder, Kimberly saw page after page of tree leaves, all richly photographed and documented with lists of words that appeared to be in Latin. Definitely not a light summer read.

'Okay, for starters we have *Betula lenta*, otherwise known as black birch, sweet birch, or cherry birch. Its leaves are approximately three to four inches long. Your picture is closer to two and a half inches long, but maybe our leaf isn't mature yet, so that's a possibility.'

'Where are black birches found?' Mac asked.

'Oh, a little bit of everywhere. You can find it in the mountains of the western half of the state, or around parts of Chesapeake Bay close to streams. Does that work?'

'I don't know yet,' Mac said. Now, he was also frowning. 'Other options?'

'The *Betula alleghaniensis*, or yellow birch, which is found generally higher up in the mountains than the black birch. It's a significantly larger tree, however, growing up to eighty feet with five-inch leaves, so I'm going to guess that it's too big to be our suspect here. Let's see . . .' Ray rapidly flipped through the book.

'Okay, consider *Betula papyrifera*, or paper birch. Leaves also grow three inches in length, which is closer in size. It's also found in the mountains, generally in clear-cut or burned-out areas. Then there's Betula nigra, or river birch, which is found in low elevations along waterways or around streams, ponds, lakes, etc. It's also a smaller birch with leaves two to three inches long. So that's a possibility.' He looked up at them sharply. 'You don't have any catkins?'

'Cat what?'

'The flowers that are generally found with the leaves. In birches, they resemble long, cone-like structures, dangling down from amid the leaves. Flower size varies dramatically, which would help narrow the scope. Better yet, would be a twig with bark. As you can guess from the names, black versus yellow versus paper, one of the key distinguishing features of birch is the color of the tree's bark.'

'I only have a leaf,' Mac said, then muttered under his

breath, 'Because our guy also likes a challenge.' He turned toward Kimberly, the tension building in his shoulders.

'He wouldn't do something common,' she said quietly. 'No compass, remember? So this time, the clues must narrow down a region. Or it's really not that much of a game.'

'Good point.' Mac turned back toward the geographer. 'You said birches are commonly found in Virginia. Are there any that *aren't* common? Maybe a type that is rare or endangered?'

Ray's dark eyes brightened. He stroked his chin. 'Not a bad question . . . Nope, this isn't going to help.' He flipped the book shut, seemed to think for a second, then turned abruptly to his computer and swiftly hit a bunch of keys. 'See, what you guys really need is a dendrologist. I'm just a lowly geographer who's spent some time dabbling with botany. A dendrologist, on the other hand . . .'

'Has a bigger name?' Kimberly asked.

'No, is a botanical expert on trees. See, I'm a generalist. Come on, ask me about a flower. I'm really good with flowers. Or ferns, for that matter. A dendrologist, on the other hand, could tell you anything you ever wanted to know about trees.'

'My God, there is an ologist for everything,' Kimberly muttered.

'You have no idea,' Mac said.

'See, you guys have come to the Richmond field office. Here, we're mostly geographers and hydrologists. Most of us have other backgrounds as well – botany, biology, geology, etc., and we're happy to help you out, but maybe we're not as specific as you need. Now, up in Reston at our national headquarters, we got botanists, palynologists, geologists, karsts geologists, you name it. That's where the big dawgs live.'

'Where is Reston?' Mac asked.

'Two hours north of here.'

'I don't have two hours.'

'Suit yourself.' Ray's fingers danced over his keyboard. 'Then for the time-conscious researcher, we have the greatest marvel of the twentieth century. Ta dah! The Internet, where for every ology, there is almost always a website. Let's face it. Geeks love technology.' He hit return, and sure enough, a website of the US Department of Agriculture site labeled Dendrology of Virginia appeared on the screen.

'As I live and breathe,' Kimberly said.

'And how,' Mac seconded.

'And we have a final suspect for your consideration,' Ray announced. 'Lady and gentleman, may I introduce *Betula populifolia*, otherwise known as gray birch. This smaller member of the birch family grows only thirty feet high, with leaves of approximately three inches in length. The bark may appear brown in color, but is in fact gray-white. It is also smooth, and not peeling, unlike the yellow birch and paper birch members of the family, which frankly, always look like they're sporting a bad case of bed head. The wood is light and soft, used mostly for pulpwood spools and fuel. Better yet, it is located in only one area of the state. Huh, well here's the kicker. It doesn't say where that is.'

Ray stopped, scrunching up his nose and wiggling it from side to side as he continued to study the screen. Mac hunkered down behind the botanist, his face taking on the intent expression Kimberly was coming to know so well.

'Are you saying this birch could be the one in our picture?'

'Could be.'

'And it's found in only one spot in the entire state of Virginia?'

'That's what the dendrologists say.'

'I need to know that spot.' Mac paused a heartbeat. '*Now.*'

'Mmm hmmm, mmm hmmm, mmm hmmm. Well, here's a thought.' Ray tapped the computer screen with his pencil. 'Look at the other ranges of distribution. The gray birch is common in New York, Pennsylvania, and New Jersey. All states north of us. Which means, this tree probably prefers cooler temperatures. So if it's growing somewhere in Virginia . . .'

'The mountains,' Kimberly filled in.

He nodded. 'Yeah. Now the question is, which range? Are we talking the Blue Ridge Mountains, the Shenandoah Mountains, the Appalachians? Hang on, I have an idea.' His chair shot across the room again. He found a directory on top of his bookcase, flipped through several pages, grabbed a phone and made a call. 'Kathy Levine, please. She's out? When do you expect her back? I'll leave a message.' And in another moment, 'Kath, hey it's Ray Lee Chee from USGS. Got a question about gray birch. Where is it in the state? It's actually important, very Sherlock Holmes. When you get in, give me a buzz. We'll be waiting. Bye.'

He hung up the phone, then met their expectant gazes. 'Kathy's the botanist with Shenandoah National Park. She's more familiar with the trees in that area and if anyone knows about the gray birch, it's her. Unfortunately, she's out in the field right now.'

'For how long?' Mac demanded to know.

'Four days.'

'We don't have four days!'

Ray held up a hand. 'Yeah, yeah, yeah. Kind of got that. Give her until around noon. Come lunch, she'll check messages, give me a call, and then I can give you a call. Noon's only four hours away.'

'Four hours can be a long time,' Mac said grimly.

'What can I say? It's not easy when you only have a picture of a leaf.'

'I have a question,' Kimberly spoke up. 'From all of your various studies . . . Is there any connection between Virginia and Hawaii?'

'Virginia and Hawaii?'

'Yes.'

'Huh. Hell if I know. From a plant perspective, I can't think of a thing. Hawaii's kind of tropical, you know. And Virginia isn't. Well, except for this week, of course. We're always prepared to make an exception.'

'No other way they might be related?' Kimberly prodded.

Ray did the nose wiggle again. 'You might ask a geologist. We have mountains, they have mountains. We have Chesapeake Bay with its multitude of barrier islands, which might be similar to their barrier islands. But from a flora and fauna perspective, I don't see a relationship.'

'And where in this building might we find a geologist?'

'We don't have geologists, you'd have to go to Reston. Wait!' He read her expression and immediately held up a hand. 'I know, I know you don't have time for Reston. Okay . . . Jennifer York. She's one of our core samplers, and I believe she has a background in geology.'

'Where's her office?'

'Other side of the building, third office on the left.'

'Okay.' She turned toward Mac, who was looking at her with a puzzled expression. 'You heard the man,' she said crisply, 'let's go find a geologist.'

19

'Why are we asking about Hawaii?' Mac asked thirty seconds later when they were back in the halls of the USGS building.

'Because the ME's assistant said the victim had a travel brochure for Hawaii in her purse.'

He grabbed her arm and they both came to a sudden halt. Mac looked cool. She was already breathing hard and gazing with lethal intent at his fingers on her wrist.

'I don't recall you mentionin' that yesterday,' he said ominously.

'I didn't think of it. The brochure was something the ME's assistant brought up in passing and I took it in kind. But then last night, I remembered what you said. That for some of the victims, the man put things in their purses – a business card, a cocktail napkin with a name. And that got me wondering.'

Mac slowly released her. 'Anything else you remembered last night?'

'Yes. I remembered to strap on my knife.'

He grinned. 'Where is it this time? Ankle? Inside of a thigh?

I swear it's the first thing I thought when I saw you this morning. So few clothes and yet somewhere on that lean little body, I know there rests a three-inch blade. I swear, honey, I never met a woman who could make a man think of knives quite the way you do.'

Mac leaned a little closer. He smelled of soap again. Clean, strong. Kimberly instantly took a small step back. Funny how it felt as if all the air had just been sucked from her lungs.

'If I'm a good boy,' Mac murmured softly, 'do I get to search you later? Or would you prefer it, if I were bad?'

'Hey. Hey, hey, hey.' Kimberly finally found her bearings, getting up her hands and placing them firmly between them. 'I am not flirting with you!'

'Of course not.'

'Now what is *that* supposed to mean?'

'You're not the type for a casual social gesture, Kimberly. I know that. Nah, with you, I imagine it would be very serious.' He nodded at her, his blue eyes suddenly somber and affecting far more strongly than any of his teasing ever had. Then he was straightening up and turning back toward the hall. 'So where's that geologist?'

He strode forward, and Kimberly had to scramble to follow suit.

Five minutes later Mac rapped on a closed door bearing the nameplate Jennifer York. The door almost immediately opened up.

'Yes?' a young woman asked. Like Ray Lee Chee, she was dressed casually – khaki shorts, white-scooped collar shirt, and heavy duty hiking boots.

Mac flashed a smile, and went to work. 'Jennifer York, I presume? Special Agent Mac McCormack, ma'am. And this here is . . . Special Investigator Quincy. We were just asking your associate Ray Lee Chee some questions relevant to a case, and he highly recommended you as an expert in the field of geology.'

The woman blinked her eyes a few times. Her gaze had started on Mac's face, but now it had drifted to the broad expanse of his chest where it seemed to have taken root. 'Special Agent? As in police?'

'Yes, ma'am. We're working on a special situation, a kidnapping, if you will. We have a few items from the scene – tree leaves, rocks, etc. – that we need to identify to help find the victim. Could we take a moment of your time? It sure would be a big help.'

Mac gave the woman one last charming smile, and she practically tripped over herself getting the door all the way open and inviting Mac inside. Briefly, she seemed to notice Kimberly was in tow, but then her gaze was all Mac all the time. Not that the man didn't have a way with women.

Inside the office, Jennifer York's workspace appeared very similar to Ray Lee Chee's – a modest arrangement of over-stuffed bookshelves, crammed filing cabinets, and a utilitarian desk. Now she stood with one hand lightly touching her desk and the other supporting her lower back, which she had arched in a not so subtle attempt to emphasize her chest.

'So,' Kimberly spoke up curtly, finally earning York's attention. 'We were wondering if there is any connection between Hawaii and Virginia.'

'You mean the two states?'

'I believe they are states, yes. So are they related or what?'

The brunette stared at Kimberly a moment longer, then abruptly abandoned her feline pose, and took a seat in her desk chair. Now that they were on the subject of work, her expression had grown serious.

'Actually, from a geologist's perspective there is quite a connection. We often compare the Blue Ridge Mountains in Shenandoah National Park with the Hawaiian Islands – both were partially formed by flows of basaltic lava. Essentially, one billion years ago, what we now call the Blue Ridge Mountains were actually the Grenville Mountains, which we believe may have stretched from Newfoundland to Texas and may have reached as high as the present-day Himalayas. This mountain range eroded over time, however, until by six hundred million years ago it was little more than a series of rolling hills. Then, however, we had the Catoctin volcanics.'

'A volcano?' Mac asked with surprise. 'In Virginia?'

'More or less. A large rift opened up in the valley and basaltic magma from the earth's mantle seeped to the surface, flooding the valley and forming the Catoctin Formation, which you can view in the northern section of the park.'

'The Catoctin Formation still exists?' Mac asked. 'And its geology is similar to Hawaii?'

'Yes, the Catoctin Formation still exists,' Jennifer said, flashing him a warm smile. 'The geology, however, isn't exact. The basalts in Hawaii are black, while the rocks in the Shenandoah National Park are dark green. Basically, a process called metamorphism caused the basalts in Shenandoah to recrystallize with new minerals, such as chlorite, epidote, and albite, which help give the rocks their greenish hue. In fact, we no longer call the rocks in Shenandoah basalts, but metabasalts, due to this alteration.'

Mac turned toward Kimberly. She could read the question in his eye. The victim had been found holding a rock. Had it been greenish in color? She couldn't remember. They hadn't gotten a good look at it and the ME had already catalogued it before she'd arrived at the morgue.

'Are metabasalts rare in the park?' Mac asked York.

'Not at all. You can view them as road outcroppings as you drive from the northern entrance of the park all the way to Thornton Gap, then there's another good twenty-mile stretch from Stony Man to Swift Run Gap, then there's more all the way to the southern point of the park.'

'Are there *any* kinds of rocks that are rare in the park?' Kimberly spoke up.

York had to think about it. 'Well, the Shenandoah National Park actually involves *three* major types of bedrock. The metabasalts are found in the north and south, which we've discussed. But there are also siliciclasts, which are found in the southern section of the park or around Thornton Gap. Then we have the granites, which are in the central part of the park. The siliciclasts, which are sedimentary rocks containing abundant amounts of silica, probably have the smallest area of distribution. The granites probably have the most definable area, however, being bunched in the middle to north section of the park. Now within each bedrock type, there are variances. For example, certain kinds of granites will have more of one mineral or another, depending on where they are found in the park. Same with the metabasalts and same with the siliciclasts.'

'Not all rocks are created equal?' Mac asked.

'Exactly.' She gave him another warm smile, a teacher bestowing praise on her favorite student. 'Geologists analyze rocks all the time. Basically, you take a cross section of the rock sample and view it under a polarizing microscope. By breaking the rock down to its mineral components, you could pinpoint more precisely from where in the park it probably came. In some cases, in fact, the distribution range might be very small. Of course, we don't have that kind of equipment here, but if you had a rock, I'd be happy to make a few phone calls . . .'

'Well, we don't exactly have a rock . . .'

She arched a brow. 'No rock?'

'No.' He added helpfully, 'But we do have a travel brochure for Hawaii.'

York blinked her eyes, obviously trying to follow that thought, then finally gave up. 'Well, without an actual rock sample, I'm not sure what to tell you. Yes, there are lots of rocks in the Shenandoah National Park. And yes, some of them are similar to geology found in Hawaii. But I don't know how to break things down for you any more than that. The wilderness area of the Shenandoah National Park encompasses nearly eighty thousand acres, you know. That's a lot of rock types and areas of geologic interest.'

'Do you have a book or a rock guide we could take with us?' Kimberly asked. 'You know, that way once we did have a sample, we could look up more information.'

'It wouldn't be specific enough. With your naked eye, the best you would be able to determine was if the stone in question were basalt versus granite versus siliciclast. That would only cut your search area in half, leaving you with forty thousand acres. No, to truly analyze a rock, you need to be able to look at its mineral components through a microscope.'

'Do you have a microscope we could borrow?' Kimberly attempted weakly.

'They cost a couple pennies. I think the US government might notice.'

'Darn government.'

'Get the rock,' York said. 'Give me a call. I'd be very happy to help.' Her gaze was once more locked on Mac.

'We'll try,' Mac said diligently, but Kimberly knew he was just being polite. They would never have access to the rock found in the victim's hand; they were outsiders no longer privy to such helpful little tidbits as real evidence.

'One last question,' Kimberly said. 'Are there rattlesnakes in the Shenandoah National Park?'

York appeared surprised. 'More than a few. Why do you ask?'

'Just checking. Guess I better put on a thicker pair of boots.'

'Watch out for rocks,' York advised. 'They like to curl up in the nooks and crannies between boulders. Or even sleep out on the sun-warmed surface once it's dusk.'

'Got it.'

Mac shook the woman's hand. York gave him a dazzling smile, while managing to once more arch her back. Kimberly engaged in a significantly stiffer handshake, which is apparently what happened when you didn't have a Southern drawl – or Mac's muscled chest.

They made their way back to the front doors, where the blue sky already stretched bright and hot beyond the glass. 'That wasn't so good,' Mac said, pausing before the entrance-way. He seemed to be bracing himself for leaving the cool comfort of air conditioning behind and bursting once more into the heat.

'We have a start,' Kimberly said firmly. 'All signs point to the Shenandoah National Park.'

'Yes, all eighty thousand acres. You're right, we should find this girl in no time at all.' He shook his head in disgust. 'We need choppers. Hell, we need search and rescue, the National Guard, and about half a dozen dogs. This poor woman . . .'

'I know,' Kimberly said quietly.

'It doesn't seem fair, does it? A kidnapped victim deserves all the help in the world. And instead . . .'

'She's only going to get us.'

He nodded and the lines of frustration etched into his dark face almost made her reach out her hand. She wondered who that sort of unsolicited contact would shock more – her or him?

'We need supplies,' Mac said. 'Then we'd better hit the road. It's a long drive to Shenandoah, particularly when we don't know where we're going yet.'

'We're going to find her,' Kimberly said.

'We need more information. Damn, why didn't I just take that rock?'

'Because that would've been crossing the line. The leaf had

already been mishandled by the ME. The rock on the other hand . . .'

'Has been properly bagged and tagged and even now is wasting away in some crime lab,' Mac finished bitterly.

'We're going to find her,' Kimberly said again.

He finally stilled in front of the glass door. His blue eyes were still dark, fired by frustration and determination. For just a moment, however, the look on his face softened. 'Earnest Kimberly,' he whispered.

'Yes.'

'I hope you're right.' He glanced at his watch. 'Ten A.M.,' he said softly, then abruptly pushed through the heavy door. 'And boy, is it getting hot.'

Tina woke up slowly, becoming aware of two things at once: a deep, wracking thirst that had left her tongue swollen and cottony in her mouth and the incessant sound of buzzing around her head.

She opened her eyes, but couldn't see a thing through the thick tangle of her long blond hair, now glued uncomfortably to her sweat-slicked face. She roughly pushed back her hair, only to encounter a fuzz black haze. And then abruptly, she knew what that buzzing was.

Tina leapt to her feet, already waving her arms frantically while a scream built in her throat. Mosquitoes. She was covered, head to toe, with hundreds of swarming, buzzing, biting mosquitoes.

Malaria, she thought instantly. The West Nile Virus. Hell, the bubonic plague, as far as she was concerned. She had never seen so many bugs, fluttering in her hair, sinking their hungry mouths into her skin. Oh God, oh God, oh God.

Her feet landed in mud, her three-inch high platform sandals immediately sinking into the watery marsh. She had a faint sensation of cool relief as the mud hit her toes, then she made the mistake of looking down and this time she did scream. Right there, slithering by her ankle in the muck, went a long black snake.

Tina scrambled back onto the rock that had apparently been her perch. The mosquitoes swarmed hungrily. And now she could see other hunters as well. Yellow flies, gnats, buzzing creatures of all sorts and sizes. They swarmed her head and shoulders, seeking the unprotected skin of her throat, the corners of her mouth and the whites of her eyes. Fresh welts rose on her ears, her eyes, her cheeks. Her legs were covered in red marks, some still oozing fresh blood as more mosquitoes were drawn to the scent. She started clapping her hands. Then she slapped them against her entire body.

'Die, die, die,' she gasped. And they did. She felt plump, overfed bodies explode between her fingers, staining her palms with her own blood as she took out dozens. Then hundreds more insects swooped in to take their place, biting painfully at her tender skin.

She was crying now. She gasped for breath. Then in the middle of her frenzy, the inevitable happened. Her stomach rolled, she just got down on her hands and knees, and then she vomited over the edge of the rock into the foul-smelling muck below.

Water. Green bile. Precious little food. Her stomach heaved anyway, her head dropping between her shoulders as she dry-heaved. The mosquitoes used the opportunity to swarm her shoulders, her elbows, her calves. She was being eaten alive, and there wasn't a thing she could do to save herself.

Minutes passed. The knot eased in her stomach. The cramping nausea released its hold on her bowels. Shakily, she straightened, brushing back her long, sweaty hair, and feeling new welts already rise up on her ears.

The mosquitoes danced in front of her eyes, seeking skin. She batted them away, but her movements were already half-hearted, the actions of a woman who realized she was no match for the enemy. She could kill hundreds of insects. A thousand would simply take their place. Oh God . . .

Her throat burned. Her skin felt as if it were on fire. She raised her trembling hands to her face and saw that they were also covered in red, angry bites. Then her gaze went all the way up to white-hot sky, where the sun was already starting to blaze overhead. Her dog crate was gone. Instead, from all appearances she had been cast into some kind of swampy pit, fodder for insects, snakes, and God knows what.

'Good news,' Tina whispered to herself. 'He's not a sexually deranged pervert after all.'

And then she started to laugh. And then she started to cry. And then she whispered in a voice probably heard only by the mosquitoes and snakes, 'I'm so sorry, Ma. Oh God, somebody, help me please.'

20

At eight A.M., Special Agent Kaplan escorted Rainie and Quincy to the roped-off crime scene where the victim had been found yesterday morning. At eight ten, Kaplan took off to attend to his own tasks for the day, leaving Rainie and Quincy alone. That was fine by Quincy. He liked to walk a scene unescorted, without the murmur of voices, incessant clicking of cameras, or the needling scratching of pencil on paper to divert his attention. Death inevitably took on a life of its own, and Quincy preferred the calm after the storm. When all the other investigators had left and he could be alone with his musings.

Rainie stood a good thirty feet away from him, walking soundlessly around the fringes of the forest. She was used to his ways by now, and worked as quietly as he did. They had been at this for two hours already, falling seamlessly into the usual grid pattern, slowly and methodically dissecting each inch of the roped-off area, and then, because even the best cops missed things, moving outside of the cordoned-off space, searching for what the others may have missed, for that one clue which would magically bring it all together. If such a thing really existed.

Underneath the relative shade of the thick oak trees, the heat hammered down on them relentlessly. They shared one bottle of water, then another, and were now almost done with the lukewarm third. Quincy's white dress shirt, sharply pressed just this morning, was now plastered against his chest while thin trickles of sweat beaded down his face. His fingers left damp stains on his small notepad while his pencil slid wetly between his fingers.

It was a brutal morning, serving as a brutal start to what would be no doubt an extremely brutal day. Was this what the killer wanted? Overheated law enforcement officers struggling to function in damp, unbearable weather that glued their uniforms to their bodies and robbed them of breath? Some killers picked extremely harsh or disgusting places to dump bodies because they relished the thought of homicide detectives picking through dumpsters or wading through swamps. First they humiliated the victims. Then they reveled in the thought of what they could do to the police.

Quincy stopped and turned once more, frowning in spite of himself. He wanted to know this space. He wanted to *feel* this space. He wanted a glimpse into why, of all places on this nearly four-hundred-acre base, had the killer dumped the body *here*.

The area was sheltered, the thick canopy of trees making the path invisible at night. The path itself was wide enough for a car, but four tires would have definitely left at least a faint impression and there were none. No, their unidentified subject – UNSUB – had selected a spot half a mile from the road. And then he'd walked that half mile in pitch-black night while staggering beneath the awkward weight of a hundred-and-ten-pound body. Surely there were dozens of spots more accessible and less physically demanding.

So again: why had their UNSUB chosen here?

Quincy was beginning to have some ideas. He bet Rainie would also have a few opinions on the subject.

'How are you making out?' Kaplan called out.

He was coming down the dirt path, looking fresher than them, so wherever he'd been, it had had air-conditioning. Quincy found himself resentful already.

'Brought you bug spray,' Kaplan said merrily.

'You're the king of men,' Quincy assured him. 'Now look behind you.'

Kaplan obediently stopped and looked behind him. 'I don't see anything.'

'Exactly.'

'Huh?'

'Look down,' Rainie said impatiently, from twenty feet back. 'Check out your footsteps.'

Rainie had pulled her heavy chestnut hair back in a ponytail first thing this morning. It had come loose about an hour ago and was now plastered in sweaty tendrils against her neck. She looked wild, her hair curly with the humidity and her gray eyes nearly black with the heat. Having grown up on the Oregon coast with its relatively mild climate, Rainie absolutely loathed high heat and humidity. Quincy figured he had about another hour before she'd be driven to violence.

'There aren't any footsteps,' Kaplan said.

'Exactly.' Quincy sighed and finally pulled his attention away from the scene. 'According to reports on the Weather Channel, this area received two inches of rain five days ago. And if you venture off the path into the woods, there are patches where the ground is still marshy and soft to the touch. The thick trees protect the dirt from baking in the sun, plus I don't think much can dry out given this humidity.'

'But the path is solid.'

'Yes. Apparently, nothing hard packs soil quite like the

daily grind of a few hundred pounding Marine and FBI trainees. The path is hard as a rock. It would take more than a two-hundred-pound person, plus a hundred-pound-body, to dent it now.'

Kaplan frowned at them both, still obviously confused. 'I already said there weren't any footprints. We looked.'

Quincy wanted to sigh again. He so preferred working with Rainie, who was now regarding the NCIS special agent with a fresh level of annoyance.

'If you simply walked off the road into the woods around here, what would happen?'

'The ground is still soft; you'd leave a footprint.'

'So to a casual visitor, the woods are marshy?'

'Yeah, I guess.'

'And what's thirty feet to my left?' Quincy asked crisply.

'The PT course.'

'The paved PT course.'

'Sure, the paved PT course.'

Quincy looked at him. 'If you were carrying a body into the woods, wouldn't you take the paved path? The one that offered you better footing? The one that would be guaranteed not to leave footprints, given the soft soil you see all around?'

'The wooded path has less traffic,' Kaplan said slowly. 'He's better hidden.'

'According to the ME's report, the UNSUB probably dumped the body in the small hours of the morning. Given the late hour, the man's already well hidden. Why take the dirt path? Why risk footprints?'

'He's not very bright?' But Kaplan was no longer convinced.

Rainie shook her head impatiently, crossing over to them. 'The UNSUB knew. He's been on this path. He knew the ground was hard and would protect him, while the wide scope makes it less likely he'd bump the body against a tree limb or accidentally leave a scrap of fabric on a twig. Face it, Kaplan.

The UNSUB isn't some random guy. He knows this place. Hell he's probably run this course sometime in the last five days.'

Kaplan was clearly discouraged as they trudged back to the Academy.

'I spoke with the four Marines on duty Tuesday night,' he reported. 'They had nothing out of the ordinary. No unusual vehicles, no suspicious drivers. Only thing they could think of was that it was a particularly busy night. A bunch of the National Academy students had hightailed it for air-conditioned bars, so they had cars coming and going right up until two A.M. Everyone showed proper ID, however. Nothing stood out in their minds.'

'Do they keep a log of who comes and goes?' Rainie asked, walking beside Quincy.

'No. All drivers have to show proper security passes, however. The Marine sentries may also ask for a license and where's the final location.'

'What does a security pass look like?'

Kaplan gestured to Rainie's shirt, where a white plastic card dangled from her collar. 'It looks like that, except in a variety of colors. Some are blue, some are white, some yellow. Each color indicates a certain level of clearance. A yellow card indicates an unescorted guest pass, someone who's allowed full access. We also have cards reading "escorted guests" which means they wouldn't be allowed back onto the base without being in the company of the proper person. That sort of thing.'

Rainie glanced down. 'They don't look that complicated to me. Couldn't someone just swipe one?'

'You have to sign a badge in and out. And believe me, the FBI police keep tabs on that sort of thing. None of us would feel particularly good if just any Tom, Dick, or Harry could swipe a card.'

'Just asking,' Rainie said mildly.

Kaplan scowled at her anyway. Their earlier conversation had obviously wounded his ego. 'You can't steal a badge. You can't just walk onto this base. For God's sake, we take this kind of thing very seriously. Look, you're probably right. It probably is an insider. Which really depresses me, though I don't know why. If all the good guys were really good people, I wouldn't have a job, would I?'

'That's not an encouraging thought,' Rainie said.

'Ma'am, it's the worst thought in the world.' He glanced at Quincy. 'You know, I've been thinking . . . Given the lack of sexual assault, and that the "weapon" so to speak, was a drug, shouldn't we be looking at women, too?'

'No,' Quincy said.

'But women are the ones who predominantly kill with poison. And the lack of sexual assault bothers me. And a guy doesn't just OD a woman and dump her body in the woods. Men are sexual predators. And did you see how this girl was dressed?'

Quincy drew up short. 'The victim,' he said curtly, 'was wearing a short skirt, not uncommon for this time of year. To imply that a certain manner of dress invites sexual assault—'

'That's not what I was saying!' Kaplan interrupted immediately.

'It's not about sex, for any predator,' Quincy continued as if Kaplan hadn't spoken. 'It's about power. We've had many serial killers who were not sexual-sadist predators. Berkowitz, for one, was strictly a triggerman, so to speak. He picked his victims, walked up to the car, opened fire on the couple, and walked away. Kaczynski was content to kill and maim long distance. Even more recently, we had the Beltway Snipers who held most of the East Coast in absolute terror by picking off victims from the trunk of their car. Murder isn't about sex. It's about power. And in this context then, drugs make perfect sense, as drugs are weapons of control.'

'Besides,' Rainie spoke up, 'there's no way a woman carried a dead body half a mile into the woods. We don't have that kind of upper-body strength.'

They finally emerged from the relative comfort of the woods. Immediately, the sun struck them like a ball peen hammer while waves of heat shimmered above the paved road.

'Holy Lord,' Kaplan said. 'And it's not even noon.'

'It's going to be a hot one,' Quincy murmured.

And Rainie said, 'Fuck the Academy, I'm putting on shorts.'

'One last thing,' Kaplan said, holding up a hand. 'Something you should both know.'

Rainie halted with an impatient sigh. Quincy waited with a far more prescient sense of something significant about to break.

'We have the tox report back on the victim. Two drugs were found in her system. A small dose of ketamine, and a significantly larger dose – no doubt lethal dose – of the benzodiazepine, Ativan. In other words . . .'

'Special Agent McCormack listed them both last night,' Quincy murmured.

'Yeah,' Kaplan said slowly. 'McCormack knew the drugs. Now how about that?'

21

Mac drove until they'd left the concrete columns of Richmond behind them. He headed west on Interstate 64, where a towering line of dark green mountains stood out in vivid contrast to the bright blue sky and drew them steadily forward.

They stopped at Texaco for gas. Then they stopped at a Wal-Mart to cover the essentials: bug spray, first aid kit, hiking socks, energy bars, chocolate bars, extra water bottles, and a complete case of water. Mac already had a compass, Swiss Army knife, and waterproof matches in his backpack. They grabbed an extra set for Kimberly to carry, just in case.

When they returned to his rented Toyota, Mac discovered a message on his cell phone from Ray Lee Chee. The botanist, Kathy Levine, would meet them at Big Meadows Lodge in the Shenandoah National Park at one-thirty. Without a word, they started driving again.

Cities came and went. Major housing developments bloomed alongside the road, then slowly withered away. They headed deeper west, where the land opened up like an emerald sea and took Mac's breath away.

'God's country,' his father would say. There wasn't much of this kind of land left.

As Kimberly navigated they turned off the interstate for the rolling lanes of US 15, leading to US 33. They swept by vast fields, each dotted by a single, red brick ranch house boasting a fresh-painted white porch. They passed dairy farms, horse stables, vineyards, and agricultural spreads.

Outside the car, everything took on a green hue, a rolling patchwork of square fields, seamed by groves of dark green trees. They passed horses and cows. They came upon tiny towns defined by run-down delis, old gas stations, and pristine Baptist churches. Then, in the blink of an eye, the towns disappeared and they headed deeper into the growing shade cast by a towering mountain range. Slowly but surely, they started to climb.

Kimberly had been quiet since their meeting with the geologist. Her visor was down, casting a shadow across the top half of her face and making it difficult to read her expression.

Mac was worried about her. She'd shown up bright and early this morning with the gaunt cheeks and feverish eyes of a woman who'd had little sleep. She wore linen trousers, topped with a white dress shirt and matching linen jacket. The outfit looked sharp and professional, but he suspected she'd chosen the long pants to hide her knife, and the jacket to cover the discreet bulge of the Glock strapped to her waist. In other words, she was a woman going to war.

He suspected she went to war a lot. He suspected that since the deaths of her mother and sister, life for her had essentially been one long battle. The thought pained him in a way he hadn't expected.

'It's beautiful,' he said at last.

She finally shifted in her seat, giving him a brief glance before stretching out her legs. 'Yes.'

'You like the mountains? Or are you a city gal?'

She shook her head. 'City gal. Technically speaking, I grew up in Alexandria, close to these mountains. But Alexandria functions more as a suburb of D.C. than Richmond. And let's just say my mother's interests ran more to the Smithsonian Institution than the Shenandoah Mountains. Then I went off to school in New York. You?'

'I love mountains. Hell, I love rivers, fields, orchards, streams, woods, you name it. I was lucky growing up. My grandparents – my mother's parents – own a hundred-acre peach orchard. As their kids married, they gifted each one with three acres of land to build a home, that way all the siblings could live close by. Basically, my sister and I grew up in booneyville, surrounded by a dozen cousins, and a ton of open space. Each day my mom would kick us out of the house, tell us not to die, and come home in time for dinner. So we did.'

'You must have liked your cousins.'

'Nah, we annoyed the snot out of each other. But that was half the fun. We made up games, we got into trouble. We basically ran around like heathens. And then at night,' he slanted her a look, 'we played board games.'

'Your whole family? Every night?' Her voice was skeptical.

'Yep. We'd rotate around each aunt and uncle's house and off we'd go. My mom started it. She hates TV, thinks it rots the brain. The Boob Tube, she calls it. When I turned twelve, she threw ours out. I'm not sure my father's ever recovered from the loss, but after that we had to do something to pass the time.'

'So you played games?'

'All the good ones. Monopoly, Scrabble, Yahtzee, Boggle, Life, and my personal favorite, Risk.'

Kimberly raised a brow. 'And who won?'

'I did, of course.'

'I believe that,' she said seriously. 'You attempt this whole laid-back Southern routine, but deep down inside, you're a natural-born competitor. I can see it every time you talk about this case. You don't like to lose.'

'The person who said there are no winners or losers, obviously lost.'

'I'm not disagreeing.'

His lips curved. 'I didn't think you would.'

'My family didn't play board games,' she volunteered finally. 'We read books.'

'Serious stuff or fun stuff?'

'Serious, of course. At least when my mother was watching. After lights out, however, Mandy used to sneak in copies of Sweet Valley High. We'd read them under the covers using a flashlight. Oh, we giggled ourselves sick.'

'Sweet Valley High? And here I figured you for a Nancy Drew kind of gal.'

'I liked Nancy, but Mandy was better at smuggling contraband, and she preferred Sweet Valley High. And booze for that matter, but that's another story.'

'You rebel.'

'We all have our moments. So.' She turned toward him. 'Big charming Southern man. You ever been in love?'

'Uh oh.'

She stared at him intently, and he finally relented with a sigh. 'Yeah. Once. One of my sister's friends. She set us up, we hit it off, and things went pretty well for a while.'

'What happened?'

'I don't know.'

'That's no kind of answer.'

'Honey, coming from a man, that's the only kind of answer.'

She resumed staring and he caved again. 'I was probably an idiot. Rachel was a nice girl. Funny, athletic, sweet. She taught second grade and was really good with kids. I certainly could've done worse.'

'So you ended it, broke your sister's best friend's heart?'

He shrugged. 'More like I let it trickle out. Rachel was the kind of girl a guy should marry, then settle down and raise two point two kids. And I . . . I wasn't there yet. You know how this job is. You get a call, you have to go. And God knows when you're comin' home. I had visions of her waiting more and more and smiling less and less. It didn't seem the thing to do.'

'Do you miss her?'

'Honestly, I hadn't thought of her in years.'

'Why? She sounds perfect.'

Mac shot her an impatient glance. 'Nobody's perfect, Kimberly, and if you must know, we did have a problem. A significant problem, in my mind. We never fought.'

'You never fought?'

'Never. And a man and woman should fight. Frankly, they should have a good head-to-head battle about every six months, then make love until they break the box springs. At least that's my opinion.'

'Well, I . . . I never thought about it that way.'

'Your turn. What was his name?'

'I don't have a name.'

'Honey, everyone's got a name. The boy you sat behind in math class. The college quarterback who got away. Your sister's boyfriend who you secretly wished was your own. Come on. Confession's good for the soul.'

'And I still don't have a name. Honest. I've never been in love. I don't think I'm the type.'

He frowned at her. 'Everyone falls in love.'

'That's not true,' she countered immediately. 'Love's not for everyone. There are people who live their whole lives alone and are very happy that way. To fall in love . . . It involves giving. It involves weakening. I'm not very good at that.'

Mac gave her a slow, lingering look. 'Ah honey, you obviously haven't met the right man yet.'

Kimberly's cheeks grew red. She turned away from him and resumed staring out the window. The road was steep now, they'd officially hit the Blue Ridge Mountains and were now making the grinding climb through Swift Run Gap. They zigzagged around sharp corners, getting teasing glimpses of million-dollar views. Then they were up the side, cresting at twenty-four hundred feet and watching the world open up like a deep green blanket. Before them, green valleys plunged, gray granite soared, and blue sky stretched for as far as the eye could see.

'Wow,' Kimberly said simply and Mac couldn't think of a better response.

He took the entrance into the Shenandoah National Park. He paid the fee and in turn they got a map of all the various lookout points. They headed north, toward Big Meadows, on Skyline Drive.

The going was slower here, the speed limit a steady 35 mph, which was just as well because suddenly there were a million things to see and not nearly enough time to look. Wild grass bordered the winding road, thickly dotted with yellow and white flowers, while deeper in the woods a vast array of ferns spread out like a thick green carpet. Towering oak trees and majestic beeches wove their branches overhead, breaking the sun into a million pieces of gold. A yellow butterfly darted in front of them. Kimberly gasped, and Mac turned just in time to see a mother and fawn cross the road behind them.

He spotted two yellow finches playing tag in a grove of pine trees. Then they were already upon the first viewing platform, where the trees gave way and half of Virginia once again opened up before them.

Mac pulled over. He was no neophyte to the great outdoors, but sometimes a man just had to sit and stare. He and Kimberly absorbed the panorama of emerald forest mixing with gray stone outcrops and brightly colored wildflowers. The Blue

Ridge Mountains really knew how to put on a show.

'Do you think he's really an environmentalist?' Kimberly murmured quietly.

Mac didn't need to ask to know whom she meant. 'I'm not sure. He certainly picks some great places.'

'The planet is dying,' she said softly. 'Look over to the right. You can see patches of dead hemlocks probably killed by the wooly adelgid, which is infesting so many of our forests. And while this range is protected as a national park, how long will the valley before us remain untouched? Someday, those fields will probably become subdivisions, while all of those distant trees will be turned into yet more strip malls to feed hungry consumers. Once upon a time, most of the U.S. looked like this. Now you have to drive hundreds of miles just to find this kind of beauty.'

'Progress happens.'

'That's nothing but an excuse.'

'No,' Mac said abruptly. 'And yes. Everything changes. Things die. We probably should fear for our kids. But I still don't know what that has to do with why one man kills a bunch of innocent women. Maybe this guy *wants* to think he's different. Hell maybe he does have some sort of conscience and it bothers him to kill for killing's sake. But the letters, the environmental talk . . . Personally, I think it's nothing but a bunch of bullshit designed to give the Eco-Killer permission to do what he really wants to do – kidnap and kill women.'

'In psychology,' Kimberly said, 'we learn that there are many different reasons for why people behave certain ways. This applies to killers as well. Some killers are driven by ego, by their own overdeveloped id, which puts their needs first and refuses to accept limits on their behavior. It's the serial killer who kills because he likes to feel powerful. It's the stockbroker who murders his mistress after she threatens to tell his wife, because he honestly believes his own desire for security is more important than another person's life. It's the kid who pulls the trigger, just because he wants to.

'There's another kind of killer, though. The morality killer. That's the fanatic who walks into a synagogue and opens fire because he believes it is his duty. Or the person who shoots abortion doctors because she believes they are committing a sin. These people don't kill to satisfy their inner child, but because they believe such an act is right. Perhaps the Eco-Killer falls into the morality category.'

Mac arched a brow. 'So these are our choices? Immature whackos on the one hand and righteous whackos on the other?'

'Technically speaking.'

'All right. You want psychobabble? I can play this game. I believe it was Freud who said everything we do communicates something about ourselves.'

'You know Freud?'

'Hey, don't let the good looks fool you, honey. I have a brain in my head. So all right, according to Freud, the tie you pick, the ring you wear, the shirt you buy, all say something about you. Nothing is random, everything you do has intent. Fine, now let's look at what this guy does. He kidnaps women traveling in pairs. Always young females leaving a bar. Now why does he do that? Seems to me that the terrorist type of killer goes after people of a certain faith – but then will equally target man, woman, or child. The moral killer goes after the abortion doctor for his occupation, not for his sex. And yet then we got our guy again. Eight victims in Georgia, ten if you think he struck here, and always a young, college-aged girl leaving a bar. Now what does that communicate about him?'

'He doesn't like women,' Kimberly answered softly. 'Particularly women who drink.'

'He hates them,' Mac said flatly. 'Loose women, fast women, I don't know how he categorizes them in his mind, but he hates women. I don't know why. Maybe he doesn't know why. Maybe he honestly believes this is about the environment. But if our guy was really about saving the world, then we should see some variety in his targets. We don't. He only goes after women. Period. And in my mind, that makes him just another garden-variety very dangerous whacko.'

'You don't believe in profiling?'

'Kimberly, we've had a profile for four years. Ask that poor girl in the morgue if it's done a thing to help us yet.'

'Bitter.'

'Realistic,' he countered. 'This case isn't going to be solved in the back room by some guy in a suit. It's going to be solved out here, roaming these mountains, sweating buckets, and dodging rattlesnakes. Because that's what Eco-Killer wants. He hates women, but every time he sticks one in a dangerous location, he's also targeting *us*. Law enforcement officers, search-and-rescue workers – we're the ones who have to walk these hills and sweat this terrain. Don't think he doesn't know it.'

'Have any search-and-rescue workers been hurt?'

'Hell yes. In the Tallulah Gorge we had several falls and broken limbs. The cotton field caused two volunteers to succumb to heat stroke. Then we had a wonderful search along the Savannah River, where one guy tangled with a gator, and two people were bitten by cottonmouth snakes.'

'Fatalities?' she asked sharply.

Mac looked back out at the vast, plunging terrain. He murmured, 'Well honey, not yet.'

22

Shenandoah National Park, Virginia
1:44 P.M.
Temperature: 97 degrees

Kathy Levine was a petite, no-nonsense woman with short-cropped red hair and a dash of freckles across her nose. She greeted Mac and Kimberly briskly as they entered the glass-and-beam expanse of Big Meadows Lodge and beckoned them immediately toward a back office.

'Ray said you had a picture of a leaf. Not a real leaf, mind you, but a picture.'

'Yes ma'am.' Mac dutifully provided the scanned image. Kathy plopped it down on the desk in front of her and snapped on a bright overhead light. It barely made a dent in a room already lit by an entire wall of sunshine.

'It could be a gray birch,' the botanist said at last. 'It would be better if you had the real leaf.'

'Are you a dendrologist?' Kimberly asked curiously.

'No, but I know what's in my park.' The woman snapped off the light and regarded them both frankly. 'Are you two familiar with refugia?'

'Refugee what?' Mac said.

'That's what I thought. Refugia is a term for plants that

exist as glacial relics in a climate where they no longer belong. Essentially, millions of years ago, this whole area was ice. But then the ice melted and certain plants got left behind. In most cases, those plants moved high up in the mountains, seeking the cool conditions they need to survive. Balsa fir and red cedar are both examples of refugia found in this park. And so is gray birch.'

'Ray said it was only found in one area.' Mac spoke up intently.

'Yes. Right outside the door. Let me get a map.' The botanist climbed out of her chair and rifled the bookshelf along the wall. Then, he proceeded to unfold the largest map Kimberly had ever seen. It was labeled, Geologic Map of Shenandoah County, and it was filled with enough streaks of bright purple, deep fuchsia, and neon orange to hurt a person's eyes.

'This is the geologic map which includes this section of the park. We are here.' Levine plopped the massive spread of paper on the jumbled surface of the desk, and promptly tapped a lime-green spot near the bottom of the page. 'Now, gray birch grows thickest in the swampy plateau across the street from the Big Meadows camp, but can also be found here and there in this whole one-mile area. So basically, if you're looking for the only gray birch in Virginia, you're standing in the middle of it.'

'Wonderful,' Mac murmured. 'Now if only we were sure we were looking for gray birch. How populated is this area this time of year?'

'You mean campers? We have thirty or so people signed in at the moment. Generally it would be more, but the heat has chased a lot away. Also we get a fair number of day hikers and the like. Of course, in this weather, we're probably doing mostly drive-throughs – people coming to the park, but never leaving the air-conditioned comfort of their cars.'

'Do guests have to sign in?'

'No.'

'Do you have park rangers or any kind of monitors working the area?'

'We have enough personnel if trouble should come up, but we don't go looking for it, if that's what you mean.'

'So a person could come and go, and you'd never know he'd been here?'

'I would imagine most people come and go, and we never know they were here.'

'Damn.'

'You want to tell me what this is about?' Levine nodded toward Kimberly. 'I can already tell she's armed. You might as well fill in the rest.'

Mac seemed to consider it. He looked at Kimberly, but she didn't know what to tell him. He might be out of his jurisdiction, but at least he was still a special agent. As of six A.M. this morning she had become no one at all.

'We're working a case,' Mac told Levine tersely. 'We have reason to believe this leaf may tie into the disappearance of a local girl. Find where the leaf came from, and we'll find her.'

'You're saying this girl may be somewhere in my park? Lost? In this kind of heat?'

'It's a possibility.'

Levine crossed her arms over her chest while regarding both of them intently. 'You know,' she said at last, 'right about now, I think I'd like to see some ID.'

Mac reached into his back pocket and pulled out his credentials. Kimberly just stood there. She had nothing to show, nothing to say. For the first time, the enormity of what she had done struck her. For all of her life, she'd wanted to be one thing. And now?

She turned away from both of them. Through the windows, the bright sunlight burned her eyes. She closed them tightly, trying to focus on the feel of heat on her face. A girl was out there. A girl needed her.

And her mother was still dead and her sister was still dead. And Mac was right after all. Nothing she did would change anything so what was she really trying to prove? That she could self-destruct as completely as Mandy?

Or that just once, she wanted to get something right. Just once, she wanted to find the girl, save the day. Because anything had to be better than this six-year ache.

'This says Georgia Bureau of Investigation,' Levine was saying to Mac.

'Yes, ma'am.'

'If my memory serves, we're still in Virginia.'

'Yes, ma'am.'

'Ray didn't ask you nearly enough questions now, did he?'

'Ray was very helpful in our investigation. We appreciate his efforts and are happy you were able to talk to us.'

Levine wasn't fooled. She drew a bead on Kimberly. 'I'm guessing you have no ID at all.'

Kimberly turned back around. She kept her voice even. 'No, I don't.'

'Look, it's gotta be a good hundred degrees in the shade right now, and while I'm not a big fan of doing field work in this kind of heat, that's my lot in life. So you both had better start talking fast, because I'm not amused to be yanked from my federally required duties to talk to two wanna-be cops who seem to be way out of their jurisdiction.'

'I am pursuing a case,' Mac said crisply. 'The killer started in Georgia. He's attacked ten girls. You wanna see photos, I can give you all your stomach can take. I have reason to believe he's operating in Virginia. The FBI are involved, but by the time they figure who did what to whom, this girl will probably have fed ten bears for a week. I, on the other hand, have been working this case for five years. I know this man. And now, I have legitimate reason to believe that he has kidnapped a young woman and abandoned her all alone in the middle of your park. Yes, it's hot outside. Yes, she is lost. And no, I don't plan on standing idly by and waiting for a bunch of Feds to complete all the required paperwork. I plan on finding this girl, Ms. Levine, and Ms. Quincy has agreed to assist. So that's why we're here and that's what we're doing. And if that offends you, well too bad. Because this girl probably is in your park, and boy oh boy, does she need some help.'

Kathy Levine appeared troubled. 'Do you have references?' she asked at last.

'I can give you the name of my supervisor in Georgia.'

'He knows about this case?'

'He sent me here to pursue it.'

'If I cooperate with you, what does that mean?'

'I have no jurisdiction, ma'am. Officially speaking, I can't ask you to do anything.'

'But you think the girl might be here. For how long?'

'He would've abandoned her yesterday.'

'It was nearly a hundred degrees yesterday,' Levine said curtly.

'I know.'

'Does she have gear?'

'He kidnaps women from bars. The best she has is her purse and her party clothes.'

Levine blinked twice. 'Sweet Jesus. And he's done this before?'

'Eight girls. So far, only one has survived. Today, I'd like to make that two.'

'We have a search-and-rescue team for the park,' Levine said briskly. 'If . . . if you had strong reason to believe there was say, a lost hiker, in the Big Meadows area, and if you reported that lost hiker, I would have authority to call the team.'

Mac stilled. The offer was both unexpected and desperately needed. A search-and-rescue team. Multiple people. Trained experts. In other words, the first genuine chance at success they'd had all day.

'Are you sure?' Mac asked sharply. 'It could be a wild goose chase. I could be wrong.'

'Are you wrong often?'

'Not about this.'

'Well, then . . .'

'I'd like to report a lost hiker,' Mac said immediately.

And Kathy Levine said, 'Let me make a call.'

23

Quantico, Virginia
2:23 P.M.
Temperature: 99 degrees

Kaplan had scheduled a two-thirty meeting with Dr Ennunzio to follow up on Mac's conversations with the forensic linguist. Rainie didn't think Kaplan believed Dr Ennunzio was a link to Georgia's Eco-Killer, as much as he wanted to grill a new person about the various doings of Special Agent McCormack.

Still, she and Quincy followed gamely along. Kaplan had his questions, they would have theirs. Besides, the BSU offices would probably be only eighty degrees, and that sure as hell beat the places they'd been thus far.

The offices of the Behavioral Science Unit were located in the basement of the indoor firing ranges building. Rainie had only been there once before, but she always thought it was a little funny. Not just because people were literally firing weapons two floors above you, which should give anyone pause, but because the elevators going down to the highly esteemed BSU offices were tucked in an isolated corner next to the laundry room. Walk by bins of dirty linens and used flak vests. Go to work for the day.

In the basement, the elevator door opened to a wood-paneled lobby area, with corridors going off every which way. Here visitors could sit on the leather sofa, while admiring various posters advertising BSU projects. 'Domestic Violence by Police Officers,' declared one, promoting an upcoming seminar. 'Suicide and Law Enforcement,' said another. 'Futuristics and Law Enforcement: The Millennium Conference,' advertised a third.

When Rainie had first met Quincy seven years ago, he'd been conducting research for the BSU. His project of choice – developing a schema for the effective profiling of juvenile mass murderers. Never let it be said that the BSU researchers were a bunch of lightweights.

And just in case someone thought the group was without a sense of humor, a new addition had been included in the line-up of agent photographs adorning the wall. Last photo in the middle row – a lovingly framed headshot of an extraterrestrial. Complete with a cone-shaped head and big black eyes. Really, it was the best-looking photo of the bunch.

Kaplan took off down the middle corridor and Rainie and Quincy followed in his wake.

'Miss it?' Rainie whispered in Quincy's ear.

'Not in the least.'

'It's never as dreary as I expect.'

'Wait until you've spent an entire week working without any natural light.'

'Whiner.'

'Be nice, or I'll lock you in the bomb shelter.'

'Promises, promises,' Rainie murmured. Quincy squeezed her hand, the first contact he'd made with her all day.

From what Rainie could determine, the space down here was basically a large square, bisected by three rows of hallways sprouting narrow offices. Kaplan came to the last door of the middle row, knocked twice and a man promptly opened it as if he were expecting them. 'Special Agent Kaplan?' he asked.

Rainie bit her lower lip just in time. Wow, she thought. A Quincy clone.

Dr Ennunzio wore a trim-fitting navy-blue suit with proper Republican-red tie. In his mid-forties, he had the lean build of an avid runner and the intense gaze of an academic who always took work home at night. His short-cropped hair was dark, but beginning to lighten at the temples. His manner was direct, his expression slightly impatient, and Rainie already had a feeling he considered this meeting a waste of his very valuable time.

Kaplan made the introductions. Ennunzio shook Rainie's hand briefly, but paused with genuine sincerity in front of Quincy. Apparently, he was familiar with the former agent's work.

Rainie simply kept gazing from the linguist to Quincy back to the linguist. Maybe it was an FBI hiring requirement, she thought. You must wear these suits and have eyes this intense to ride this ride. That could be.

Ennunzio gestured to his cramped office, much too small to house four grown adults, then ushered them back down the hallway to an unused conference room.

'This used to be the director's office,' he explained, his attention returning to Quincy. 'Back in your day. Now it's a conference room, while the bigwigs are across the way. It's not so hard to find their new offices. Just follow all the posters for the *Silence of the Lambs*.'

'Everyone loves Hollywood,' Quincy murmured.

'Now then,' Ennunzio said, taking a seat and placing a manila folder in front of him, 'you had questions about Special Agent McCormack from the GBI?'

'Yes,' Kaplan spoke up. 'We understand you were supposed to meet with him.'

'Tuesday afternoon. It didn't happen. I got held up at a conference in DC, the Forensic Linguistics Institute.'

'A conference for linguists,' Rainie muttered. 'That had to be a blast.'

'Actually it was quite fascinating,' Ennunzio told her. 'We had a special presentation on the anthrax envelopes sent to Senator Tom Daschle and Tom Brokaw. Were the envelopes sent by someone whose first language was English or Arabic? It's an extremely interesting analysis.'

Rainie startled, intrigued in spite of herself. 'Which one was it?'

'Almost certainly a native English speaker trying to impersonate an Arabic speaker. We call that "trick mail", when the sender attempts certain devices to mislead the receiver. In this case, the definitive evidence is the seemingly random mix of uppercase and lowercase letters throughout the text on the envelope, as well as a mixing of large and small caps. While this is meant to appear sloppy and childlike – someone uncomfortable with proper English syntax – in fact, it indicates someone so comfortable with the Roman alphabet he can manipulate it at will. Otherwise, it would be difficult to construct such a varied combination of letter styles. And while the messages in the two envelopes are short and filled with misspellings, this is again an attempt to deceive. Short missives actually involve a very concise use of the English language and are consistent with someone of higher, not lower, education. All in all, it was a first-rate presentation.'

'Okay,' Rainie said. She looked at Kaplan helplessly.

'So you didn't actually see Special Agent McCormack on Tuesday?' Kaplan asked.

'No.'

'But you had spoken to him before?'

'When Special Agent McCormack arrived at the National Academy, he stopped by my office asking if I would have time to consult on an old homicide case. He had copies of some letters that had been sent to the editor, and he wanted any information on them I could provide.'

'Did he give you copies of the letters?' Quincy spoke up.

'He gave me what he had. Unfortunately the GBI was only able to recover the original document for the last letter, and frankly, there's not much I can do with published versions. The newspapers sanitize too much.'

'You wanted to see if the guy also mixed small and large caps?' Rainie asked.

'Something like that. Look, I'll tell you the same thing I told Special Agent McCormack. Forensic linguistics is a broad field. As an expert, I'm trained to study language, syntax, spelling, grammar. I don't analyze penmanship per se – you need a handwriting expert for that – but how a document is prepared and presented provides context for my own analysis, so it is relevant. Now, within the field, we all have our own domains. Some linguists pride themselves on a sort of forensic profiling – you give them a document, and they can tell you the probable race, gender, age, education, and street address of who wrote it. I can do that to a certain degree, but my own subspecialty is authorship. You give me two samples of text and I can tell you if the person who wrote the threatening letter is the same person who wrote that second note to his mom.'

'How do you do that?' Rainie quizzed him.

'In part, I look at format. Mostly, however, I'm looking at word choice, sentence structure, and repeated errors or phrases. Everyone has certain expressions they favor, and these phrases have a tendency to appear over and over again in our writings. Are you familiar with the cartoon sitcom *The Simpsons*?'

Rainie nodded.

'All right, if you were the chief of police in Springfield and you received a ransom note including repeated uses of the expression "D' oh!," you'd probably want to start your investigation with Homer Simpson. If, on the other hand, the letter contained the phrase "Eat my shorts", you'd be better off looking at the younger Simpson, Bart. All people have phrases they like to use. When writing text, they are even more likely to repeat these catchphrases. The same goes with grammatical mistakes and spelling errors.'

'And in the case of the Eco-Killer?' Quincy spoke up.

'Not enough data points. Special Agent McCormack presented me with three copies and one original. With only one original, I can't compare penmanship, ink, or paper choice. In terms of content, all four letters contain the exact same message: "Clock ticking . . . planet dying . . . animals weeping . . . rivers screaming. Can't you hear it? Heat kills . . ." Frankly, to compare authorship, I need additional material, say another letter you believe may have been written by the suspect, or a longer document. Are you familiar with Ted Kaczynski?'

'The Unabomber? Of course.'

'That case was largely broken on the writings of Mr Kaczynski. Not only did we have the writing on the packages he used to mail out his bombs, but we also had several notes he included in the packages, many letters he wrote to the press, and finally the manifesto he demanded be run in the papers. Even then, it wasn't a forensic linguist who made the connections, but Kaczynski's own brother. He recognized parts of the manifesto from his brother's letters to him. Without such an extensive amount of material to analyze, who knows if we ever would have identified the Unabomber?'

'But this guy hasn't given the police much to work with,' Rainie said. 'Isn't that unusual? I mean, according to your own example, once these guys get talking, they have a lot to say. But this guy is implying he's earnest about the environment, while on the other hand, he's pretty quiet on the subject.'

'That is actually the one thing that jumped out at me,' Ennunzio said, his gaze going to Quincy. 'This is getting more into your domain than mine, but four short, identical messages are unusual. Once a killer makes contact with the press, or someone in authority, generally the communication becomes more expansive. I was a little surprised that by the last letter to the editor, at least, the message didn't include more.'

Quincy nodded. 'Communication by a killer with either the press or an officer in charge of the investigation is almost always about power. Sending letters and watching those messages be retold by the media gives certain subjects the same kind of vicarious thrill other killers experience when revisiting the scene of the crime or handling a souvenir from one of their victims. Killers will generally start small – an initial note or phone call – but once they know they have everyone's attention, the communication becomes about boasting, bragging, and constantly reasserting their sense of control. It's all part of their ego trip. This message . . .' Quincy frowned. 'It's different.'

'He distances himself from the act,' Ennunzio said. 'Notice the phrase, "heat kills." Not that he kills, that *heat* kills. It's as if he has nothing to do with it.'

'Yet the message is filled with short phrases, which you said earlier indicates a higher level of intelligence.'

'He's smart, but guilty,' Ennunzio told them. 'He doesn't want to kill, but feels driven to do it, and thus seeks to lay the blame elsewhere. Maybe that's why he hasn't written more. For him, the letters aren't about establishing power, but seeking absolution.'

'There's another possibility,' Quincy said shortly. 'Berkowitz also wrote extensively to the press in an attempt to explain his crimes. Berkowitz, however, suffered from mental illness; he falls into a different category than the organized killer. Now people suffering from some kind of mental incapacity such as delusions or schizophrenia—'

'Often repeat a phrase,' Ennunzio filled in. 'You also see that in stroke victims or people with brain tumors. They'll have anything from a word to a mantra they repeat over and over again.'

'You're saying this guy is insane?' Rainie spoke up sharply.

'It's one possibility.'

'But if he's nuts, how has he successfully eluded the police while kidnapping and killing eight women?'

'I didn't say he was stupid,' Quincy countered mildly. 'It's possible that he's still functional in many ways. People close to him, however, would know there was something "not right" about him. He's probably a loner and ill at ease with others. It could help explain why he has spent so much time outdoors, and also why he employs an ambush style of attack. A Ted Bundy-styled killer would rely on his social skills to smooth-talk his way inside a prey's defenses. This man knows he can't.'

'This man builds elaborate riddles,' Rainie said flatly. 'He targets strangers, communicates with the press, and plays games with the police. That sounds like a good old-fashioned organized psychopath to me.'

Kaplan held up a hand. 'Okay, okay, okay. We're getting a little off track here. This so-called Eco-Killer is Georgia's problem. We're here about Special Agent McCormack.'

'What about him?' Dr Ennunzio asked with a frown.

'Do you think McCormack could've written these notes?'

'I don't know. You'd have to give me something else he's written. Why are you looking at Special Agent McCormack?'

'You haven't heard?'

'Heard what? I've been out of town at the conference. I haven't even had time to clear all my voice mail yet.'

'A body was found yesterday,' Kaplan said curtly. 'Of a young girl. On the Marine PT course. We have reason to believe McCormack might be involved.'

'There are elements of the case similar to the Eco-Killer,' Rainie added, ignoring Kaplan's dark look. 'Special Agent McCormack thinks the murder is the work of the Eco-Killer, starting over here in Virginia. Special Agent Kaplan thinks maybe McCormack is our guy, and merely staged the scene to match an old case.'

'A body was found *here*? At Quantico? Yesterday?' Ennunzio appeared dazed.

'You should leave the bomb shelter every once in a while,' Rainie told him.

'This is horrible!'

'I don't think the young girl enjoyed it much, either.'

'No, you don't understand.' Ennunzio was looking down at his notes wildly. 'I did have a theory, one thing I was going to suggest to Special Agent McCormack if I ever got a chance. It was a long shot, but . . .'

'What?' Quincy asked intently. 'Tell us.'

'Special Agent McCormack mentioned in passing that he'd started getting phone calls about the case. Some anonymous tipster trying to help them out. He believed it might be someone close to the killer, a family member or spouse. I had another idea. Given that the letters to the editor were so brief, and that most killers expand their communication over time . . .'

'Oh no,' Quincy said, closing his eyes and obviously tracking the thought. 'If the UNSUB feels guilty, if he's dissociating himself from the act . . .'

'I wanted Special Agent McCormack to either attempt to tape those calls, or write down the conversations verbatim the minute he hung up the phone,' Ennunzio said grimly. 'That way I could compare language from the caller with wording from the letters. You see, I don't think he's hearing from a family member. It's possible . . . Special Agent McCormack may be hearing from the killer himself.'

24

Tina dreamed of fire. She was tied to a stake in the middle of a pile of kindling, feeling the flames wick up her legs while the gathered crowd cheered. 'My baby,' she screamed at them. 'Don't hurt my baby!'

But no one cared. The people laughed. The fire lapped her flesh. Now it seared her fingers, starting at the tips and racing up to her elbows. Then her hair was ablaze, the flames licking her ears and singeing her eyelashes. The heat gathered and built, forcing its way into her mouth and searing her lungs. Her eyeballs melted. She felt them run down her face. Then the fire was inside her eye sockets, greedily devouring her flesh, while her brains began to boil and her face peeled back from her skull . . .

Tina awakened with a jolt. Her head flew up from the rock and she became aware of two things at once. Her eyes were swollen shut and her skin felt as if it were burning.

The mosquitoes still swarmed her head. Yellow flies, too. She batted at them feebly. She had no blood left. They should leave her alone and seek fresher prey, not some exhausted girl on the verge of dehydration. The bugs didn't seem to care. She was bathed from head to toe in sweat, which apparently in the insect world made her a feast fit for kings.

Hot, so hot. The sun was directly overhead now. She could feel it beating down on her, burning her bite-sensitive skin and parching her lips. Her throat was swollen and dry. She could feel the skin on her arms and legs shrinking beneath the harsh glare and pulling uncomfortably at her joints. She was a piece of meat left too long in the sun. She was, quite literally, being cured into a piece of human jerky.

You have to move. You have to do something.

Tina had heard the voice before, in the back of her mind. In the beginning, it had given her hope. Now, it just filled her with despair. She couldn't move, she couldn't do anything. She was nothing but mosquito fodder and if she moved off this rock, then she'd be snake fodder, too. She was sure of it. Before her eyes had swollen shut from mosquito venom, she'd taken inventory as best she could. She was in some kind of open pit, with sides that stretched out ten to fifteen feet, while the broad mouth yawned twenty feet overhead at least. She had a rock. She had her purse. She had a one-gallon jug of water the son of a bitch had probably thrown in just to toy with her.

That was it. Pit, rock, water. Only other thing around was the foul-smelling muck that oozed out from under her rocky perch. And no way was she stepping off her boulder into that slime. She'd seen things move in the marsh around her. Dark, slimy things she was certain would love to feast on human flesh. Things that genuinely frightened her.

Drink.

Can't. I won't have water, and then I'll die.

You are dying. Drink.

She groped around for the bottle of water. It too felt hot to the touch. She'd had a little when she'd first woken up, but then quickly recapped the precious supply. Her resources were limited. In her purse, she had a pack of gum and a package of six peanut-butter crackers. She also had a little baggy filled with twelve saltines, the perks of being a pregnant woman.

Pregnant woman. She was supposed to be drinking at least eight glasses of water a day to help support the whole new infrastructure being built in her tummy. She should also be eating an extra three hundred calories a day, as well as getting plenty of rest. Nowhere in the preparing-for-parenthood book had it talked about surviving on three sips of water and a couple of crackers. How long could she go on like this? How long could her baby?

The thought both discouraged her and brought her strength. Her inner voice was right. She wasn't going to make it on this god-forsaken rock in this god-forsaken pit. She was already dying. She might as well put up a fight.

Tina worked grimly with her swollen fingers at the plastic cap of the water jug. At the last minute, it popped off wildly and went soaring somewhere in the muck. No matter. She brought the jug to her lips and drank greedily. The water was hot and tasted of cooked plastic. She downed it gratefully, each giant gulp soothing her rusty throat. Second turned into wonderful, indulgent second. At the last minute, she tore the jug from her lips, gasping for breath and already desperate for more.

Her thirst felt like a separate beast, freshly awakened and now ravenous.

'Crackers,' she told herself firmly. 'Salt is good.'

She set the jug down carefully, feeling along the rock for a stable spot. Then she found her purse and after painful minutes fumbling with the zipper, got it open.

The mosquitoes had returned, attracted by the smell of fresh water. Yellow flies buzzed her lips, settling on the corners as if they'd sip the moisture straight from her mouth. She slapped savagely, and had the brief satisfaction of feeling plump insect bodies burst against her fingers. Then more flies were back, crawling on her lips, her eyes, the soft tissue of her inner ear, and she knew she had to let them go. Ignore the constant pricking bites, the awful dreadful hum. Give up this battle, or most certainly lose the war.

Grimly, she set about searching her purse. Her fingers found the baggy of saltines and drew them out. She counted out six. A dozen bites later, they were gone. The salty, dry texture immediately intensified her thirst.

Just one sip, she thought. To chase down the saltines. To soothe her pain, because oh God, the flies, the flies, the flies. They were everywhere, buzzing and biting and the more she tried to ignore them the more they skittered across her skin and sank little teeth deep into her flesh. She wasn't going to make it after all. She was going to go insane and the least a crazy person could do was drink.

She reached for the bottle, then snatched back her hand. No, she'd had water. She'd had sustenance. Not much, but enough. After all, she didn't know how long she'd been down here. Earlier, she'd screamed for a full hour without any luck. Best she could tell, the rat bastard had dropped her somewhere remote and isolated. If that was true, it was up to her. She had to be smart, stay calm. She had to think of a plan.

She rubbed her eyes. Bad idea. They immediately burned. Some of that water would feel so nice on her face. She could rinse out her eyes, maybe get them to crack open so she could see. Rinse off the sweat, then maybe the mosquitoes would finally leave her alone.

Stupid. Pipe dream. She was sweating down to her toes, her green sundress plastered to her skin and her underwear soaked straight through. She hadn't been this hot since she'd sat naked in a Swedish sauna. Rinsing her face would buy her respite for about two seconds. And then she'd be sweat-soaked and miserable again.

The key was to marshal her resources and use them sparingly.

She also had to get out of the sun. Find someplace shady and relatively cool for the day. Then she could make her escape at night.

She remembered the weather forecast now. Hot, working toward even hotter. Probably breaking triple digits by the end of the week. Not much time, especially if she was already feeling this exhausted.

She had to get moving. Get out of this pit, or die here.

Tina wasn't ready to die yet.

She used her fingers on her puffy eyelids, prying open the painful, swollen flesh. Some kind of thick liquid drained down her face. She held her eyelids open resolutely, permitting only a few short blinks.

In the beginning, nothing. And then . . . the goo cleared from her eyes and the world slowly came into focus. Bright, harsh, punishing.

Tina inspected her surroundings. Below her was some kind of thick, wet muck. Above her, fifteen to twenty feet overhead, was the mouth of the pit. And beyond that? She had no idea. She could see no signs of bushes, trees, or shrubs. Whatever was up there, however, it surely had to be better than what was down here.

She turned her inspection to the walls. Balancing herself carefully on the edge of the boulder, she counted to three, then let her upper body fall forward. Her red, inflamed hands hit the surface hard. She felt a moment of stunning, cracking pain. Then she was there, feet on the boulders, the rest of her leaning against the side of the pit.

The side was cooler than she would've thought. Wet with something she didn't understand. Green, she decided at last. Slippery. Like a rock covered with algae or maybe mold. Tina wanted to yank back her hand in revulsion. Instead, she forced her fingers to spread, feeling around for handholds.

Not rock, she determined after a moment. The rough texture was too consistent, without any protruding knobs or zigzagging crevices. It was gravelly, lightly scraping her palms. Concrete, she realized abruptly. Oh my God, she was in a man-made pit. The son of a bitch had dropped her into his own homemade hell!

Did that mean she was in a backyard? Her thoughts raced. Maybe some kind of residential area? If she could just climb up, then, find some way to the surface . . .

But if she was in a populated area, why hadn't someone responded to all of her screams? And what about the muck? That oozy, swampy mud, teaming with things she didn't want to know . . .

He probably had a place out in the country, or deep in the woods. Someplace far from civilization, where no one would ever be the wiser. That would make more sense, given the things he liked to do.

But still, if she could climb out . . . Once on the surface she could run, hide, find a road, follow a stream. Even if she was deep in the middle of nowhere, up top she had a chance. It was more than she could say down here.

She resumed scouring the bumpy walls with her hands. Faster now. More determined. A moment later, she found it. A vine. Long and green and tangled. Then another, and another. Some kind of invasive species, either seeking the mud or trying to escape. It didn't matter to her.

Tina wrapped three vines around her hand and gave them an experimental tug. They seemed strong and resilient. She could use them like rope. Balance her feet against the wall and use the vines to pull her way up. Why not? She'd seen it dozens of times on TV.

Fired with purpose now, she got serious. She pushed herself back onto her rocky perch and examined her worldly goods.

She needed her purse; it had food and who knows what else might come in handy. Easy enough. She slung it over her shoulder and tried not to wince as the leather rubbed against her sunburned flesh. The water was trickier. It didn't fit in her purse and she didn't think she could grip a gallon jug and the vines in the same hand.

Briefly, she considered drinking all of it. Why not? It would feel so good going down her throat. Wonderful and wet. And she was making a break for it. Escaping from this hell. If she got on top, she wouldn't need supplies anymore, would she?

Of course, she had no way of knowing that. She didn't even know what was up there. No, no more drinking. The water needed to go with her. Even if it was heavy and hot to the touch. It was the only supply she had.

Her dress. The material was thin and wispy. She could tear it into strips and use them to tie the jug to her purse. She reached down with both hands and yanked at her hem. The material immediately slid undamaged from her grip. Her fingers were swollen and refused to cooperate. She tried again and again, panting hard, working herself into a frenzy.

The damn material refused to tear. She needed scissors. Of all the things not to have in her purse.

She bit back a sob. Feeling defeated again as the mosquitoes welcomed her stillness by once more resuming to feed. She had to move, she had to do something!

Her bra. She could take that off and loop it through the gallon jug with the shoulder straps serving as a handle. Or better yet, she could wrap the bra around her purse strap and let the water hang from her purse. Then her hands would be free for climbing. Perfect.

She lifted the hem of her sundress and peeled it from her skin. The flies and mosquitoes instantly got excited. Fresh, white flesh. New, unbloodied areas. She tried not to think about it as she worked on removing her sweat-soaked bra. The nylon fabric was sticky to the touch. She grimaced and finally got it off with a sigh.

It seemed pure cruelty to yank back on her dripping, stinky dress. It felt so much better to be naked in this heat, no uncomfortable fabric rubbing her raw, salty skin. The faintest of breezes wafting against her breasts, her back . . .

She gritted her teeth, and forced her dress back on, the fabric rolling and twisting uncooperatively as she wiggled. For one moment, her foot slipped on the rock. She teetered precariously, looking down at the oozing mud. She dropped down on the rock and held on tight.

Her heart hammered against her ribs. Oh she wanted done with this. She wanted to go home. She wanted to see her mother. She wanted a wonderful Minnesotan winter, when she could run outside and fling herself into the deep white snow. She remembered how the flakes tasted on the tip of her tongue. The sensation of fresh icy crystals melting in her mouth. The delicate tickle of more flakes feathering across her eyelashes.

Was she crying now? It was so hard to know with all the sweat on her face and the flies encrusting the corners of her eyes.

'I love you, Ma,' Tina whispered. And then she had to break off the thought before she definitely wept.

She looped her bra around the jug handle, fastened it around her purse and pushed it behind herself. The dragging weight of it was awkward, and the water sloshed up dangerously close to the uncapped top, but it was the best she could do. She had her supplies. Next.

She balanced on the rock, then grimly fell forward against the wall. Her hands scraped against the surface, catching her weight. Then she searched for vines. She found six. She wrapped three around each hand, feeling them bite into her sunburned hands. Time to grin and bear it.

Tina stepped out of her highly impractical shoes. One last

deep breath. The sun beating down on her head. The sweat rolling down her cheeks. The bugs, buzzing, buzzing, buzzing.

Tina pulled on the vines with both arms while simultaneously throwing her right foot at the wall. Her toes scrabbled for traction against the algae-slick surface, found a drier patch and dug in. On the count of three, she heaved up with her arms.

And simultaneously felt the vines give way. She was falling back, her leg already kicking back, trying to find her rocky perch. The water gallon jug swung wildly, further upsetting her balance. She wasn't going to make it, she was going to fall into the stroking muck.

Tina pushed desperately with her hands, releasing her panicked grip on the vines. She went careening back onto her rock. Windmilling, twisting, then suddenly, gratefully, collapsing down onto the stable surface. The water, water, water. Her hands frantically found the jug, still magically upright and holding the last of her precious supply.

She was back on her rock, she had some water, she was safe.

The vines collapsed into the muck below. As they did so, she noticed their edges. Cut clean halfway through. And then came the fluttering piece of white paper, as if loosened by the turbulence above.

Tina reached up a tired hand and felt the paper fall into her palm.

She drew it toward her.

It read: heat kills.

'You son of a bitch,' Tina tried to scream, but her throat was too dry, rendering. The words a mere whispered rasp. She licked her lips. It did no good. And then she hung her head tiredly, and felt the last of her strength leech from her body.

She needed more food. She needed more water. She needed a break from this desperate heat if she was ever going to survive. And now the bugs were back, the mosquitoes, the yellow flies, feasting, feasting, feasting.

'I'm not going to die down here,' she muttered resolutely, trying to summon some force of will. 'Dammit, I won't do it.'

But if she couldn't make it up out of the pit . . .

Very slowly, Tina's gaze went to the thick, slithering muck.

25

'The search area has been divided into ten different sections. Each team of two should analyze their section on the map, then work it in the standard grid pattern. In the good news department, since the hiker has been missing for only twenty-four hours, she shouldn't have wandered beyond a thirty-mile radius, giving us a fairly contained target for search. In the bad news department, this thirty-mile radius contains some of the harshest, steepest terrain in the entire park. Here's what you need to know:

'One, lost hikers inevitably head down. They're tired, they're fatigued and once they lose their sense of direction, they'll head down the mountain even when help lies just twenty feet away over the next hill. Two, hikers will also gravitate toward the sound of running water. Everyone knows how important water is, especially someone who is disoriented. If there is water in your section of the grid, check the areas around the streams carefully and follow them for as long as you can. Three, once off the groomed hiking trails, this is rough country. The underbrush is thick, the footing treacherous. Be on the lookout for upturned rocks, broken branches, and trampled underbrush. If this woman is still on the trails, chances are someone would've seen her by now. So most likely she's in the wild and we're going to have to do this the hard way.'

Kathy Levine paused for a moment, gazing out somberly over the group of twenty search-and-rescue volunteers now gathered at Big Meadows Lodge. 'It's hot out, people. Yeah, no kidding, you're thinking. But I mean it. In this kind of heat index, dehydration is a constant threat. The rule of thumb is that two quarts of water a day keeps dehydration away. Unfortunately, in these conditions your body can easily lose a quart of water per hour through your lungs and pores, so two quarts isn't going to cut it. Frankly, each person should carry two gallons of water, but since that weight would be prohibitive, we're requiring each rescue team to carry either water tablets or a water purification system. Then you can refill your water supply at the various streams you encounter along the way. *Don't drink untreated stream water.* Sure the water looks clear and pretty up here, but most of it is contaminated by *Giardia lamblia* – a parasite which is guaranteed to give you a bad case of the seven-day trots. Drink often, but drink smart.

'Now assuming that you stay properly hydrated, don't slip down a steep hillside, or stumble upon a sleeping bear, there are a few final things to keep in mind. For example, rattlesnakes. We have plenty. Every now and then, you'll come to a clear meadow with a pile of rocks from an old landslide. Looks like a terrific place to sit down. Don't. The snakes think so, too, and most of those rocks are their homes. Let's not argue with them. Second, we have hornets. They like to build nests in old hollows in the ground or in rotten logs. If you leave them alone, they'll leave you alone. If you step into a nest, however . . . Might I recommend *not* running back to your partner. You'll only drag him into the mess and one of you will need to be able to hike back for help. Finally, we have stinging nettles. If you haven't ever seen one, they are about thigh-high with broad green leaves. If you boil them, they actually make a pretty good green to go with dinner. Walk into them, however, and welcome to nature's version of fiberglass. The prickers get immediately under the skin and emit a poison that remains long after the thistles are gone. It takes a good thirty to sixty minutes for the inflammation to subside and by then, you'll have renounced everything you once held dear.

'This park is beautiful. I've walked almost every inch of it in the last five years and I can't think of a more beautiful spot on earth. But nature also commands respect. We need to be focused. We need to move fast. But in these conditions, I also need each and every one of you to always be using your head. Our goal is to find one person, not lose anymore. Any questions?' Levine paused. There were none. 'Good,' she said crisply. 'Let's move. We have only four and a half hours of daylight left.'

The group broke up, people finding their search partners and heading out of the lodge. Everyone had received their assignment, and most seemed to understand the drill. Mac and Kimberly were probably the biggest rookies of the bunch and Mac had done his fair share of search and rescue work by now. Kimberly, he could tell, was more uncomfortable. She had the gear, she had the fitness. But by her own admission, she'd never spent much time in the woods.

If what Kathy Levine had said was correct, this was going to be quite an adventure.

'What do you think she meant by the hornets?' Kimberly said now as they trudged out of the wonderfully air-conditioned lodge into the searing heat. 'If the hornets build their nests in the ground and we're walking on the ground, how are we supposed to avoid them?'

'Look where you step,' Mac said. He stopped, held up the

map they'd been given, and worked on orienting it to their surroundings. They were officially Search Team D, assigned to search the three square miles of, logically enough, Search Area D.

'But if I'm looking at the ground, how am I supposed to look for a lost woman or broken branches or whatever?'

'It's just like driving. You look ahead ten feet to know what's coming, then gaze around all you want, then scope out the next ten feet. Look, glance, look, glance, look, glance. Okay, according to the map, we enter the trailhead there.'

'I thought we weren't on a trail. Levine said we were in the "wild country" – whatever the hell that means.'

'We are,' Mac said patiently. 'But the first quarter of a mile is on a trail. Then we veer off into the wild underbelly of the beast.'

'How will we know which way to go?'

'We chart and map usin' compass points. It'll be slow, but thorough.'

Kimberly barely nodded. She was gazing nervously at the dark forest before them, carpeted in nine shades of green. Mac saw beauty. Kimberly, however, obviously saw something worse.

'Tell me again how often you've done this?' she whispered.

'I assisted with two of the search operations in Georgia.'

'You said people got hurt.'

'Yep.'

'You said he sets up scenarios like this, just to torture us.'

'Yep.'

'He's a real son of a bitch, isn't he?'

'Oh, yeah.'

Kimberly nodded. She squared her shoulders, her chin coming up in that set he already knew so well. 'All right,' she said stiffly. 'We're going to find this girl, we're going to save the day, and then we're going to walk out of this park so we can nail the bastard. Deal?'

'You are a woman after my own heart,' Mac said soberly.

They pushed ahead into the thick, dark woods.

Footing was easy on the dirt trail. Steep, but manageable, with rocky ledges and worn tree roots forming a natural cascade of stairs. Shady, with the dense canopy of trees blocking out the sun. The heat and humidity, however, were harder to escape. Mac was already short of breath, his lungs laboring as they headed down the path. Within minutes, his face was drenched in sweat, and he could feel moisture beading uncomfortably between his shoulder blades, where his backpack pressed against his shirt. The sun was bad, but the humidity was their true enemy. It turned the high mountain woods from a shady reprieve to a steaming jungle where each footstep required hard physical effort and four hours of intense hiking would be about three hours too much.

Both Mac and Kimberly had changed clothes for the operation. Kimberly now wore khaki shorts and a short-sleeved cotton T-shirt, the casual outfit of an amateur day hiker. More experienced, Mac had donned nylon shorts and a quick-drying nylon top. As he began to sweat, the synthetic material wicked the moisture away from his body, allowing him a small degree of comfort. Kimberly's cotton T-shirt, on the other hand, was already plastered against her body. Soon, the shirt, as well as her shorts, would start to chafe her skin painfully. He wondered if she would complain, but already figured she wouldn't.

'Do you think she's still alive?' Kimberly asked tersely. Her breath also came out in short pants, but she was matching stride with stride. When called upon to perform, the lady didn't disappoint.

'I read a study once of search-and-rescue operations,' Mac replied. 'Of the fatalities, seventy-five percent died in the first forty-eight hours. Assuming this girl was abandoned yesterday, that gives us another twenty-four hours to find her.'

'What,' *pant, pant,* 'generally kills' *pant, pant,* 'lost people?'

'Hypothermia. Or on a day like this, heat stroke. Basically, it's exposure that does a person in. Here's a fact for you: Did you know that children under the age of six actually have the highest survival rate when lost in the woods?'

Kimberly shook her head.

'Kids are better at listening to their instincts,' Mac explained. 'When they're tired, they sleep. When they're frightened, they seek shelter. Adults, on the other hand, are always convinced they can regain control. So rather than get out of the rain or the cold or the sun, they keep walking, determined that safety is just around the corner. It's exactly the wrong thing to do. Your odds are much better if you remain calm and stay in one place. After all, the average person can last up to five days with no water and up to a month without food. Wear yourself out walking, however, and you'll succumb to exposure, fall off a cliff, stumble into a bear's den, etc., etc. Next thing you know, the lost hiker's dead in forty-eight hours, when any old schmuck should be able to last a week.'

Mac stopped abruptly. He looked at the map again, then his compass. 'Hang on. Yep. We head off here.'

Kimberly came to a halt beside him and he could feel her uneasiness immediately increase tenfold. There was no clearly marked trail in front of them. Instead, the earth opened up, then plummeted down, a tumbling mess of boulders, bushes, and grass. Fallen trees lay directly in their way, overgrown with shaggy moss and brilliant ferns. Jagged branches stuck out dangerously low, while some kind of thick green vine covered half the trees in sight.

The woods were dense, dark, green. Kathy Levine was right: they held secrets that were both beautiful and deadly.

'If we get separated,' Mac said quietly, 'just stay in one place and blow your whistle. I'll find you.'

All the search-and-rescue operatives had been given shrill

plastic whistles. One blow was to communicate between partners. Two blows meant a team had found the girl. Three shrills was the international call for distress.

Kimberly's gaze had gone to the ground. Mac could practically see her eyes scouring each rock and thicket for signs of rattlesnakes or hornets. Her hand now rested on the top of her left thigh. Where she had the knife strapped, he guessed, and immediately felt his gut tighten with a shot of good, old-fashioned male lust. He did not know why an armed woman should be so arousing, but man oh man, this one was.

'We're going to be fine,' he said.

Kimberly finally looked at him. 'Don't make promises you can't keep,' she said. Then she stepped off the path into the wild underbrush.

Footing quickly grew rough. Twice Kimberly slipped and tumbled halfway down a steep slope. Long, thick grass offered little traction, even for her hiking boots, and rocks and tree roots stuck up in the damnedest places. If she looked down for obstacles, then a stray tree limb would catch her up high. If she looked up high, she risked taking a fallen log in the shin. If she tried looking everywhere at once, she fell, a lot, regularly, and with generally painful, bloody results.

Within two hours, her legs wore a crisscross of scratches to match the ones still healing on her face. She avoided hornets, but blundered into a patch of poison ivy. She stopped running into dead logs, but twice twisted her ankles on slippery rocks.

All in all, she wasn't enjoying the woods much. She supposed it should be beautiful, but to her it wasn't. She felt the loneliness of this place, where the sound of your companion's footsteps was swallowed up by moss-covered rocks, and even knowing there was another search party within three miles, she didn't hear a peep. She felt the disorientation of the towering trees that blocked out the sun and made it difficult to get a sense of direction. The rough, undulating landscape meant they were often walking down to go up, or walking up to go down. Which way was north, south, east, west? Kimberly didn't know anymore, and that left her feeling anxious in a way she couldn't fully explain.

The immense size of the woods swallowed her up as effectively as any ocean. Now she was drowning in greenness, not sure how to get her head up, or which way to head for shore. She was a city girl who was way out of her league. And in a place like this, so much could go wrong without anyone ever finding your body.

She tried to focus on the missing woman to distract herself. If the girl had started the night at a bar, then she was probably wearing sandals. Had she gotten smart and ditched them right away? Kimberly had already slipped several times in hiking boots. Sandals would be impossible. Bare feet not great, but at least more manageable.

Where would she strike out first? Head down is what Kathy Levine had said; lost hikers seek the easier path. In Kimberly's mind, this path wasn't that easy. Having to pick and choose for footing required slow, laborious work. Maybe it wasn't as aerobic as hiking up, but the muscles in her legs and butt were already screaming while her heart beat furiously.

Would the girl try to seek shelter? Someplace she could stay cool and not wear herself out? Mac had implied that staying put was the key. Be calm, in control, don't just wander around in a daze.

Kimberly looked around her, at the arching trees, the looming shadows, and the deep crevices with all their unknown inhabitants.

She bet the girl had started out at a dead run. She bet she'd torn through these bushes and trees, desperately seeking some sign of civilization. She'd probably screamed for hours, wearing herself hoarse with the need for human contact. And when night had fallen, when the woods had filled with the louder sounds of bigger beasts and buzzing insects . . .

The girl had probably run again. Tripped. Fallen. Maybe gone headfirst into a poison ivy patch or into a hornet's nest. And what would have happened to her then? Stung, terrorized, half-dressed, and lost in the dark?

She'd seek water, anything to cool her wounds. And because whatever lurked in the streams had to be less dangerous than the creatures that stalked the woods.

Kimberly halted abruptly, holding up a hand. 'Do you hear it?' she asked Mac sharply.

'Water,' Mac agreed. From his backpack, he retrieved his map. 'There's a stream directly to the west.'

'We should follow it. That's what Levine said, right? Hikers are drawn to water.'

'Sounds like a plan to me.'

Kimberly stepped left . . .

And her foot went totally out from under her. One moment she was on solid ground. The next, her leg shot out and she went careening butt-first down the slippery slope of grass. Her hip bounded over a rock. Her thigh scraped by a fallen log. Desperately she tried to get her hands beneath her, while vaguely she was aware of Mac shouting her name behind her.

'Kimberly!!!'

'Ahhhhhhhhhh.' Thump. Thunk. Another dead log reared up ahead, and she slammed into it with all the grace of a rhino. Stars burst in front of her eyes. A buzzing roared through her ears. She was acutely aware of the rusty taste of blood in her mouth where she had bitten her tongue. And then, all at once, her body caught fire.

'Shit. Damn. Oh what the hell!' She was on her feet, slapping at her arms and legs. It hurt, it hurt, it hurt, like a million little fire ants biting her skin again and again and again. She bolted out of the weeds and went scrambling back up the hillside, grabbing at tree limbs with her hands while churning up the grass with her feet.

She made it fifteen feet back up and not a single inch of it helped. Her skin burned. Her blood roared. She watched helplessly as her body suddenly bloomed with a bright red rash.

Mac finally came crashing to a halt in front of her. 'Don't scratch, don't scratch, don't scratch.'

'What the hell is it?' she cried frantically.

'Congratulations, honey, I think you just found the stinging nettles.'

26

'So what do we have?' Quincy asked. It was after eight o'clock now. He, Rainie, Special Agent Kaplan, and Supervisor Watson had taken over an unused classroom for their ad hoc meeting. No one looked particularly cheerful. For one thing, half of them were still wrung out from working the crime scene in this heat. For another, they had nothing to show for their fourteen-hour day.

'I think we still have to look harder at McCormack,' Kaplan insisted. 'In this business, you know there is no such thing as coincidence. And him being here at the same time one of his old cases heats up . . . That's too much coincidence for me.'

'It was not coincidental, it was planned.' Rainie spoke up in exasperation. Her opinion on this matter was clear, and now she shook her head in disgust at Kaplan. 'You spoke to his boss. You know what McCormack said was true.'

'People cover for their own.'

'So the entire GBI is in on the crime? We've simply gone from coincidence to conspiracy theory.'

Lisa Gardner

Quincy held up his hand, attempting to cut off this argument before it got going. Again. 'What about the ad?' he asked Kaplan.

'According to the Public Affairs Officer, the ad arrived yesterday, with instructions to run in today's paper. The *Quantico Sentry*, however, is a weekly paper. Next edition doesn't come out until this Friday. Besides, the officer didn't like the look of the ad. Seemed like code to him, maybe something drug related, so he passed it my way.'

Kaplan pushed a photocopy of the ad in question across the table. It was a small, two-by-two inch box, outlined with a black border and containing one block of text. The text read: Dear Editor, Clock ticking . . . planet dying . . . animals weeping . . . rivers screaming. Can't you hear it? Heat kills . . .

'Why an ad?' Watson spoke up.

'*Quantico Sentry* doesn't do letters to the editor.'

'What are the rules for ad submissions?' Quincy asked.

Kaplan shrugged. 'The newspaper is a civilian enterprise, published in cooperation with the Public Affairs Office here on the base, so it covers anything topical to the area. Lots of local merchants advertise, charities reach out, services for military personnel, etc. It's no different really than any other small, regional paper. Ads must be submitted typeset and with a payment. Otherwise, you're pretty much good to go.'

'So our guy took the time to learn the submission requirements for an ad, but still didn't realize the paper wouldn't print it today?' Watson asked skeptically. 'Doesn't seem too bright to me.'

'He got what he wanted,' Quincy said quietly. 'It's the next day, and we're reading his message.'

'Pure chance,' Watson said dismissively.

'No. This man does everything with a purpose. *Quantico Sentry* is the Corps' oldest newspaper. It's part of their tradition and pride. Putting his message in this paper is the same as dumping a body on the base. He's bringing his crime close to home. He's demanding our attention.'

'It fits the pattern,' Rainie said. 'So far we have the same MO as with the Eco-Killer, and now we have the letter too. I'd say the next step is pretty obvious.'

'And what would that be?' Watson asked.

'Call McCormack! Get him back in on this thing. He knows this guy better than we do. And, since there's probably another girl out there, maybe we ought to get some experts looking once more at the body, let alone those little details like the rattlesnake, leaf, and rock. Come on. As the ad says, clock is ticking, and we've already wasted the entire day.'

'I sent them to the lab,' Kaplan said quietly.

'You did what?' Rainie asked incredulously.

'I sent the rock, the leaf and well, the various snake bits to the Norfolk crime lab.'

'And what the hell is a crime lab going to do with them? Dust them for prints?'

'It's not a bad idea—'

'It's a fucking horrible idea! Weren't you listening to McCormack before? We've got to find the *girl!*'

'Hey!' Quincy's hand was up again, his voice loud and commanding across the table. Not that it did much good. Rainie was already half out of her chair, her hands fisted. And Kaplan appeared just as eager for a battle. It had been a long day. Hot, tiring, wearing. The kind of conditions that led to an increase in bar brawls, let alone a deterioration of cooperation in multi-jurisdictional homicide cases.

'We need to proceed along two tracks,' Quincy continued firmly. 'So shut up, sit down, and pay attention. Rainie's correct – we need to move quickly.'

Rainie slowly sank back down into her chair. Kaplan, too, grudgingly gave him his attention.

'One, let's assume that perhaps this man is the Eco-Killer. Ep, ep, ep!' Kaplan was already opening his mouth to protest. Quincy gave him the same withering look he'd once used on junior agents, and the NCIS agent shut right up. 'While we cannot be one hundred percent certain of this, the fact remains that we have a homicide that fits a pattern previously seen in Georgia. Given the similarities, we need to consider that another woman has also been abducted. If so, according to what happened in Georgia, we need to start approaching the evidence we've found on the body as pieces of a geographic puzzle.' He looked at Kaplan.

'I can arrange for some experts in botany, biology, and geology to look at what we have,' the special agent said grudgingly.

'Quickly,' Rainie spoke up.

Kaplan gave her a look. 'Yes, ma'am.'

Rainie merely smiled at him.

Quincy took another deep breath. 'Secondly,' he said, 'we need to explore some broader avenues. While I've read summaries of the Georgia case notes, it seems clear to me that they've never come close to knowing much about the killer. They generated a profile and a list of suppositions, none of which have ever been proven either way. I think we should start clean-slate, generating our own impressions based on *this* crime. For example, why plant the body on Quantico grounds? That seems clearly like a man who is making a statement against authority. He feels so invincible, he can operate even within the heart of America's elite law enforcement agency. Then we have the UNSUB's various letters to the editor, as well as his phone calls to Special Agent McCormack. Again this raises several questions. Is this an UNSUB seeking to reassert his feelings of power and control? Or is this a conflicted man, who is reaching out to law enforcement in the dim hope that he will be caught? Also, is the anonymous caller really our UNSUB, or someone else entirely?

'And there is a third motive we should also contemplate. That this killer's game is not targeted at either the Marines or the FBI, but rather, at Special Agent McCormack specifically.'

'Oh you have got to be kidding me,' Kaplan grumbled.

Quincy gave the man his cool, hard stare. 'Assume for a moment that the anonymous caller is the UNSUB. Through his comments, he brought Special Agent McCormack to Virginia. It stands to reason then, that the UNSUB already had a plan of attack in mind for this area. And furthermore, as part of this plan, he knew of Special Agent McCormack's whereabouts and thus made sure to start the game here. The ad in the *Quantico Sentry* would fit this pattern. As of Friday, the paper would be distributed all over the base. Surely McCormack would get the hint.'

Rainie appeared troubled. 'That's getting out there,' she said quietly.

'True. Killers rarely target a specific member of law enforcement. But stranger things have happened, and as the lead officer, McCormack was the most visible member of the Georgia task force. If the UNSUB *were* going to identify with a specific target, McCormack would be the logical one.'

'So we have two options,' Rainie murmured. 'A garden-variety psychopath trying to mess with McCormack's head. Or a more troubled, guilt-stricken nut who's still murdering girls, but showing signs of remorse. Why doesn't either one of these theories help me sleep better at night?'

'Because either way, the man is deadly.' Quincy turned toward Kaplan. 'I assume you sent out the ad to the *Quantico Sentry* to be analyzed?'

'Tried,' Kaplan said. 'Not much to work with. Stamp and envelope are both self-adhesive, so no saliva. Latent found no prints on the paper, and the ad was typeset, so no handwriting.'

'What about form of payment?'

'Cash. You're not supposed to send it through the mail, but apparently our killer is a trusting soul.'

'Postmark?'

'Stafford.'

'The town next door?'

'Yeah, sent yesterday. Local job all the way. Guy's in the area to murder a woman, might as well send his note as well.'

Quincy raised a brow. 'He's smart. Done his homework. Well, stationery is a good place to start. Dr Ennunzio said that Georgia had sent him one original letter to the editor. I'd like you to turn over this ad to him as well. Perhaps that gives him two data points to consider.'

Kaplan had to think about it. 'He can have it for a week,' he conceded at last. 'Then I want it back at my lab.'

'Your cooperation is duly noted,' Quincy assured him.

There was a knock on the door. Quincy thinned his lips, frustrated by the intrusion when they were finally getting somewhere, but Kaplan was already climbing to his feet. 'Probably one of my agents,' he said by way of explanation. 'I told him I'd be around here.'

He opened the classroom door, and sure enough, a younger buzz-cut man entered the room. The agent was holding a piece of paper and his body practically thrummed with excitement.

'I thought you'd want to see this right away,' the younger officer said immediately.

Kaplan took the paper, glanced at it, then looked up sharply. 'Are you sure about this?'

'Yes sir. Got it confirmed fifteen minutes ago.'

'What?' Rainie was asking. Even Watson strained in his chair. Kaplan turned back to them slowly.

'We got an ID on the girl,' he said, and his gaze went to Quincy. 'It's not just like Georgia after all. Sweet Jesus, this is much, much worse.'

* * *

'Water break.'

'Soon.'

'Kimberly, water break.'

'I want to see what's around the next corner—'

'Honey, stop and drink some water, or I will tackle you.'

Kimberly scowled at him. Mac's face remained resolute. He'd halted ten feet back, at a boulder jutting out from the stream they were following down the steep slope.

After three hours of hard hiking, half of her body was covered in a bright red rash – poison ivy, stinging nettles, take your pick. Her T-shirt was sweated through. Her shorts were drenched. Even her socks squished as she walked. Then there was the sodden skullcap that now passed as her hair.

In contrast, Mac stood with one knee bent comfortably on a large boulder. His damp gray nylon shirt molded his impressive chest. His short dark hair was slicked back to better highlight his bronzed, chiseled face. He wasn't breathing hard. He didn't have a scratch on him. Three hours of brutal trekking later, the man looked like a damn L.L.Bean cover model.

'Bite me,' Kimberly said, but she finally stopped and grudgingly dug out her water bottle. The water was tepid and tasted of plastic. It still felt good going down her throat. She was hot. Her chest heaved. Her legs trembled. She'd had easier times on the Marine's obstacle course.

'At least the heat keeps the ticks down,' Mac said conversationally.

'What?'

'The ticks. They don't like it when it's this hot. Now if it were spring or fall . . .'

Kimberly gazed down frantically at her bare legs. Beneath the red rash, were any of her freckles moving? Blood-sucking parasites, that ought to top off the day . . . Then she registered the underlying humor in Mac's voice and looked up suspiciously.

'You're living dangerously,' she growled.

He merely grinned. 'Are you thinking of going for your knife? I've been waitin' all day.'

'Not to put a damper on your male fantasies, but I'm sorry I wore the knife. It's rubbing off all the skin on my thigh and damn near killing me.'

'Would you like to remove it? I could assist.'

'Oh, for heaven's sake.'

She turned away from him, swiping a hand through her short-cropped hair. Her palm came back wet and salty, disgusting even her. She must look like a wreck. And still he flirted with her. The man was obviously insane.

Her gaze went to the sun. From this vantage point, she could just see it sinking low in the sky. Funny, it was easy to lose track of night around here. The trees already cast so much of the landscape into shadow, and it wasn't as if the temperature was magically cooling down. But the sun was definitely retreating, the hour growing late.

'Not much time,' she murmured.

'No,' he agreed, his voice now as somber as her own.

'We should get going.' She bent to put her water bottle away. He stepped toward her and halted her hand with his own.

'You need to drink more.'

'I just had water!'

'You're not drinking enough. You've only gone through a quart. You heard Kathy Levine. In these conditions you're probably sweating through at least that much an hour. Drink more, Kimberly. It's important.'

His fingers were still on her arm. Not gripping, certainly not bruising. She felt his touch anyway, more than she should. His fingertips were calloused. His palm was damp, probably as sweaty as the rest of him, as the rest of her. She still didn't move away.

And for the first time . . .

She thought about moving closer. She thought about kissing him. He was the kind of man who would be very good at kissing. She imagined he would be slow and thorough. Kissing for him would be like flirting, a fun bit of foreplay he'd been practicing for most of his life.

And for her?

It would be desperate. She knew that without having to think why. It would be need and hope and anger. It would be a vain attempt to leave behind her own body, to break free of the relentless anxiety that shadowed every step she took. To forget for a moment that a young woman was lost out here, and she was trying so hard, but maybe she still wasn't good enough. She hadn't saved her sister. She hadn't saved her mother. Why did she think this time would be different?

She needed too much. She wanted too deeply. This man could laugh his way through life. While Kimberly would one day simply die trying.

Kimberly stepped away. After another moment, she brought back up her water bottle and took a long, deep drink.

'Times like these,' she said after drinking, 'you should be able to push yourself harder.'

Her tone was goading, but Mac merely arched a brow.

'You think I'm soft?'

She shrugged. 'I think we're running out of daylight. I think we should be moving more, and talking less.'

'Kimberly, what time is it?'

'A little after eight.'

'And where are we?'

'Somewhere in our three-mile grid, I guess.'

'Honey, we've been hiking *down* for three hours now. We're about to go down more, because like you, I also want to see what's around that next bend. Now, you want to tell me how we're going to complete our three-hour hike down *and* magically make it back up to base camp in the one hour of daylight we have left?'

'I . . . I don't know.'

'It can't be done,' he said flatly. 'Come dark, we'll still be in these woods, plain and simple. Good news, according to my map, we're close to a trail due west. I figure we finish off this section of the stream, leave a marker, then find the trail before dark. Footing there will be better, and we can use my flashlight to pick our way back up. That way, it'll only be hard and dangerous, versus downright foolhardy. Don't think I don't know how to push the envelope, honey. I've just had a few more years to perfect the act than you.'

Kimberly studied him. And then, abruptly, she nodded. He was putting their lives at risk and perversely, she liked him better for it.

'Good,' she said, and hefted her pack. She turned down the streambed, calling out casually over her shoulder, 'Old fart.'

That got him crashing down behind her. It also put a smile on her face. It made her feel better all the way around the next bend, where they finally got their first lucky break for the day.

Kimberly saw it first.

'Where are we?' she asked wildly.

'We're in our section, there shouldn't be any overlap . . .'

Kimberly pointed to the tree, with its freshly broken branch. And then she saw the crushed fern, followed by the flattened-down grass. She started walking faster, following the un-mistakable signs of human passage as the coarse trail began to zigzag through the woods. It was wide. It was clearly marked. A single person, crashing down nearly out of control. Or perhaps even a man, doubled over from the weight of carrying a heavily drugged body.

'Mac,' she said with barely contained excitement.

He was looking at the sun. 'Kimberly,' he said grimly. 'Run.'

She went careening down the path with Mac hot on her heels.

27

Virginia
8:43 P.M.
Temperature: 94 degrees

Tina hated the mud. It oozed and popped and smelled. It rippled and writhed with things she couldn't see and didn't want to know. It undulated slowly, like a living beast, just waiting for her to succumb.

She didn't have a choice. She was dangerously exhausted and dehydrated. Her skin burned from too much sun and too many bug bites. On the one hand, she felt as if her entire body were on fire. On the other hand, she had started shivering, her overheated skin breaking out incongruously with wave after wave of goosebumps.

She was dying; it was that simple. Weren't people comprised of something like eighty percent water? Which made her a pond, now literally drying up from drought.

Curled up against the hot surface of the rock, she thought of her mom. Maybe she should've told her about the pregnancy. Sure, her mother would've been upset, but only because she personally knew how hard the life of a young, single mother could be. Once the shock wore off, she would've helped Tina, offered some support.

And it would've been something else, too. Bringing a little life into the world, seeing her baby's scrunched up, squalling face, and tiny waving hands. She could see her and her mom crying together in the delivery room, exhausted and proud. She could see them picking out cute little baby clothes and fussing over midnight feedings. Maybe she'd have a girl, one more tough cookie to continue the family tradition. The three Krahns, ready to take over the world. Oh the state of Minnesota had better look out.

She would've tried so hard to be a good mother. Maybe she wouldn't have succeeded, but she would've tried.

Tina finally turned her head, looking up at the sky. Through the slits of her swollen eyes, she could see the yawning blue canvas of her prison. The horizon seemed to be darkening now, the sun finally sinking from view and leeching away the white-hot glare. Funny, it didn't feel any cooler. The humidity was still a stifling wet blanket, as oppressive as the cloud of mosquitoes and yellow flies that continued to swarm her face.

Her head fell back down. She stared at her hand, inches from her face. She had open sores from scratching the hundreds of mosquito bites. Now, she watched a yellow fly land on her skin, dig into her open wounds, and lay a pile of tiny, shiny white eggs.

She was going to be sick. No, she couldn't be sick. It was an inefficient use of the little water she had left. She was going to throw up anyway. Not even dead yet and already being used for maggot bait. How much longer could she possibly go on like this. Her poor baby. Her poor mom.

And then, that calm, practical Minnesotan voice from the back of her head, started speaking to her again: *You know what, girl? It's time to get tough. 'Cause you either do something now, or you really do get to forever hold your peace.*

Tina's gaze went to the oozing black mud.

Just do it, Tina. Be tough. Show the rat bastard what you're made of. Don't you dare go down without a fight.

She sat up. The world spun; the bile rose immediately in her throat. With a gagging cough, she choked it back down. Then, she pulled herself wearily to the edge of the boulder and gazed at the muck. Looks like pudding. Smells like . . .

No throwing up!

'All right,' Tina whispered grimly. 'I'll do it. Ready or not, here I come!'

She stuck her right foot in the muck. Something promptly slithered against her ankle, then darted away. She bit her lower lip to keep from screaming and forced her foot deeper into the muck. It felt like sliding her body into rotted-out guts. Warm, slimy, slightly chunky . . .

No throwing up!

She thrust her left foot into the ooze, saw the clear outline of a black snake slide away and this time she did scream, long, hoarsely, and helplessly. Because she was afraid and she hated this and oh God why had this man done this to her? She'd never hurt anyone. She didn't deserve to be cast in a pit where she was baking alive while flies laid shiny white eggs into the deep sores of her skin.

And she was sorry for having sex now, and she was sorry for not taking better precautions and she was sorry she had messed up her young life, but surely she didn't deserve this kind of torture. Surely she and her baby at least deserved a shot at making a better life.

The mosquitoes swarmed. She batted at them again and again and again, while standing mid-calf in the muck and gagging hopelessly. The smell, the feel. The smell, the feel.

Drop down, Tina. It's like plunging into a cold pool. Just grit your teeth, and plunge into the muck. It's the only option you have left.

And then . . .

There, in the distance. She heard it again. A sound. Footsteps? No, no. Voices. Someone was around.

Tina jerked back her head to the mouth of the open pit. 'Hey,' she tried to scream, 'hey, hey.'

All that came out of her parched throat was the croak of a frog. The voices were fading. People were around, but walking away, she was sure of it.

Tina grabbed her half-empty gallon of water. She took giant, greedy gulps, desperate for help and careless of rationing. Then, with her newly lubricated throat, she threw back her head and screamed in earnest.

'Hey, hey. I'm down here! Someone, anyone! Oh please, come here . . .'

Kimberly was running. Her lungs were burning; a stitch had developed in her side. Still she powered down the slippery slope, crashing through thick brush, jumping over rotting logs, careening around boulders. She could hear the hot, heavy breathing of Mac, racing by her side.

It was a suicidal pace. They could twist an ankle, plummet over a ledge, crash into a tree, or suffer things that would be much, much worse.

But the sun was setting fast now, daylight slipping through their fingers to be replaced by a fiery dusk that shot the sky blood-red. And the path, so distinguishable only fifteen minutes ago, was already slipping into shadow, vanishing before their eyes.

Mac surged ahead. Kimberly put her head down and forced her shorter legs to keep up.

They came crashing down the heavily wooded slope into a sudden, broad clearing. Thorny bushes and tightly squeezed trees gave way to knee-high grass. The ground flattened out and footing eased up.

Kimberly didn't slow. She was still tearing forward at full throttle, trying to pick out the trail in the fading light, when she registered two things at once: The jagged tumble of hundreds of boulders off to her left and then, just fifteen feet up the pile, a startling strip of red. A skirt, her mind registered. And then . . . A human body. The girl!

They had found the girl!

Kimberly streaked toward the pile of rocks. Vaguely, she heard Mac yelling at her to halt. He grabbed at her wrist. She pulled away.

'It's her,' she shouted back triumphantly, springing onto the pile. 'Hey, hey you! Hello, hello, hello!'

Three sharp whistles sounded behind her. The international call for distress. Kimberly didn't understand why. They had found the girl. They had saved the day. She had been right to leave the Academy. She had finally done it.

And then the girl came fully into view and then any bit of triumph Kimberly had ever felt burst like a proverbial bubble and left her halted short in her tracks.

The streak of red was not a piece of brightly dyed cotton, but a pair of white shorts, now stained darkly with dried blood. The sprawling white limbs – not a young girl lying peacefully down to rest, but a bruised and bloated body, now twisted beyond recognition. And then, as Kimberly watched in the dusky pall, she swore she saw one of the girl's limbs suddenly move.

The sound hit her all at once. A constant, building thrum. The deep vibration of dozens upon dozens of rattlesnakes.

'Kimberly,' Mac said quietly from the ground behind her. 'For the love of God, please don't move.'

Kimberly couldn't even nod. She just stood there, perfectly frozen, while all around her, the shadows of the rocks uncurled into the shapes of snakes.

'The girl's dead,' Kimberly said finally. Her voice sounded hoarse and faint, the tone of a woman already in shock. Mac eased closer to the boulders. By his third footstep, a fresh round of rattling shook the pile. He stopped instantly.

The sound seemed to be coming from everywhere. Ten, twenty, thirty different vipers. They seemed to be everywhere. Sweet Jesus, Mac thought, and reached back slowly for his gun.

'She must have been tired and dazed,' Kimberly murmured. 'Saw the rocks. Climbed up for a better view.'

'I know.'

'My God, I think they bit every inch of her body. I've never . . . I've never seen anything like it.'

'Kimberly, I have my gun out. If something moves, I'm going to shoot it. Don't flinch.'

'It won't work, Mac. There are too many of them.'

'Shut up, Kimberly,' he growled.

She turned her head toward him and actually smiled in at him. 'Now which one of us is being earnest?'

'Snakes don't like us anymore than we like them. If you just remain calm and don't move, most of them will disappear back into the rocks. I've sounded the whistle; help will be here shortly.'

'I almost died once. Did I ever tell you that? A man I thought I knew well. It turned out he was just using me to get to my father. He cornered Rainie and me in a hotel room. He held a gun to my head. There was nothing Rainie could do. I still remember just how the barrel felt. Not cold, but warm. Like living flesh. It's strange to feel so helpless. It's strange to be trapped in the arms of another human being and know he's going to take your life.'

'You're not dead, Kimberly.'

'No, my father surprised him. Shot him in the chest. Thirty seconds later, everything had changed and I was the one still alive, wearing his blood in my hair. And my father was telling me everything would be all right. It was nice of him to lie.'

Mac didn't know what to say. Light was fading fast, the

pile of boulders quickly becoming another world, filled with too much black.

'She never stood a chance,' Kimberly murmured, her gaze returning to the woman's body. 'Look at her in her shorts and silk blouse. She was dressed to have fun in a bar, not fend her way in a wilderness. It's beyond cruel.'

'We're going to find him.'

'Not until another girl is dead.'

Mac closed his eyes. 'Kimberly, the world's not as bad as you think.'

'Of course not, Mac. It's worse.'

He swallowed. He was losing her. He could feel Kimberly slide deeper into fatalism, a woman who had escaped death once and didn't expect to get that lucky again. He wanted to yell at her to buck up. And then he wanted to take her into his arms, and promise her everything would be all right.

She was right: when men tried to protect the people they cared about, they inevitably resorted to lies.

'Do you see the snakes?' he asked shortly.

'There's not enough light. They blend into the boulders.'

'I don't hear them.'

'No, they've fallen silent. Maybe they're tired. They've had a busy day.'

Mac edged closer. He wasn't sure how near the old landslide he could get. He didn't hear any fresh rounds of hissing. He crept to within five feet, then took out his flashlight, flaring it over the pile of boulders. It was difficult to tell. Some rocks seemed clear. Others had bulging outlines that could very well be more rattlers.

'Do you think you can jump to me?' he asked Kimberly.

She was at least twenty feet away, at an awkward angle in the rock pile. Maybe if she bounded quickly from boulder to boulder . . .

'I'm tired,' Kimberly whispered.

'I know, honey. I'm tired, too. But we need to get you off those rocks. I've sort of grown attached to your sunny smile and gentle disposition. Surely you wouldn't want to disappoint me now.'

No answer.

'Kimberly,' he said more sharply. 'I need you to pay attention. You're strong, you're bright. Now, focus on how we're going to get out of this.'

Her gaze went off in the distance. He saw her shoulders tremble. He didn't know what she thought about, but, finally, she turned back to him. 'Fire,' she told him quietly.

'Fire?'

'Snakes do hate fire, right? Or have I watched too many Indiana Jones movies? If I make a torch, maybe I can use it to scare them away.'

Mac moved quickly. He wasn't an expert on snakes, but it sounded like a plan to him. Good God, anything was better than feeling so damn helpless. He used his flashlight and quickly found a decent-sized fallen limb. 'Ready?'

'Ready.'

He lofted the branch into the air with an easy underhand. A moment later, he heard the small thump as she caught it in her hands. They both held their breaths. A slight buzzing rattle, low and to the right.

'Stay still,' Mac warned.

Kimberly dutifully froze and after several long minutes, the sound faded away.

'You need to get into your pack for the other supplies,' Mac instructed. 'If you have an extra pair of wool socks, wrap one around the end of the branch. Then you'll notice a small film canister in your front pocket. I added that. It contains three cotton balls dipped in Vaseline. They make an excellent fire starter. Just tuck them into the folds of the sock and hit 'em with a match.'

He held the flashlight, illuminating her in its beam of light as she went to work. Her movements were slow and subdued, trying not to call attention to herself.

'I can't find my extra socks,' she called back at last. 'What about an extra T-shirt?'

'That'll do.'

She had to set her pack down. Mac briefly lit up the ground beside her. It appeared free of snakes. She gingerly lowered her pack. Another hiss as the snakes sensed the disturbance and voiced their disapproval. She stilled again, straightening at the waist and now Mac could see the fresh sheen of sweat on her brow.

'You're almost done,' he told her.

'Sure.' Her hands were shaking. She fumbled the stick briefly, nearly dropped it, and a fresh rattle, close and loud, reverberated through the dark. Mac watched Kimberly squeeze her eyes shut. He watched her battle for composure, and he wondered if she was now remembering another truth about that day in the hotel room – that when the man had held a gun to her head, her first thought had been that she didn't want to die.

Come on, Kimberly, he willed her. *Come back to me.*

She got the T-shirt wrapped around the end of the stick. Then tucked in the cotton balls. Then found the matches. Her trembling hand found the first, small wooden match. The raspy sound of the tip scratching against the box. The match flared to life, she touched it on the cotton balls, and a torch was born in the night.

Immediately, the space around her blazed with fresh light, illuminating not one, but four coiled rattlers.

'Mac,' Kimberly said clearly. 'Get ready to catch.'

She thrust the torch forward. The snakes hissed, then recoiled sharply from the flames, and Kimberly bolted off the first boulder. She bounded down, one, two, three, four, as the crevices came alive with low rattles and slippery shapes tumbling off the boulders as the snakes sought to escape the flame. The rocks were alive, hissing, curling, rattling. Kimberly plunged through the writhing mess.

'Mac!' she yelled. She came catapulting off the final rock and crashed against his hard frame.

'Gotcha,' he said, grabbing her shoulders and already removing the torch from her shaking hand.

For one moment, she just stood there, pale, shell-shocked and dazed. Then, she collapsed against his chest and he held her more gratefully and desperately than he should.

'Mandy,' Kimberly murmured. And then she began to cry.

28

Professionals arrived and took over the scene. Lanterns were brought in, along with battery-powered lights. Then volunteers, armed with sticks, served as emergency snake wranglers, while men wearing thick boots and heavy-duty pants waded onto the rock pile and removed the victim's body in a litter.

Kathy Levine stood by as Mac officially reported their latest find to the powers-that-be. As a national park, Shenandoah fell under FBI jurisdiction; Watson would have his case after all, and Mac and Kimberly would once again be relegated to the role of outsiders.

Kimberly didn't care. She sat alone on the sidewalk in front of Big Meadows Lodge, watching the emergency vehicles pile up in the parking lot. Ambulances and EMTs with no one to save. A fire department with no blaze to extinguish. Then finally, the ME's van, the only professional who would get to practice his trade tonight.

It was hot. Kimberly felt moisture roll down her face like tears. Or maybe she was still crying. It was hard to know. She felt empty in a way she'd never felt empty before. As if everything she had ever been had simply disappeared, been flushed down a drain. Without bones, her body would have no weight. Without skin, she would cease to have form. The wind would come, blow her away like a pile of burnt-out ash, and maybe it would be better that way.

More cars came and went. Exhausted search volunteers returned and headed for a makeshift canteen where they downed buckets of ice water, then sank their teeth into pulpy slices of orange. The EMTs treated them for minor cuts and small sprains. Most people simply collapsed into the metal folding chairs, physically exhausted by the hike, and emotionally drained by a search that had ended with bitter disappointment.

Tomorrow all of this would be gone. The search-and-rescue volunteers would disperse back to their everyday lives, returning to mundane rituals and routine concerns. They would rejoin their families, hiking parties, fire departments.

And Kimberly? Would she go back to the Academy? Fire shotgun rounds at blank targets and pretend it made her tough? Or play dress up in Hogan's Alley, dodging paint shells and matching wits with overpaid actors? She could pass the last round of tests, graduate to become a full-fledged agent, and go through the rest of her life pretending her career made her whole. Why not? It had worked for her father.

She wanted to lay her head down on the hard sidewalk bordering the parking lot. She wanted to melt into the cement until the world ceased to exist. She wanted to go back to a time when she did not know so much about violent death, or what dozens of rattlesnakes could do to the human body.

She had told Mac the truth earlier. She was tired. Six years' worth of sleepless, bone-weary nights. She wanted to close her eyes and never open them again. She wanted to disappear.

Footsteps grew closer. A shadow fell between her and the

ambulance headlights. She looked up, and there was her father, striding across the steam-filled parking lot in one of his impeccably tailored suits. His lean face was set. His dark eyes inscrutable. He bore down on her fiercely, a hard, dangerous man come to collect his own.

She didn't have the strength anymore to care.

'I'm fine,' she started.

'Shut up,' Quincy said roughly. He grabbed his daughter's shoulder. Then he shocked them both by pulling her roughly off the sidewalk and folding her into his embrace. His arms went around her trembling form. He pressed his cheek against her hair. 'My God, I have been so worried about you. When I got the call from Mac . . . Kimberly, you are killing me.'

And then she shocked them both by bursting once more into tears. 'We didn't make it. I thought for sure this time I would be right. But we were slow and she was dead. Oh God, Daddy, how can I always be too late?'

'Shhh . . .'

She pulled back slightly, until she could gaze into his hard-lined face. For so much of her childhood, he had been a cool, remote figure. She respected him, she admired him. She strove desperately for his praise. But he remained out of reach, a larger-than-life figure, who was always rushing out the door to assist other families, and rarely around for his own. Now, it was suddenly, frantically important to her that he understand. 'If I'd just known how to move faster. I have no experience in the mountains. How could I grow up around here and not know anything about the woods? I kept tripping and falling, Dad, and then I stumbled into the stinging nettles and God, *why couldn't I have moved faster*?'

'I know, sweetheart. I know.' His thumb brushed her cheek, finding all the errant tears.

'Mac was right after all. I wanted to save Mandy and Mom, and since I can't help them, I honestly thought saving this girl would make a difference. But they're still dead and she's still dead, and God what is the point?'

'Kimberly, what happened to your mother and Mandy wasn't your fault—'

She wrenched away from him. Screaming now, her words carrying across the parking lot, but she was beyond noticing. 'Stop saying that! You always say that! Of course it was my fault. I'm the one who trusted him. I'm the one who told him all about my family. Without me, he never would've known how to reach them. Without me, he never would've killed them! So stop lying to me, Dad. What happened to Mom and Mandy is exactly my fault. I just let you take the blame because I know it makes you feel better!'

'Stop it!' Quincy grabbed her again, gripping her face so she couldn't look away. 'You were only twenty. A young girl. You can't saddle yourself with this kind of guilt.'

'Why not? You do.'

'Then we're both idiots, all right? We're both idiots. What happened to your mom and Mandy . . . I would've died for them, Kimberly. Had I known, if I could've stopped it, I would've died for them.' His breathing grew harsh. She was shocked to see the glitter of tears in his eyes.

'I would've died, too,' she whispered.

'Then we did the best we could, all we could. He was the enemy, Kimberly. *He* took their lives. And God help both of us, but sometimes, the enemy is simply that good.'

'I want them back.'

'I know.'

'I miss them all the time. Even Mandy.'

'I know.'

'Dad, I don't know why I'm still alive . . .'

'Because God took pity on me, Kimberly. Because without you, I think I would've gone insane.'

He held her tight against him. She sobbed against his chest, crying harder. And she could feel him crying, too, her father's tears falling onto her hair. Her stoic father, who didn't even cry at funerals.

'I wanted to save her so badly,' Kimberly whispered.

'I know. It's not bad to care. Someday, that will be your strength.'

'But it hurts. And now I have nothing left. The game is over, and the wrong person has won, and I don't know how to simply go home and wait for the next match. It's life and death. It shouldn't be this cavalier.'

'It's not over, Kimberly.'

'Of course it is. We didn't find the second girl. Now all we can do is wait.'

'No. Not this time.' Her father took a deep breath, then gently pulled away. He looked at her in the dark, breathless night, and his face was as sad as she'd ever seen. 'Kimberly,' he said quietly. 'I'm so sorry sweetheart, but this time, there weren't just two girls. This time, the man took four.'

Rainie was huffing badly by the time she made it down to the crime scene. Lanterns marked the trail, so footing wasn't bad, but geez Louise, it was a ways down the mountain. And for the record, while it was now after midnight and the moon ruled the sky, apparently no one had bothered to tell the heat. She'd soaked through both her T-shirt and hiking shorts, ruining her third outfit of the day.

She hated this weather. She hated this place. She wanted to go home, and not to the high-rise coop she shared with Quincy in downtown Manhattan, but home to Bakersville, Oregon. Where the fir trees grew to staggering heights, and a fresh ocean breeze blew off the water. Where people knew each other by first names, and even if it made it hard to escape the past, it also gave you an anchor in the present. Bakersville, where she'd had a town, a community, a place that felt like home . . .

The pang of longing struck hard and deep. As it had been doing so often these days. A ghost pain for the past. And it filled her with a restlessness she was having a harder and harder time trying to hide. Quincy could sense it, too. She caught him watching her sometimes with a question in his eyes. She wished she could give him an answer, but how could she, when she didn't have one herself?

Sometimes she ached for things she couldn't name. And sometimes, when she thought of how much she loved Quincy, it simply hurt her more.

She found Mac standing with a cluster of three people over by the body. The first guy appeared to be the medical examiner. Second guy had the look of an assistant. Third person was a woman with short red hair and lots of freckles. She was built like a firecracker, with the muscled legs and broad shoulders of a serious hiker. Not the ME's office. Probably leader of the search-and-rescue operations.

Thirty seconds later, Mac made the introductions, and Rainie was pleased to find out she was right. ME turned out to be Howard Weiss, his assistant was Dan Lansing, and the redhead was Kathy Levine, a botanist at the park who had indeed organized the search.

Levine was still talking to the ME, so the three of them broke away, leaving Mac and Rainie standing over the partially wrapped body.

'Where's Quincy?' Mac asked.

'He said he needed to have a fatherly chat with Kimberly. I took one look at his face and decided not to argue.'

'They fight a lot?'

'Only because they're too much alike.' She shrugged. 'Someday they'll figure that out.'

'What about Kaplan and Watson? Are they gonna join the party, or are they not allowed off the base?'

'Not known yet. Watson has a full-time job at the Academy,

Lisa Gardner

so while the FBI is definitely assembling a team, it probably won't involve him personally. Kaplan, on the other hand, is lead investigator on the Quantico homicide. So he has plenty of time; but lacks jurisdiction. Given that he's a resourceful man, I figure in another hour or two, he'll crack that nut and show up with full NCIS entourage. Oh, aren't we the luckiest duckies in the whole wide world?'

She peered down into the black plastic body bag, the contents clearly lit by one of the generator-powered overhead lights. 'Whoa.'

'Nearly two dozen puncture wounds,' Mac said. 'And countin'. Poor girl must've wandered right into the thick of things. After that, she never stood a chance.'

'Her purse? The gallon of water?'

'No signs yet. We don't know where she was abandoned, though. In daylight, we can find her trail and backtrack. Probably discover her things along the way.'

'Seems strange she'd drop the water.'

He shrugged. 'In this heat, a gallon of water is good for about two to four hours. She's been out here for at least twenty-four, so . . .'

'So even when the guy plays nice, he's still a total bastard.' Rainie straightened. 'Well, do you want the good news or the bad news first?'

Mac was silent for a moment. She could see fresh lines on his forehead, a gaunt set to his jaw. He'd been pushing himself hard and he looked it. Still, he didn't blink an eye. 'If it's all the same, I think I'd like to start with the good news tonight.'

'We might have a name.' Rainie dug out her spiral notepad from her fanny pack and started flipping through. She glanced once more at the body. 'Brunette, twenty years old, brown eyes, distinguishable by a birthmark on her upper left breast.' She bent down, then paused, with a meaningful glance at Mac. He was already looking away. She approved. Some people handled bodies as if they were nothing more than dolls. Rainie had never liked that. This was a girl. She'd had a family, a life, people who deeply loved her. There was no need to disrespect her anymore than necessary.

Gently, she lifted the top of the girl's blouse. She had to move her head to let in the light. Then she could see it clearly, the top edge just peeking out from beneath the edge of the girl's black satin bra – a dark brown clover-shaped birthmark.

'Yeah,' Rainie said quietly. 'It's Vivienne Benson. She was a student at Mary Washington College in Fredericksburg, spending the summer working for her uncle. He called her landlady yesterday when she didn't show up for work. Landlady went up to the apartment, found it empty, and the dog howling to be let out of its crate. She took pity on the poor beast, then called the police. According to her, it's not like Vivienne, or her roommate, Karen Clarence, to stay out all night. Particularly because of their dog, whom apparently they love madly.'

'Karen is a blonde?'

'Actually, Karen's a brunette.'

Mac immediately frowned. 'The body we found at Quantico had blond hair.'

'Yeah.'

'It's not Karen Clarence?'

'No. Betsy Radison. Her brother made the ID just a few hours ago.'

'Rainie, honey, I'm a little tired right now. Can you take pity on an exhausted GBI agent and start your story over in English?'

'I'd be delighted. Turns out the landlady is a real font of information. She was sitting out two nights ago, when Vivienne and Karen came downstairs to wait for their ride. According to her, Viv and Karen were picked up by two other friends from college, and the four of them were going to a bar in Stafford.'

'The four of them?'

'Enter Betsy Radison and Tina Krahn, also living in Fredericksburg and taking some summer courses. All four girls went out Tuesday night in Betsy's Saab convertible. None have been seen since. Fredericksburg PD went into Betsy and Tina's apartment late tonight. All they could find were a dozen messages from Tina Krahn's mother on the answering machine. Apparently she didn't like her last conversation with her daughter. She's been frantically trying to reach Tina ever since.'

'I gotta sit down,' Mac said. He moved away from Vivienne Benson's body, found a tree stump and collapsed on the rough shape as if he'd abruptly lost all the strength in his legs. He ran a hand through his damp hair, then did it again and again. 'He ambushed four girls at once,' he said at last, trying out the words, feeling his way into the horrible concept. 'Betsy Radison, he dumped at Quantico, Vivienne Benson he abandoned here. Which leaves us with Karen Clarence and Tina Krahn, who he may have taken . . . Goddamn . . . The gray birch leaf. I thought that was too easy for him. But of course. It wasn't an end. Just a strange beginning.'

'Like Quincy said, serial killers have a tendency to escalate the violence of their crime.'

'Did you find a letter to the editor?' he asked sharply.

'No letter. An ad in *Quantico Sentry*.'

'The Marines' newspaper?' Mac frowned. 'The one distributed all over the base?'

'Yeah. We have the original of what was sent in, but it didn't give up much in the way of forensic evidence. Quincy had it turned over to Ennunzio to analyze the text.'

'You got to meet with the forensic linguist? Hell, you *have* been busy.'

'We try,' Rainie said modestly. 'You're going to see him again soon, too. Quincy's requested that Ennunzio join the case team. The two of them are working on a theory that your caller isn't an anonymous tipster, but the man himself. We're just not entirely sure why.'

'He doesn't gloat. If I'm getting calls from the Eco-Killer, don't you think he'd want to take the credit?'

'Well, maybe and maybe not. One theory is that he feels guilty about what he's doing, so this is his roundabout way of getting you to stop him. Second theory, he's mentally incapacitated – hence his love of repeating the same message over and over again. Third, you're part of this game now, too, and he's luring you into the wild, just like he does with the girls. Look at the body, Mac. Can you be a hundred percent certain, that wouldn't have been you?'

'It wasn't almost me,' Mac said quietly. 'It was almost Kimberly.'

Rainie's expression became very gentle. 'Yeah, and then he wins, too, right, Mac? Either way, he wins.'

'Son of a bitch.'

'Yeah.'

'I'm getting too old for this shit, Rainie,' he said. And then almost on cue, his phone rang.

29

Shenandoah National Park, Virginia
1:22 A.M.
Temperature: 89 degrees

'Special Agent McCormack.'

'Heat kills.'

'Shut the fuck up. You really think this is a game? We found your latest victim dead from two dozen rattlesnake bites. Does that make you feel good? Is feeding young girls to pit vipers how you get your jollies? You're nothing but a sick son of a bitch and I'm not talking to you anymore!'

Mac flipped his phone shut. He was mad. Madder than he'd ever been in his life. His heart thundered. He could hear the roar of blood in his ears. He wanted to do more than yell into a tiny phone. He wanted to find the man, and beat him into a bloody pulp.

Rainie was staring at him in mild shock. 'While I am impressed, was that really a good idea?'

'Wait.' His phone immediately rang again. He gave her a look. 'Contacting the authorities is about exercising control, right? He's not gonna let it end on my terms. But that doesn't mean I can't make him work for it.'

He flipped his phone open. 'Now what?' he said. Good cop was definitely gone for the night.

'I'm only trying to help,' the distorted voice echoed peevishly.

'You're a liar and a killer. And guess what, we know for a fact that makes you a bed wetter, too. So stop wasting my time, you little prick.'

'I'm not a killer!'

'I got two bodies that say otherwise.'

'He struck again? I thought . . . I thought you might have more time.'

'Hey, buddy, stop the lies. I know you're him. You want to gloat? Is that what this is about? You drugged two young girls and then killed them. Yeah, you are just the biggest badass in town.'

Rainie's eyes went wide. She shook her head furiously. She was right, of course. If the guy did want to boost his ego, it wasn't a good idea to egg him on.

'I am not the killer!' the voice protested shrilly, and then in the next instant, the voice grew an edge of its own. 'I'm trying to help. You can either listen and learn, or continue this game on your own.'

'Who are you?'

'He's getting angrier.'

'No shit. Where are you calling from?'

'He's going to strike again. Soon. Maybe already.'

Mac took a gamble. 'He's already struck again. This time he didn't take two girls. This time, he took four. So what about it?'

A pause, as if the caller was genuinely surprised. 'I didn't realize . . . I didn't think . . .'

'Why is he now in Virginia?'

'He grew up here.'

'He's from Virginia?' Mac's voice picked up. He swapped

concerned glances with Rainie.

'His first sixteen years,' the caller replied.

'When did he move to Georgia?'

'I don't know. It's been . . . years. You have to understand. I don't think he really wants to hurt the victims. He wants them to figure it out. If they would just remain calm, be smart, show some strength—'

'For Christ's sake, they're only kids.'

'So was he once.'

Mac shook his head. The killer as a victim. He didn't want to hear this shit. 'Listen, I have two dead girls and two more at risk. Give me his name, buddy. End this thing. You have it in your power. You can be the hero. Just give me his damn name.'

'I can't.'

'Then send it in the mail!'

'Did the first body lead you to the second?'

'*Give me his goddamn name!*'

'Then the second body will lead you to the third. Move quickly. I don't . . . I'm not even sure what he'll do next.'

The signal went dead. Mac swore and hurled his phone into the brush. It spooked a scavenging raccoon and didn't do a thing to calm his temper. He wanted to run back up the mountainside. He wanted to plunge into an ice-cold stream. He wanted to throw back his head and howl at the moon. Then he wanted to swear every obscenity he'd ever learned as a child and collapse into a pile and weep.

He'd been working too long on this case to keep seeing so much death.

'Damn,' he said at last. 'Damn, damn, damn.'

'He didn't give you a name.'

'He swears he's not the killer. He swears he's just trying to help.'

Rainie looked at the body. 'Could've fooled me.'

'No kidding.' Mac sighed, straightening his shoulders and

moving resolutely toward the body. 'All four girls disappeared at once, from the same car?'

'That's what we're assuming.'

'Then we don't have much time.' He hunkered down, already pulling the black plastic body bag away from the girl.

'What are you doing?'

'Looking for clues. Because if the first girl led us to the second, then the second will lead us to the third.'

'Ahh, shit,' Rainie said.

'Yeah. You know what? Go find Kathy Levine. We're gonna need some help here. And a boatload of coffee.'

'No rest for the weary?'

'Not tonight.'

Nora Ray was dreaming again. She was in the happy place, the land of fantasy where her parents smiled and her dead dog danced, and she floated in a pool of cool, silky water, feeling it lap peacefully against her skin. She loved this place, longed to come here often.

She could listen to her parents laugh. Watch the pure blue sky, which never contained a red-hot sun. Feel the crystalline cleanness of pure water against her limbs.

She turned her head. She saw the door open. And without hesitation, she left the pool behind.

Mary Lynn was riding her horse. She drove Snowfall through miles of green pasture, racing through fields of wild daisies, and jumping fallen logs. She sat forward in the saddle, her body tight and compact like a jockey's, her hands light and steady on the reins. The horse soared. She soared with it. It was as if they were one.

Nora Ray crossed to the fence. Two other girls sat on the top rail. One blonde. One brunette.

'Do you know where we are?' the blonde asked Nora Ray.

'You're in my dream.'

'Do we know you?' the brunette asked.

'I think we knew the same man.'

'Will we get to ride the horse?' the brunette asked.

'I don't know.'

'She's very good,' said the blonde.

'There's never been anything my sister couldn't ride,' Nora Ray replied proudly.

'I have a sister,' said the brunette. 'Will she dream of me?'

'Every night.'

'That's very sad.'

'I know.'

'I wish there's something we could do.'

'You're dead,' Nora Ray said. 'You can't do anything at all. Now, I think it's up to me.'

Then her sister was gone, the pasture had vanished, and she was spiraling away from the pond long before she was ready. She woke up wide-eyed in her bed, her heart beating too fast and her hands knotted around her comforter.

Nora Ray sat up slowly. She poured herself a glass of water from the pitcher on her nightstand. She took a long drink and felt the cool liquid slide down her throat. Sometimes, she could still feel the salt building like rime around her mouth, coating her chin, covering her lips. She could remember the deep, unquenchable thirst that ran cell-deep, as the sun pounded and the salt built and she went mad with thirst. *Water, water everywhere, and not a drop to drink.*

She finished her glass of water now. Let the moisture linger on her lips, like dew on a rose. Then she left her room.

Her mother slept on the couch, her head crooked awkwardly to the side, while on the TV Lucille Ball crawled into a vat of grapes and gamely stomped away. In the neighboring bedroom, Nora Ray glimpsed her father, slumbering alone on the queen-sized bed.

The house was silent. It filled Nora Ray with a loneliness

that threatened to cut her heart in two. Three years later, and no one had healed. Nothing was better. She could still remember the harsh grit of salt, leaching the last moisture from her body. She could remember her rage and confusion as the crabs nibbled on her toes. She could remember her simple desire to survive this hell and return to her family. If she could just see them again, slide into her parent's loving embrace . . .

Except her family had never returned to her. She had survived. They had not.

And now, two more girls in the pastureland of her dream. She knew what that meant. The heat had arrived on Sunday, and the shadowy man from her nightmares had resumed his lethal game.

The clock glowed nearly two A.M. She decided she didn't care. She picked up the phone and dialed the number she knew by heart. A moment later, she said, 'I need to reach Special Agent McCormack. No, I don't want to leave a message. I need to see him. Quick.'

Tina didn't dream. Her exhausted body had given out, and now she was collapsed in the mud in a sleep that bordered on unconsciousness. One arm still touched the boulder, a link to relative safety. The rest of her belonged to the muck. It oozed between her fingers, coated her hair, slithered up her throat.

Things came and went in the sucking muck. Some had no interest in prey quite that large. Some had no interest in a meal that wasn't already dead. Then, up above, a dark shadow lumbered along the path, stopping at the edge of the pit. A giant head peered down, dark eyes gleaming in the night. It smelled warm-blooded flesh, a fine, delectable meal that was just his size.

More sniffing. Two giant paws raked one side of the hole. The depth was too deep, the terrain not manageable. The bear grunted, lumbered on. If the creature ever came up, he'd try again. Until then, there were other fine things to eat in the dark.

The man didn't sleep. Two A.M., he packed his bags. He had to move quickly now. He could feel the darkness gathering at the edges of his mind. Time was becoming more fluid, moments slipping through his fingers and disappearing into the abyss.

Pressure was growing in the back of his skull. He could feel it, a true physical presence at the top of his spine, with another tendril starting to press against the inner canal of his left ear. A tumor, he was pretty sure. He'd had one before, years ago when he'd had his first 'episode' of vanishing time. Had it been only minutes he'd lost in the beginning? He couldn't even remember that anymore.

Time grew fluid, black holes took over his life. One tumor was removed. Another came back to eat his brain. It was probably the size of a grapefruit by now. Or maybe even a watermelon. Maybe his brain wasn't even his brain anymore, but a giant malignant mass of constantly dividing cells. He didn't doubt it. That would explain the bad dreams, the restless nights. It would explain why the fire came to him so often now, and made him do things he knew he shouldn't.

He found himself thinking of his mother more. Her pale face, her thin, hunched shoulders. He thought of his father, too, and the way he always strode through their tiny cabin in the woods.

'*A man's gotta be tough, boys, a man's gotta be strong. Don't you listen to no government types, they just want to turn us into mealy-mouthed dependents who can't live without a federal handout. Not us boys. We got the land. We will always be strong, as long as we got the land.*'

Strong enough to beat his wife, abuse his kids and wring the neck of the family cat. Strong enough, and isolated enough, to live as he goddamned pleased, without even a neighbor to hear the screams.

The black storm clouds built, rolled and roared. Now he was sitting tied to a chair, while his father took a strap to his brother, his mother washed the dishes, and his father told them both that next it would be their turns. Now he and his brother were huddled under the front porch, planning their big escape, while above their heads their mother wept and their father told her to go inside and wipe that goddamn blood off of her face. Now it was late at night and he and his brother were sneaking out the front door; at the last minute they turned, and saw their mother standing pale and silent in the moonlight. Go, her eyes told them. *Run away while you still can.* Her bruised cheeks were streaked with wordless tears. They crept back inside. And she clutched them to her breast as if they were the only hope she had left.

And he knew then that he hated his mother as much as he had ever loved her. And he knew then that she felt the same about him and his brother. They were the crabs, stuck together in the bottom of a bucket, and pulling each other down so no one ever made it to freedom.

The man swayed on his feet. He felt the dark roll in, felt himself totter on the edge of the abyss . . . Time was slipping through his fingers.

The man turned. He drove his fist forcefully into the wall, and let the pain bring him back. The room came into focus. The dark spots cleared from his eyes. Better.

The man crossed to his dresser. He got out his gun.

He prepared for what must happen next.

30

Rainie and Mac were still working the victim's body when Quincy materialized before them. His gaze went from them to Kathy Levine then back to them.

'She's one of us,' Rainie said, as if he'd asked a question.

'Definitely?'

'Well, she risked ordering a search team based solely on Mac's hunch, and now she's picking rice out of a corpse's pocket. You tell us.'

Quincy raised a brow and glanced at Levine again. 'Rice?'

'Uncooked white,' she said briskly. 'Long grain. Then again, I'm a botanist, not a chef, so you may want a second opinion.'

Quincy switched his attention to Mac, who was carefully going over the girl's left foot. 'Why rice?'

'Damned if I know.'

'Anything else?'

'She's wearing a necklace – some kind of vial filled with a clear fluid. That might be a hint. Then we got about nine different bits of leaves, four or five samples of dirt, half a dozen kinds of grass, some crushed flower petals and a whole lotta blood.' Mac gestured to a stack of evidence containers. 'Help yourself to a sample. And good luck figuring out if it came from her hike through the woods or from him. This new strategy of his definitely puts a wrinkle in things. What'd you do with Kimberly?'

'Feds got her.'

Three heads shot up. Quincy smiled grimly. 'I believe there's been a change of plans.'

'Quincy,' Mac said curtly. 'Tell me what the hell you're talking about.'

Quincy didn't look at him directly. Instead, his gaze went to Rainie. 'The FBI case team arrived. No Kaplan, no Watson. In fact, I don't recognize anyone on the team. They pulled in, spotted Kimberly, and immediately pulled her aside for questioning. I'm supposed to be waiting outside the lodge.'

'Those assholes!' Rainie exploded. 'First they want nothing to do with this. Now it's suddenly their party, and no one else is invited to play. What are they going to do? Start all over at this stage of the game?'

'I imagine they are going to do exactly that. The FBI can launch a pretty good search, you know. They'll bring in computer operators, stenographers, dog handlers, search-and-rescue teams, topography experts, and recon pilots. Within twenty-four hours, they'll have a full ops center set up roadside, while planes search the surrounding areas with infrared photography and volunteers stand by to assist. It's not too shabby.'

'Infrared photography is bullshit this time of year,' Mac said tightly. 'We tried it ourselves. Every damn boulder and wandering bear shows up as a hit. Not to mention deer also look roughly like humans in the still photos. We ended up with hundreds of targets and not a single one of them was ever the missing girl. Besides, that assumes the next victim is somewhere in these woods, and I already know she isn't. The man doesn't repeat an area, and the whole point of his game is to ramp up the challenge. The other girl is somewhere far from here, and believe it or not, someplace even more dangerous.'

'Judging from what I've seen so far, you're probably correct.' Quincy turned around, looking back up the darkened path. 'I give the new federal agents ten minutes before they arrive down here, and that delay is only because Kimberly promised to be unforthcoming with her answers. I know she's good at that.' He grimaced, then turned back. 'All right, for the next ten minutes at least, I'm part of this case and have authority over evidence. So, Ms. Levine, as a botanist, are any of these samples definitely out of place?'

'The rice,' she said immediately.

'I'll take half.'

'The vial with fluid, maybe. Though that could be a personal possession.'

'Do we have an inventory of what any of the girls were last seen wearing?'

'No,' answered Rainie.

Quincy mulled it over. 'I'll take half the fluid.'

Mac nodded, and immediately produced a glass vial from the evidence processing kit. Quincy noticed his hands were shaking slightly. Maybe fatigue. Maybe rage. Quincy knew from his own experience that it didn't really matter. Just as long as you got the job done.

'Why take only half the samples?' Levine asked.

'Because if I took the whole sample, something would be missing. The other agents might notice and ask, and then I might feel compelled to hand it over. If, on the other hand, nothing's obviously missing . . .'

'They'll never ask.'

'And I'll never tell,' Quincy said with a grim smile. 'Now, what else?'

Levine gestured helplessly to the pile of bags. 'I honestly

don't know. Lighting's not great, I don't have a magnifying glass on me. Given the state of half of this stuff, I'd say she picked it up crashing through the underbrush. But without more time for analysis . . .'

'He generally leaves three to four clues,' Mac said quietly.

'So we're missing something.'

'Or he's making it harder,' Rainie commented.

Mac shrugged. 'I'd say the stack of false positives makes it hard enough.'

Quincy glanced at his watch. 'You have five minutes. Sort through, then go. Oh, and Rainie, love, better turn off your cell phone.'

Mac had finished with the girl's foot and was moving up the body. He tilted back the girl's head, cracked open her mouth, then inserted a gloved finger into the abyss. 'He's twice hidden something in a victim's throat,' he said by way of explanation. He twisted his hand left, then right, then sighed and shook his head.

'I got something.' Rainie looked up sharply. 'Can I get some better light? I don't know if this is just bad dandruff or what.'

Quincy adjusted his flashlight. Rainie parted the girl's hair. There appeared to be a fine powder dusted over the strands. As Rainie shook the victim's head, more residue fell onto the plastic bag she had laid beneath it.

Levine moved closer, catching some of the dust on her finger and sniffing experimentally. 'I don't know. Not dandruff. Too gritty. Almost . . . I don't know.'

'Take a sample,' Quincy ordered tersely, his gaze returning to the path. There, he heard it again. Not far off anymore. The thump of descending footprints.

'Rainie . . .' he murmured tightly.

She hastily scraped a small bit of the shavings into a glass vial, corked it, and threw it in her fanny pack. Kathy added some of the rice; Mac had already claimed half of the water.

They were scrambling to their feet as Quincy moved toward Levine. 'If they ask, you started working the scene under my orders. This is what you found, properly catalogued and waiting for them. As for me, last you knew, I was heading away from the scene. Trust me, you won't be lying.'

The footsteps pounded closer. Quincy shook the botanist's hand. 'Thank you,' he told Kathy Levine.

'Good luck.'

Quincy headed down the hillside and Rainie and Mac quickly followed suit. Levine watched as the darkness opened up, and then there was no one there at all.

'For the last time, how did you know to come to the park? What led you and Special Agent McCormack straight to Big Meadows and another girl's body?'

'You'd have to ask Special Agent McCormack about his reasoning. Personally, I was in the mood for a hike.'

'So you just magically discovered the body? Your second corpse in twenty-four hours?'

'I guess I have a gift.'

'Will you be asking for another hardship leave? Do you need more time to *grieve*, Ms Quincy, in between finding all these dead bodies?'

Kimberly thinned her lips. They'd been at this for two hours now, her and Agent Tightass, who had introduced himself with a real name, though she'd long forgotten what it was. He'd thrust, she'd parry. He'd punch, she'd dodge. Neither one of them was having much fun, and in fact, given the late hour and lack of sleep, both of them were getting more than a little pissed.

'I want water,' she said now.

'In a minute.'

'I hiked five hours in nearly a hundred-degree heat. Give me water, or when I succumb to dehydration, I'll sue your ass, end your career, and keep you from ever having that fat government pension to fund your golden years. Are we clear?'

'Your attitude doesn't speak well for an aspiring agent,' Tightass said curtly.

'Yeah, they didn't care for it much at the Academy either. Now I want my water.'

Tightass was still scowling, obviously debating whether he should give in, when the door opened and Kimberly's father strode in. Funny, for the first time in years, she was genuinely happy to see him, and they'd only parted ways hours ago.

'The EMTs will see you now,' Quincy said.

Kimberly blinked her eyes a few times, and then she got it. 'Oh, thank God. My aching . . . everything.'

'Wait a minute,' Tightass started.

'My daughter has had a very long day. Not only has she been instrumental in finding a lost woman but, as you can tell by looking at her arms and legs, it was at great personal cost to herself.'

Kimberly smiled at Tightass. It was true. She did look like hell. 'I walked into a patch of stinging nettles,' she volunteered cheerfully. 'And some poison ivy. And about a dozen trees. Not to mention what I did to my ankles. Oh yeah, I need some medical attention.'

'I have more questions,' Tightass said tersely.

'When she's done being treated, I'm sure my daughter would be delighted to cooperate.'

'She's not cooperating now!'

'Kimberly,' her father said in a chastising tone.

She shrugged. 'I'm tired, I'm hot, and I'm in pain. How am I supposed to think clearly when I've been denied water and proper medical attention?'

'Of course.' Quincy was already crossing the room and helping her out of the metal folding chair. 'Really, Agent, I know my daughter is a very strong young lady, but even you should know better than to question someone without first getting them proper treatment. I'm taking her straight to the EMTs. You can ask your questions again after that.'

'I don't know—'

Quincy already had them to the door, his right arm wrapped around Kimberly's waist, his left hand holding her arm around his shoulder, as if she was in desperate need of support. 'Come to the medic station in thirty minutes. I'm sure she'll be ready for you then.'

Then Quincy and Kimberly were out the door, Quincy half bearing her weight and Kimberly managing a truly impressive limp.

In case Tightass was watching, Quincy took her straight to the first-aid station. And as long as she was there, Kimberly had some water, grabbed four oranges and then saw an EMT – for approximately thirty seconds. He gave her salve for her legs and arms, then she and Quincy were striding rapidly away from the station and into a remote section of the parking lot.

Rainie was waiting. So was Mac. They each had a vehicle.

'Get in the car,' Quincy said. 'We talk again on the road.'

31

Mac followed Quincy's taillights, leading them away from the buzzing chaos of Big Meadows, and into the inky black of a winding road lit only by the moon and stars.

Kimberly didn't speak right away. Neither did Mac. She was tired again, but in a different sort of way now. This was the physical fatigue that came after a long, arduous journey and too few hours' sleep. She liked this kind of tired better. It was familiar to her. Almost comforting. She had always pushed her body hard and it had always recovered quickly. Her battered emotions, in contrast . . .

Mac reached over and took her hand. After another moment, she squeezed his fingers with her own.

'I could sure use some coffee,' he said. 'About four gallons.'

'I could use a vacation. About four decades.'

'How about a nice cool shower?'

'How about air-conditioning?'

'Fresh clothes.'

'A soft bed.'

'A giant platter of buttermilk biscuits smothered in gravy.'

'A pitcher of ice water, topped with sliced lemon.'

She sighed. He joined suit.

'We're not going to bed anytime soon, are we?' she asked quietly.

'Doesn't look it.'

'What happened?'

'Not sure. Your father showed up, said an official FBI case team had arrived and that we were no longer invited to the party. Damn those feds.'

'They pulled Dad and Rainie off the case?' Kimberly was incredulous.

'Not yet. The fact they both turned off their cell phones and made a quick getaway probably helped. But it looks like the feds are trying to reinvent the wheel again, and even your father knows better. We worked with Kathy Levine to identify which items might be clues on the victim's body, then we took half the evidence. And now, just for the record, I believe we're officially AWOL. Did you really want to be an FBI agent, Kimberly? 'Cause after this . . .'

'Fuck the FBI. Now tell me the plan.'

'We work with your father and Rainie. We see if we can't find the remaining two girls. Then we track down the son of a bitch who did this, and nail him to the wall.'

'That's the nicest thing I've heard all night.'

'Well,' he said modestly. 'I do try.'

Shortly, Quincy's car turned in at one of the scenic vistas, and Mac followed suit. Given the hour, no other cars were around, and they were far enough off Skyline Drive to be invisible from the road. They all got out of the two vehicles and congregated around the hood of Mac's rental car.

The night still felt hot and heavy. Crickets buzzed and frogs croaked, but even those sounds were curiously subdued, as if everything were hushed and waiting. There should be heat lightning and thunder. There should be an impressive July thunderstorm, bringing cleansing rain and cooler temperatures. Instead, the heat wave pressed down on them, blanketing the world in stifling humidity and silencing half the creatures of the night.

Quincy had taken off his jacket, loosened his tie and rolled up his sleeves. 'So we have three possible clues,' he said by way of starting things off. 'A vial of liquid, rice, and some kind of dust from the victim's hair. Any ideas?'

'Rice?' Kimberly asked sharply.

'Uncooked, white, long grain,' Mac informed her. 'At least that was Levine's best guess.'

Kimberly shook her head. 'That doesn't even make sense.'

'He likes to make it harder,' Mac said quietly. 'Welcome to the rules of the game.'

'How far away do you think the other two victims are?' Rainie spoke up. 'If he's taken multiple victims, maybe the first victim speaks for all three. He's only one man after all, working with a limited amount of time to set this up.'

Mac shrugged. 'I can't be sure of this new format, of course. In Georgia, he definitely moved around a lot. We started at a state park famous for its granite gorge, then moved to cotton fields, then the banks of the Savannah River, and finally to the salt marshes on the coast. Four clearly diverse regions of the state. Here, however, you're right – he has some practical issues involved in placing bodies all over the state, particularly in twenty-four hours or less.'

'The logistics of hauling multiple bodies are complicated,' Quincy commented.

'Vehicle of choice is probably a cargo van. Gives him a place to stash kidnapped women, inject poison in their veins, and then haul them around. In this case, he'd also need plenty of room, given four victims.'

'How did he manage to snatch four women at once?'

Kimberly murmured. 'You'd think at least one of them would put up a fight?'

'I doubt they had a chance. His favorite method of ambush is using a dart gun. He closes in on the car, darts the women with fast-acting ketamine, and they're drifting off to la-la land before anyone can protest. If another car drives by, he can pose as the designated driver with four passed out passengers. Then, once the coast is clear, he loads the women into his van, ramps up the ketamine to keep them unconscious for as long as he needs, and he sets off for stage two of his master plan. He's not a flashy killer, but he certainly gets the job done.'

They all nodded morosely. Yes, the man certainly got the job done.

'Rainie said you got a call again,' Quincy said to Mac.

'At the scene. Caller swears he's not actually the killer, though. He got mad when I accused him of the crimes, swore he was just trying to help, and said he was sorry more girls had died. Not that he volunteered his name or the killer's name, mind you, but he still swears he's a stand-up guy.'

'The caller's lying,' Quincy said flatly.

'You think?'

'Consider the timing of both your recent calls. First one comes the night before the first victim is found – incidentally, right around the same time the killer must have been plotting his ambush, if he had not already taken the four girls. Then the second call comes tonight, when you're at the scene of the second victim. I believe that is what Special Agent Kaplan would consider a suspicious coincidence.'

'You think the Eco-Killer's close?' Mac asked sharply.

'Killers like to watch. Why should this UNSUB be different? He's left a trail of breadcrumbs for us. Perhaps he also likes to note our progress.' Quincy sighed, then squeezed the bridge of his nose. 'Earlier, you said the GBI attempted several times to find the Eco-Killer. You tried tracing the drugs that were used.

You did the standard victim profiling, you looked at veterinarians, campers, hikers, birdwatchers, all sorts of outdoorsmen.'

'Yes.'

'And you created a profile. It describes the killer as being male, white, above-average intelligence, but probably stuck in a menial job. Travels often, has limited social skills and is prone to fits of rage when frustrated.'

'That's what the expert told us.'

'Two things strike me,' Quincy said. 'One, I think the killer is even smarter than you think. By definition, his game forces your immediate attention and resources on finding the second victim – instead of pursuing him.'

'Well, in the beginning, sure—'

'A path grows cold, Mac. Every detective knows that. The more time has passed, the more difficult it is to find a suspect.'

Mac nodded his head more grudgingly. 'Yeah, okay.'

'And second, we now know something very interesting that you didn't know before.'

'Which is?'

'The man has access to the Marine base at Quantico. That narrows our suspect pool down to a relatively small group of people within the state of Virginia. And that's a lead we shouldn't squander.'

'You think a Marine or an FBI agent did this?' Mac asked with a frown.

Quincy had a faraway look in his eye. 'I don't know yet. But the emphasis on Quantico, the phone calls to you ... There's something significant there. I just can't see it yet. Can you write down the conversation you had tonight? Word by word, all of the caller's comments? Dr Ennunzio will want to see it.'

'You think he'll still help us?' Kimberly spoke up.

'You assume he knows we've been taken off the case.' Quincy shrugged. 'He's a backroom academic; field agents never think to keep those kind informed. They live in their world, the BSU lives in its own. Besides, we're going to need Dr Ennunzio. So far, those letters and phone calls are the only direct link we have to the Eco-Killer. And that's important. If we're going to break this pattern, we must identify the UNSUB. Otherwise, we're only ever treating the symptoms, not the disease.'

'You're not going to abandon the other two girls?' Mac asked sharply.

'I am,' Quincy said calmly. 'But you're not.'

'Divide and conquer?' Rainie spoke up.

'Exactly. Mac and Kimberly, you work on finding the girls. Rainie and I will continue our pursuit of the man himself.'

'That could be dangerous,' Mac said quietly.

Quincy merely smiled. 'That's why I'm taking Rainie with me. Let him just dare to tangle with her.'

'Amen,' Rainie said soberly.

'We could try the USGS again,' Kimberly said. 'Bring them the samples we have. I'm not sure what to make of the rice, but a hydrologist is a good start for the fluid.'

Mac nodded thoughtfully. 'They might know something about the rice. Maybe it's like the Hawaii connection. Wouldn't mean anything to a layman, but to the proper expert . . .'

'Where are those offices?' Quincy asked.

'Richmond.'

'What time do they open?'

'Eight A.M.'

Quincy glanced at his watch. 'Well, good news, everyone. We can all grab a few hours sleep after all.'

They drove out of the park. They found a chain motel in one of the nearby towns and booked three rooms. Quincy and Rainie disappeared into their tiny quarters. Mac went into his. Kimberly went into hers.

The furniture was sparse and dingy. The bed was covered by a faded blue comforter and already had a crater in the middle from one too many guests. The air was motel air, stale, reeking of old cigarettes, and mixed with undertones of Windex.

It was a room. It had a bed. She could sleep.

Kimberly cranked the air-conditioning. She stripped off her sweat-soaked clothes, climbed into the shower and scrubbed her battered body. She shampooed her hair again and again, while trying to forget the rocks, the snakes, that poor girl's tortuous death. She scrubbed and scrubbed and scrubbed. And she knew then that it would never be enough.

She was thinking of Mandy again, and of her mother and the unidentified girl at Quantico. And of Vivienne Benson. Except the victims got all tangled in her mind. And sometimes the body in the Quantico woods bore Mandy's face, and sometimes the girl in the rocks was actually Kimberly in disguise, and sometimes her mother was fleeing through the woods, trying to escape the Eco-Killer, when she had already been butchered by a madman six years before.

An investigator should have objectivity. An investigator should be dispassionate.

Kimberly finally got out of the shower. She pulled on a T-shirt. She used the dingy towel to wipe the steam from the mirror. And then she regarded her reflection. Pale, bruised face. Sunken cheeks. Bloodless lips. Oversized big blue eyes.

Jesus. She looked too scared to be herself.

She almost lost it again. Her hands gripped the edge of the washbasin tightly. She sank her teeth in her lower lip and fought bitterly for some trace of sanity.

All of her life, she'd been focused. Shooting guns, reading homicide textbooks. She had genuinely liked crime, sought it out as her father's daughter. All cases were puzzles to be solved. She wanted the challenge. Wear a badge. Save the world. Always be the one in control.

Tough, cool-as-a-cucumber Kimberly. She now felt her own mortality as a hollow spot deep in her stomach. And she knew she wasn't so tough anymore.

Twenty-six years old, all the defenses had finally been stripped away. Now here she was. A young, overwhelmed woman, who couldn't eat, couldn't sleep, and had a fear of snakes. Save the world? She couldn't even save herself.

She should just quit, let her father, Rainie and Mac go at it alone. She'd already bailed from the Academy. What would it matter if she simply disappeared now? She could spend the rest of her life curled up in a closet, hands clasped around her knees. Who could blame her? She'd already lost half of her family, and almost been killed twice. If anyone was entitled to a nervous breakdown, surely it was Kimberly.

But then she started thinking of the two missing girls again. Mac had told her their names. Karen Clarence. Tina Krahn. Two young college students who'd simply wanted to hang out with friends on a hot Tuesday night.

And then she knew she wouldn't quit. She was frightened, she was weepy, she wasn't as tough as she thought she should be. She felt as if she'd plunged over some psychic edge this afternoon, and was still making her way gingerly to shore. Her nerve-endings were raw, her skin felt as if it no longer suited her, and still . . .

Karen Clarence. Tina Krahn. Someone had to find them. Someone had to do something. And maybe she was her father's daughter after all, because she couldn't just walk away. She could quit the Academy, but she could not quit this case.

A knock sounded on the door. Kimberly's gaze came up slowly. She knew who had to be standing there. Ignore it and he will go away. She was already walking across the room.

She opened the door. Mac had obviously used the past thirty minutes to shower and shave.

'Hey,' he said softly, and strode into her room.

'Mac, I'm too tired—'

'I know. I am, too.' He took her arm and led her over to the bed. She followed only grudgingly. Her face was too pale, her eyes too bloodshot. Maybe she did like the smell of his soap, but she also wished desperately to just be alone.

'Have I mentioned yet that I don't sleep well in strange motel rooms?' he asked.

'No.'

'Have I mentioned that I think you look really good wearing just a T-shirt?'

'No.'

'Have I mentioned how good I look wearing nothing at all?'

'No.'

'Well, that's a shame, because it's all true. But you're tired and I'm tired, so this is all we're gonna do tonight.' He sat on the bed and tried to pull her down with him. She, however, finally dug in her heels.

'I can't do this,' she whispered.

He didn't force the issue. Instead, he reached up a large hand, and cradled her cheek. His blue eyes weren't laughing anymore. Instead, he studied her intently, his eyes dark, his expression somber. When he looked at her like this, she could barely breathe.

'You scared me tonight,' he told her quietly. 'When you were up on those rocks, surrounded by all those snakes, you scared me.'

'I scared me, too.'

'Do you think I'm toying with you, Kimberly?'

'I don't know.'

'It bothers you, that I can flirt, that I can smile.'

'Sometimes.'

'Earnest Kimberly.' His thumb stroked her cheek. 'You are honestly the most beautiful woman I've ever met, and I don't know how to tell you that, without you thinking it's just some kind of line.'

She closed her eyes. 'Don't.'

'Would you like to hit me?' he murmured. 'Would you like to yell and scream at the world, or maybe hurl your knife? I don't mind it when you're angry, honey. Anything's better than seeing you sad.'

That did it. She sank down on the bed beside him, feeling something big and brittle give way in the middle of her chest. Was this weakening? Was this succumbing? She didn't know anymore. She didn't care. Suddenly, she wanted to press her head against the broad expanse of his chest. She wanted to wrap her arms tightly around his lean waist. She wanted his warmth all around her, his arms holding her close. She wanted his body above her body, demanding and taking and conquering. She wanted something fierce and fast, where she didn't have to think and didn't have to feel. She could simply be.

She would blame him for it all in the morning.

Her head came up. She brushed her lips over his, feeling his breath tickle her cheek and, being rewarded, his tremor. She kissed his jaw. Smooth. Square. She followed its line to his throat, where she could see his pulse pounding. His hands were on her waist, not moving. But she could feel his tension now, his body hard and tightly leashed with his effort at control.

She caught the fragrance of his soap again. Then the trace of the mint on his breath. The spicy tones of his aftershave on his freshly razored cheek. She faltered again. The elements were personal, powerful. Things he had done just for her, and had no place in raw, meaningless sex.

She was going to cry again. Oh God, she hated this hard lump in her chest. She didn't want to be this creature anymore. She wanted to return to cold, logical Kimberly. Anything had to be better than to be this weepy all the time. Anything had to be better than to feel this much pain.

Mac's hands had moved. Now, they found her hair, gently feathering it back. Now his fingers ran from her temples all the way down to the taut lines of her neck.

'Shhh,' he murmured. 'Shhh,' though she wasn't aware she'd ever made a sound.

'I don't know who I am anymore.'

'You just need sleep, honey. It'll be better in the morning. Everything's better in the morning.'

Mac pulled her down beside him. She fell without protest, feeling his arousal press hard against her hip. Now he would do something, she thought. But he didn't. He merely tucked her into the curve of his body, his chest hot against her back, his arms like steel bands around her waist.

'I don't like strange motel rooms, either,' she said abruptly, and could almost see his grin against her hair. Then in another minute, she could tell he had drifted off.

Kimberly closed her eyes. She curled her fingers around Mac's arms. She slept the best she had in years.

32

Front Royal, Virginia
6:19 A.M.
Temperature: 88 degrees

Mac woke first, the tinny bleat of his cell phone penetrating his deep slumber. He had a moment of disorientation, trying to place the dimly lit room with its sagging bed and stale-smelling air. Then he registered Kimberly, still curled up soft and snug in the crook of his arm, and the rest of the evening came back to him.

He moved quickly now, not wanting to wake her. He slid his right arm from beneath her head, felt the resulting tingle shoot up from his elbow as various nerve endings fired to life, and swallowed a rueful curse. He shook out his hand, realizing now he didn't know where his phone was. He had a vague memory of throwing it across the room during the night. Frankly, given his recent treatment of his phone, it was a miracle it was working at all.

He dropped to the floor, scrambling on all fours until he finally came up with the palm-sized object. He flipped it open, just as it was ringing for the fourth time.

'Special Agent McCormack here.' He glanced at the bed. Kimberly still hadn't stirred.

'Took you long enough,' a distinctly male voice said.

Mac relaxed immediately. No more distorted voices to mess with his head. This was simply his boss, Special Agent in Charge Lee Grogen. 'Been a long night,' Mac replied.

'Successful?'

'Not especially.' Mac filled in the details of the last twelve hours. Grogen listened without interruption.

'It's definitely him then?'

'No doubt in my mind. Of course, for an official opinion you'd have to consult the feds. They probably think it's a terrorist act.'

'You sound bitter, Mac.'

'Three hours of sleep will do that to a guy. Now, best we can tell, we got two more girls out there. Pardon my French, but fuck the feds. I have some leads, and I'm goin' after them.'

'And I'm going to pretend I didn't hear that. In fact, I'm going to pretend we're talking about fishing.' Grogen sighed. 'Officially speaking, Mac, there's nothing I can offer you. My boss can press their boss for cooperation, but given that it's the feebies . . .'

'We're frozen out.'

'Probably. At least they'll refer to us one day – at the press conference when they announce their big catch, we'll be the local yokels who had a shot at the guy the first time around and couldn't get the job done. You know the drill.'

'I can't give up.' Mac said it quietly.

'Don't let me come between a man and some fishing,' Grogen said.

'Thank you, sir.'

'We have another complication.'

'Uh oh.' Mac rubbed his hand over his face, feeling the sandpaper of his beard. He was already tired again and so far he'd only been awake ten minutes. 'What's up?'

'Nora Ray Watts.'

'Huh?'

'She called me in the middle of the night. She wants to talk to you. She claims she has information about the case and she'll only give it to you, in person. Mac: she knew two girls were dead.'

'Has there been something in the papers?'

'Not a peep. Mac, I didn't even know two girls were dead until ten minutes ago when I called you. Frankly, I'm a little freaked out.'

'He's contacted her,' Mac murmured.

'It's possible.'

'It's the only thing that makes sense. Writing his letters isn't enough anymore. Calling me is probably just frustrating him. Hell, I hope so. So now he's contacting a past victim . . . Son of a bitch!'

'What do you want to do?'

'I can't go back to Atlanta. I don't have time.'

'I told Nora Ray you were out of town.'

'And?'

'And she said she would come to you. In all honesty, Mac, I think that's what she wants.'

Mac blinked his eyes, dumbfounded. After everything Nora Ray had been through. To drag her back into this mess. A civilian. A victim. 'No,' he said gruffly.

His supervisor was quiet.

'No way,' Mac said again. 'She doesn't deserve this. He messed with her life once already. Now it's time for her to be free of him, to heal and be with her family. Hell, to forget this ever happened.'

'I don't think that's working for her.'

'I can't protect her, Lee! I don't know where this guy is, I don't know where he's gonna strike next. It's a long story, but I've been working with a former FBI profiler, and he thinks the killer may be keeping tabs on us.'

'I'll tell her that.'

'Damn right!'

'And if she still wants to come?'

'She's a damn fool!'

'Mac, if she knows something, if she has a lead . . .'

Mac hung his head. He raked his hand through his hair. God there were times he hated his job. 'I can meet her at the airport in Richmond,' he said at last. 'Sooner versus later. Day's young and a lot can happen yet.'

'I'll be in touch. And Mac – good luck fishing.'

Mac flipped his phone shut. He rested his forehead against the cool silver shape. What a mess. He should go back to bed. Or at the very least, crawl back into a shower. When he got up the second time, maybe this day would make more sense.

But the fuzz was already clearing. He was thinking of water and rice, and obscure clues that had to lead to real and terrible places. They had been lucky to sleep at all last night. God knows when they'd sleep again.

He rose and crossed to the bed. Kimberly's arms were wrapped around her waist, her body held tightly together, as if she were protecting herself even when asleep. He sat down on the edge of the mattress. He touched the curve of her jaw with his thumb, then feathered back her short, dusty blond hair. She didn't stir.

She looked more vulnerable in sleep, her fine features delicate and even a trace fragile. He didn't let the image fool him. A guy could spend years, just working on learning the curve of her smile. And still, one day, she'd walk out the door and never look back. Probably think she'd done him a favor.

In her world, guys like him didn't fall for girls like her. Funny, 'cause in his world, he was already long gone.

He stroked his fingers down her arm and her eyes finally fluttered open.

'I'm sorry, sweetheart,' he whispered.

'Did someone else die?'

'Not if we keep moving.'

Kimberly sat up, and without another word, headed for the bathroom. He lay down on the bed and placed his hand on the spot still warm from the heat of her body. He could hear the sound of running water now, the rattle of old, rusty pipes. He thought again of yesterday, and the sight of Kimberly surrounded by dozens of rattlesnakes.

'I'm going to take better care of you,' he vowed in the quiet of the room.

But he already wondered where the day would lead, and if that promise could be kept.

33

'Sure as hell looks like water to me.'

Kimberly sighed with relief, while Mac visibly sagged against the wall of the tiny office. Neither of them had realized just how tensely they'd been awaiting that news until USGS hydrologist Brian Knowles had delivered it.

'Could it be holy water?' Kimberly asked.

Knowles shot her a look. 'I don't exactly have a test for that. I'm just a mere government employee, you know, not the Pope.'

'But can you help them out?' Ray Lee Chee prodded him. He'd personally brought Mac and Kimberly to Knowles's office just ten minutes earlier. Now he was perched on the edge of a gunmetal gray filing cabinet, swinging his feet rhythmically.

Mac spoke up. 'We'd like to be able to test the sample. Ideally, we need to trace it to a source such as a specific pond or stream or watering hole. Can you do that?'

Knowles yawned, rolled out one sleepy shoulder and seemed to consider it. He appeared to be in his mid-thirties, a good-looking guy with a thick head of woolly brown hair and the world's rattiest jeans. Like Ray Lee Chee, he appeared remarkably fit. Unlike the geographer, however, mornings weren't his thing. Brian Knowles looked as tired as Kimberly felt.

'Well,' he said shortly, 'we can test a water sample for all sorts of things: pH, dissolved oxygen, temperature, turbidity, salinity, nitrogen, ammonia, arsenic, bacteria . . . Then there's water hardness, tests for various inorganic constituents such as iron, manganese, and sulfates, as well as tests for various water pollutants. So testing, yeah, we can do that.'

'Good, good,' Mac said encouragingly.

'Just one hitch though.' Knowles spread his hands in a helpless gesture. 'We're not out in the field, and you can't do squat with six drops of water.'

Mac raised a startled brow. He glanced at Kimberly, who shrugged. 'At least we brought you water,' she commented. 'We only gave Ray a picture of a leaf.'

'Damn right. And I did good,' Ray boasted. 'So don't you ruin our track record now, Knowles. We keep this up, and maybe we can get our own TV show. You know, *Law & Order: US Geological Survey Unit*. Think of the chicks, Ryan. Think of the chicks.'

Knowles, however, didn't appear convinced. He leaned back in his desk chair and locked his hands behind his head. 'Look, I'm just being practical here. To get accurate results from any sort of water test, you need to be at the source, looking at the sample *in situ*. The minute you bottled up this water, a couple of things happened. One, you changed the temperature. Two, you removed it from its oxygen source, rendering a test for diffused oxygen useless. Three, the pH is going up from off-gas. Four, you may have contaminated the sample from the container itself, and five . . . Well, hell, I can't think of five at the moment, but let's just agree it's not good.

Whatever I do to this sucker, the results are about as meaningful as a sixth toe – gives you something to look at, but doesn't do a damn thing.'

'But we don't have a source,' Mac reminded him curtly. 'That's the whole damn point. This sample is what we've been given, the source is what we gotta find. Come on, surely there's something you can do.'

Mac just stared at the man with mute appeal. After another moment, Knowles caved with a sigh. 'It won't be accurate,' he warned.

'At this point, we'll take an educated guess.'

'I don't know if I'd even call it that.' But Knowles was fingering the glass tube bearing their precious sample. 'You're sure you don't have more? I'd prefer about forty milliliters.'

'The best I could do would be six more drops.'

Knowles blinked. 'Damn, whoever gave you this was definitely feeling stingy.'

'He likes a challenge.'

'No kidding. I don't suppose you're gonna tell me anything more about this case.'

'Nope.'

'Ah well, never hurts to ask.' Knowles sighed again, sat up in his chair and stared intently at the sample. 'Okay. It's possible to test for salinity. We just need enough water to cover the end of the probe. I could also do pH, which also uses a meter. Of course, the probe on the pH meter can deposit a tiny amount of potassium chloride in a sample, raising the electrical conductivity and screwing the salinity test . . . So we do salinity first, I guess, then examine pH. As for mineral testing . . . Hell, I don't know if any of our test equipment is even calibrated for a sample this small. Bacteria tests . . . You have to run the water through a sieve, not sure that would do much here. Same with testing for plant matter.' He looked up. 'Salinity and pH it is then, though I'm telling you now, the sample size is too limited, the methodology flawed, and all the results will be too relative to draw any sort of accurate conclusions. Other than that, what the hell, I'm game. I've never worked a murder case before.'

'Any information is helpful,' Mac said grimly.

Knowles pulled open a drawer. He pulled out a small plastic box with a well-worn label that read, Field Kit. He popped open the container and started pulling out handheld meters complete with long metal probes. 'Salinity first,' he murmured to himself, fiddled around, then stuck the probe in the water.

He didn't say anything right away. Just grunted a few times.

'What does a salinity test measure?' Kimberly asked. 'If it's freshwater or salt water?'

'It can.' Knowles glanced up at her. 'Basically, I'm measuring the amount of microsiemens per centimeter in the water, which gives me an idea of the dissolved content. Water on its own has no electrical conductivity. But water that has a lot of salt or other dissolved minerals in it will have a higher level of conductivity. More microsiemens per centimeter. So, in a roundabout way, we're trying to tell where this water has been.'

He looked at the meter, then pulled the probe from the sample. 'All right. According to my handy dandy salinity meter, this water has a reading of fifteen thousand microsiemens per centimeter. So, bearing in mind all my earlier objections, what does that tell us?'

They all looked at him blankly, and he generously filled in, 'The water has good conductivity. Not high enough to be salt water, but there's a fair amount of dissolved content in this sample. Maybe minerals or ions. Something that conducts electricity better than water alone.'

'The water is contaminated?' Mac asked hesitantly.

'The water is high in dissolved content,' Knowles reiterated stubbornly. 'At this moment, we can't conclude anything more than that. Now, the logical thing would be to run tests for various minerals, which might answer your question. But we can't do that, so let's try pH.'

He set aside the first meter and inserted a second. He watched the meter, then frowned at the meter, then pulled out the tip and muttered, 'Goddamn probe. Hang on a sec.'

He wiped the tip. Blew on the tip. Then gave the whole thing a small whack with his hand. With a grunt of satisfaction, he finally returned the probe to the water. The second time didn't make him any happier.

'Well shit on a stick, this is no good.'

'What's wrong?' Kimberly asked.

'Sample must be too small for the probe, or my meter's out of whack. To believe this thing, the pH is three-point-eight, and that just ain't happening.'

This time, he banged the probe twice against the desk. Then he tried again.

'What does three-point-eight mean?' Mac asked.

'Acidic. Very acidic. Eat-holes-in-your-clothes level of acidic. Basic is a perfect seven-point-oh. Most fish and algae need at least six-point-five to survive; snails, clams and mussels require seven-point-oh; while insects, suckers, and carp can go as low as six. So when we're testing ponds and streams with any sort of aquatic life, generally we're at least in the sixes. Now in Virginia, rainfall has a pH of four-point-two to four-point-five, so pure rainwater would test low, but we know this isn't pure rainwater thanks to the salinity test. Three-point-eight,' he was still shaking his head. 'That's ridiculous.'

He glanced at the meter again, gave a final growl of disgust, and yanked out the probe.

'What's it saying?' Mac asked intently.

'Same garbage as before, three-point-eight. I'm sorry, but the sample has got to be too small. That's all there is to it.'

'You're three for three.' Kimberly spoke up quietly. 'Three tests, three similar results. Maybe the water is that acidic.'

'It doesn't make any sense, especially when you consider that any pH reading we're getting now, is actually *higher* than the original pH at the source. Frankly, we just don't see pH reading below four-point-five. It doesn't happen. Well, except maybe in cases of acid mine drainage.'

Mac straightened immediately. 'Tell us about acid mine drainage.'

'Not much to tell. Water spills out of the mine or goes through tailings of the mine, getting contaminated as it goes. The pH ends up extremely low, possibly in the twos.'

'And that would be extremely rare? Something unusual in this state?'

Knowles gave Mac a look. 'Buddy, there aren't many places in the *world* that have pH readings in the twos, let alone in the state of Virginia.'

'Where is this mine?' Kimberly spoke up urgently.

'You mean mines, *s* as in plural, as in coal mines. We're loaded with them.'

'Where?'

'Southwestern Virginia mostly. There's a good seven counties, I think.' Knowles was looking at Ray for confirmation. 'Let's see . . . Dickenson, Lee, Russell, Scott. Hell, I'm never going to be able to do this off the top of my head; let me look 'em up.' He pushed back toward his filing cabinet, gave Ray's legs a prodding shove, then rifled through some manila files.

'How big is the area?' Kimberly pressed him.

Knowles shrugged, then looked again at Ray. 'Most of the southwestern corner of the state,' Ray offered up. 'It's not small, if that's what you mean.'

'But the water probably came from there,' Mac asserted.

'I will not say that,' Knowles warned him. 'Sample too

small, results too subjective, too many variables beyond my control.'

'But it is a strong possibility.'

'*If* you accept that reading of three-point-eight to be correct, then yes, a mine would be a good place to look for this kind of contaminated water supply. The only other possible theory . . .' He stopped, chewed on his lower lip. 'It's gotta be contamination of some kind,' he muttered at last. 'That's the only thing that could reduce the pH level so dramatically. Now it could be from a mine. It could also be pollution from organic wastes. Basically, a large dose of biodegradable organic material gets in the water. Bacteria feed off the waste, bacterial population explodes, and now the bacteria consume oxygen faster than the algae or aquatic plants can replace it. *Badda bing, badda boom*: anything that needs oxygen to live – say, fish, insects, plants – dies, and anaerobic bacteria take over the water source; they're about the only thing that can live at pH that low.'

'But you can't test it for bacteria, can you?' Kimberly quizzed him.

'Nah, sample's too small.'

'Is . . . is there anything else you can do?'

'Well, I could *try* testing for minerals. We got a guy around here who's been squeezing water out of core samples going back thousands of years and running that stuff through the equipment. I know those water samples have gotta be small, but he's gotten some results. I don't know how good—'

'We'll take anything,' Mac interrupted him.

'It's very important,' Kimberly reiterated. 'We need to narrow down this water to the smallest geographic region possible. Seven counties is a start, but seven miles would be better.'

'Seven miles huh?' Knowles gave her a doubtful look. 'Even if I did get lucky and identify a bunch of minerals . . .

Well,' he caught himself. 'Then again, there are some key physiographic differences between the mine counties. A lot of sandstone and shale in some areas. Karsts in others. So minerals results might help. Not seven miles, mind you, but I might be able to get you down to a county or two. I guess we'll find out.'

'How long?' Mac pressed him.

'First I'm going to have to talk to the guy, figure out how to set up the equipment . . . I'd say give me a couple of days.'

'I'll give you two hours.'

'Say what?'

'Listen to me. Two women are missing. It's been nearly forty-eight hours now, and one woman is somewhere around that water. We either find her soon, or it won't much matter anymore.'

Knowles's mouth was ajar. He looked pale and troubled at the news, then glanced at the tiny sample with a fresh distrust. 'All right,' he said abruptly. 'Give me two hours.'

'One last item.' Mac's attention went to Ray Lee Chee. 'We have one more sample we need tested. Problem is, we don't know what it is.'

He held out the glass vial bearing the residue from the second victim's hair. Ray took it first, then handed it over to Knowles. Neither man knew what it was, but decided a palynologist would be their best bet – an expert in pollen. And they were in luck. One of the best in the state, Lloyd Armitage, was due in this afternoon for a team meeting.

'Anything else?' Ray asked.

'Rice,' Kimberly said. 'Uncooked long grain. Does that mean anything to either of you?'

That brought a fresh round of bemused looks. Knowles confessed he was a pasta man. Ray Lee Chee said he'd always hated to cook. But hey, they'd ask around.

And that was that. Knowles would attempt to test their

water for mineral samples; Ray would inquire about rice; and Mac and Kimberly would hit the road.

'The leaf was easier,' Kimberly said shortly, as they walked down the hall.

'That was probably the point.' Mac pushed through the exterior door and led them back into the wall of heat. He glanced at his watch and Kimberly caught the gesture.

'Time?'

'Yep.' They got into his car and headed for the airport.

34

Kimberly's first glimpse of Nora Ray Watts was not what she had expected. In her mind, she had pictured a young, deeply traumatized girl. Head bowed, shoulders hunched. She would wear nondescript clothes, trying desperately to blend in, while her furtive gaze would dash around the crowded airport, already seeking the source of some unnamed threat.

They'd handle the girl with kid gloves. Buy her a Coke, pick her brain for what she claimed to know about the Eco-Killer, then send her back to the relative safety of Atlanta. That's how these things were done, and frankly, they didn't have time to dick around.

Nora Ray Watts, however, had another plan in mind.

She strode down the middle of the airport terminal, with an old flowered bag slung over her shoulder. Her head was up, her shoulders square. She wore a pair of slim-fitting jeans, a wispy blue shirt over a white tank top, and a pair of heavy-duty hiking boots. Her long brown hair was pulled back into a ponytail, and she hadn't a shred of makeup on her pale, composed face. She headed straight for them, and the other travelers immediately gave way.

Kimberly had two impressions at once. A young girl, grown up too fast, and a remote woman who now existed as an island in the sea of humanity. Then Kimberly wondered, with almost a sense of panic, if that's what people saw when they peered into her own face.

Nora Ray walked up and Kimberly looked away.

'Special Agent McCormack,' she said gravely and shook Mac's outstretched hand.

He introduced Kimberly, and Nora Ray took her hand as well. The girl's grip was firm, but quick. Someone who didn't like touching.

'How was the flight?' Mac asked.

'Fine.'

'How are your parents?'

'Fine.'

'Uh huh. And what kind of story did you feed them about today?'

Nora Ray brought her chin up. 'I told them I was going to spend a few days with an old college friend in Atlanta. My father was happy I was going to see a friend. My mother was busy watching *Family Ties*.'

'Lying's not good for the soul, little girl.'

'No. And neither is fear. Shall we?'

She headed toward the food court, while Mac arched a brow.

'She's not your typical victim,' Kimberly murmured as they fell in step behind the girl. Mac merely shrugged.

'She has a good family. Least she did before this.'

In the food court, Mac and Kimberly got large cups of bitter coffee. Nora Ray purchased a soda and a banana muffin, which she then proceeded to pick at with her fingers as they sat at a small plastic table.

Mac didn't ask anything right away. Kimberly, too, took her time. Sipping the foul-tasting brew, looking around the Richmond airport as if she hadn't a care in the world. Nothing better to do than sit around in air-conditioned glory. Nothing more urgent today than getting that perfect cup of coffee. If only her heart hadn't been beating so hard in her chest. If only they all hadn't been so unbearably aware of the fleeting nature of time.

'I want to help,' Nora Ray said abruptly. She'd finished destroying her muffin, and now she looked at them with a nervous, shaky expression. Closer to the young girl again, not so much the remote woman.

'My boss tells me you know something about the current situation,' Mac said neutrally.

'He's at it again. Taking girls. Two are dead, aren't they?'

'How do you know that, honey?'

'Because I do.'

'He call you?'

'No.'

'Send you letters?'

'No.' She stiffened her spine. Her voice grew stubborn. 'You answer my question first. Are two more girls dead? Is he doing it again?'

Mac was silent, letting the moment drag out. Nora Ray's fingers returned to the bits of her muffin. She kneaded them back together, then tore them apart into a fresh round of small, doughy balls. But the girl was good. She outlasted both of them.

'Yeah,' Mac said, tersely. 'Yeah, he's killing again.'

The fire left her all at once. Nora Ray's shoulders slumped, her hands fell heavily on the table. 'I knew it,' she whispered. 'I didn't want to know, I wanted to believe it was only a dream. But in my heart . . . In my heart I always knew. Poor girls. They never stood a chance.'

Mac leaned forward. He folded his arms on the table and studied her intently. 'Nora Ray, you have to start talking. How do you know these things?'

'You won't laugh?'

'After the last thirty-six hours, I don't have the strength left in me to smile.'

Nora Ray's gaze flickered to Kimberly.

'I'm even more tired than he is,' Kimberly told her. 'So your secret's safe with us.'

'I dreamed them.'

'You *dreamed* them?'

'I dream of my sister all the time, you know. I never tell people. It would only upset them. But for years I've watched Mary Lynn. She's happy, I think. Wherever she is, there are fields and horses and plenty of sunshine. She doesn't see me; I don't know if I exist in her place. But I get to see her, from time to time, and I think she's doing all right. But then, a few days ago, another girl appeared. And last night, a second girl joined her on the fence. I think they're still figuring out that they're dead.'

Mac's expression had gone blank. He rubbed one large hand over his face, then did it again and again. He doesn't know what to do, Kimberly realized. He doesn't know what to say. However either one of them had imagined this conversation going, this wasn't it.

'Are these girls aware of you?' Kimberly asked at last. 'Do they talk to you?'

'Yes. One of them has a younger sister. She wanted to know if her sister would also dream about her at night.'

'Can you describe the girls?'

Nora Ray rattled off two descriptions. They weren't exactly right, but neither were they wrong. A blonde, a brunette. People who claimed to have psychic ability often relied on generic descriptions to get your own imagination to fill in the blanks. Kimberly was feeling tired again.

'Do you see the man?' Mac asked Nora Ray sharply.

'No.'

'You just dream of the girls?'

'Yes.'

Mac spread his hands. 'Nora Ray, I don't see how that helps us.'

'I don't either,' she admitted, her tone suddenly sodden and on the edge of tears. 'But it's something, isn't it? I have a connection. Some kind of . . . I don't know what! But I'm seeing these girls. I know they died! I know they're hurt and confused and angry as hell at this man for what he did to them. Maybe I can use that. Maybe I can ask them more questions, get information on the killer, find out where he lives. I don't know. But it's something! I know it's something!'

Her voice broke off raggedly. Her hands were now compulsively mashing muffin bits into the tabletop. She squished the soft dough harder and harder with her thumbs. It appeared to be her last link to sanity.

Kimberly looked at Mac. He seemed sorry to have agreed to this meeting. She couldn't blame him.

'I appreciate you coming out and telling me this,' he said at last, his tone grave.

'You're not sending me home.'

'Nora Ray—'

'No. I can help! I don't know how yet. But I can help. If you're still looking, then I'm staying.'

'Nora Ray, you're a civilian. Now, I'm in the middle of a formal police investigation. It's demanding and time-consuming and while I'm sure you mean well, your presence in fact will only slow me down, and – if you'll pardon my French – fuck things up. So go home. I'll call you when we've learned something.'

'He's going to strike again. That last summer, he struck twice. He'll do the same now.'

'Nora Ray, honey . . .' Mac spread his hands. He seemed to be searching for some way to get through to the girl, to make her understand the futility of her efforts. 'The killer's already struck twice in a manner of speaking. This time, instead of taking two girls, he ambushed four. Now two are dead, two are missing, and so help me, God, I can't keep sitting here and having this conversation. We are in the middle of serious business. Go home, Nora Ray. I'll be in touch.'

Mac rose from the table. Kimberly took that as her cue to join him. But once again, Nora Ray did not conform to type. She also got up from the table, and this time her brown eyes held a bright, feverish light.

'That's it, then,' the young girl breathed. 'We're going to find the missing girls. That's why I'm seeing the first two in my dreams. I was meant to come. I was meant to help.'

'Nora Ray—'

The girl cut him off with a firm shake of her head. 'No. I'm twenty-one, I'm an adult. I've made my choice. I'm going with you, whether I have to follow you in a taxi or latch on to your trunk. You're in a hurry, so just nod yes and we can all get on with this. Three heads are better than two. You'll see.'

'Get on that plane or I will call your parents.'

'No. You look me in the eye and tell me that I'm wrong. Go on: Tell me you're one hundred percent certain I can't help. Because this man's been killing a long time, Special Agent McCormack. This man, he's been killing for years, and you *still haven't stopped him*. Given all that, maybe dreams aren't such a bad place to start.'

Mac visibly faltered. As guilt trips went, the girl was good. And there was a nugget of truth to what she said. More than a few reputable police departments had brought in psychics and soothsayers over the years. Detectives got to a point in a case where everything logical had been done. Timelines had been analyzed and overanalyzed. Evidence traced and retraced. And cops grew frustrated and trails grew cold and next thing they knew, the mad hatter on the other end of the phone saying *I've had a vision*, was the best lead they'd gotten all year.

Kimberly found she was suddenly very into the idea of dreams and she'd only been working the case thirty-six hours. She couldn't imagine how Mac must feel after five brutal years. And now here they were. Two girls dead. Two girls missing. Clock ticking . . .

'You know the kind of terrain this man picks,' Mac said at last.

Nora Ray hefted the pack by her side, then kicked out one hiking boot. 'I came prepared.'

'It's dangerous.'

She merely smiled. 'You don't have to tell me that.'

'You were lucky three years ago.'

'I know. I've practiced since then. Read survival books, studied nature, got in shape. You'd be amazed how much I know now. I might even be helpful to you.'

'This isn't your battle to fight.'

'It's my only battle to fight. My sister's never coming home, Special Agent McCormack. My family has fallen apart. I've spent three years shut inside a dead house, waiting for the day I'd magically stop being afraid. Well you know what? It's never going to happen on its own. So I might as well come here.'

'It's not a vendetta. We find him and you try to touch a hair on his head . . .'

'I'm a twenty-one-year-old girl, traveling with a pack that's been cleared by airport security. What do you think I'm going to do?'

Mac still looked very uncomfortable. He glanced at Kimberly. She shrugged. 'You do attract a certain kind of woman,' she told him.

'I'm changing my cologne,' he said seriously.

'And until then?'

He sighed. Stared down the terminal. 'Fine,' he said suddenly, shortly. 'What the hell. I'm illegal on this case. Kimberly's illegal on this case. What's one more member of unsanctioned personnel? Goddamn strangest investigation I've ever led. Know anything about rice?' he asked Nora Ray sharply.

'No.'

'What about pollen?'

'It makes you go ahchoo.'

He shook his head. 'Grab your bag. We've got a lot more ground to cover and it's already getting late.'

Nora Ray fell in step beside Kimberly as both of them scrambled to keep up with Mac's long, angry strides.

'Feel better?' Kimberly asked Nora Ray at last.

'No,' the young girl answered. 'Mostly, I feel afraid.'

35

Quincy and Rainie drove to Quantico in silence. They did that a lot these days. Ate in silence, traveled in silence, shared a room in silence. Funny how Rainie hadn't noticed it much in the beginning. Maybe it had seemed like personable silence back then. Two people so comfortable with one another they no longer needed words. Now, it seemed more ominous. If silence was a noise, then this silence was the sharp crack of an iceberg, suddenly tearing apart in the middle of an ancient glacier field.

Rainie pressed her forehead against the warm glass of the passenger side window. She rubbed her temples unconsciously and wished she could get these thoughts out of her head.

Outside, the sun beat down relentlessly. Even with the AC cranked in the tiny rental car, she could feel the heat gathering just beyond the vents. Her bare legs were hot from sunbeams. She could already feel sweat trickle uncomfortably down her back.

'Thinking of Oregon?' Quincy asked abruptly. He was wearing his customary blue suit; jacket draped neatly in the backseat for now, but tie still knotted around his throat. She didn't know how he did it every morning.

'Not exactly.' She straightened in her seat, stretching out her bare legs. She wore a fresh pair of khaki shorts and a white collared shirt that desperately needed ironing. No suits for her. Not even if they were returning to Quantico. The place wasn't her hallowed ground and they both knew it.

'You're thinking of Oregon a lot these days, aren't you?' Quincy asked again. She looked at him more carefully, surprised by his tenacity. His face was impossible to read. Dark eyes peering straight ahead. His lips set in a tight line. He was going for the neutral, psychologist-on-duty approach, she decided.

'Yeah,' she said.

'It's been a long time. Nearly two years. Maybe after this, we should go there. To Oregon. Have a vacation.'

'All right.' Her voice came out thicker than she intended. Dammit, she had tears in her eyes.

He heard it, turned toward her and for the first time, she saw the full panic on his face. 'Rainie . . .'

'I know.'

'Have I done something wrong?'

'It's not you.'

'I know I can be distant. I know I get a little lost in my work . . .'

'It's my work, too.'

'But you're not happy, Rainie. It's not just today either. You haven't been happy in a long, long time.'

'No.' It shocked her to finally say it out loud, and in the next instant, she felt a curious sensation in the middle of her chest. Relief. She had gotten the word out. She had said it, had acknowledged the elephant that had been lurking in the room for a good six months now. Someone had to.

Quincy's gaze returned to the road. His hands flexed and

unflexed on the wheel. 'Is there something I can do?' he asked at last, already sounding more composed. That was his way, she knew. You could hit the man in the gut, and he'd merely square his shoulders. If you hurt his daughter, on the other hand, or threatened Rainie . . . That's when the gloves came off. That's when his dark eyes gleamed feral, and his runner's body fell into the stance of a long, lean weapon, and he emerged not as Quincy, top criminology researcher, but as Pierce, an extremely dangerous man.

That was only when you harmed someone he loved, however. He had never done much of anything to protect himself.

'I don't know,' Rainie said bluntly.

'If you want to go to Oregon, I'll go to Oregon. If you need a break, we can take a break. If you need space, I'll give you space. If you need comfort, then just tell me and I'll pull over this car right now and take you into my arms. But you have to tell me something, Rainie, because I've been floating in the dark for months now, and I think I'm losing my mind.'

'Quincy . . .'

'I would do anything to make you happy, Rainie.'

And she said in a small voice, 'I'm so sorry, Quincy, but I think I want a baby.'

Kaplan was already waiting for them when they pulled into the parking lot outside the Jefferson Dormitory. He looked hot, tired, and already pissed as hell with the day.

'A little birdie told me I'm not supposed to be talking to you two,' he said the moment they climbed out of their car. 'Said, I should deal only with some new guy, who's now heading the investigation.'

Quincy shrugged mildly. 'I haven't been notified of any change in staffing. Have you, Rainie?'

'Nope,' she said. 'Never heard a thing.'

'That little birdie must be pulling your leg,' Quincy told Kaplan.

Kaplan raised a brow. In a surprising quick move for a big guy, he swiped the cell phone clipped to Quincy's waist, eyed its lack of power, and grunted. 'Smart. Well, as long as they're fucking their own people, welcome to my happy little club. I got a body, I still have jurisdiction, and I'm not giving it up.'

'Amen,' Quincy said. Rainie merely yawned.

Kaplan remained scowling. 'So why do you want to reinterview my sentries? Think I couldn't possibly have gotten it right the first time?'

'No, but now we have new information on the suspect.'

That seemed to appease the special agent. He shook out his shoulders, indicated for them to climb into his car, then headed back out onto the base. 'Guys were out training this morning.' Kaplan filled them in, 'I had their CO pull them aside. Both should be waiting for us at the school. They're young, but good. If they know anything that can be of help, they'll tell you.'

'Any more activity around here?'

'Dead bodies? Thankfully, no. Ads in the *Quantico Sentry*? None that have crossed anyone's desk. I met with Betsy Radison's parents late last night. That's been about it.'

'Tough business,' Quincy said quietly.

'Yeah, it is.'

Kaplan turned into the cluster of buildings that marked Marine TBS – The Basic School. Sure enough, two young recruits sat to the side, dressed in jungle camo with hats pulled low to shield their faces and thick black utility belts strapped around their waists. Kaplan, Quincy, and Rainie climbed out of the car, and immediately the two snapped to attention.

Kaplan made the introductions, while the recruits held their rigid stance.

'This is civilian Pierce Quincy. He is going to ask you some questions regarding the night, fifteen of July. This is his partner, Lorraine Conner. She may also ask you questions regarding the same evening. You will answer both of their questions to the best of your ability. You will accord them the full respect and cooperation you would give any Marine officer requesting your assistance. Is that clear?'

'Sir, yes sir!'

Kaplan nodded at Quincy. 'You may proceed.'

Quincy raised a brow. The pomp and circumstance was a little extreme. Then again, Kaplan had taken a lot of hits recently. The FBI had forced him out of their world. Now he was showing off the power he still wielded in his.

Quincy approached the two Marines. 'You were both on duty for the night shift, July fifteenth?'

'Sir, yes sir.'

'Both of you stopped each vehicle and checked each driver for proper ID?'

'We stopped all incoming vehicles, sir!'

'Did you check passengers for proper identification?'

'All visitors to the base must show proper identification, sir!'

Quincy shot Rainie another dry look. She didn't dare meet his eye or she would start giggling or burst into tears or both. The morning had already taken on a surreal quality, and now it felt as if they were interviewing two trained seals.

'What kind of vehicles did you stop that night?' Quincy asked.

For the first time, no immediate answer was shouted forth. Both recruits were still staring straight ahead as procedure dictated, but it was clear they were now confused.

Quincy tried again. 'Special Agent Kaplan said you both reported heavy traffic that night.'

'Sir, yes sir!' both Marines cried out promptly.

'The majority of this traffic seemed to be National Academy students returning to the dorms.'

'Sir, yes sir!'

'Is it fair to say that these people mostly drove rental cars or their own personal vehicles? I would guess you saw a lot of small, nondescript automobiles.'

'Sir, yes sir.' Not quite as vehement, but still an affirmative.

'What about vans?' Quincy asked gently. 'Particularly a cargo van arriving in the early morning hours?'

Quiet again. Both sentries wore a frown.

'We did see a few vans, sir,' one finally reported.

'Did you happen to note these vehicles in your logs, or glance at the license plates?'

'No, sir.'

Quincy's turn to frown. 'Why not? I would think you'd see mostly cars coming and going off the base. A cargo van should be unusual.'

'No, sir. Construction, sir.'

Quincy looking blankly at Kaplan, who seemed to get it. 'We have a number of projects active here on the base,' the special agent explained. 'New firing ranges, new labs, new admin buildings. It's been a busy summer, and most of those crews are driving vans or trucks. Hell, we've cleared guys on forklifts.'

Quincy closed his eyes. Rainie could already see the anger building behind his deceptively quiet façade. The little details no one thought to mention in the beginning. The one little detail, of course, that could make all the difference in a case.

'You have a ton of construction personnel active on this base,' Quincy said in a steely voice. His eyes opened. He looked straight at Kaplan. 'And you never mentioned this before?'

Kaplan shifted uneasily. 'Didn't come up.'

'You have a murder on the base, and you don't think to mention that you have an abnormally high number of eighteen-to-thirty-five-year-old males engaged in transient, menial labor, in other words, men who fit the murderer's profile, passing through these gates?'

Now even the two Marine sentries were regarding Kaplan with interest. 'Each and every person who receives authorization to enter this base must first pass security clearance,' Kaplan replied evenly. 'Yeah, I got a list of the names, and yeah, my people have been reviewing them. But we don't allow people with records on this base period – not as personnel, not as contractors, not as guests, and not as students. So it's a clean list.'

'That's wonderful,' Quincy said crisply. 'Except for one thing, Special Agent Kaplan. Our UNSUB doesn't have a record – he hasn't been caught yet!'

Kaplan's face blazed red. He was definitely aware of the two sentries watching him, and he was definitely aware of Quincy's growing fury. But still he didn't back down. 'We pulled the list. We analyzed the names. No one has a history of violence or a record of assault. In other words, there is nothing to indicate any one of those contractors should be pursued as a suspect. Unless, excuse me, you want me to start attacking any guy who drives a cargo van.'

'It would be a start.'

'It would be half the list!'

'Yes, but then how many of those people once lived in Georgia!'

Kaplan drew up short, blinked, and Quincy finally nodded in grim satisfaction. 'A simple credit report, Special Agent. That's all you have to do. It'll give you previous addresses and we can identify anyone who also has ties to Georgia. And then we'd have a suspect list. Don't you think?'

'It . . . but . . . well . . . Yeah, okay.'

'There are two more girls out there,' Quincy said more quietly. 'And this UNSUB has gotten away with this for far too long.'

'You don't know that he's really a member of the construction crews,' Kaplan said stubbornly.

'No, but we should at least be asking these questions. You can't let the UNSUB control the game. Take it from me,' Quincy's gaze had taken on a faraway look. 'You have to take control, or you will lose. With these kinds of predators, it's all about gamesmanship. Winner takes all.'

'I'll put my people on the list,' Kaplan said. 'Give us a few hours. Where will you be?'

'At the BSU, talking to Dr Ennunzio.'

'Has he learned anything from the ad?'

'I don't know. But let's hope he's been lucky. Because the rest of us certainly haven't.'

36

Tina had gone native. Mud streaked her arms, her legs, her pretty green sundress. She had stinking ooze coating her face and neck, primordial slime squishing between her toes. Now she picked up another sticky handful and smeared it across her chest.

She remembered reading a book in high school, *Lord of the Flies*. According to one of the notations in the handy yellow CliffNotes, *Lord of the Flies* was really about a wet dream. Tina hadn't gotten that part. Mostly she remembered the stranded kids turning into little savages, first taking on wild boars, then taking on one another. The book possessed a fearful edgy quality that was also definitely sexy. So maybe it was about wet dreams after all. She couldn't tell if the guys in her class had read it with any more enthusiasm than they'd read the other literary classics.

But that wasn't really the point. The point was that Tina Krahn, knocked-up college student and madman's current plaything, was finally getting a real-life lesson in literature. Who said high school didn't teach you anything?

She started mucking up first thing this morning, the sun already climbing in the sky and threatening to fry her like a bug caught in the glare of a magnifying glass. The mud stank to high heaven, but it sure did feel good against her flesh. It went on cool and thick, coating her festering skin with a thick layer of protection not even the damn mosquitoes could penetrate. It filled her nostrils with a putrid, musky smell. And it made her head practically swim with relief.

The mud liked her. The mud would save her. The mud was her friend. Now she stared at the bubbling, popping mess and she wondered why she didn't eat a handful as well. Her water was gone. Crackers, too. Her stomach had a too-tight, pained feeling, like she was on the verge of the world's worst menstrual cramps. The baby was probably leaving her. She had been a bad mother, and now the baby wanted the mud, too.

Was she crying? It was so hard to tell, with the heavy weight of drying filth on her cheeks.

The mud was wet. It would feel so good sliding down her parched, ravenous throat. It would fill her stomach with a heavy, rotting mass. She could stop digesting her stomach lining, and dine on dirt instead.

It would be so easy. Pick up another oozing handful. Slide it past her lips.

Delirious, the voice in the back of her brain whispered. The heat and dehydration had finally taken their toll. She had chills even in the burning heat. The world swam uneasily every time she moved. Sometimes she found herself laughing, though she didn't know why. Sometimes she sat in a corner and sobbed, though at least that made some kind of sense.

The sores on her arms and legs had started moving this morning. She had squeezed one scabbed-over mass between her fingers, then watched in horror as four white maggots popped out. Her flesh was rotting. The bugs had already moved in to dine. It wouldn't be much longer for her now.

She dreamt of water, of ice-cold streams rippling over her skin. She dreamt of nice restaurants with white linen table-cloths, where four tuxedoed waiters brought her an endless supply of frosty water glasses, filled to the brim. She would dine on seared steak and twice-baked potatoes covered in melted cheese. She would eat marinated artichoke hearts straight from the container, until olive oil dribbled down her chin.

She dreamt of a pale yellow nursery and a fuzzy head nestled at her breast.

She dreamt of her mother, attending Tina's funeral and standing alone next to her grave.

If she closed her eyes, she could return to the world of her dreams. Let the maggots have her flesh. Let her body sink into the mud. Maybe when the end came, she wouldn't even know anymore. She would just slide away, taking her baby with her.

Tina's eyes popped open. She forced her head up. Struggled to her feet. The world spun again, and she leaned against the boulder.

No eating mud! No caving in. She was Tina Krahn and she was made of sterner stuff.

Her breath came out in feeble gasps, her chest heaving with effort to inhale the overheated, muggy air. She staggered toward one vine-covered wall, watching a snake dart out of her way, hissing at it as it passed. Then she was braced against the wall, the vines cool against her muddy cheek.

Her fingers patted the structure as if it were a good dog. Funny, the surface over here didn't feel like rough cement. In fact . . .

Tina pushed herself back. Her eyes were terribly swollen; it was so hard to see . . . She forced them wide with all of her might, while simultaneously pushing back the vines. Wood. This part of the rectangular pit was held up by wood. Railroad ties or something like that. Old, peeling railroad ties that were already rotting with age.

Frantically, she dug her fingers into one visible hole. She tugged hard, and felt the meat of the lumber start to give way. She needed more strength. Something harder, a tool.

A rock.

Then she was down on her hands and knees, once again digging in the mud while her eyes took on a feverish light. She would find a rock. She would gouge out the boards. And then she would climb out of this pit, just like Spider Man. She would get to the top, she would find coolness, find water, find tender green things to eat.

She, Tina Krahn, knocked-up college student and madman's current plaything, would finally be free.

Lloyd Armitage, USGS palynologist and Ray Lee Chee's new best friend, met them shortly after noon. Five minutes later, Mac, Kimberly, and Nora Ray were piling into a conference room Armitage had set up as his traveling lab. It was a strange entourage, Mac thought, but then this was a strange case. Kimberly looked bone-tired but alert, wearing that slightly edgy look he'd come to know so well. Nora Ray was much harder to read. Her face was blank, shut down. She'd made a big decision, he thought, now she was trying not to think about it.

'Ray Lee Chee says you're working some kind of homicide case,' Armitage stated.

'We have evidence from a scene,' Mac answered. 'We need to trace it back to the original source. I'm afraid I can't tell you much more than that, other than whatever you have to tell us, we needed to have heard it yesterday.'

Armitage, an older man with bushy hair and a thick brown beard, arched a curling eyebrow. 'So that's how it is. Well, for the record, pollen analysis isn't as specific as botany. Most of my job is taking soil samples from various field sites. Then I use a little bit of hydrochloric acid and a little bit of hydrofluoric acid to break apart the minerals in the sediment. Next, I run every-thing through sieves, mix that with zinc chloride, then place it in a medical centrifuge until voila, I have a nice little sample of pollen, fresh from the great outdoors – or from several thousand years ago, as the case might be. At that point, I can identify the general plant family that deposited the pollen, but *not* a specific species. For example, I can tell you the pollen is from locust, but not that it's from a bristly locust. Will that help?'

'I'm not sure what a locust is,' Mac said. 'So I guess what-ever you discover, it'll be more than what we knew before.'

Armitage seemed to accept that. He held out his hand and Mac gave him the sample.

'That's not pollen,' the palynologist said immediately.

'You're sure?'

'Too big. Pollen is roughly five to two hundred microns or considerably smaller than the width of human hair. This, is closer to the size of sediment.'

The palynologist didn't give up, however. He opened the glass vial, shook out a small section of the dusty residue onto a slide, then slid it under a microscope. 'Huh,' he said. Then 'huh' again.

'It's organic,' Armitage told them after another minute. 'All one substance rather than a mix of various residues. Seems to be some kind of dust, but coarser.' His bushy head popped up. 'Where did you find this?'

'I'm afraid I can't tell you that.'

'Are there other samples you found with it?'

'Water and uncooked rice.'

'Rice? Why in heaven's name did you find rice?'

'That's the million-dollar question. Got any theories?'

Armitage frowned, wagged his eyebrows some more, then pursed his lips. 'Tell me about the water. Have you brought it to a hydrologist?'

'Brian Knowles examined it this morning. It has an extremely low pH, three-point-eight, and high . . . salinity, I guess. It registers fifteen thousand microsiemens per centimeter, meaning there might be lots of minerals or ions present. Knowles believes it comes from a mine or was polluted by organic waste.'

Armitage was nodding vigorously. 'Yes, yes, he's thinking the coal counties isn't he?'

'I think so.'

'Brian's good. Close, just missed one thing.' Lloyd slid out the slide and then did the totally unexpected by dabbing his index finger into the sample and touching it to his tongue. 'It's unusually fine, that's the problem. In it's coarser form, you would have recognized it yourself.'

'You know what it is?' Mac asked sharply.

'Absolutely. It's sawdust. Not pollen at all, but finely ground wood.'

'I don't get it,' Kimberly said.

'Sawmill, my dear. In addition to coal mines, the southwestern part of the state also has a lot of timber industry. This sample is sawdust. And, if these samples are supposed to go together . . .'

'We hope so,' Mac said.

'Then your water's pH is due to organic waste. See, if mill wastes are not disposed of properly, the organic matter leaches into a stream, where it leads to bacterial buildup, eventually suffocating all other life-forms. Has Brian tested the sample for bacteria yet?'

'The amount's too small.'

'But the high salinity,' Armitage was muttering. 'Must be minerals of some kind. Pity he can't test it more.'

'Wait a minute,' Kimberly said intently. 'You're saying this is from a mill, not a mine?'

'Well, I don't generally associate sawdust with coal mines. So yes, I'm going to say a lumber mill.'

Lisa Gardner

'But that could give you acidic water?'

'Contamination is contamination my dear. And with a pH reading of three-point-eight, your water came from an extremely contaminated source.'

'But Knowles indicated this water is at a crisis,' Mac said. 'Aren't mills regulated for how they dispose of waste?'

'In theory, yes. But then, there's a lot of lumber mills in this state and I wouldn't be surprised if some of the smaller, backwoods operations fall through the cracks.'

Nora Ray had finally perked up. She was looking at the palynologist with interest. 'What if it were a closed mill?' she asked quietly. 'Some place shut down, abandoned.' Her gaze flickered to Mac. 'That would be his kind of place, you know. Remote and dangerous, like something from a B-grade horror movie.'

'Oh, I'm sure there are plenty of abandoned mills in the state,' Armitage said. 'Particularly in the coal counties. That's not a very populated area. And, frankly, not a bad location for a horror movie.'

'How so?' Mac asked.

'It's an impoverished area. Very rural. People first moved out there to get their own land and be free from government. Then the coal mines opened and attracted hordes of cheap labor, looking to make a living. Unfortunately, farming, timber, or mining hasn't made anyone rich yet. Now you just have a broad expanse of bruised and battered land, housing a bruised and battered population. People still eke out a living, but it's a hard life and the communities look it.'

'So we're back to seven counties,' Mac murmured.

'That would be my guess.'

'Nothing more you can tell us?'

'Not from a minute sample of sawdust.'

'Shit.' Seven counties. That just wasn't specific enough. Maybe if they'd started yesterday or the day before. Maybe if they had hundreds of searchers or what the hell, the entire National Guard. But three people, two of them not even in law enforcement . . .

'Mr Armitage,' Kimberly spoke up suddenly. 'Do you have a computer we can use? One with Internet access.'

'Sure, I have my laptop.'

Kimberly was already up out of her chair. Her gaze went to Mac and he was startled by the light he now saw blazing in her eyes. 'Remember how Ray Lee Chee said there was an ology for everything?' she asked excitedly. 'Well, I'm about to put him to the test. Give me the names of the seven coal-producing counties and I think I can find our rice!'

37

Dr Ennunzio was not in his office. A secretary promised to hunt him down, while Quincy and Rainie took a seat in the conference room. Quincy rifled through his files. Rainie stared at the wall. Periodically, sounds came from the hallway as various agents and admin assistants rushed by doing a day's work.

'It's not that simple,' Quincy said abruptly.

Rainie finally looked at him. As always, she didn't need a segue to follow his line of thought. 'I know.'

'We're not exactly spring chickens. You're nearly forty, I'm pushing fifty-five. Even if we wanted to have kids, it doesn't mean it would happen.'

'I've been thinking of adopting. There are a lot of children out there who need a family. In this country, in other countries. Maybe I could give a child a good home.'

'It's a lot of work. Midnight feedings if you adopt an infant. Bonding issues if you adopt an older child. Children need the sun, the moon, and the stars at night. No more jetting around

334

the world at the drop of a hat. No more dining at fine restaurants. You'd definitely have to cut back on work.'

She was silent for a moment. Then she said, 'Don't get me wrong, Quincy. I like the work that we do. But lately . . . it's not enough for me. We go from dead body to dead body, crime scene to crime scene. Catch a psychopath today, hunt a new one tomorrow. It's been six years, Quince. I think maybe I need more out of life.' She looked down at the table. 'If I do this, I'll quit the practice. I've waited too long to have a child, not to do it right.'

'But you're my partner,' he protested without thinking.

'Consultants can be hired. Parents can't.'

He turned away, then tiredly shook his head. He didn't know what to say. Perhaps it was only natural that someday she would want children. Rainie was younger than him, hadn't already weathered the domestic storm that had been his pathetic attempt at domestic bliss. Maternal instincts were natural, particularly for a woman her age, who was bound to be hearing the steady beat of her own biological clock.

And for a moment, an image came to him. Rainie with a small little bundle wrapped in her arms, cooing in that high-pitched voice everyone used with babies. Him, watching little feet and hands kick in the air. Catching that first giggle, seeing the first smile.

But the other images inevitably followed. Coming home late from work and realizing your child was already in bed – again. The urgent phone calls that pulled you away from piano recitals and school plays. The way a five-year-old could break your heart by saying, 'It's okay, Daddy. I know you'll be there next time.'

The way children grew too fast. The way they could die too young. The way parenthood started with so much promise, but one day tasted like ashes in your mouth.

And then he felt a hot, unexpected surge of anger toward Rainie. When he'd first met her, she'd said she never wanted marriage or kids. Her own childhood had been a dark, twisted tale, and she knew better than most to believe she could magically break the cycle. God knows he'd asked her to marry him twice over the past six years and each time, she'd turned him down. 'If it's not broke, don't fix it,' she'd told him. And each time, though it had hurt a little, stung more than he'd expected, he'd taken her at her word.

But now she was changing the rules. Not enough to marry him, heaven forbid, but enough to want kids.

'I've already served my time,' he said harshly.

'I know, Quincy.' Her own voice was quiet, harder on him than if she had yelled. 'I know you raised two girls and dealt with midnight feedings and adolescent angst and so much more. I know you're at the phase of your life where you're supposed to be looking forward to retirement, not your kid's first day of kindergarten. I thought I would be there, too. I honestly thought this would never be an issue. But then . . . Lately . . .' She gave a little shrug. 'What can I say? Sometimes, even the best of us change our minds.'

'I love you,' he tried one last time.

'I love you, too,' Rainie replied, and he thought she'd never looked so sad.

When Dr Ennunzio finally strode into the room, the silence was definitely awkward and strained. He didn't seem to notice, however. He came to an abrupt halt, a stack of manila files bulging under his arm. 'Up,' he told them curtly. 'Out. We're taking a walk.'

Quincy was already climbing out of his chair. Confused, Rainie was slower to follow suit.

'You got a call,' Quincy said to Ennunzio.

The agent shook his head warningly and looked up at the

ceiling. Quincy got the message. Years ago, a BSU agent had spied on his fellow members of the FBI. Elaborate surveillance systems and audio devices were found snaking through the vast crawl space above the drop ceiling. Better yet, when the FBI began to suspect espionage activity, they had responded by inserting their own surveillance devices and wiretaps to catch the man. In short, for a span of time – who knows how long – all the BSU agents were being watched by both the good guys and the bad. Nobody forgot those days easily.

Quincy and Rainie followed Ennunzio to the stairwell, where he swiped his security badge over the scanner, then led them up to the great outdoors.

'What the hell is going on?' the linguist asked the minute they were across the street from the building. Now their conversation was muffled by the steady sounds of gunfire.

'I'm not sure.' Quincy held up his dead cell phone. 'I've been a little out of touch.'

Ennunzio shook his head. He looked decidedly frayed around the edges and not happy with how things had turned out. 'I thought you guys were doing good. I thought by talking to you, I was assisting a major investigation. Not killing my own career.'

'We are doing good. And I have every intention of catching this man.'

'Things are heating up,' Rainie told him. 'We found another victim late last night. Everything matches the Eco-Killer's MO. Except this time he kidnapped four girls at once. Which means two more are out there, and if we're going to break this thing, we need to move fast.'

'Damn,' Ennunzio said tiredly. 'After meeting with you guys, I was hoping . . . Well, what do you need from me?'

'Any luck with the newspaper ad?' Quincy asked.

'I sent the paper out to the lab, so I don't have results yet.

Handwriting, however, appears to be consistent with the previous sample. As for the text, I don't have anything new to say. Author is most likely male. To look at penmanship, he's not well-educated, but to look at content, he's probably of above-average intelligence. I repeat the theory that we might be dealing with someone who is somehow mentally incapacitated. Maybe suffering from paranoia or otherwise impaired. Ritual is obviously extremely important to him. The process of killing is as satisfying as the killing itself. You know the rest of that as well as I do.' Ennunzio looked at Quincy. 'He'll never stop unless someone makes him.'

Quincy nodded his head. The news discouraged him more than it should and abruptly he was tired of everything. Worrying about Kimberly. Worrying about Rainie. And wondering what it meant when talk of babies scared him more than talk of psychopaths.

'Special Agent McCormack received another call,' Quincy said. 'He was going to write down the conversation, but with everything that's happened, I don't think he's had the time.'

'When was he contacted?'

'Late last night. When he was at the crime scene.'

Ennunzio immediately looked troubled. 'I don't like that.'

'The UNSUB has a keen knack for timing.'

'You think he's watching.'

'As you said, he likes the process. For him, it's as important as the kill itself. We have a new theory.' Quincy was watching Ennunzio's face very closely. 'The UNSUB most likely uses a cargo van as his kill vehicle. We understand from Special Agent Kaplan that there is an unusually high number of vans coming and going off the base these days – they belong to various contractors doing construction work on the base.'

Ennunzio squeezed his eyes shut. He was already nodding. 'That would fit.'

'Kaplan is now examining the list of workers for anyone with a previous address in Georgia. That may give us a name, but I think it's too late.'

Ennunzio opened his eyes, staring at them both sharply.

'The UNSUB wanted Quantico, the UNSUB got Quantico, and now he doesn't need it anymore,' Quincy continued. 'The action is out in the field, and I think that's where we're going to have to go if we're to have any chance of finding him. So, Doctor, what do you know that you're not telling us yet?'

The forensic linguist appeared genuinely startled, then wary, then carefully composed. 'I don't know why you say that.'

'You're taking a lot of interest in this case.'

'It's what I do.'

'You've gone out of your way to focus on the caller, when in fact, you deal with notes.'

'Linguistics is linguistics.'

'We're accepting all theories,' Quincy tried one last time. 'Even the fuzzy, half-baked ones.'

Ennunzio finally hesitated. 'I don't know. There's just something about this . . . A feeling I get on occasion. But feelings are not facts, and in my line of work I should know better.'

'Would it make a difference,' Rainie said, 'if we told you we had three more clues?'

'What are they?'

'Water. Some kind of residue. And some uncooked rice. We believe we can trace the water and residue. We haven't a clue about the rice.'

Ennunzio was gazing at them now with a curious smile on his face. 'Rice?'

'Uncooked long grain. What about it?'

'You said he favors dangerous terrain, correct? Unpopulated areas where there is little risk of his victims being found by accident? Oh, he is good, very, very good. . . .'

'What the hell do you know, Ennunzio?'

'I know I used to be a caver in my younger days. And now I know your UNSUB was, as well. Quick, we need to make a call!'

38

Virginia
3:12 P.M.
Temperature: 101 degrees

Sun was high in the sky. It baked Tina's little pit, until the mud flaked off her body to reveal tantalizing slices of burnt, festering skin, and the mosquitoes had themselves some lunch. Tina didn't care anymore. She barely felt the pain.

No more sweat. She didn't even have to pee and it had easily been over twelve hours. Nope, not even the tiniest drop of water could be squeezed from her body. Dehydration definitely severe now. She worked at her task, covered in goose bumps and shivering again and again from some deep, unnatural chill.

Rocks didn't work. Too large and bulky for prying away rotting wood. She'd remembered her purse and feverishly dumped out the contents in a jumbled pile on the center boulder. A metal nail file. Much better.

Now she gouged out slices of old railroad ties, desperately crafting footholds and handholds while the mosquitoes buzzed her face, the yellow flies bit her shoulders, and the world spun round and round and round.

Nail file dropped. She slithered to the ground. Panting hard. Her hand trembled. It took so much effort just to locate the file in the mud. Oh looky, another snake.

She would like to close her eyes now. She would like to sink back into the comforting stink of the muck. She would feel it slide across her hair, her cheek, her throat. She would part her lips and let it into her mouth.

Fight or die, fight or die, fight or die. It was all up to her, and it was getting so hard to know the difference.

Tina retrieved the nail file. She went back to work on the railroad ties, while the sun burned white-hot overhead.

'Where am I going? Right turn? Okay, now what? Wait, wait, you said right. No you said left. Damn, give me a sec.' Mac crammed the brakes, threw his rental car in reverse and jolted backward thirty feet on the old dirt road. Sitting beside him, Kimberly was trying desperately to find their location on a state of Virginia map. Most of these old logging roads didn't seem to show up, however, and now he had Ray Lee Chee trying to guide him by cell phone over terrain that was as spotty as the phone connection.

'What? Say that again? Yeah, but I'm only hearing every fourth word. Bats? What's this about bats?'

'Cavers . . . rescue team . . . bats . . . on cars,' Ray said.

'A batmobile?' Mac said, just as Kimberly yelled 'Look out!' He glanced up in time to see the giant tree fallen smack across the middle of the road.

He hit the brakes. In the backseat, Nora Ray went, 'Oooomph.'

'Everyone okay?'

Kimberly looked at Nora Ray, Nora Ray looked at Kimberly. Simultaneously, they both nodded. Mac gave up on the road for a second, and returned his attention to the cell phone.

'Ray, how close are we?'

' . . . two . . . three . . . zzz.'

'Miles?'

'Miles,' Ray confirmed.

All right, forget the damn car, they could walk. 'How's the team coming?' Mac asked. Ray was under strict orders to assemble the best people he could find for a down-and-dirty field team. Brian Knowles, the hydrologist, and Lloyd, the palynologist, were already on board. Now Ray was trying to round up a forensic geologist and a karst geologist. In theory, by the time Mac, Kimberly, and Nora Ray magically found and rescued victim number three, Ray's team would have arrived, ready to analyze the next round of clues and pinpoint victim number four. It was late in the game, but they were preparing to make up for lost time.

'Bats . . . cavers . . .' Ray said again.

'I can't hear you.'

'Karst . . . volunteers . . . bats . . .'

'You have volunteer bats?'

'Search and rescue!' Ray exploded. 'Cavern!'

'A volunteer group for search and rescue. Oh, in the cave!' Mac hadn't even thought that far ahead. Kimberly had searched the various county names combined with rice, and lo' and behold, up had come an article on the Orndorff's Cavern. Apparently, it was home to an endangered isopod, a tiny white crustacean that was approximately a fourth of an inch long. To make a long story short, some politician had wanted to build an airport in the area, environmentalists had tried to block it using the Endangered Species Act, and the politician had replied that no way in damn hell would progress be halted by a grain of rice. And now the Orndorff's Cavern isopod had a cool nickname among karst specialists.

So they had a location. If they could find it, and if they could get the girl back out.

'Water . . . dangerous,' Ray was saying on the other end of the phone. 'Entrance difficult . . . Ropes . . . coveralls . . . lights.'

'We need special equipment to access the cave,' Mac translated. 'Okay, so when will the search-and-rescue team arrive?'

'Making calls . . . different locations . . . Bats . . . on cars.'

'Their cars will have bats?'

'Stickers!'

'Gotcha.'

Mac popped open his car door and got out to survey the fallen tree. Kimberly was already out and walking its length. She glanced up at his approach and grimly shook her head. He saw her point. The tree trunk was a good three feet in diameter. It would take a four-wheel-drive vehicle, a chainsaw, and a winch to move this sucker now. No way was it happening with a guy, two girls and a Camry.

'We made the left turn,' Mac said into the phone. 'What do we do next?' This time he couldn't make out Ray's reply at all. Something about smell the fungus. Mac looked around sourly. They were in the middle of soaring woods, deep into the heart of nowhere. Since turning off Interstate 81 forty minutes ago, they'd drifted into the westernmost part of the state, a thin peninsula wedged between Kentucky and North Carolina. Nothing around here but trees, fields, and doublewides. Last building they'd seen was a decrepit gas station fifteen miles back. It looked like it hadn't pumped a drop since 1968. Before that had been half a dozen mobile homes and one tiny Baptist church. Lloyd Armitage hadn't been kidding. Whatever better days had come to this part of the state had departed a long time ago.

Now it was strictly backwoods country, and Mac's cell phone reception would not be getting better anytime soon.

'I'll try you again at the scene,' Mac said. Ray made some kind of reply, but Mac still couldn't hear him and finally snapped his phone shut.

'What do we do?' Nora Ray asked him.

'Now, we walk.'

* * *

Actually, first they assembled gear. True to her word, Nora Ray had come prepared. From her travel bag, she pulled out a modest daypack, complete with dried food, first aid kit, compass, Swiss Army knife, and water filtration system. She also had waterproof matches and a small flashlight. She loaded up her gear; Kimberly and Mac attended to their own.

They had three gallons of water left. Mac thought of the condition the girl would probably be in, unglued his shirt from his torso for the fourth time in the last five minutes, and stuck all three gallons in his backpack. The weight was considerable, the nylon pack feeling like a son of a bitch as it dragged against his shoulders and pressed his shirt against his overheated skin.

Kimberly came over, removed one of the gallon jugs and stuck it in her own backpack. 'Don't be an idiot,' she told him, then hefted on her pack and clipped it around her waist.

'At least the trees are providing shade,' Mac said.

'Now if only they'd soak up the wet. How far?'

'Couple of miles. I think.'

Kimberly glanced at her watch again. 'We'd better get moving.' She sneaked a peek at Nora Ray and Mac could read her thoughts. How hard could the civilian push it? They'd soon find out.

It was a surreal hike, Mac thought later. Moving down a thickly shaded logging road in the middle of a blistering afternoon. The sun seemed to chase them, peeking in and out of the trees as it dodged their footsteps and seared them with unrelenting beams of light.

Bugs came out in force. Mosquitoes the size of humming-birds. Some kind of obnoxious fly with a vicious little bite. They were batting at their faces before they'd gone fifteen feet. At thirty feet, they stopped and got out the cans of bug repellent. A quarter of a mile later, they stopped again and sprayed each other down as if the stuff were gallons of cheap perfume.

It didn't make a difference. The flies swarmed, the sun burned and the humidity covered their bodies in never-ending rivulets of sweat. No one spoke. They just put one foot in front of the other and focused on walking.

Forty minutes later, Mac smelled it first. 'What the hell is that?'

'Deet,' Kimberly said grimly. 'Or sweat. Take your pick.'

'No, no, it's worse than that.'

Nora Ray stopped. 'It's like something rotten,' she said. 'Almost like . . . sewage.'

Mac suddenly got it. What Ray Lee Chee had been trying to tell him on the phone. Smell the fungus. He picked up the pace. 'Come on,' he said. 'We're almost there.'

He started jogging now, Kimberly and Nora Ray hastily following suit. They crested the small rise of the hill, came down the other side, and then abruptly drew up short.

'Holy shit,' Mac said.

'B-grade horror movie,' Nora Ray murmured.

And Kimberly just shook her head.

Quincy was getting frustrated. He'd tried Kimberly's cell phone three or four times without success. Now he turned back to Ennunzio and Rainie.

'Do you know where this cave is?' he asked Ennunzio.

'Absolutely. It's in Lee County, a good three or four hours from here. But you two can't just crash into this cavern as if it's one of the tourist hotspots from the Shenandoah Valley. To access Orndorff's Cavern, you need serious gear.'

'Fine. Get the gear, then take us.'

Ennunzio was silent for a moment. 'Perhaps it's time to let the official case team know what's going on.'

'Really? What do you think they'll do first, Doctor? Rescue

the victim? Or call you in for a three-hour interview to corroborate every last detail of your story?'

The linguist saw his point. 'I'll get my gear.'

'What are we looking for?'

'Hell if I know. Some kind of cavern entrance. Maybe amid a pile of rocks, or a sinkhole at the base of a tree. I've never done any spelunking. Then again, how hard can it be to find the entrance to a cave?'

Pretty hard, it turned out. Mac had already been running around the sawmill for a good fifteen minutes. So had Kimberly and Nora Ray. They were probably all being stupid. The smell was the first kicker. The foul odor rose so thick in the heavy, humid air it stung their eyes and burned their throats. Mac was now holding an old T-shirt over his mouth, but even that didn't make much difference.

Next to the smell was the intense wall of heat rising from the same sky-high pile of sawdust. None of them had even recognized the wood residue at first. It had looked like a pile of white sand, or maybe dirt covered in snow. Ten minutes ago, Kimberly had gotten close enough to discern the truth. Fungus. The entire, stinking, rotten pile was covered in some kind of fungus.

When Brian Knowles had guessed their water sample came from a site in crisis, he hadn't been kidding.

Now Mac leapt belatedly over one abandoned blade saw. He weaved in and out of long, shed-style buildings with busted-out windows and sagging roof beams. The old conveyors still gleamed darkly in the shadows, complete with nasty-looking pikes used for skewering the wood as it was brought before the blade.

Litter covered the ground. Crumpled-up soda cans, discarded Styrofoam cups. Mac found a pile of old gasoline containers, probably used to fill up the handheld chain saws. He found another pile of old fluorescent lights. A faint popping sound emitted from the debris field as some of the glass exploded from the heat of the sun.

He'd never seen anything like it. Strings of rusted barbed wire clawed at his legs. Abandoned saw blades lay hidden in the overgrown weeds, waiting to do far, far worse. This place was straight out of an environmentalist's nightmare. And he was now one hundred percent sure their third girl had to be around here somewhere.

Kimberly came staggering around one of the broken-down sheds. She had tears streaming down her face from the stench. 'Any luck?'

Mac shook his head.

She nodded and went careening on by, still looking for some hint of an underground cavern.

He came upon Nora Ray soon afterward. She'd stopped running around and was now standing in one place, her eyes closed, her hands spread by her side.

'See anything?' he asked brusquely.

'No.' She opened her eyes and seemed embarrassed to find him there. 'I don't know . . . It's not like I'm a psychic or anything. I just have these dreams so I thought maybe if I closed my eyes . . .'

'Anything that works.'

'But it's not working. Nothing's working. And that's so unbelievably frustrating. I mean, if she's in a cavern, well then, aren't we literally walking on top of her right now?'

'It's possible. Search and rescue isn't easy, Nora Ray. The Coast Guard passed back and forth over your spot five times before seeing your red shirt.'

'I was lucky.'

'You were smart. You hung in there. You kept trying.'

'Do you think this girl is smart?'

'I don't know. But I'm willing to settle for lucky if that gets her home.'

Nora Ray nodded. She resumed walking and Mac zigzagged through another abandoned building. Already past four o'clock. His heart was beating too fast, his face felt dangerously hot to the touch. They were pushing too hard for the conditions. Raising their core body temperatures to dangerous levels and going too long between drinks. This was no way to manage a rescue operation and yet he couldn't bring himself to stop.

Nora Ray was right; if the girl was in the cavern, they could literally be standing on top of her right now. So close, yet so far away.

Then, through the buzzing drone of the insects, he finally heard a welcome cry. It was Kimberly, somewhere off to the left.

'Hey, hey,' she yelled. 'I found something. Over here, quick!'

39

'Hello, hello? Can you hear me?' Kimberly had found an eight-inch wide duct sticking up through the ground like a section of stovepipe. She peered down the tube, trying to see where it led, but encountered only darkness. Next, she waved her hand over the top. Definitely a draft of cooler air coming up from somewhere. She tried dropping a small pebble. She never heard it land.

Mac was running over. Nora Ray as well. Kimberly leaned closer to the pipe, cupping her mouth to amplify her voice. 'Is anyone down there?'

She lowered her ear to the mouth of the pipe. Did she hear movement? Sounds of something shifting way down in the dark, dank depths? It was hard to be sure.

'Hellooooooo!'

Mac finally drew up at her side. His hair was spiky with sweat, his shirt and shorts plastered to his skin. He dropped to his knees beside her and added his voice to the pipe.

'Is anyone down there? Karen Clarence? Tina Krahn? Are you in there?'

'She might be asleep,' Kimberly murmured.

'Or unconscious.'

'Are you sure that goes to the cavern?' Nora Ray asked.

Kimberly shrugged wearily. 'As sure as I am about anything.'

'But that can't be the entrance,' Nora Ray said. 'No one could fit down that hole.'

'No, it can't be an entrance. Maybe it's an airhole, or a skylight. Someone at least took the time to engineer the pipe. That's gotta mean something.'

'The cavern's big,' Mac muttered. He tried the pebble trick and got the exact same results. 'From the website it sounded as if it were several rooms connected by long tunnels, and some of the rooms are the size of small cathedrals. Maybe this pipe leads to one of those chambers, letting in some natural light.'

'We need an entrance,' Kimberly said.

'No kidding.'

'I'll stay here and keep yelling. You and Nora Ray see if you can't find another opening. Maybe you'll hear my voice echoing through and that will help. Besides...' Kimberly faltered. 'If one of the girls is down there, I don't want her to think we went away. I want her to know that we're coming. That it'll be over soon.'

Mac nodded, giving her a look that was hard to read. He and Nora Ray resumed their frantic scouring of the woods. Kimberly got down on the dusty ground, placing her mouth next to the rusty pipe.

'This is Kimberly Quincy,' she called. She wasn't sure what to say, so she started with the basics. 'I'm with Special Agent Mac McCormack and Nora Ray Watts. We've come to help you. Can you hear me at all? I can't hear you. Maybe, if you're too weak to yell, you could try banging on something.'

She waited. Nothing.

'Are you thirsty? We have water and food. We also have a blanket. I understand the caverns are cold, even this time of year. And boy, I bet you're sick to death of the dark.'

She thought she heard something this time. She paused, holding her breath. A thunk against the rocks? Or maybe a cold, frightened girl, trying to drag her body closer to the hole in the sky?

'A whole team is coming. Search-and-rescue specialists, karst specialists. They'll have all the proper gear to be able to get you out of there. And trust me, if you think it's cold down there, wait 'til you find out how hot it is up here. Must be a good hundred degrees in the shade. You'll be missing that cool hunk of rock in no time. But I bet you'll love seeing the sun again. And the trees and the sky and all the smiling faces of us rescue workers, who can't wait to meet you.'

She was still talking. Rambling, really. Funny, her voice had grown thick.

'You don't need to be afraid. I know it's hard to be alone in the dark. But people are here now. We've been looking for you a long time. And we're going to go into the cavern, we're going to bring you back up to the light and then we're going to find the man who did this, so it never happens again.'

Sounds now. Loud, startling noises like the crunch of gravel. Kimberly jerked her head up in excitement, then realized the noise wasn't coming from the stovepipe. Instead, she saw two dusty trucks pull in straight ahead. One had a sticker of a bat glued to the driver-side window.

A door banged open. A man sprang out, already running to the back, jerking down his tailgate, and tossing out gear.

'You the one that reported the lost caver?' the guy yelled over his shoulder. The second truck had already come to a halt and was now shedding two more men rushing for gear.

'Yes.'

'Sorry for the delay. Would've been here sooner if not for that damn tree. What can you tell us of the missing caver?'

'We believe she's been abandoned in the cavern for at least

forty-eight hours. She doesn't have proper gear, and was probably left with only a gallon of water.'

The man drew up short. 'Huh? You want to try that again?'

'She's not a caver,' Kimberly said quietly. 'She's just a girl, a victim of a violent crime.'

'You're kiddin'?'

'No.'

'Ah hell, I'm not sure I want to know anything more after that.' The man turned to his two companions. 'Bob, Ross, you catch that?'

'Girl, no gear, lost somewhere in the cavern. Don't tell you anything more than that.' The two other men didn't even look at Kimberly. They were busy pulling on long johns in hundred-degree heat. Then they grabbed pairs of thick blue coveralls and jerked them on over the long underwear. Both men were sweating profusely. They didn't seem to notice.

'I'm Josh Shudt,' the first guy said, coming over and belatedly shaking Kimberly's hand. 'I wouldn't say I'm the leader of this group, but I'm probably as close as it gets. We have two others on the way, but given what you say, the three of us should probably head on in.'

'Does this stovepipe go to the cave?'

'Yes ma'am. It's a skylight in the main chamber right beneath your feet.'

'I've been talking down it. I don't know if she can hear anything . . .'

'She probably appreciates that,' Shudt said quietly.

'Can I go with you?'

'You have any gear?'

'Just what I'm wearing.'

'That's not gear. In a cave, it's fifty-five degrees every day of the year. Feels like a fucking refrigerator, and that's before you get into the water. To enter Orndorff's Cavern, we gotta descend forty feet by rope, into knee-high water. Then we get to wiggle through thirty feet of watery tunnel that's 'bout twelve inches high. Good news is then we enter the main chamber, which has a forty-foot vault. Assuming, of course, we don't run into a rabid raccoon or a ring-necked snake.'

'Snakes?' Kimberly asked weakly.

'Yes ma'am. At least there are no bats. Orndorff's Cavern is dying, sad to say. And even if the bats had still found it an acceptable hibernacula, this time of year they're out eating bugs. October through April, it's another story. Never a dull moment being a caver.'

'I thought you guys were called spelunkers.'

'No ma'am. We're cavers. Cavers rescue spelunkers. So don't you worry. Just let us do our thing, and we'll find your missing person. She got a name?'

'Karen or Tina.'

'She has two names?'

'We don't know which victim she is.'

'Ah man, I really don't want to know more about your case. You do your thing. We'll do ours.'

Shudt walked back to his pile of gear, snapping on his coveralls, while Mac and Nora Ray finally came running over. Everyone made curt introductions, then Mac, Kimberly, and Nora Ray were left standing awkwardly to the side while the three men finished suiting up, strapped on packs, then donned thick hiking boots and tough leather gloves.

They had piles of brightly colored rope between them. In deft movements they coiled up the various heavy-duty lengths, then looped them over their shoulders. They seemed to be down to final adjustments then, testing out multiple light sources, adjusting their hard hats. Finally Shudt grunted approval at each man's gear, returned to the back of his truck, and pulled out a long backboard.

For transporting the victim out of the cave. In case she couldn't walk on her own. Or in case she was dead.

Shudt looked over at Mac. 'We could use a spotter to help man the ropes up top. Ever worked with a belay?'

'I've done some rock climbing.'

'Then you're our man. Let's go.'

Shudt turned one last time toward Kimberly.

'Keep talking down the pipe,' he told her quietly. 'You never know.'

The men turned and walked into the woods. Kimberly sank back down to the ground. Nora Ray joined her in the dust.

'What do we say?' the girl murmured.

'What did you want to hear most?'

'That it was going to end. That I was going to be okay.'

Kimberly thought about it a moment. Then she cupped her hands and leaned over the pipe. 'Karen? Tina? This is Kimberly Quincy again. I just want you to know that the search-and-rescue workers are on their way. Do you hear me? The tough part is over. Soon, we'll have you home to your family again. Soon, you'll be safe.'

Tina had gouged as much as she could gouge. She had started at knee level, digging holes up as far as she could reach. Then, as an experiment, she'd crammed her muddy toes into the first two rough holes, gripped other ragged edges with her hands, and climbed up a whole two feet.

Her legs shook violently. She felt at once light as a feather and as heavy as an anchor. She would rocket to the top like a human spider. She would plummet to the ground and never get up again.

'Come on,' she whispered through her parched cracked lips. And then she started to climb.

Three feet up. Her arms now shook as violently as her legs and her stomach contracted with a painful cramp. She rested her head against the blanket of dense green vines, prayed not to throw up, and resumed climbing again.

Up toward the sun. Light as a feather. Be like Spiderman.

Six feet up, she came to an exhausted halt. No more hand-holds and she still didn't trust the vines. Awkwardly, she tried to support herself with her feet, straining up on her tiptoes as she reached above her head with her right hand and blindly dug in her nail file. The ancient wood crumbled beneath the fumbling metal and gave her fresh courage. She gouged wildly, already envisioning herself at the top.

Maybe she'd find a lake on the surface. A vast blue oasis. She would plunge in headfirst. She would float on tranquil waves. She would dive low, letting the water wash the mud from her hair. And then she would swim to the cool depths in the middle of her fantasy lake, and drink until her belly swelled like a balloon.

Then when she reached the other side, she would be greeted by a tuxedoed waiter, bearing a silver platter piled with fluffy white towels.

She giggled out loud. Delirium didn't bother her so much anymore. It seemed the only chance of happiness she would get.

Wood rained down on her head. She was reminded of her task by the sudden, fierce pain in her overexerted arms. She explored the hole she'd made with her fingertips. She could curl her fingers into the rough opening. Time to move again. How did the old TV jingle go? Had to keep moving on up, to the top, where she would finally get a piece of the pie.

She painfully pulled her body up another step, her butt sticking out precariously, her arms shaking violently from her efforts. She moved four more excruciating inches. And then once more she was stuck.

Time for another hole. Her left arm ached too badly to bear her weight. She switched to hanging on with her right hand, while digging at the wood with her left. The motion felt awkward. She had no idea if she was working one spot, or carelessly ripping up the whole board. Too hard to look.

She clung to the wall with her trembly legs and worn-out arms. Then she had the next hole done and it was time for another step. She made the mistake of looking up then, and almost wept.

The sky. So high above her. What, a good ten to fifteen feet? Her legs already ached, her arms burned. She didn't know how much longer she could do this and she had only made it ten feet. She had spidey hands and spidey feet, but she did not have spidey strength.

She just wanted her lake. She wanted to swim through those cool waves. She wanted to step out the other side and fall into her mother's arms, where she would weep piteously and apologize for anything she'd ever done.

God give her strength to climb this wall. God give her courage. Because her mother needed her and her baby needed her and please God, she did not want to die like a rat in a trap. She did not want to die all alone.

One more hole, she told herself. Climb up, dig one more hole, and then you can return to the muck to rest.

So she made it one more hole. And then she made it another. And then she promised herself, through her labored breathing, that she just needed to do one more. Which turned into two more, then three more, until finally, she had gone ten or twelve feet up the wall.

And it was scary now. Definitely no looking down. Had to just keep pushing up, even if her shoulders felt curiously elastic, as if the joints had pulled apart and now dangled loosely. And then she swayed sometimes, having to catch herself with her fingers which made her shoulders shriek and her arms burn and she cried out in pain, though her throat was so dry it came out more like a chirpy croak, a sandpaper sound of protest.

Moving on up. To the top. Gonna finally get a piece of the pie.

She was weeping with no tears. She was clinging desperately to rotted timber and fragile vines and trying hard not to think of what she was doing. She hurt beyond pain. She pushed herself beyond endurance.

She pictured her mother. She pictured her baby and she pushed and she pushed and she pushed.

Fifteen feet up. The top ledge so close she could finally see an overhang of bushy grass. Surface vegetation. Her parched mouth watered at the thought.

She stared too long. Forgot what she was doing. And her exhausted, dehydrated body finally gave out. Her hand reached up. Her fingers failed to connect.

And then she went backwards.

For a moment, she felt herself suspended in midair. She could see her arms and legs churning, like one of those silly cartoon creatures. Then reality reasserted itself. Gravity took over.

Tina plummeted down into the muck.

No scream this time. The mud swallowed her whole and after all these days, she did not protest.

Kimberly was still talking forty-five minutes later. She talked of water and food and warm sun. She talked of the weather and the baseball season and the birds in the sky. She talked of old friends and new friends and wouldn't it be nice to meet in person?

She talked of holding on. She talked of never giving up. She talked of miracles and how they could happen if you willed them hard enough.

Then Mac came out of the woods. She took one look at his face and stopped talking.

Seventeen minutes later, they brought the body up.

40

Lee County, Virginia
7:53 P.M.
Temperature: 98 degrees

The sun started to descend, surfing bright orange waves of heat. Shadows grew longer, while remaining stifling hot. And in the abandoned saw mill, vehicles started to pile up.

First came more members of the cavers' search-and-rescue team. They finished hauling out the lifeless body of a young girl with short-cropped brown hair. Her yellow-flowered slip dress had been reduced to tatters by the acidic water. The fingernails on both of her hands were broken and ragged, as if at some point she'd clawed frantically at the hard dolomite walls.

The rest of her was blue and bloated; Josh Shudt and his men had found her body floating in the long tunnel that connected the cavern's sinkhole entrance to the main chamber. They'd pushed through to the cathedral room after pulling out her body. There, on a ledge, they'd found an empty gallon jug of water and a purse.

According to her driver's license, the victim's name was Karen Clarence, and just one week ago she had turned twenty-one.

It didn't take much to fill in the rest. The UNSUB had delivered the victim, most likely drugged and unconscious, to the main chamber. The stovepipe skylight forty feet above would've offered precious little light when the girl awoke. Enough to realize she had a shallow pond of relatively safe rainwater to her left and a stream of highly polluted, toxic water to her right. Maybe she stayed on the ledge for a while. Maybe she tried the small pond and promptly got bit by its already stressed inhabitants – the white, eyeless crayfish, or the tiny, rice-sized isopods. Maybe she even encountered a ring-necked snake.

Either way, the girl had probably ended up wet. And once you got wet in an environment that's constantly fifty-five degrees, hypothermia's only a matter of time.

Shudt told them all a story of a caver who'd lasted two weeks lost in five miles of winding underground caverns. Of course, he'd been wearing proper gear and had a pack full of protein bars. He'd also been lost in a healthy cavern, where the water was not only safe to drink, but according to local lore, brought the drinker good luck.

Karen Clarence hadn't been so lucky. She'd managed not to brain her skull on a thick hanging stalactite. She'd managed not to bruise a knee or sprain a wrist crawling in the dark amid the stalagmites. But at some point, she'd headed straight into the polluted stream. Water that acidic had had to burn her skin, just as it promptly ate holes in her dress. Was she beyond caring at that point? Had the cold set in so deep, the burning liquid felt good against her flesh? Or had she simply been that determined? She would die sitting on the ledge. The shallow pond led nowhere. That left only the stream to guide her back to civilization.

Either way, she immersed herself into the stream, her clothes eroding, her face streaming with tears. She had followed the stream to the narrow tunnel. She had pushed her head and shoulders into that long, skinny space. And then she had died in the darkness there.

Ray Lee Chee showed up shortly after seven. With him came Brian Knowles, Lloyd Armitage, and Kathy Levine. They unloaded two Jeep Cherokees filled with field equipment, camping packs, and bins of books. Their mood in the beginning was giddy, bordering on festive. Then they saw the body.

They put down their field kits. They held a moment of silence for a girl they'd never met. Then, they got to work.

Thirty minutes later Rainie and Quincy arrived, bearing Ennunzio in tow. Nora Ray left the camp shortly thereafter. And Kimberly followed suit.

The nature experts had the clues. The law enforcement professionals had the body. She wasn't sure what was left for her to do.

She found Nora Ray sitting on a tree stump deeper in the woods. A fern sprouted green shoots nearby and Nora Ray was running her hands through the fronds.

'Long day,' Kimberly said. She leaned against a nearby tree trunk.

'It's not over yet,' Nora Ray said.

Kimberly smiled thinly. She'd forgotten – this girl was good. 'Holding up?'

Nora Ray shrugged. 'I guess. I've never seen a dead person before. I thought I would be more upset. But mostly I'm just . . . tired.'

'It has the same effect on me.'

Nora Ray finally looked up at her. 'Why are you here?'

'In the woods? Anything's better than the sun.'

'No. On this case, working with Special Agent McCormack. He said you were illegal, or something like that. Did you . . . Are you?'

'Oh. You mean, am I a relative of one of the victims?'

Nora Ray nodded soberly.

'No. Not this time.' Kimberly slid down the tree trunk. The dirt felt cooler against her legs. It made it easier to talk. 'Until two days ago, actually, I was a new agent at the FBI Academy. I was seven weeks from graduation, and while my supervisors will tell you I have trouble with authority figures, I think I would've made it in the end. I think I would've graduated.'

'What happened?'

'I went for a run in the woods and I found a dead body. Betsy Radison. She was the one driving that night.'

'She was the first?'

Kimberly nodded.

'And now we're finding her friends.'

'One by one,' Kimberly whispered softly.

'It doesn't seem fair.'

'No, it's not meant to be fair. It's meant to be about one man. And our job is to catch him.'

They both drifted off to silence again. There wasn't much sound in the woods. A faint breeze crinkling the damp, heavy trees. The distant rustle of a squirrel or bird, foraging in a pile of dead leaves.

'My parents must be worried by now,' Nora Ray said abruptly. 'My mom . . . Ever since what happened to my sister, she doesn't like me to be away for more than an hour. I'm supposed to check in by phone every thirty minutes. Then she can yell at me to come home.'

'Parents aren't meant to outlive their children.'

'And yet it happens all the time. Like you said, life isn't fair.' Nora Ray jerked impatiently on the fern frond, tearing the tender leaves. 'I'm twenty-three years old, you know. Frankly, I should be back at college. I should be planning a career, going on dates, drinking too hard some nights and studying diligently on others. I should be doing smart things and stupid things and all sorts of things to figure out my own life. Instead . . . My sister died, and my life went with her. No one in my house does anything anymore. We just . . . exist.'

'Maybe three years hasn't been long enough. Maybe your family needs longer to make it through the stages of grief.'

'Make it through?' Nora Ray's voice was incredulous. 'We're not making it through. We haven't even started the process. Everything's stagnant. It's like my life has been cut in half. There's everything that was before that one night – college classes and a boyfriend and an upcoming party – and now there is everything after. Except after doesn't have any content. After is still an empty slate.'

'You have your dreams,' Kimberly said quietly.

Nora Ray immediately appeared troubled. 'You think I'm making them up.'

'No. I'm absolutely sure you dream of your sister. But some hold that dreams are the unconscious's way of working things out. If you're still dreaming of your sister, then maybe your unconscious has something to work out. Maybe your parents aren't the only ones who aren't over her yet.'

'I don't like this conversation very much,' Nora Ray said.

Kimberly merely shrugged. Nora Ray narrowed her eyes. 'What are you? Some kind of shrink?'

'I've studied psychology, but I'm not a shrink.'

'So you've studied psychobabble and you've attended half of the FBI Academy. What does that make you?'

'Someone who also lost her sister. And her mother, too, for that matter.' Kimberly smiled crookedly in the falling light. 'Trump. In the contest of who has gotten dumped on more by life, I believe I just won.'

Nora Ray had the good grace to appear ashamed. Her hand was back on the fern. Now she methodically picked off its leaves. 'What happened?'

'Same old story. Bad man believes my father, an FBI profiler, ruined his life. Bad man decides to seek revenge by destroying my father's family. Bad man targets my older sister first – she is troubled and has never been a great judge of character. He kills her and makes it look like an accident. Then he uses everything she has told him to befriend my mother. Except my mother is smarter than he thinks. In the end, there is nothing accidental about her death. The blood spray goes on for seven rooms. Finally, bad man goes after me. Except my father gets him first. And now I've spent the last six years much like you – trying to figure out how to go on merrily living a life that's already been touched by too much death.'

'Is that why you joined the FBI? So you could help others?'

'No. I joined the FBI so I could be heavily armed, and also help others.'

Nora Ray nodded as if that made perfect sense. 'And now you're going to catch the man who killed my sister. That's good. The FBI is lucky to have you.'

'The FBI doesn't have me anymore.'

'But you said you were halfway through training . . .'

'I took a personal leave to pursue this case, Nora Ray. The FBI Academy is not fond of that sort of thing. I'm not sure I'll ever be allowed back.'

'I don't understand. You're going after a killer, you're trying to save people's lives. What more can they want from an agent?'

'Objectivity, professionalism, a clear understanding of the big picture, and an ability to make tough decisions. When I left the Academy, I did it to help one life. Staying, on the other hand, and completing my training, would have given me the opportunity to save hundreds. My supervisors are tiresome at times, but they aren't stupid.'

'Then why did you do it?'

'Because Betsy Radison looked just like my sister, Mandy.'

'Oh,' Nora Ray said quietly.

'Oh,' Kimberly agreed. She leaned her head back against the rough bark of the tree and sighed deeply. It felt better than she would've thought to say the words out loud. It felt good to finally confront the truth.

She had lied to Mac when she'd told him this wasn't about her family. She had lied to her father when she had told him she could handle things. But mostly, she had lied to herself. Young, passionate Kimberly, fighting valiantly for the underdog in a jurisdiction-mad case gone wrong. It sounded so good, but in fact, her decision to help Mac had had nothing to do with Betsy Radison, or the Eco-Killer or even her supervisor Mark Watson. All along, it had been about herself. Six years of grieving and growing and telling herself she was doing just fine, and all it had taken was one victim who looked slightly like Mandy for her to throw it all away. Her career, her dreams, her future. She hadn't even put up much of a fight.

Betsy Radison had died, and Kimberly had run back to the heavy burden of her past as if it were the ultimate comfort food. Why not? As long as she kept obsessing about her family's death, she'd never have to face the future. As long as she kept dwelling on her mother and Mandy, she would never have to define Kimberly. She had wondered what her life would've been like if her mother and sister had never died. In truth, her life could still be about whatever she wanted it to be. If she was that strong. If she was that courageous.

'What happens now?' Nora Ray asked softly.

'Short-term now, or long-term now?'

'Short-term now.'

'Ray and the team from the USGS figure out the clues left with this victim. Then we try to find the fourth girl. And then we try to find the Eco-Killer and light up his ass.'

Nora Ray nodded with satisfaction. 'And long-term now?'

'Long-term now, you and I finally realize that none of it has made a difference. Your sister is still dead, my family is still gone, and we still have to get on with the rest of our lives. So we start seriously wading through the grief and seriously wading through the guilt and see if we can't make something out of this mess. Or, we do nothing at all, and let a couple of killers take what little we have left.'

'I don't like long-term now very much,' Nora Ray said.

'No. The dead suffer no more. The living, however, must always struggle to find a way.'

41

Lee County, Virginia
8:53 P.M.
Temperature: 96 degrees

The bats came out. In the inky hues of fading daylight, they glided gracefully among the trees, dive-bombing clusters of fireflies and scattering the flickering lights. The humidity was still unbearable, but with the sun low in the sky and the bats feasting silently overhead, dusk took on a peaceful, almost soothing feel.

When Kimberly was younger, she and her sister had loved to catch fireflies. They would run around their back lawn with Mason jars, trying desperately to capture the shooting darts of lights. Mandy had been horrible at it, but Kimberly had gotten pretty good. They'd sit around the patio table, trying to feed the fireflies stalks of fresh-cut grass or tender stems of dandelions. Then they'd let the flies go again; their mother didn't allow bugs in the house.

Now Kimberly sat in the circle they had formed around a Coleman lantern, her knee brushing Mac's, while Rainie and Quincy talked of contacting the local coroner. Ennunzio and Nora Ray sat across from Kimberly. Ray and his team remained off to one side, still working the body.

'We've done the best we can,' Quincy was saying. 'Now we need to notify the official case team.'

'It'll only piss them off,' Mac said.

'Why? Because we've moved the body, destroyed chain of custody for the evidence, and made the crime scene perfectly useless for basic investigative procedures?' Quincy regarded the younger man drolly. 'Yes, I'm sure they will have a few thoughts on the subject.'

'Saving a life always takes priority over preserving a scene,' Mac insisted stubbornly.

'I'm not questioning what we did,' Quincy said. 'I'm simply trying to bring us back to reality. We found the body, we brought in professionals to analyze the clues, and now we need to start thinking about what should happen next. I certainly hope none of you are suggesting that we return the body to the cavern. Or worse, leave it unattended.'

Everyone shifted uncomfortably. Quincy was right; none of them had thought that far ahead.

'You contact the official case team, and we'll spend the rest of the night in jail,' Kimberly pointed out. 'Which pretty much defeats the purpose of coming here in the first place.'

'Agreed. I was thinking you and Mac should continue. Rainie and I will wait here for the proper authorities. Sooner or later, someone must face the music.' His gaze rested on Rainie's face.

'If it's all the same,' Ennunzio said, 'I'd like to continue on with the others. I want to be around if Special Agent McCormack gets another call.'

Mac glanced at the cell phone clipped to his waist and grimaced. 'Fat chance, with the signal strength around here.'

'As we get closer to civilization, however . . .'

'I'm going, too.' Nora Ray was regarding Ennunzio steadily, as if daring the FBI agent to deny her.

'This is outside your responsibility,' Quincy spoke up. 'In

all honesty, Ms. Watts, the biggest help you could give this team right now is to go home. Your parents must be worried.'

'My parents are worried even when I am home. No. I can help and I'm going to stay.'

The tone of her voice was set and none of them had the energy left to argue. Instead, Kimberly turned to Ennunzio, regarding him curiously. 'How did you know about this cave? I understand from Josh Shudt that Orndorff's Cavern isn't exactly a common cavern for exploration.'

'Not after what the mill did to it,' Ennunzio said, 'but twenty, thirty years ago, it used to be beautiful.' He shrugged. 'I grew up in this area. Spent my free time running wild among these mountains and caverns. It's been a long time now, but I like to think it'll come back to me. And maybe the little bits and pieces I remember can be of help. I hardly know the whole state, but I know this one corner of Virginia fairly well.'

'Do you have any idea where he might have placed the fourth victim?' Quincy spoke up quietly, his gaze on Mac.

The special agent rolled out his shoulders, contemplating the question. 'Let's see! . . . he's done a national forest and an underground cavern. So what do we have left? Chesapeake Bay rates high on the geological interest scale. I read about scuba diving in some reservoirs formed by flooding old mining towns – that's gotta float his boat. Then there are a variety of rivers – last time he liked the Savannah.'

'There are two more major mountain ranges,' Ennunzio considered, but Mac shook his head.

'He's done forests. He'll go for something different.'

'What about the coast line?' Nora Ray asked. She was still staring at Ennunzio.

'Beaches around here are more populated than the Georgia coastline,' Mac said. 'It's possible, but I think he'll look for someplace more remote. We can check with Ray.'

He waved his hand, and after a moment, the USGS man

came on over. Ray's face was pale and covered with a fine sheen of sweat. Now that he'd seen an actual body, working a murder case had clearly lost some of its appeal.

'Any luck?' Mac asked him.

'Some. It's hard to know what to look for on the girl . . . body . . . victim. Body.' He seemed to decide. 'It um, it was in the water for a bit, and who knows what that washed away. Kathy found some kind of crumpled leaf in a dress pocket. She's trying to extract it now without doing more damage; tissue tears easily when this wet. Also, Josh Shudt went in and checked the ledge for us. Lloyd's now working on some soil samples he took from the girl's . . . body's shoes. I'm trying to go through her purse, since you said he sometimes puts things there.'

'Have you tried the back of the throat?'

'Nothing.'

'I wonder about her stomach,' Mac murmured. 'With the first victim, the map, he was very inventive. I'm not sure how he would consider these next ones in line. Maybe we should consider cutting her open.'

Nora Ray got up abruptly and moved away from the lantern light. Mac watched her go, but didn't apologize.

Ray Lee Chee had turned green. 'You didn't uh . . . you didn't mention anything like that before.'

'We need the coroner,' Quincy said.

'You can't ask a geologist to serve as ME,' Rainie seconded.

'Oh good,' Ray said. ''Cause I think I'm gonna barf.' He didn't though. He just turned in a dazed little circle, then returned to them even paler, but with his expression set. 'Look, we've done about as much as we can here. Best bet is to find a hotel, hole up for a few hours with our equipment, and see what we can figure out. I know you're in a hurry, but if we gotta guarantee that we're not sending you off on a wild goose chase, then we need a shot at doing this right.'

'You're the boss,' Mac said. 'Pack up if that's what you'd like. Rainie and Quincy are going to remain here with the body. The rest of us will follow you.'

Ray nodded gratefully, then returned to his team.

There didn't seem much more to say, or much more to do.

Quincy was looking up at the sky. 'One more girl to go,' he murmured. 'And it's already dark.'

Tina woke up to the sound of someone's whimper. It took her a moment to realize it was her own.

The world was black, refusing to come into focus. She almost panicked. Her eyes had swollen shut again or worse, she'd gone blind. Then she realized the black wasn't pitch black, but only the deep, purple shadows of night.

Hours had passed with her lying in the mud. Now she lifted one arm and attempted to move. Her whole body groaned. She could feel muscles tremble with effort. Her left hip ached, her ribs throbbed. For a moment, she didn't think anything was going to happen, then she finally rolled over in the mud. She got her arms beneath her for leverage, pushed up weakly, and staggered to her feet.

The world promptly spun. She staggered over to the pit wall, dragging her feet through the heavy muck and grasping desperately at the vines for support. She leaned too far left, then lurched too far right, then finally got her hands planted against the wall. Her stomach rolled and cramped. She bent in agony and tried not to think about what must be happening now.

She cried. She cried all alone in her pit, and it was all that she could do.

Things came back to her in bits and pieces. Her glorious attempt at being a human spider. Her not-so-glorious fall. She lifted her arms again. Tried out her legs and inspected for damage. Technically speaking at least, she was still in one piece.

She tried to take a step. Her right leg buckled and she immediately sank back into the mud. Gritting her teeth, she tried again, only to get the same results. Her legs were too weak. Her body had simply had enough.

So she lay with her head in the cool, soothing muck. She watched the slime ooze and pop inches from her face. And she decided maybe dying wouldn't be so bad after all.

If she could just get water . . . Her mouth, her throat, her shriveled stomach. Her parched, festering skin.

She stared at the mud a minute longer, then she staggered up onto her hands and knees.

She shouldn't . . . It would kill her. But did that matter anymore?

Spreading her fingers, she flattened them into the muck. The small indent instantly filled with putrid, stinking water.

Tina put down her head and drank like a dog.

42

Kimberly checked them into the tiny, roadside motel. Ray and his team got their rooms. Kimberly booked another for Nora Ray, plus one for Dr Ennunzio. Then she reserved one room for her and Mac to share.

She couldn't meet his eye when she returned to the car. She distributed keys, deliberately omitting him, which earned her a curious glance. Then she was busy unloading bags from the trunk. They needed a game plan. Ray would ring Mac or Kimberly's room when the team had a theory. They, in turn, would rouse the others. In the meantime, Mac had his cell phone on and seemed to be receiving a faint signal. Kimberly also turned hers on, in case her father needed her.

Nothing left to do now but grab a shower and snatch a few hours' sleep. Soon enough, they would all be up again.

Kimberly watched Nora Ray disappear behind the plain white door of the single-story structure. Then she watched as Dr Ennunzio crossed the parking lot to his wing of the motel. She waited until he was gone from view before finally turning toward Mac.

'Here,' she said. 'I got us a room.'

If he was surprised, he didn't say anything. He simply took the key from her trembling hand. Then he picked up their bags and carried them through the doorway.

Inside she almost lost her courage again. The room was too beige, too generic, too worn. It could've been any room in any hotel in any part of the country, and for some reason that nearly broke her heart. Just once she wanted something more out of life than desperate attempts at happiness. They should go to a bed-and-breakfast. One of those places with rose-patterned wallpaper and red quilted comforters and a giant four-poster bed. Where you could sink deep into the mattress and sleep well past noon and forget the real world ever existed.

They didn't have that kind of luxury. She supposed she wouldn't have known what to do with it if she had.

Mac set their bags down at the foot of the bed. 'Why don't you shower first,' he suggested quietly. She nodded and disappeared gratefully into the solitude of the tiny bath.

She showered. First, hot and steamy to relax her tired muscles, then cool and crisp to eradicate all memories of the heat. She didn't cry this time. She didn't stand there with haunted images of her mother or sister. The worst of her grief had passed, and in some ways, she felt the most composed she'd been in weeks.

They had tried again. They had failed again. And soon, maybe in a day, maybe in an hour, they would try again. That's the way life worked. She could either quit now, or forge ahead, and for whatever reason, she wasn't the quitting type. So that was it then. She had chosen her path. She would keep trying, and keep trying, even if some days it broke her heart.

She took her time drying off. She searched her small toiletry bag for the bottle of perfume she didn't own. She wondered if she should do something with her hair, or put makeup on her pale face. She wished she possessed even a bottle of lotion to smooth over her, sun-battered skin.

But she wasn't that kind of girl. She didn't travel with those kinds of things.

She walked back into the bedroom with a threadbare white towel wrapped self-consciously around her breasts. Mac still didn't say anything. He merely grabbed his shaving kit and disappeared into the bathroom.

She put on a plain gray FBI T-shirt and waited as he showered.

It was pitch black outside now. Still hot, she imagined. Was that easier on a missing person than being someplace cold and dark? Or by now, was the girl delirious with her need for something cool and soothing against her overheated skin? It must seem like a ridiculous joke for the air to remain so hot, long after the sun had retreated from the sky.

Nora Ray had survived out there. She'd protected herself from the sun; she'd found a way to keep cool as endless day shipped into day. How small she must have felt, how absolutely insignificant, as she dug deeper into the marsh and waited for someone, anyone, to find her in the vast line of a coastal horizon. She'd never given up hope, however. She'd never succumbed to panic. And in the end, she'd survived.

Only to lose sight of the victory in her grief for her sister. She had won the battle, then lost the war. It was such an easy thing to do.

The shower shut off. Kimberly heard the rake of metal as the shower curtain was pulled back. Her breathing grew uneven. She took a seat in the broken-down chair next to the TV. Her hands trembled on her thighs.

The sound of running water in the sink. A toothbrush sudsing across teeth. Now some fresh splashes. He was probably shaving.

Kimberly got up, paced the room. She had had final exams

easier than this. She had held her first loaded firearm with less trepidation. Oh, how could this be so hard?

Then the door opened. Then Mac was standing there, freshly showered, freshly shaven, with just a towel wrapped around his lean, tanned waist.

'Hey, beautiful,' he said softly. 'Come here often?'

She crossed to him, placed her hands on his bare shoulders and it wasn't so difficult after all.

Nora Ray didn't sleep. Alone at last in a hotel room, she plopped down in an old chair and contemplated her traveling bag. She knew what she needed to do. Funny, now that the moment was at hand, she was stalling. She was nervous.

She hadn't thought it would feel like this. She'd expected to be stronger, more triumphant. Instead, she was terrified.

She got up out of the chair, idly inspecting the room. The lumpy double bed. The cheap TV cabinet, covered in fresh nicks and ancient water rings. The TV itself, so old and small no one would even consider it worth stealing. She counted the cigarette burns in the carpet.

Three years was such a long time. She could be wrong, but she didn't think so. You didn't forget your last moments with your sister. And you never stopped etching those details into your mind.

So now here she was. And now here he was. What was she going to do?

She crossed to her bag, unzipped the canvas top, reached in and pulled out the plastic zip-lock bag that passed as her toiletry kit. She hadn't lied to Mac. There wasn't much a young girl could get past airport security.

But there was something. In fact, she had learned it straight from him.

She pulled out the bottle of eye drops. Then from the inside of her hiking boot, she found the long needle slipped between the sides of the rubber sole. It took her only a moment longer to retrieve the plastic syringe from her bottle of shampoo.

She assembled the needle first. And then, very carefully, she squeezed out the liquid from the bottle of Visine. Once the tiny bottle had contained genuine eye drops, but she had replaced the contents just last week.

Now, it held ketamine. Fast acting. Powerful, and in the proper dosage, quite, quite deadly.

The man was dreaming. He thrashed from side to side. Waved his hands and kicked his feet. He hated this dream, fought to bring himself back to waking. But the dream memory was stronger, sucking him back into the abyss.

He was at a funeral. The sun burned starkly overhead, an unbearably hot day in an unbearably hot graveyard, while the priest droned on and on at a service no one else had bothered to attend. His mother gripped his hand too tightly. Her only black dress – long-sleeved and woolen – was too heavy for this weather. She rocked from side to side, panting pitifully, while he and his younger brother fought to keep her standing.

It was finally done. The priest shut up. The coffin sank down. The sweaty gravedigger moved in, looking relieved to get his task underway.

They went home, and the man was grateful.

He used the last of the coal to light their oven when they returned to the cabin. The air was too stuffy for the heat, but without electricity, it was the only way to get supper on the table. Tomorrow he'd have to find wood to feed the stove. And tomorrow after that, he'd have to think of something else. That was okay. This was now, and he just wanted to get food on the table and see some color in his mother's cheeks.

His brother was waiting with a saucepan to heat broth.

They fed their mother wordlessly. Didn't take a drop for themselves, but spooned beef bouillon past her bloodless lips, while tearing up chunks of stale bread. Finally she sighed, and he thought the worst had passed.

'He's gone, Mama,' he heard himself say. 'Things will be better now. You'll see.'

And then her bloodless face came up. Her lifeless eyes turned vibrant, snapping blue, and her cheeks filled with a color that was frightening to behold.

'Better? *Better?* You ungrateful little bastard! He put a roof over your head, he put food on the table. And what did he ever ask for in return? A little respect from his wife and kids? Was that too much, Frank? Was that really too goddamn much?'

'No, Mama,' he tried to say, already frantically backing up from the table. His nervous gaze darted to his equally nervous brother. They had never seen her like this.

She rose from the table, too pale, too thin, too bony, and stalked her older son across the room.

'We have no food!'

'I know, Mama—'

'We have no money!'

'I know, Mama—'

'We will lose this house.'

'No, Mama!'

But she would not be placated; closer she came and closer. And now he had backed up all the way across the room, his shoulders pressed against the wall.

'You are a bad boy, you are a filthy boy, you are a rotten, ungrateful, selfish little boy. What did I ever do to deserve a boy as bad as you!'

His brother was weeping. The broth grew cold on the table. And the man-child realized now that there truly was no escape. His father had gone. A new monster had already arisen to take his place.

The man lowered his hands. He exposed his face. The first

blow didn't even feel that bad, nothing like his father's. But his mother learned very quickly.

And he did nothing. He kept his hands at his side. He let his mother beat him. Then he slid down, down, down to the hot, dusty floor while his mother went to get his father's belt.

'Run away,' he told his brother. 'Run now, while you still can.'

But his brother was too terrified to move. And his mother was back soon enough, snapping the strip of leather through the air, and already getting a feel for its cutting hiss.

The man woke up harshly. His breathing was ragged, his eyes were wild. Where was he? What had happened? For a moment, he thought the black void had taken over completely. Then he got his bearings.

He was standing in the middle of a room. And in his hands, he held a box of matches, the first match already clutched between his fingers . . .

The man gently laid the matches back on the table. Then he quickly stepped away, grabbing at his head and trying to tell himself he wasn't yet insane.

He needed aspirin. He needed water, he needed something far more potent than that. Not yet, not yet, no time. His fingers clawed his rough-shaven cheeks, sinking into his temples as if through sheer force of will he could keep his skull from shattering apart.

He had to hold it together. Not much longer. Not much more time.

Helplessly, he found himself staring at the matches again. And then he knew what he must do. He retrieved the box from the table. He held the precious sticks in the palm of his hand, and he thought of things he had not thought of now, in a long, long time.

He thought of fire. He thought that all things of beauty must die. And then he allowed himself to remember that day in the cabin, and what had happened next.

43

'This is the most irresponsible handling of a case I've ever seen in my life. It's inappropriate and frankly, it's goddamn criminal! We lose this man, Quincy, and I swear to God I will spend the next two years making your life a living hell. I want you off this property as fast as you can drive. And don't bother heading back to Quantico. I know about your little chats with special agents Kaplan and Ennunzio. So much as step one foot onto Academy grounds, and I'll have you arrested at the gate. Your work on this case is over. As far as I'm concerned, your whole fucking career is over. Now get out of my sight.'

Special Agent Harkoos finally wrapped up his tirade and stormed away. His navy-blue blazer hung limply in the heavy heat. His face, covered in sweat before he'd started yelling, was dripping. In other words, he looked about the same as the other FBI agents now swarming the abandoned sawmill.

'I don't think he likes you much,' Rainie said to Quincy.

He turned toward her. 'Be honest with me. Do I look that ridiculous in a navy-blue suit?'

'Most of the time.'

'Huh. The things you learn forty years too late.'

They started walking toward their car. Their light tones fooled neither of them. Harkoos's dressing-down had been thorough and honest. They were fired from the case, banned from the Academy, and once word of this disaster spread, probably finished as consultants in the tight, incestuous world of high-profile law enforcement investigations. Reputations were built in a lifetime, but ruined in only a matter of minutes.

Quincy had a hollow, sick feeling in his stomach, one he hadn't had in a very long time.

'When we catch the Eco-Killer, they'll quickly forget about this,' Rainie offered.

'Perhaps.'

'Irresponsible is only irresponsible if you fail. Succeed, however, and irresponsible quickly becomes merely unorthodox.'

'True.'

'Quincy, those guys had the same body and same evidence we did last night, and they weren't even in the area when you gave them a call. Frankly, if we hadn't gone off the deep end, that girl would still be floating in a cavern, and the fourth victim would be no closer to discovery. Harkoos is just mad because you beat him to the punch. There's nothing more embarrassing than being upstaged, especially by a bunch of outsiders.'

Quincy stopped walking. 'I'm sick of this,' he said abruptly.

'Politics are never fun.'

'No! I don't mean this damn case. Fuck this case. You're absolutely right. Failure today, hero tomorrow. It's always changing and none of it means a thing.'

Rainie had stopped moving completely. He could see her pale face in the thin moonlight. He rarely swore, and the fact he was driven to it now had her both fascinated and frightened.

'I don't want things to be like this between us, Rainie.'

Her expression faltered. She looked down at the ground. 'I know.'

'You are the best thing that ever happened to me, and if I don't tell you that enough, then I am a total idiot.'

'You're not a total idiot.'

'I don't know about kids. I'll be honest: the very thought scares me to death. I was not a great father, Rainie. I'm still not a great father. But I am willing to talk about it. If this is what you really, truly want, then I can at least explore the notion.'

'I want.'

'All right, then you have to be honest with me. Is it only kids you want? Because I tried . . . I thought . . . Rainie, each time I've asked you to marry me, why have you never said yes?'

Her eyes filled with tears. 'Because I thought you'd never stop asking. You're not the idiot, Quincy. It's me.'

He felt the world spin again. He had thought . . . Had been so sure . . . 'Does that mean . . .'

'You think you're scared of kids? Hell, Quince, I'm scared of everything. I'm scared of commitment and I'm scared of responsibility. I'm afraid I'll disappoint you and I'm afraid one day I'll physically harm my child. We all get a little older, but we never completely outgrow our past. And mine is looming behind me now, this big giant shadow I want so desperately to leave behind.'

'Oh, Rainie . . .'

'I tell myself to be happy with what I've got. You, me, this is a good gig, better than anything I thought I'd have. And we do important work and meet important people, and hey, that's not bad for a woman who used to be a human punching bag. But . . . but I get so restless now. Maybe happiness is like a drug. You get a little, then you want a lot. I don't know, Quincy. I want so badly not to want so much, but I think I can't help it anymore. I want more you. I want more me. I want . . . kids and white picket fences and maybe tea cozies, except I'm not sure I know what a tea cozy is. Maybe you're frightened. But I'm pretty sure I've lost my mind.'

'Rainie, you are the strongest, bravest woman I know.'

'Oh, you're just saying that so I don't kick your ass.'

She kicked at the ground in disgust, and Quincy finally smiled. It amazed him how much better he already felt. The world had righted. His hands had steadied. It was as if a crushing weight he didn't even know he'd been carrying had suddenly been lifted off his chest.

This was not the time, he knew. This was not the place. But then he'd spent too much of his life waiting for perfect moments that had never come. And he knew better than most how fleeting opportunity could be. Life gave, but life also took away. He was older, wiser, and he didn't want any more regrets.

He went down on his knee, a crush of dirt and pine needles staining his suit. He took hold of Rainie's hands. She was crying openly now, tears streaming down her face, but she didn't pull away.

'Grow old with me, Rainie,' he whispered. 'We'll adopt some children. We'll cut back on cases, create a home, then do the fashionable thing and write our memoirs. I'll be terrified. You can help show me the way.'

'I don't know if I'll be a good mother!'

'We'll learn together.'

'I don't know if I'll be a good wife!'

'Rainie, I just need you to be you. And then I'm the happiest man in the world.'

'Oh for God's sake, get up off the dirt.' But she was clasping his hands with both of hers now, and crying harder, and since he wouldn't get up, she sank down to the ground with him. 'We have to talk more.'

'I know.'

'I mean about something other than work!'

'I understand that, too.'

'And you have to tell me when you're frightened, Quincy. I can't stand it when you pull away.'

'I'll try.'

'Okay.'

'Okay?'

She sniffed. 'I mean, better than okay. I mean yes, I'll marry you. What the hell. If we can catch a few killers, we oughtta be able to figure out this domestic thing.'

'You would think so,' Quincy agreed. He pulled her closer, wrapped his arms around her shoulders. He could feel her trembling now and understood for the first time that she was as nervous as he. It gave him strength. You didn't have to know all the answers. You just had to be brave enough to try.

'I love you, Rainie,' he whispered in her ear.

'I love you, too.'

She gripped him tighter and he kissed all the tears from her face.

The call came almost an hour later. They had made it back to I-81 and were heading north, seeking a more populated Virginia. They had both turned on their cell phones. No reason to dodge the FBI anymore and Quincy wanted to be ready when Kimberly and Mac had new information.

The caller wasn't Kimberly, however. It was Kaplan.

'I have some news from the name game,' the special agent said.

'It's only fair to tell you, we've been officially removed from the case,' Quincy replied.

'Well then, you didn't hear this from me. But I've had my people scouring every contractor with ties to Georgia in the past ten years. Good news, we got a few hits. Bad news, none of them panned out. Better news, then I expanded the search.'

'Expanded?'

'I started looking at everyone on the whole damn base. Now we got lots of hits, but I thought there was one you should know about right away. Dr Ennunzio. The linguist.'

'He used to live in Georgia?'

'Worked there. A high-profile string of kidnappings that had him flying in and out of Atlanta for a good three years. Say ninety-eight to two thousand. Which would be . . .'

-'The same time the Eco-Killer started up his game. Dammit.' Quincy smacked the wheel. He already had Kaplan on the phone, so he turned to Rainie. 'Quick, dial Kimberly! Tell her it's Ennunzio, and get Nora Ray away from him quick!'

Kimberly wasn't sleeping. Sleeping would be the smart thing to do. Recharge while she had a chance. Catch some desperately needed shut-eye. But she didn't sleep.

She was tracing lines on Mac's bronzed shoulder with her index finger. Then she ran her fingers through the light smattering of hair on his chest. She couldn't get over the feel of him, his skin like warm satin to the touch.

He snored. She'd learned that right away. He was also unbearably hot and heavy. Twice he'd flung his large frame over, tossing one arm across her chest or over her hip in a highly proprietary manner. She thought she should break him of that habit, while finding it secretly endearing.

And then she suspected she was experiencing the same downward slide she'd witnessed in other women – they started out strong and independent with firm beliefs on how to manage men, then caved like spun sugar when tall, dark, and handsome crooked his little finger.

Well, she wasn't going to cave, she decided. Not totally, anyway. She was going to demand her own side of the bed. Space where she could sprawl comfortably and sleep. Just as soon as she stopped tracing the ripple of his triceps, or the hard line of his jaw . . .

Now her fingers wandered down to his hip and were rewarded by a growing length against the juncture of her thighs.

Her phone rang. Her hand stilled. She swore a word nice young girls probably weren't supposed to use in bed. Then she was frantically trying to kick off the tangle of sheets.

'I fucking hate cell phones,' Mac said clearly.

'Cheater! You were awake.'

'Delightfully so. Wanna punish me? I could use a good spanking.'

'This had better be good,' Kimberly declared, 'or I'll break every microchip in this damn phone.'

But they already knew it would be urgent. Given the early morning hour, it was probably Ray Lee Chee with news on the fourth victim. They'd had their reprieve. Now, time was up.

Kimberly flipped open the phone, already expecting the worst, and then was genuinely startled to hear Rainie's voice on the other end of the line.

'It's Ennunzio!' she said without preamble. 'Where the hell are you?'

Kimberly rattled off the name of the motel and the exit number, still in shock.

'Get him secured,' Rainie was saying. 'We're on our way. And Kimberly – take care of Nora Ray.'

The phone went click. Mac and Kimberly scrambled for clothes.

Dark out. Very hot. They pressed against the wall of the motel, working their way down to Ennunzio's room with weapons drawn and faces tense. They came to Nora Ray's room first. Kimberly knocked. No answer.

'Deep sleeper,' Mac murmured.

'Don't we both wish.'

They cut across the parking lot, moving now with anxious speed. Ennunzio's room was in the other wing of the L-shaped building. Door closed. Lights off. Kimberly pressed her ear against the door and listened. First nothing. Then, the sudden, crashing sound of furniture – or a body – being thrown around the room.

'Go, go, go!' Kimberly cried.

Mac heaved up a leg and kicked in the cheap wooden door. It snapped back, caught on the chain. He gave it one more thunderous whack, and the door ricocheted into the wall.

'Police, freeze!'

'Nora Ray, where are you?'

Kimberly and Mac rolled into the room, one taking high, another taking low. In the next instant, Kimberly's groping fingers snapped on the light.

In front of them, two people were clearly involved in a struggle. Chairs had been tossed, the bed destroyed, the TV toppled. But it was not Dr Ennunzio bearing down on a frightened girl. It was Nora Ray who had the special agent, clad in just a pair of boxers, backed into a corner. Now she loomed over him, brandishing a giant, gleaming needle.

'Nora Ray!' Kimberly said in shock.

'He killed my sister.'

'It wasn't me, it wasn't me. I swear to God!' Ennunzio pressed harder against the wall. 'I think . . . I think it was my brother.'

44

Wytheville, Virginia
3:24 A.M.
Temperature: 94 degrees

'You have to understand, I don't think he's well.'

'Your brother may have kidnapped and killed over ten women. Being not well is the least of his problems!'

'I don't think he meant to hurt them—'

'Holy shit!' Mac drew up short. He was looming above Ennunzio, who was now slumped on the edge of his bed. Quincy and Rainie had arrived and guarded the door, while in the right-hand corner, Kimberly kept watch over Nora Ray. Kimberly had taken the girl's needle away. Hostility in the small room, however, remained sky-high. 'You're the caller!'

Ennunzio bowed his head.

'What the hell? You've been playing me from the start!'

'I was not trying to play you. I've been trying to help—'

'You said the caller might be the killer. What was that all about?'

'I wanted you to take the calls more seriously. Honest to God, I've been trying very hard to assist, I just don't know much myself.'

'You could've given me your brother's name.'

'It wouldn't have done you any good. Frank Ennunzio doesn't exist. However he's living now, it's under an assumed name. Please, you have to understand, I haven't actually spoken to my brother in over thirty years.'

That brought them all to attention. Mac frowned, not liking this newest bit of news. He crossed his arms over his chest and started to pace the tiny room.

'Maybe you should start from the beginning,' Quincy said quietly.

Ennunzio tiredly nodded his head. 'Five years ago, I started work on a case in Atlanta, a kidnapping involving a young doctor's child. I was called in to analyze notes being delivered to the house. While I was there, two girls from Georgia State University also vanished. I clipped the articles from the newspaper. At the time, I chalked it up to an investigative hunch. I was working a disappearance, here was another disappearance, you never knew. So I started to follow the case of the missing college girls as well. That summer and then the next summer, when two other girls also went missing during a heat wave.

'By now, I knew the case of the young girls had nothing to do with my own. I was dealing with what turned out to be a string of ransom cases. A very cool, young man who worked at one of the more prominent golf clubs was using his position to identify and stalk wealthy young families. It took us three years, but we finally identified him, in a large part from his ransom notes.

'The heat-wave kidnappings, however, were an entirely different beast. The UNSUB always struck young, college-aged girls traveling in pairs. He'd leave one body next to a road and the second in some remote location. And he always sent a note to the press. Clock ticking . . . heat kills. I've remembered that note for a long, long time. It's not the sort of thing you forget.'

Ennunzio's voice broke off. He stared down at the carpet, lost now in his own thoughts.

'What did your brother do?' Rainie spoke up quietly. 'Tell us about Frank.'

'Our father was a hard man.'

'Some fathers are.'

'He worked in the coal mines, not far from where we were today. It's an unforgiving life. Backbreaking labor by day. Brutal poverty by night. He was a very angry person.'

'Angry people often become physical,' Rainie commented.

Ennunzio finally looked up at her. 'Yes. They do.'

'Did your brother kill your father?'

'No. The mines got him first. Coal dust built up in my father's lungs, he started to cough, and then one day we didn't have to fear him anymore.'

'Ennunzio, what did your brother do?'

'He killed our mother,' Ennunzio whispered. 'He killed the woman we had spent all of our childhood trying to protect.'

His voice broke again. He didn't seem capable of looking at anyone anymore. Instead his shoulders sagged, his head fell forward, and on his lap he began to wring his hands.

'You have to understand . . . After the funeral, our mother went a little crazy. She started yelling at Frank that he was ungrateful, and next thing we both knew, she went at him with my father's belt. At first, he didn't do anything. He just lay there until she wore herself out. Until she was so exhausted from hitting him that she couldn't even lift her own arm. And then he got off the floor. He picked her up. So gently. I remember that clearly. He was only fourteen, but he was already big for his age and my mother was built like a bird. He cradled her in his arms, carried her to her room and laid her down on the bed.

'He told me to get out of the house. But I couldn't leave. I stood in the middle of the cabin, while he got down the oil lamps and started pouring the oil around the rooms. I think I knew then what he was going to do. My mother just watched.

Lying on the bed, her chest still heaving. She didn't utter a word. Didn't even lift her head. He was going to kill her, maybe kill all of us, and I think she was grateful.

'He covered the cabin in oil. Then he went to our stove and dumped the burning coals onto the floor. The whole house went up with a single whoosh. It was an old wood cabin, dry from age, never burdened by insulation. Maybe the house was grateful, too; it had never been a very happy place. I don't know. I just remember my brother grabbing my hand. He pulled me through the door. Then we stood outside and watched our house burn. At the last minute, my mother started screaming. I swore I saw her standing right in the middle of those flames, her arms over her head, shrieking to high heaven. But there was nothing anyone could do for her by then. Nothing anyone could do for any one of us.

'My brother walked me to the road. He told me someone would be by soon. Then he said, "Just remember, Davey. Heat kills." He disappeared into the woods and I haven't seen or talked to my brother since. One week later, I was placed with a foster family in Richmond and that was that.

'When I turned eighteen, I returned to the area briefly. I wanted to visit my parents' headstone. I found a hole had been gouged into the marker, and inside I found a rolled-up piece of paper that read, "Clock ticking . . . planet dying . . . animals weeping . . . rivers screaming. Can't you hear it? Heat kills." I think that summarizes my brother's last thoughts on the subject.'

'Everything must die?' Kimberly spoke up grimly.

'Everything of beauty.' Ennunzio shrugged. 'Don't ask me to explain it completely. Nature was both our refuge – where we went to escape our father – and our prison – the isolated area where no one could see what was really happening. My brother loved the woods, he hated the woods. He loved our father, he hated our father. And in the end, he loved my mother and he loathed her. For him, I think the lines are all blurred. He hates what he loves and loves what he hates and has himself tangled in a web he'll never escape.'

'So he seeks heat,' Quincy murmured, 'which purifies.'

'And uses nature, which both saved him and betrayed him,' Rainie filled in. She turned troubled eyes toward Nora Ray. 'Does this help you any?'

'What?' the girl spoke up angrily. 'So the guy had a rough life. Lots of people have rough lives. That still doesn't give him the right to murder my sister. And you.' Her hard, over-bright gaze swung toward Ennunzio. 'You should be ashamed of yourself! You're an FBI agent, you're supposed to be protecting people. Instead, you knew something about a killer and you said nothing.'

'I had nothing to add, not a name, not a location—'

'You knew his past!'

'I didn't know his present. All I could do was watch and wait. And I swear, the minute I saw my brother's note suddenly resurface in a Virginia paper, I mailed a copy to the GBI. I wanted Special Agent McCormack involved. I did everything in my power to get the police involved early and actively. Surely that must count for something—'

'Three girls are dead,' Nora Ray spat out. 'You tell me how valuable your efforts have been.'

'If I could've been sure . . .' Ennunzio murmured.

'Coward,' Nora Ray countered savagely and Ennunzio finally shut up.

Quincy took a deep breath. He regarded Rainie, Mac and Kimberly. 'So where does this leave us?'

'Still short one killer and still short one victim,' Mac said. 'Now we've got motive, but that's only going to help us at trial. Bottom line is that it's the middle of the night, scary hot, and another girl's still out there. So cough it up, Ennunzio. He's your brother. Start thinking like him.'

The forensic linguist, however, merely shook his head. 'I understood some of the clues in the beginning, only because I've also spent a lot of time outdoors. But the evidence you're seeing now – water samples, sediment, pollen. That's way over my head. You need the experts.'

'Doesn't your brother have any favorite places?'

'We grew up dirt poor in the foothills of the Appalachian Mountains. The only favorite places we knew were the ones we could walk to.'

'You knew the cave.'

'Because I used to be into caving. And of all the places Frank's chosen, that's been the most local.'

'So we should look at the Appalachian Mountains, stay in the area,' Rainie spoke up.

Both Mac and Ennunzio, however, were shaking their heads.

'My brother's methodology may be influenced by the past,' Ennunzio told them, 'perhaps even triggered by the trauma of heat spells, but the places themselves aren't tied to our family. I didn't even know he lived in Georgia.'

'Ennunzio's right,' Mac said. 'Whatever hang-ups got this guy started, he's moved beyond them now. He's sticking to his game plan, and that means diversity. Wherever we are now, the last girl will be the farthest point away.'

'We need Ray's team,' Kimberly said.

'I'll go check on them,' Mac said.

But in the end, he didn't have to. Ray met him halfway across the parking lot, already on his way to Mac's room.

'We have a winner,' the USGS worker said excitedly. 'Lloyd's soil samples turned out to contain three kinds of pollen from three types of trees – bald cypress, tupelo gum, and red maple – while the crushed plant matter is actually a sorely abused log fern. The shoes were also covered in peat moss. Which could only mean . . .'

'We're going to DisneyLand?'

'Better. The Dismal Swamp.'

Four A.M., the group made their decision to divide and conquer. Quincy, as elder statesman, once more inherited the responsibility of contacting the official FBI case team. He and Rainie also assumed watch of Nora Ray, whom nobody trusted alone.

The USGS team members were packing up their gear and loading up their vehicles. According to Kathy Levine's debriefing, the Dismal Swamp was six hundred square miles of bugs, poisonous snakes, black bears, and bobcats. Trees grew to stupendous sizes, while a dense underbrush of brier bushes and wild vines made sections of the swamp virtually impassable.

They needed water. They needed insect repellent. They needed machetes. In other words, they needed all the help they could get.

Mac and Kimberly had Ennunzio in the back of their car. They would follow Ray's team to the site. That gave them seven bodies to search an area that had daunted even George Washington. While the sun once again peeked over the horizon, and the mosquitoes started to swarm.

'Ready?' Mac asked Kimberly as he climbed into the car.

'Ready as I'm gonna get.'

His gaze rested on Ennunzio in the rearview mirror. The agent was wearily rubbing his head; he looked like he had just aged twenty years. 'Why didn't they arrest your brother after the fire?' Mac asked crisply.

'I don't think they ever found him.'

'Did you tell anyone what happened?'

'Of course.'

'Because you never hold back the truth.'

'I'm a federal agent,' Ennunzio said curtly. 'I know what needs to be done.'

'Good, because finding this next girl is only half the battle.

After that we go after your brother, and we don't stop until we've found him.'

'He'll never surrender. He's not the type to spend the rest of his life in a cage.'

'Then you'd better be prepared,' Mac said grimly. He looked over at Kimberly.

'It would be better if we had a rifle,' she said, and they both unsnapped the holsters with their guns.

45

Her mother was yelling at her. 'I sent you to college for an education. So you could make something of yourself. Well, you've certainly made something now haven't you?'

Tina yelled back. 'Woman, bring me a goddamn glass of water. And get those tuxedoed waiters out of here.'

Then she sat down and watched the blue butterfly.

Water. Lakes. Ice cold streams. Potato chips. Oh, she was hot, hot, hot. Skin on fire. She longed to peel it off in strips. Peel down to the bone and roll in the muck. Wouldn't that feel good?

The flesh on her forearm squirmed. She watched bloody sores ripple and ooze. Maggots. Horrible little white worms. Writhing under her flesh, feasting on meat. She should pull them out and pop them in her mouth. Would they taste like chicken?

Pretty blue butterfly. How it glided along the air. Dancing up, up, and away. She longed to dance like that. To dance and glide and soar. To drift off to the comforting shade of a giant beech tree . . . or lake . . . or cool mountain stream.

Itched. Her skin itched and itched. She scratched and scratched. Didn't make a difference. Hot, hot, hot. So thirsty. Sun, coming up. Going to burn, burn, burn. She would cry, but no moisture left. She slathered on the mud, flattened out puddles and sought desperately to wet her tongue.

Her mother was hollering at her again. *Now look at what you've done.* She didn't have the strength to yell back.

'I'm sorry,' she whispered. Then she closed her eyes. She dreamed of deep Minnesotan winters. She dreamed of her mother holding out her arms to her. And she prayed the end would happen quick.

It took over two hours to drive due east to the swamp. The visitors' entrance was in North Carolina on the east side. Operating under the assumption that the killer would stick to the Virginian playing field, however, Kathy Levine led their little caravan to a hiking entrance in Virginia, on the west side. All three vehicles pulled into the dirt parking lot and Kathy, the official search-and-rescue member of their party, assumed command. First, she handed out whistles.

'Remember, three blasts signifies the international call for distress. Get in trouble, stay put, blow away, and we will find you.'

Next, she handed out maps. 'I downloaded these from the Internet before we left the hotel. As you can see, the Dismal Swamp is basically a rectangle. Unfortunately for us, it's a very large rectangle. Looking at only the Virginia half, we're still talking over a hundred thousand acres. That's going to be a bit much for seven people.'

Mac took one of the maps. The printout showed a large, shadowed area, crisscrossed by a maze of lines. He followed the various markings with his finger. 'What are these?'

'The dashed lines represent hiking and biking trails bisecting the swamp. The broader lines here are unpaved roads. The thin dark lines reveal the old canals, most hand-dug by slaves hundreds of years ago. When the water levels were higher, they would use the canals to harvest the cypress and juniper trees.'

'And now?'

'Most of the canals are marshy messes. Not enough water for a canoe, but not dry enough to walk.'

'What about the roads?'

'Wide, flat, grassy; you don't even need four-wheel drive.' Levine already understood where he was going with this. She added, 'Technically speaking, visitors aren't permitted to bring vehicles onto the roads, but as for what happens under the cover of night . . .'

Mac nodded. 'Okay. So our guy needs to get an unconscious, hundred-and-twenty-pound body into the heart of the swamp. He'd want to take her someplace remote, where she wouldn't immediately be found by others. He'd need a road for access, however, because carrying a woman through a hundred thousand acres would be a bit much. Where does that leave us?'

They all studied the map. The marked hiking paths were fairly centralized, with a clear grid pattern occupying most of the west side of the swamp. Closest to them was a simple loop labeled a boardwalk trail. They immediately dismissed that as too touristy. Farther in lay the dark oval shadow of Lake Drummond, also highly populated with hiking trails, roads, and feeder ditches. Beyond the lake, however, moving farther east, north and south, the map became a solid field of gray, only periodically bisected by old, unpaved roads. This is where the swamp became a lonely place.

'We need to drive in,' Kimberly murmured. 'Make it to the lake.'

'Branch off from there,' Mac agreed. He looked at Levine intently. 'He wouldn't leave her by a road. Given the grid pattern, it would be too easy for her to walk out.'

'True.'

'He wouldn't use a canal either. Again, she could just follow it straight out of the swamp.'

Kathy nodded silently.

'He took her into the wild,' Mac concluded softly. 'Probably in this north eastern quadrant, where the trees and thick underbrush are disorienting. Where the predator population is higher and that much more dangerous. Where she can scream all she wants; and no one will hear a thing.'

He fell silent for a moment. It was already so hot out this morning. Sweat trickled down their faces, staining their shirts. The air felt too heavy to breathe, making their hearts beat faster and their lungs labor harder, and it was barely sunrise. Conditions were harsh, bordering on brutal. What must the girl be going through, trapped here for over three days?

'Going there ourselves will be dangerous,' Kathy said quietly. 'We're talking brier thickets so dense in places you can't even hack your way through. One minute you might be walking on hard-packed earth; the next you'll have sunk down to your knees in sucking mud. You need to be on the lookout for bears and bobcats. Then there's the matter of cotton-mouth snakes, copperhead snakes, and the canebrake rattler. Normally they keep to themselves. But once off the trails, we're intruding in their terrain, and they won't take it kindly.'

'Canebrake rattler?' Kimberly spoke up nervously.

'Shorter than its cousin, with a thick, squat head that will scare the piggy out of you. Cottonmouth and copperhead will be around the wet, swampy patches. The canebrake rattler will prefer rocks and piles of dead leaves. Finally, we have the bugs. Mosquitoes, yellow flies, gnats, chiggers, and ticks . . . Most of the time, none of us consider the insect population. But the overwhelming swarms of mosquitoes and yellow flies are what help the Dismal Swamp to be considered one of the least hospitable places on earth.'

Lisa Gardner

'No kidding,' Ray muttered darkly. He was already swatting at the air around his face. The first few mosquitoes had picked up their scents, and judging from the growing buzz in the air, the rest were on their way.

Ray and Brian dug in their packs for bug repellent, while the mood grew subdued. If the girl was in the wild lands of the swamp, then of course that's where they would go. No one liked it, but no one was arguing it either.

'Look,' Kathy said surely, 'the biggest danger today is dehydration and heat stroke. Everyone needs to be drinking at least one liter of water an hour. Filtered water is best, but in a pinch, you can drink the swamp water. It looks like something that's been used to wash dirty socks, but the water is actually unusually pure, preserved by the tannic acids in the bark of the juniper, gum, and cypress trees. As a matter of fact, they used to fill barrels with this water for long sea voyages. The habitat and water have changed some since then, but given today's temperatures . . .'

'Drink,' Mac said.

'Yes, drink a lot. Liquids are your friends. Now, assume for a moment that we get lucky and find Tina. First priority with anyone suffering severe heat stroke and dehydration is to reduce core body temperature. Douse her with water. Massage her limbs to increase circulation. Give her water, but also plenty of salty snacks, or better yet a saline solution. Don't be surprised if she fights you. Victims of extreme heat stroke are often delusional and argumentative. She may be ranting and raving, she may seem perfectly lucid, then lash out at you the next instant. Don't try to reason with her. Get her down, and get her hydrated as fast and efficiently as you can. She can blame you for the bruised jaw later if need be. Other questions?'

No one had any. The mosquitoes were arriving in force now, buzzing their eyes, their ears, their mouths. Ray and Brian took some half-hearted swipes at the winged-insects with their hands. The mosquitoes didn't seem to notice. They all hosed down with bug repellent. The mosquitoes didn't seem to mind that either.

Last minute check of gear, now. Everyone had water, first aid kits, and whistles. Everyone had a map and plenty of bug spray. That was it then. They loaded their packs back into their vehicles. Ray opened the gate to the main road leading to Lake Drummond. And one by one, they drove into the swamp.

'Scary place,' Ennunzio murmured as the first dark, muddy canal appeared on their right and snaked ominously through the trees.

Mac and Kimberly didn't say anything at all.

Things grow bigger in a swamp. Kimberly ducked her head for the fourth time, trying to wind her way through the thick woods of twisted cypress trees and gargantuan junipers. Tree trunks grew wider than the span of her arms. Some leaves were bigger than her head. In other places, tree limbs and vines were so grossly intertwined, she had to take off her backpack to squeeze through the narrow space left between.

Sun was a distant memory now, flickering in a tree canopy far above. Instead, she, Mac, and Ennunzio walked through a silent, boggy hush. The spongy ground absorbing the sound of their footsteps, while the rich scent of overripe vegetation filled their nostrils and made them want to gag.

On a different day, in different circumstances, she supposed she would've found the swamp beautiful. Bright orange flowers from the trumpet vines dappled the swamp floor. Gorgeous blue butterflies appeared in the beams of sunlight, playing tag among the trees. Dozens of green and gold dragonflies darted along their path, offering delicate flashes of color amid the deepening gloom.

Mostly, however, Kimberly was aware of the danger. Piles of dried leaves bunched at the base of trees and made the perfect home for sleeping snakes. Predatory vines, the same thickness as her arm, bound trees in tight, suffocating coils. Then there were clearings, sections of the swamp that had been logged out decades ago, and now just worn, rounded tree stumps dotted the shadowed landscape like endless rows of miniature gravestones. The ground would be softer there, marshy and popping as toads and salamanders leapt out of their hiding places to escape the encroaching footsteps.

Things moved in the dark recesses of the swamp. Things Kimberly never saw but felt like a whisper in the wind. Deer, bear, bobcat? She couldn't be sure. She just knew she jumped at the random, distant noises and was aware of the hair rising at the nape of her neck.

It had to be over a hundred degrees out. And still she battled a chill.

Mac led their little party. Then came Kimberly, then Ennunzio. Mac was trying to work a rough grid, sweeping between two unpaved roads. It seemed like a good idea at the time. Thickets and dense trees often made passage impossible, however, so they started having to veer a little more to the right, then a little more to the left. Then they had to take this detour and then that detour. Mac had a compass. Maybe, he knew where they were. From what Kimberly could tell, however, the swamp now owned them. They walked where it let them, passed where it let them pass. And increasingly, that path was taking them to a dark, decaying place, where the tree branches grew denser, and they had to round their shoulders to fit through the tight, cramped space.

They didn't speak much. They slogged their way through the hot, wet vines, searching for signs of broken twigs, scuffed ground, or bruised vegetation that might indicate recent human passage. They took turns issuing single blasts on their whistles or calling out Tina Krahn's name. Then they heaved themselves over giant, lightning-felled trees. Or wiggled between

particularly large boulders. Or hacked their way futilely
through dense, prickly thickets.

While they downed more and more of their precious supply
of water. While their breathing became hard and panting, and
their footsteps grew unsteady, and their arms started to tremble
visibly from the heat.

Kimberly's mouth had gone dry, a sure sign she wasn't
drinking enough water. She found herself stumbling more,
having to catch herself on tree limbs and tangled brush. The
sweat stung her eyes. The yellow flies constantly swarmed her
face, trying to feast on the corners of her mouth or the tender
flesh behind her ears.

She didn't even know how long they had been hiking anymore. It seemed as if she'd been in the steaming jungle forever,
pushing her way through thick, wet leaves only to encounter
another choking eternity of vines, briers, and bushes.

Then, all of a sudden, Mac held up his hand.

'Did you hear that?' he asked sharply.

Kimberly stopped, drew in a ragged gasp of air, and strained
to hear: There, for just an instant. A voice in the wind.

Mac turned, his sweat-covered face at once triumphant and
intent.

'Where is that coming from?'

'Over there!' Kimberly cried, pointing to her right.

'No, I think it's more like over there,' Mac said, pointing
straight ahead. He frowned. 'Damn trees; they're distorting the
sound.'

'Well, somewhere off in that direction.'

'Let's go!'

Then, a new and sudden realization sucked the last of the
moisture from Kimberly's mouth. 'Mac,' she said sharply.
'Where is Ennunzio?'

46

'I'm telling you, the fourth girl, Tina Krahn, has been abandoned somewhere in the Dismal Swamp.'

'And I'm telling you, you have absolutely no authority in this case.'

'I know I have no authority!' Quincy started yelling, caught the outburst, and bitterly swallowed it back down. He had arrived at the FBI's Richmond field office just thirty minutes ago, seeking a meeting with Special Agent Harkoos. Harkoos wouldn't grant him permission to come to his office, but instead had grudgingly agreed to meet with him in a downstairs alcove. The blatant lack of hospitality was not lost on Quincy. 'I'm not seeking authority,' Quincy tried again. 'I'm seeking help for a missing person.'

'You tampered with evidence,' Harkoos growled.

'I arrived late at the scene, the USGS personnel had already started analyzing data, and there was nothing I could do.'

'You could've forced them away until the real professionals arrived.'

'They are experts in the field—'

'They are not trained forensic technicians—'

'They've identified three different sites!' Quincy was yelling again and about to start swearing, too. Really, the last twenty-four hours had been a banner day of emotional outbursts for him. He forced himself to take another deep breath. Time for logic, diplomacy, and calm rationality. Failing that, he'd have to kill the son of a bitch. 'We need your help,' he insisted.

'You fucked this case.'

'This case was already fucked. Four girls missing, three now dead. Agent, we have one last shot at doing this right. One girl, in the middle of a hundred-thousand-acre swamp. Call in the rescue teams, find that girl, get the headlines. It really is that simple.'

Special Agent Harkoos scowled. 'I don't like you,' he said, but his voice had lost its vehemence. Quincy had spoken the truth, and it was hard to argue with headlines. 'You have behaved in an unorthodox manner which has put prosecuting this case in jeopardy,' Harkoos grumbled. 'Don't think I'm going to forget that.'

'Call in the rescue teams, find that girl, get the headlines,' Quincy repeated.

'The Dismal Swamp, huh? Is it as bad as its name sounds?'

'Most likely, yes.'

'Shit.' Harkoos dug out his cell phone. 'Your people had better be right.'

'My people,' Quincy said tersely, 'haven't been wrong yet.'

Quincy had no sooner left the building to rejoin Rainie and Nora Ray at the car when his cell phone rang. It was Kaplan, calling from Quantico.

'Do you have Ennunzio in custody?' the special agent demanded to know.

'It's not him,' Quincy said. 'Try his brother.'

'Brother?'

'According to Ennunzio, his older brother murdered their mom thirty years ago. Burned her to death. Ennunzio hasn't seen him since, but his brother once left a note on their parents' grave, bearing the same message as the notes now sent by the Eco-Killer.'

'Quincy, according to Ennunzio's personnel records, he doesn't have a brother.'

Quincy drew up short, frowning now as he stood beside Rainie. 'Maybe he doesn't consider him family anymore. It's been thirty years. Their last time together was hardly a Kodak moment.'

There was a pause. 'I don't like this,' Kaplan said. 'Something's wrong. Look, I was calling because I just got off the phone with Ennunzio's secretary. Turns out, two years ago, he took a three-month leave of absence to have major surgery. The doctors removed a tumor in his brain. According to his secretary, Ennunzio started complaining of headaches again six months ago. She's been really worried about him.'

'A tumor . . .'

'Now, you're the expert, but brain tumors can impact behavior, right? Particularly ones growing in the right place . . .'

'The limbic system,' Quincy murmured, closing his eyes and thinking fast. 'In cases of brain trauma or tumors, you often see a marked change in behavior in the subject – increased irascibility, we call it. Normally mild-mannered people become violent, aggressive, use foul language.'

'Maybe even go on a murder spree?'

'There have been some instances of mass murder,' Quincy replied. 'But something this cold and calculated . . . Then again, a tumor might trigger psychotic episodes, paving the way. Special Agent, are you at a computer? Can you look up the name David Ennunzio for me? Search birth and death records, Lee County, Virginia.'

Rainie was watching him curiously now. Nora Ray as well.

'Isn't David Dr Ennunzio's first name?' Rainie whispered.

'That's what we all assumed.'

'Assumed?' Her eyes widened and he knew she was getting it, too. Why should you never assume something when working an investigation? Because it made an ass out of you and me. Kaplan was already back on the line.

'According to the obits, David Joseph Ennunzio died July 14, 1972, at the age of thirteen. He was killed in a house fire along with his mother. They are survived by . . . Christ! Franklin George Ennunzio. Dr Frank Ennunzio. Quincy, Ennunzio doesn't have a brother.'

'He had a brother but he killed him. He killed his brother, his mother – hell, maybe he killed his father, too. Then he spent all these years covering it up and trying to forget. Until something else went even more wrong in his head.'

'You have to get him in custody now!' Kaplan shouted.

And Quincy whispered, 'I can't. He's in the Dismal Swamp. With my daughter.'

The man knew what he must do. He was letting himself think again, remembering the old days and old ways. It hurt his head. Brought on raging bolts of pain. He staggered as he walked and clutched his temples.

But remembering brought him clarity, too. He thought of his mother, the look on her face as she lay so passively on the bed and watched him splatter kerosene on the floor of their wooden shack. He thought of his younger brother, and how he'd cowered in the corner instead of bolting for safety.

No fighting from either of them. No protest. His father had beat the resistance out of them over all those long, bloody years. Now, death came and they simply waited.

He had been weak thirty years ago. He had tossed the match, then outrun the flames. He had thought he would stay. He'd been so sure death was what he wanted, too. Then, at the last moment, he couldn't do it. He'd broken from the fire's mesmerizing spell. He had dashed out the door. He had heard his mother's raw, angry screams. He had heard his brother's last pitiful cries. Then he had run for the woods and begged the wilderness to save him.

Mother Nature was not that kind. He had been hungry and hot. He had spent weeks dazed and desperate with thirst. So finally he had emerged, walking into town, waiting to see what would happen next.

People had been kind. They fawned over him, hugged him, and fussed over this lone survivor of a tragic fate. How big and strong he must have been to survive in the woods all this time, they told him. What an amazing miracle he'd made it out of the house in time. God must surely favor him to show him such compassion.

They made him a hero; he was much too tired to protest.

But fire still found him in his dreams. He ignored it for years, wanting to be the proverbial phoenix rising from the ash in a new and improved life. He worked hard and studied hard. He swore to himself he would do good. He would *be* good. As a child he had committed a horrible act. Now, as an adult, he would do better.

Maybe for a while it had worked. He'd been a good agent. He'd saved lives, worked important cases, advanced critical research. But then the pain started and the flames grew more mesmerizing in his dreams and he let the fire talk to him. He let it convince him to do things.

He had killed. Then he had begged the police to stop him. He had kidnapped girls. Then he'd left clues for someone else to save them. He hated himself; he serviced himself. He had sought redemption through work; he committed bigger sins in his personal life. In the end, he had been everything his family had raised him to be.

Everything of beauty betrayed you. Everything of beauty

lied. All you could trust was the flame.

He ran around now, in the dark recesses of the swamp. He listened to the deer dash out of his way, the stealthy foxes race for cover. Somewhere in the leaves came an ominous rattle. He didn't care anymore.

His head throbbed, his body begged for rest. While his hands played with matches, raking them across the sulfur strips and letting them fall with hissing crackles into the bog.

Some matches were immediately squelched by muddy water. Others found dry patches of leaves. Still others found the nice, slow-burning peat.

He ran by the pit. He thought he heard sound far below.

He dropped in another match just for her.

Everything of beauty must die. Everything, everyone, and him.

Mac and Kimberly were running now. They could hear frantic crashes in the underbrush, the pounding of footsteps that seemed to come from everywhere and nowhere. Someone was here. Ennunzio? His brother? The swamp had suddenly come alive, and Kimberly had her Glock out, holding it desperately with sweat-slicked hands.

'To the right,' Mac said, low under his breath.

But almost immediately the sound came again, this time from their left.

'Woods are distorting it,' Kimberly panted.

'We can't lose our bearing.'

'Too late.'

Kimberly's cell phone vibrated on her hip. She snatched it with her left hand, still holding her gun in her right, and trying to look everywhere at once. The trees swirled darkly around her, the woods closing in.

'Where's Ennunzio?' her father said in her ear.

'I don't know.'

'There is no brother, Kimberly. He died thirty years ago in

Lisa Gardner

the fire. It's Ennunzio. It sounds as if he may have a brain
tumor and has now experienced a psychotic break. You must
consider him armed and dangerous.'

'Dad,' Kimberly said softly. 'I smell fire.'

Tina's head came up sharply. Her eyes were swollen shut
again; she couldn't see, but her hearing was just fine. Noise.
Lots of noise. Footsteps and panting and crashing underbrush.
It was as if the swamp overhead had suddenly exploded with
activity. Rescuers!

'Hello?' she tried weakly. Her voice came out as nothing
more than a croak.

She swallowed, tried again, and got little better results.

Desperate now, she attempted to pull herself up. Her arms
trembled violently, too exhausted to bear her weight. But then
she heard a fresh pounding of footsteps and adrenaline surged
through her veins. She heaved herself half upright, groping
around vainly in the mud. Something squished between her
fingers, something plopped by her hand.

She gave up on caution, and brought a big handful of muck
to her mouth, sucking greedily at the mud. Moisture for her
parched throat, lips. So close, so close, so close.

'Hello,' she tried again. 'Down here!'

Her voice was slightly louder now. Then she heard a faint
pause, and sensed a presence suddenly close.

'Hello, hello, hello!'

'Clock ticking,' a clear voice whispered from above. 'Heat
kills.'

And the next thing Tina knew, she felt a sharp pain on her
hand, as if a pair of fangs had finally found her flesh.

'Ow!' she slapped at her hand, feeling the heat of the flames.
'Ow, ow, ow.' She beat at the heat frantically, squashing the
match into the mud. Son of a bitch. Now he was trying to burn
her out!

That did it. Tina staggered to her feet. She raised her tired arms over her head, balling her hands into fists. Then she screamed at the top of her sandpaper dry throat. 'You come down here and face me, you bastard. Come on. Fight like a man!'

Her legs promptly collapsed beneath her. She lay there in the mud, dazed and panting. She heard more sounds, this time the man running away. Perversely, she missed him; it was the closest to a human connection she'd had in days.

Hey, she thought weakly. She smelled smoke.

Kimberly was blowing frantically on her whistle. Three sharp blasts. Mac was whistling, too. They could see smoke now directly ahead. They raced to the pile of leaves, kicking them open and stomping furiously on the burning embers.

More smoke spiralled from the left, while a sputtering sound came from the right. Kimberly blew futilely on her whistle. Mac, too.

Then they were off to the right and off to the left, dashing through the woods and desperately seeking the dozens of burning piles.

'We need water.'

'None left.'

'Damp clothing?'

'Only what I'm wearing.' Mac peeled off his soaked shirt and used it to smother a burning stump.

'It's Ennunzio. No brother. Has a brain tumor. Apparently has gone insane.' Kimberly kicked frantically at yet another pile of smoldering leaves. Snakes? She didn't have time to worry about them anymore.

A fresh sound of rustling tree limbs came from their right. Kimberly jerked toward the noise, already raising her gun and trying to site a target. A deer raced by, followed swiftly by two more. For the first time, she became aware of the full activity around them. Squirrels scrambling up trees, birds taking to the air. Soon they would probably see otters, raccoons, and foxes, a desperate exodus of all creatures great and small.

'He hates what he loves and loves what he hates,' Kimberly said grimly.

'They have the right idea. Two of us alone can't stop this. We have to think of bailing out.'

But Kimberly was already running to a fresh batch of curling smoke. 'Not yet.'

'Kimberly . . .'

'Please, Mac, not yet.'

She tore apart a rotting tree limb, stomping on the scattering flames. Mac tended to the next hot spot, then they both heard it at once. Yelling. Distant and rough.

'Hey . . . Down here! Somebody . . . Help.'

'Tina,' Kimberly breathed.

They ran toward her voice.

Kimberly nearly found Tina Krahn the hard way. One moment she was running forward, the next her right foot peddled through open air. She staggered at the edge of the rectangular pit, frantically windmilling her arms until Mac grabbed her by the backpack and yanked her to firmer footing.

'I gotta start looking before I leap,' she muttered.

Drenched in sweat and covered with soot, Mac managed a crooked smile. 'And ruin your charm?'

They dropped down on their stomachs and gazed intently into the hole. The pit seemed quite large, maybe a ten-by-fifteen-foot area, at least twenty feet deep. It obviously wasn't new. Thick, tangled vines covered most of the walls, while beneath Kimberly's fingertips, she could feel old, half-rotted railroad ties. She didn't know who had built the pit, but given that slaves had been used to dredge most of the swamp, she had her theories as to why. Don't want to watch the help too much at night? Well, talk about restricted sleeping quarters . . .

'Hello!' she called down. 'Tina?'

'Are you for real?' a feeble voice called back from the shadows. 'You're not wearing a tuxedo, are you?'

'Noooo,' Kimberly said slowly. She glanced at Mac. They were both thinking about what Kathy Levine had said. Heat stroke victims were often delusional.

The smell of smoke was growing thicker. Kimberly narrowed her eyes, still trying to pick out a human being below. Then, she saw her. All the way down in the muck, curled tight against a boulder. The girl was covered head to toe in mud, blending in perfectly with her surroundings. Kimberly could just barely make out the flash of white teeth when Tina spoke.

'Water?' the girl croaked hopefully.

'We're going to get you out of there.'

'I think I lost my baby,' Tina whispered. 'Please, don't tell my mom.'

Kimberly closed her eyes. The words hurt her, one more casualty in a war they never should have had to fight.

'We're going to throw you a rope.' Mac's voice was steady and calm.

'I can't . . . No Spiderman. Tired . . . So tired . . .'

'You go down,' Mac murmured to Kimberly. 'I'll haul up.'

'We don't have a litter.'

'Loop the end of the rope to form a swing. It's the best we can do.'

Kimberly looked at his arms wordlessly. It would take a tremendous amount of strength to pull up a hundred pounds of deadweight, and Mac had been hiking for nearly three days straight, on virtually no sleep. But Mac merely shrugged. In his eyes she saw the truth. The smoke was thickening, the deadly fire taking root. They didn't have many options left.

'I'm coming down,' Kimberly called into the pit.

Mac pulled out the vinyl coil, worked a rough belay using a clamp around his waist, then gave her the go-ahead. She repelled down slow and easy, trying not to recoil at the stench, or to think about what kind of things must be slithering in the muck.

At the bottom, she was startled by her first close-up glance at the girl. Tina's bones stood out starkly. Her skin was shrink-wrapped around her frame in a macabre imitation of a living mummy. Her hair was wild and muddy, her eyes swollen shut. Even beneath the coating of mud, Kimberly could see giant sores oozing blood and pus. Was it just her imagination, or did one of those sores just wiggle? The girl hadn't been lying. In her shape, she was never going to be able to climb up the pit walls on her own.

'It's very nice to meet you, Tina,' Kimberly said briskly. 'My name is Kimberly Quincy, and I've come to get you out of here.'

'Water?' Tina whispered hopefully.

'Up top.'

'So . . . thirsty. Where's the lake?'

'I'm going to loop this rope. You need to sit in it like a swing. And then Special Agent McCormack up there is going to pull you up. If you can use your legs against the wall to assist him, that would be very helpful.'

'Water?'

'All the water you want, Tina. You just have to make it to the top.'

The girl nodded slowly, her head bobbing back and forth almost drunkenly. She seemed dazed and unfocused, on the edge of checking back out. Kimberly moved quickly, wrapping the rope around Tina's hips and getting it in place.

'Ready?' she called up.

'Ready,' Mac replied, and Kimberly heard a new urgency in his voice. The fire was obviously sweeping closer.

'Tina,' she said intently. 'If you want that water, you gotta move. And I mean *now*.'

She hefted the girl up, felt the slack immediately tighten in the rope. Tina seemed to half get it; her feet kicked weakly at the wall. A groan from up top. A heaving gasp as Mac began to pull.

'Water at the top, Tina. Water at the top.'

Then Tina did something Kimberly didn't expect. From deep in her haze, she roused her tired limbs, stuck her feet in what appeared to be small gaps between the railroad ties and actually tried to help.

Up, up, up she went, climbing toward freedom. Up, up, up out of her dark hellhole.

And just for a moment, Kimberly felt something lighten in her chest. She stood there, watching this tired, exhausted girl finally make it to safety and she felt a moment of satisfaction, of sublime peace. She had done good. She had gotten this one right.

Tina disappeared over the edge. Within seconds the rope was back down.

'*Move!*' Mac barked.

Kimberly grabbed the rope, spotted the toeholds and bolted for the top.

She crested the pit just in time to watch a wall of flames hit the trees and bear down upon them.

47

Dismal Swamp, Virginia
2:39 P.M.
Temperature: 103 degrees

'We need choppers, we need the manpower, we need help.'

Quincy pulled up at the cluster of cars and spotted the thin columns of smoke darkening the bright blue sky. One, two, three – there had to be nearly a dozen of them. He turned back to the forestry official who was still barking orders into a radio.

'What the hell has happened?'

'Fire,' the man said tersely.

'Where is my daughter?'

'Is she a hiker? Who is she with?'

'Dammit.' Quincy spotted Ray Lee Chee staggering out of a vehicle and made a beeline for him, Rainie hot on his heels. 'What happened?'

'Don't know. Drove into Lake Drummond to start the search. Next thing I know, I'm hearing whistle blasts and smelling smoke.'

'Whistle blasts?'

'Three sharp blows, the international call for distress. Sounded from the northeast quadrant. I was headed in that direction, but man, the smoke got so thick so fast. Brian and I figured we'd better bug out while we still had the chance. We're not equipped with that kind of gear.'

'And the others?'

'Saw Kathy and Lloyd headed toward their vehicle. I don't know about Kimberly, Mac, or that doctor dude.'

'How do I get to Lake Drummond?'

Ray just looked at him, then the clouds of smoke. 'Now, sir, you don't.'

Mac and Kimberly had Tina slung between them, one of her arms over each of their shoulders. The girl was a fighter, trying vainly to help them by moving her feet. But her body had been pushed beyond its limits days ago. The more she tried to run with them, the more she stumbled and careened sluggishly, throwing them all off balance.

The awkward motions were getting them nowhere and the fire was gaining fast.

'I got her,' Mac said tersely.

'It's too much weight—'

'Shut up and help.' He stopped and hunkered down. Tina wrapped her arms around his neck, Kimberly boosted the muddy girl up onto his back.

'Water,' the girl croaked.

'When we're out of the woods,' Mac promised. Neither of them had the heart to tell Tina that they had no water left. For that matter, if they didn't magically find their vehicle in about the next five minutes, all of the water in the world would make no difference.

They were off and running again. Kimberly had no sense of time or place. She was stumbling around trees, battling her way through choking underbrush. Smoke stung her eyes and made her cough. In the good news department, the bugs were gone. In the bad news department, she didn't know if she was heading north or south, east or west. The swamp had closed in on her and she'd long ago lost any sense of direction.

Mac seemed to know where he was going, however. He had a hard, lean look on his face, pushing himself forward and determined to take them both with him.

A lumbering shape appeared to their left. Kimberly watched in awe as a full-grown black bear went running by not ten feet away. The big animal didn't spare them a glance, but kept on trucking. Next came deer, foxes, squirrels, and even some snakes. Everything was clearing out, and normal food chain rules did not apply in the face of this far greater foe.

They ran, sweat streaming down their arms and legs. They ran more, Tina beginning to mumble incoherently, her head lolling forward on Mac's shoulder. They ran harder, the smoke penetrating their lungs, making them all gasp.

They squeezed through a narrow space between two towering trees, rounded a large patch of thickets and came face-to-face with Ennunzio. He was on the ground, propped up against a tree trunk. He seemed unsurprised to see them burst through the roiling smoke.

'You shouldn't run from the flames,' he murmured, and then Kimberly saw what was at his feet. A coiled nest of brown mottled skin. Two pinpricks of red showed on Ennunzio's calf where the rattler had bit him.

'I shot him,' he said, in reply to their unasked question. 'But not before he got me. Just as well. Can't run anymore. Time to wait. Must take your punishment like a man. What do you think my father thought about, each time he heard us scream?'

His gaze went to the muddy shape on Mac's back. 'Oh good, you found her. That's nice. Out of four girls, I was hoping you'd get at least one right.'

Kimberly took a furious step forward and Ennunzio's hand immediately twitched by his side. He was holding his gun.

'You shouldn't run from the flames,' he said sternly. 'I tried it thirty years ago, and look what happened to me. Now sit. Stay a while. It only hurts for a short time.'

'You're dying,' Kimberly told him flatly.

'Aren't we all?'

'Not today, Look – sit here all you want. Die in your precious fire. But we're out of here.'

She took another step, and Ennunzio immediately raised the gun.

'Stay,' he said firmly and now she could see the light flaming in his eyes, a feverish, rabid glow. 'You must die. It's the only way to find peace.'

Kimberly pressed her lips into a thin, frustrated line. She shot a glance at Mac. He had a gun somewhere, but with his hands full trying to keep Tina on his back, he was in no position to do anything quickly or stealthily. Kimberly shot her gaze back to Ennunzio. This one was up to her.

'Who are you?' she asked. 'Frank or David?'

'Frank. I've always been Frank.' Ennunzio's lips curled weakly. 'But do you want to hear something stupid? I tried to pretend in the beginning that it wasn't me. I tried to pretend the killer was Davey, come back to do all those terrible things, because I was big brother Frank and I'd gotten out and I wasn't going to be anything like my family. But of course it wasn't Davey. Davey got beat one too many times. Davey stopped having any hope. Davey, given a choice between running and dying, chose dying. So of course it could only be me, hunting down innocent girls. Once I had the tumor removed, I could see that more clearly. I had done bad things. The fire had made me do it, and now I must stop. But then the pain came back and all I could dream of was bodies in the woods.'

The smoke was growing thicker. It made Kimberly blink owlishly and become even more aware of the intense heat growing at her back. 'If we fashioned a tourniquet above the bite, you could still live,' Kimberly tried desperately. 'You could walk out of this swamp, get yourself some antivenom, and then get yourself some serious psychological help.'

'But I don't want to live.'

'I do.'

'Why?'

'Because living is hope. Trying is hope. And because I come from a long line of people who have excelled at being earnest.' Ennunzio's gaze had drifted to Mac. It was the opportunity she'd been waiting for. Choking back a harsh cough, Kimberly brought up her Glock and leveled it at Ennunzio's face. 'Throw down your weapon, Frank. Let us pass, or you won't have to worry about your precious fire.'

Ennunzio merely smiled. 'Shoot me.'

'Put down your weapon.'

'Shoot me.'

'Shoot your own goddamn self! I wasn't put on this earth to end your misery. I'm here to save a girl. Now we have her and we're getting out.' The smoke was so thick now, Kimberly could barely see.

'No,' Ennunzio said distinctly. 'Move, and I'll shoot. The flames are coming. Now take your punishment like a man.'

'You're a coward,' Kimberly told him, harshly. 'Always taking your rage out on others, when all along you know who you truly hate the most is yourself.'

'I saved lives.'

'You killed your own family!'

'They wanted me to do it.'

'Bullshit! They wanted help. Ever think who your brother could've been? I'm sure he would've done better than turn into a serial murderer who preyed on young girls.'

'Davey was weak. Davey needed my protection.'

'Davey needed his family and you took them away from him! It's always been about you, Ennunzio. Not what your brother needed, not what your mom needed and sure as hell

420

not what the environment needed. You kill, because you want to kill. Because killing makes you happy. And maybe that's why Davey stayed in the house that day. He already knew the truth – that of the whole family, you are the worst of the bunch.'

Kimberly leaned forward. Ennunzio's face had turned a mottled shade of scarlet while his Glock trembled in his hand. The fire had grown dangerously close. She could smell the acrid odor of singeing hair. Not much time left. For him, for her, for any of them.

Kimberly took a deep breath. She waited, one, two, three. A popping sound came from the woods, an old tree trunk exploding. Ennunzio jerked his head toward the noise. And Kimberly descended upon him with a vengeance. Her foot connected with his hand, the Glock went flying out of his grasp. A second hard kick had him holding his gut. A third whipped his head around.

She was moving in for the kill, when she heard his rough laugh.

'Take it like a man,' he cackled. 'By God boys, don't you waste your pathetic cries on me. Hold your chin up when I beat you. Square those shoulders. Look me in the eye, and take your punishment like a man.' Ennunzio laughed again, a hoarse, hollow sound that sent shivers up her spine.

His head came up. He peered straight at Kimberly. 'Kill me,' he said, very clearly. 'Please. Make it quick.'

Kimberly walked over. She picked up his gun. Then she threw it deep into the heart of the oncoming flames.

'No more excuses, Ennunzio. You want to die, you go do it yourself.'

She turned back toward Mac and Tina. The fire was so close now, she could feel its heat on her face. But mostly she was aware of Mac, his calm blue eyes, his big strong body. His absolute faith that she could handle Ennunzio. And now his readiness to take her and Tina Krahn straight out of here.

Life was filled with choices, Kimberly thought. Living, dying, fighting, running, hoping, dreading, loving, hating. Existing in the past or living in the present. Kimberly looked at Mac, then looked at Tina, and she had no problem with her choices anymore.

'Let's go,' she said crisply.

They started running. Ennunzio howled behind them. Or maybe he simply laughed. But the fire was moving fast now. The flames would no longer be denied.

The firewall descended, and one way or another, Ennunzio had his peace at last.

They found the car ten minutes later. Tina was piled into the backseat, Mac and Kimberly plunked down in the front. Then Mac had the keys out and the engine running and they were tearing down the flat, grassy road, dodging fleeing animals.

Kimberly heard a roar that sounded like an inferno, while overhead the skies filled with rescue choppers and forestry planes. The cavalry coming, bringing in professionals to fight the blaze and save what could be saved.

They tore out of the swamp, coming to a screeching halt in a parking lot now piled high with vehicles.

Mac jumped out first. 'Medical attention, quick, over here.'

Then EMTs were working on Tina with water and cooling packs, while Quincy and Rainie were running across the parking lot toward Kimberly, and Mac was beating them both to the punch by taking her into his arms. She rested her head against his chest. He put his arms around her, and things finally felt all right.

Nora Ray appeared out of the crowd, moving toward Tina's side.

'Betsy?' Tina murmured weakly. 'Viv? Karen?'

'They're happy that you're safe,' Nora Ray said quietly, squatting down next to Tina's prostrate form.

'Are they okay?'

'They're happy that you're safe.'

Tina understood then. She closed her eyes. 'I want my mother,' she said, and then she started to cry.

'You'll be okay,' Nora Ray said. 'You have to take it from me. A bad thing happened, but you survive it. You won.'

'How do you know?'

'Because three years ago, the same man kidnapped me.'

Tina finally stopped crying. She looked at Nora Ray through bloodshot eyes. 'Do you know where they're going to take me?'

'I don't know, but I can stay with you if you'd like.'

'Buddy system?' Tina whispered.

And Nora Ray finally smiled. She squeezed Tina's hand and said, 'Always.'

Epilogue

She was running, tearing through the woods at breakneck speed. Dangling leaves snatched at her hair, low branches tore at her face. She leapt fallen tree trunks, then threw herself full throttle at the fifteen-foot wall. Her hands found the rope, her feet scrabbled for footing. Up, up, up she went, heart pounding, lungs heaving and throat gasping.

She crested the top, had an absolutely stellar view of the lush, green Virginia woods, then flipped herself down the other side. Tires coming up. Bing, bing, bing, she punched one foot through the center of each rubber mass. Then she was hunched over like a turtle, scrambling down a narrow, metal pipe. Now out the other end, racing down the home stretch. Sun on her face. Wind in her hair.

Kimberly careened over the finish line, just as Mac clicked off the stopwatch and said, 'Ah honey, you call that a time? Hell, I know guys that go twice as fast.'

Kimberly launched herself at his chest. He saw the attack coming and tried to brace his feet. She'd learned a new move in

424

combat training just last week, however, and had him flat on his back in no time.

She was still breathing hard, sweat glistening across her face and dampening her navy blue FBI Academy T-shirt. For a change, however, she wore a smile.

'Where's the knife?' Mac murmured with a wicked gleam in his eyes.

'Don't you wish.'

'Pretty please, I can insult you more, if you'd like.'

'No way can you do that course twice as fast.'

'Well, I might have been exaggerating.' His hands were now on her bare legs, tracing the lines from her ankles, up to the hem of her nylon shorts. 'But I'm at *least* two seconds faster.'

'Upper body strength,' Kimberly spat out. 'Men have more and it comes in handy at the wall.'

'Yep, ain't life unfair?' He rolled swiftly with a surprise move of his own, now she was the one on the dirt and he was the one looming above. Trapped, she did the sensible thing; she lunged up, grabbed his shoulders and nailed him with a long, lingering kiss.

'Miss me?' he gasped three seconds later.

'No. Not much.'

Other voices were coming from the woods now. More students, taking advantage of this beautiful Saturday to train. Mac got up grudgingly. Kimberly vaulted up with more energy, hastily wiping dirt and leaves from her hair. The students were almost in view now, about to top the wall. Mac and Kimberly bolted for the shelter of the neighboring woods.

'How's it going?' Mac asked as they drifted into the lush, green shade.

'Hanging in there.'

He stopped, took her arm, and made her face him. 'No, Kimberly. I mean for real. How is it going?'

She shrugged, wishing the sight of him didn't make her

want to throw her arms around his waist or bury her head against his shoulder. Wishing the sight of him didn't make her feel so damn giddy. Life was still life, and these days, hers carried a lot of obligations.

'Some of the students aren't wild about my presence,' she admitted at last. She had resumed her studies nearly a month ago. Some of the powers-that-be weren't wild about it, but Rainie had been right: everybody blamed a failure, nobody argued with a hero. Kimberly and Mac's dramatic rescue of Tina Krahn had been front-page news for nearly a week. When she'd called Mark Watson about returning to the Academy, he'd even gotten her her own room.

'Not easy being recycled?'

'No. I'm the outsider who showed up halfway through the school year. Worse, I'm an outsider with a reputation half want to challenge and the other half don't want to believe.'

'Are they mean to you?' he asked soberly, thumb beneath her chin.

'Someone actually short-sheeted my bed. Oh my God, the horrors. I should write home to Daddy.'

'Uh oh, what did you do in retaliation?' Mac asked immediately.

'I haven't decided yet.'

'Oh dear.'

She resumed walking. After a moment, he fell in step beside her. 'I'm going to make it, Mac,' she said seriously. 'Five weeks to go, and I'm going to make it. And if some people don't like me, that's okay. Because others do, and I'm good at this job. With more experience, I'm going to be even better at the job. Why someday, I might even follow a direct order. Think of what the Bureau will do then.'

'You'll be like a whole new secret weapon,' Mac said with awe.

'Exactly.' She nodded her head with pride. Then, not being

stupid, she regarded him intently. 'So why are you here, Mac? And don't tell me you missed my smile. I know you're a little too busy for social calls these days.'

'It's always something, isn't it?'

'At the moment.'

He sighed, looked as if he wished he could say something clever, then must've decided to get on with it. 'They found Ennunzio's body.'

'Good.' It had taken weeks to completely annihilate the swamp fire. In the good news department, crews had contained the blaze fairly quickly, limiting damage. In the bad news department, the smoldering peat moss continued to flare up for nearly a month, requiring constant vigilance on the part of the US Forestry Service.

During that time, volunteers worked the site, tending the woods and seeking some sign of Ennunzio's body. As week had grown into week, they had all started getting a little nervous, especially Kimberly.

'He made it farther than any of us would've guessed,' Mac was saying now. 'True to his natural ambivalence, he must have decided at the last minute that he wanted to live. He actually hiked a good mile with his bitten leg. Who even knows what got him in the end? The venom pumped into his heart, or the smoke, or the flames.'

'They do a postmortem?'

'Completed it yesterday. Kimberly, he didn't have a tumor.'

She halted, blinked her eyes a few times, then had to run a hand through her hair. 'Well that figures, doesn't it,' she murmured. 'Guy's such a fuck-up, he's gotta blame his actions on everything but himself. His mother, his brother, and a medical condition he doesn't even have. Doesn't that take the cake?'

'For the record, he did have a tumor once,' Mac said. 'Doctors confirmed his operation three years ago to remove the mass. According to them, a tumor could affect someone's propensity for violence. I understand there was even a mass murderer in Texas who claimed his actions were caused by a tumor.'

'Charles Whitman,' Kimberly murmured. 'Stabbed his mother to death, then murdered his wife, then climbed a clock tower at the University of Texas and opened fire on the population below. In the end, he killed eighteen people and wounded thirty others before being shot and killed himself. He left a note, didn't he? Said he wanted an autopsy performed because he was sure there was something physically wrong with him.'

'Exactly. The autopsy revealed a small tumor in his hypothalamus, which some experts say could have contributed to his rampage, while others claim it could not. Who knows? Maybe Ennunzio liked that story. Maybe it made an impression upon him, especially when he found out he had a tumor himself. But there was no tumor this time, so once again, he was just giving himself an excuse.'

'You had him nailed in the beginning,' Kimberly said. 'Why does the Eco-Killer target and murder young women? Because he wants to. Sometimes, it really is as simple as that.'

'The guy did feel some level of guilt,' Mac said with a shrug. 'Hence leaving us clues to find the second girl. Hence contacting the police as an anonymous tipster and getting us all into the game. Hence his personal involvement as an FBI agent, keeping us on track. When he analyzed the letters, he described the author as someone who felt compelled to kill, but who also wanted to be stopped. Maybe that was his way of trying to explain himself to us.'

Kimberly, however, vehemently shook her head. 'Did he really want to help, Mac, or did he just want more people to hurt? This is the guy who started out hating his father, but killed his mother and brother. He targeted young women, but also set up hazardous conditions for the search-and-rescue volunteers. I don't think he placed those anonymous phone calls because he wanted you to catch him. He was seeking more persons in the game. He obviously didn't mind collateral damage. And if he could have, he would've killed us in the swamp that day.'

'You're probably right.'

'I'm glad he's dead.'

'Honey, I'm not so sad about it myself.'

'Any sign of the girls' cars?' she asked.

'Funny you should mention it; we think we've found one.'

'Where at?'

'In the Tallulah Gorge, camouflaged with netting, green paint, and a whole-lotta leaves. We're revisiting the other sites now, to see if we'll find the victims' vehicles nearby. We also discovered Ennunzio's home base – he has a cabin in the woods not far from here. Very rustic, like an old hunting shack. In it, we found a cot, gallons of water, boxes of crackers, a tranquilizer gun, and tons of drugs. He really could've kept doing this for a very long time.'

'Then I'm doubly glad he's dead. And Tina?'

'At home in Minnesota with her mom,' Mac reported immediately. 'I understand from Nora Ray that Tina had just discovered she was pregnant before the kidnapping. Unfortunately, she lost the baby and is taking it rather hard. But I hear her mother's been a pillar of strength and Tina's gonna spend the rest of the summer recuperating at home, then see what she wants to do. She lost her three best friends; I'm not sure exactly how you recover from something like that. She and Nora Ray seem to have grown close, however. Maybe they can help each other out. Nora Ray's talking of visiting her in a few weeks. Minnesota has cooler summers. Nora Ray likes that. Okay, your turn. How're your father and Rainie?'

'They're in Oregon. They're planning on doing absolutely

nothing but stroll on beaches and play a little golf until my graduation in five weeks. I give my father two days, and he'll be working the first local homicide case he can find. The Oregon cops will never know what hit them.'

'Have dead body, will travel?' Mac teased her.

'Something like that.'

'And you?' His finger traced a slow, gentle line down her cheek. Then both his hands settled on her waist. 'What are you going to do in five weeks?'

'I'm a new agent,' Kimberly said quietly. Her hands had come up, resting on the hard curve of his arms. 'We don't have much say in things. You get assigned where you get assigned.'

'Can you list preferences?'

'We can. I said Atlanta might be nice. No reason, of course.'

'No reason?' Mac's hands stroked up her sides, his thumbs feathering across her breasts.

'Okay, I have a little bit of a reason.'

'When will you know?'

'Yesterday.'

'You mean . . .'

She smiled, feeling a little bit ridiculous now, and ducked her head. 'Yeah, I got lucky. Atlanta's a big field office and they needed a fair amount of agents. I guess I'm going to have to learn to talk with a drawl, and drink a lot of Coke.'

'I want you to meet my family,' Mac said immediately. He was holding her tighter now. She hadn't been 100 percent sure of what he would think. They had both been so busy lately, and you never knew . . .

But he was grinning. His blue eyes danced. He bobbed his head and nailed her with a second kiss. 'Oh, this will be fun!'

'I'm bringing my knife,' she warned weakly.

'My sister will be thrilled.'

'I'm not trying to rush you. I know we'll both be very busy.'

'Shut up and kiss me again.'

'Mac . . .'

'You're beautiful, Kimberly, and I love you.'

She barely knew what to say anymore. She took his hand. She whispered the words. She pressed her lips against his.

Then they walked together through the woods, with the wind sighing in the trees and the sun shining softly overhead.